Crown of the Sundered Empire

A Legends of Tivara Epic Sword and Sorcery

JC Kang

To JC Nelson, the best author buddy a writer could have.

This is a work of fiction. Names, places, characters, and events are either fictitious or are used fictitiously. Any resemblance to actual events, locations, organizations, or persons, alive or dead, is entirely coincidental and unintended.

http://jckang.dragonstonepress.us
jc.kang.author@gmail.com

Cover Art by Polar Engine

Maps by Laura Kang

Logos by Emily Jose Burlingame

CONTENTS

MAPS

TIVARALAN
Listuvi
Rotuvi
Cathay
Ankira
Dragon Lands
Teleri Empire
Kanin
Arkothi City States
Chapter 1 Insert
Chapter 4 Insert
Serikoth
Tarkoth
Korynth

The Sundered Empire

Enlarged Maps And More at:
http://tivara.dragonstonepress.us/crown-of-the-sundered-empire-resources/

Who's Who In Crown of the Sundered Empire

Lorium and Twins Island

Tomas Larelli	A fisherboy with mismatched eyes
Antonius	Constable, son of the mayor
Sofia	The town beauty
Julius	Sofia's father
Old Gian	A fisherman from Lorium
Joacquin	A fisherman originally from Twins Island

Bovyans of the Teleri Empire

Keris	Commander
Fethos	Soldier on a special mission
Sathis	Soldier on a special mission

Serikoth

Koryn	Crown Prince
Damaryn	Cavalier captain
Fleet	Madaeri Scout

Tarkoth

Elrayn	Crown Prince
Aryn	Second Prince
Karyna	Princess
Aelward	Bastard son of the king, navy lieutenant
Peris	Aide to Aryn
Tharis	Aide to Elrayn

Eldaeri of Korynth

Selayna	Queen
Alaena	Princess of Serikoth, adopted by Korynth

Others

Jie Yan	Black Fist Spy from Cathay
Melas	Rogue Aksumi Mystic

PROLOGUE:

Light of Solaris

Stuck in human form for the past decade, Avarax had suffered indignities no dragon should ever have to endure. Toe fungus. Hangnails. Body odor. The new perspective, closer to the ground, had made him almost sympathetic to the bottom-feeders' plight.

Almost. Now they were proliferating again, after the Hellstorm and Long Winter had culled the herd. Only the best had survived—which was not to say their best were all that good. A line of the pathetic roaches marched in the meadow ahead, mostly scruffy men with fair skin. None of their makeshift spears bore magic runes. They were just plain sticks, as fragile as their wielders.

One, in chainmail, rode a horse. He turned and pointed at Avarax. "You, the bronze-skinned one."

All eyes turned to him. Murmurs erupted.

"Brownie." A particularly filthy specimen spat at his feet.

Avarax yawned. It never ceased to amaze him how humans made such a big deal out of skin color, when it all looked and tasted the same when roasted. Underneath, they were all succulent flesh and thirst-quenching blood.

"Can you fight?" the horseman asked, shielding his eyes from the afternoon sun.

"Yes." Shrugging, Avarax kicked a rock through the ankle-high grass. "But why would I?"

"Because you are on my land, and I order you to do so." The man pointed a rune-inscribed gladius shortsword, a much better weapon than any of his underlings carried.

Avarax laughed. So wretched. After the Hellstorm had laid low empires, all these warlords scrambled for land and power. Now, these peasants pined for the safety and order those dead empires had provided. "I don't take orders from you."

The lord's face flushed a delicious shade of red. "Seize him!"

His men broke ranks, jogged through the browning grass, and started to encircle him.

Avarax grinned. The Dragonstone in his chest buzzed. Its energy might be constrained by a ward, but he still had more power than all these vermin, combined. He'd start by activating the rune in the leader's sword, and turn it against him. That would be entertaining. He opened a hand, ready to unleash his magic.

"Look!" A young man pointed. "The Eldaeri!"

All eyes turned in that direction.

Closing his hand and snuffing the energy growing there, Avarax looked.

A thousand soldiers, both men and women, formed a wall of green tunics on a hilltop. Shorter and frailer than the local Arkothi humans, they looked like no other people Avarax had seen in this world. White banners emblazoned with a nine-pointed gold star fluttered above them. They all carried bizarre-looking crossbows with boxes on top.

In the center, a man with a circlet on his brow lifted a white rod. Atop it sparkled a twelve-faceted crystal the size of a fist.

"The Light of Solaris." The warlord spoke in awed tones.

"We don't stand a chance," another man said, backing away. He trembled like a small wet dog.

"Form up!" the warlord snarled.

More wide-eyed soldiers took steps back, then started to flee.

"We're going to die!"

"They've never lost a battle with the Light at the head of their army."

Magic! Avarax's ears tingled. Perhaps it could help remove the ward on his power and restore his magnificent form. Dragonstone pulsing with excitement, he turned to the warlord, whose curses and threats did little to rally his panicking men. "I will fight..."

...For himself, of course.

A downpour of crossbow bolts began.

CHAPTER 1:

Inauspicious Start to the Day

Despite his mismatched eyes, sixteen-year-old Tomas Larelli had never seen the future. That didn't keep everyone from assuming he could, nor did his scruples compel him to deny it. After all, with a face that only a monkey could love, he had to find ways to get people to like him.

"Oi, Tomas." Old Gian waved from a neighboring boat. "Thanks again for teaching me that knot you invented. It's helped secure my nets. How did you ever figure it out?"

Tomas raised his oars and tapped under his green eye. "Diviner's Sight!"

Or a little bit of imagination. His mind had painted the image of the rope, weaving its way through its own loops. The result was the dozens of fish flopping at his feet. With a nod, he resumed his rowing.

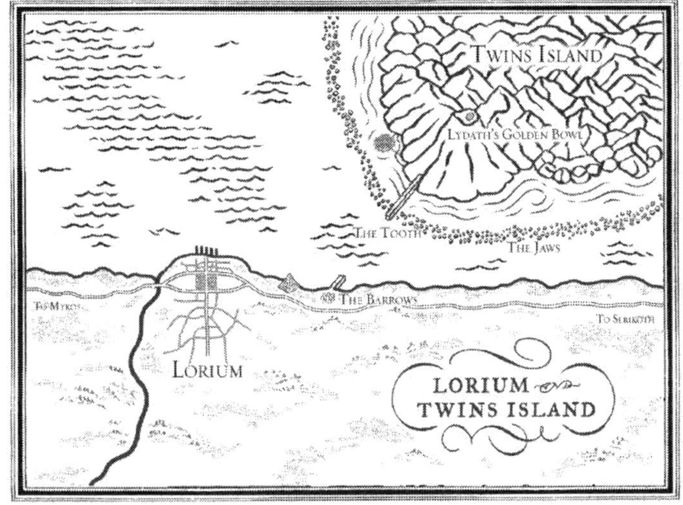

His boat glided through the Inland Sea's placid blue waters, passing between his island village on the right and the Barrows on the mainland to the left. He shuddered and formed a ring with his thumb and finger to ward off evil. Tortured spirits of humans, sacrificed to the orc gods a thousand years ago, still haunted the towering mounds.

On the other side of the Barrows the wooden pyramid of Solaris came into view, and then beyond it, the red-tiled roofs of the town of Lorium. His stomach fluttered. Soon...

"Oi, Tomas," a croaking voice called from the docks.

Tomas squinted as he rowed closer. A sablewood bireme, flying a crimson flag with a nine-pointed silver sun, loomed large over the far wharf. Its black hull made it difficult to pick out the figure waving from the closest dock. Probably Mauritizio, since he was always the first out to buy the best catches. The fine linen shirt and trousers he wore didn't match his sun-roughened skin.

Mauritizio craned his neck. "Another bumper catch, I see."

Grinning, Tomas tapped beneath his eye yet again. "Diviner's Sight can't go wrong." Nor could studying the currents and tides, the way they swept lines through the Inland Sea. Nobody else had to know his secret, though. He gestured to his boat's bottom, where the fish continued their desperate thrashing.

Mauritizio took hold of a pylon and leaned over. "Whitefins. Very nice. I'm feeling generous today. I'll give you a copper *draka* for two." He tossed a rope.

Catching it, Tomas moored his boat to the pylon. He looked up and grinned. The foreign bireme in town would drive up the price of fish. "Two copper *draka*s for three is generous. What you offer is banditry."

Mauritizio looked over his shoulder to where the other fishmongers were now approaching like sharks to blood. He turned back. "Deal."

It was a fair exchange, and though he could've waited for the other fishmongers to come and haggle for more, Mauritizio had always been kind.

Not to mention, there was somewhere Tomas had to be. His hand strayed to the vial in his pocket. "You'll find thirty-three fish in there."

Making a show of counting with his fingers, Mauritizio nodded. "Then two silver and one copper *draka* for you."

"*Two* coppers." Tomas chuckled.

Mauritizio threw his hands up. "Ah, can't get anything past your nets. Darn Diviner's Sight!"

Or math. Coppers grouped into tens in his mind's eye.

Imitating the Diviners of old, Tomas looked past the setting Blue and White Moons to the Iridescent Moon. It waxed toward its third crescent.

The market would open soon.

"Good for both of us," he said. "I know where the fish will be, and you get to sell them for profit. My Diviner's Sight says you'll make at least four silvers from them today."

Mauritizio bowed. "You're never wrong, of course."

If only because Tomas paid attention to market prices. He held out his hand with an arch of his eyebrow.

Mauritizio opened his purse, pulled out two silver and two copper coins, and pressed them into Tomas' palm. "Nice doing business with you."

Tucking his slingshot into the back of his pants, Tomas climbed onto the dock. He hurried along the main road deeper into town, trusting Mauritizio to collect the fish. Again, he looked up at the Iridescent Moon, never moving from its reliable spot in the sky, always cycling through its twenty-four phases in a single day. There wasn't much time left. His heart pattered.

The creaks, thumps, and fishy reek of the docks gave way to the rich textures of the marketplace: The earthy smell of spring vegetables from several stalls. The hammering of the blacksmith on the east. The bright colors of cloth in the shops to the south.

Burly men, whose crimson tunics marked them as rowers from the Serikothi ship, mingled among the townsfolk and catcalled the women. Ethnically Arkothi, like the locals, these foreigners had olive complexions.

They stood in contrast to their officers in their high-collared jackets, who had lithe builds, brown hair, and bronze complexions. These smaller, shorter men belonged to the Eldaeri, a long-lived race who proclaimed themselves to be the sun god's Chosen People. In his limited experience, Tomas had found them to be as arrogant as their claim.

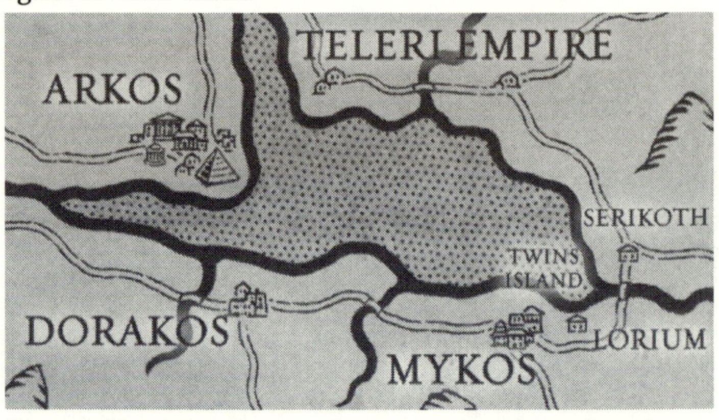

"Tomas!" cried a farmer from a vegetable stall as he entered the marketplace. "Can you tell me when the next rain will be?"

"Two days," Tomas said. At least, that's what the earthworm activity suggested. He locked his eyes on a kiosk at the far end.

A shock of golden hair flashed among the trays of magic light baubles and lamps.

A smile tugged at his lips. Patting the vial in his pocket, he quickened his pace.

"When will a Runemaster Imperator return with the Crown of Arkos?"

After three hundred years since the sundering of the Arkothi Empire, probably never. Tomas laughed. Let them believe in long-lost emperors and their equally missing crowns. "I can't have you betting against me in the gambling dens."

"Tomas," yelled out the baker from across the way. "Are we safe from the Teleri?"

"I'll be back with your answer, and I expect a fresh loaf of your best bread in return." Tomas flashed a smile. It would give him time to ask around and find out more about the aggressive empire's latest positions.

In this, Constable Antonius would know more. The mayor's son—and indeed, the town's favorite son—was striding from the other end of the market. The shiny buttons on his crisp blue uniform glinted in the morning light, and a sword dangled from his hip. Their eyes met, and the constable's smirk punctuated his strong jaw, heavy brows, and high nose. Then his gaze shifted toward their mutual destination, just ten paces away.

Tomas had to get there first.

At the kiosk, stocky Julius spread out rune-inscribed antiques and modern light bauble lamps. He stepped to the side, revealing his daughter.

Time seemed to slow as Sofia tossed her hair over a shoulder. Sunlight caught silver highlights in the sea of gold. Unlike everyone else's sun-darkened olive skin, hers was as fair as the sandy beaches back home. It made her bright blue eyes stand out. The neckline of her green velvet dress plunged low enough to hint at her budding curves. She was like the Goddess Ayara arriving on earth for the first time. Temple bells chimed in Tomas' imagination.

You brighten my day more than the sun. Tomas rehearsed the greeting in his mind, gulping hard in hopes he'd actually be able to articulate it. *You brighten my day more than the sun.* He covered the last ten paces in just eight strides. *You brighten my day more than the sun.* Math, logic, market trends, and tides were easy compared to talking to a woman. "You...sun. Brighten... Good morning, Sofia."

She flashed him a radiant smile, which indeed brightened the day more than the sun. "Good morning, Tomas. How are things on Twins Island?"

Tomas' gut twisted. While everyone else asked him about their future, the town beauty was the only one who ever inquired about his well-being. "Fine...uh, just wonderful."

"You said you'd have a surprise for me today?" She batted her eyelashes.

Tomas' face flushed as hot as sand in afternoon sun. He reached for the vial in his pocket. "I brought—"

"Ah, Monkey Face Tomas, ever the rube." A deep laugh boomed behind him. A huge hand clapped him on the back.

It just about knocked his heart out of his chest. Tomas gritted his teeth. Every instinct screamed to lay a fake curse on Antonius, but it would only make Tomas look petty. He relaxed his jaw. "Good morning, Antonius."

Sofia's father, Julius, paused in polishing a rune-infused fire starter and turned around. His wide shoulders bulged from his blue vest. With his thinning black hair, craggy nose, and small eyes, it was hard to believe he'd sired such a beauty. A friendly smile formed on his lips. "Good morning, Antonius. Sofia, give Antonius a trinket, will you?"

Tomas stifled a growl. Of course, Antonius was the most desired man in town, son of the mayor, who was mayor only because he'd married some lord's cousin's nephew's sister-in-law. With Antonius' good looks and status, he already had enough girls to fill the long-departed Runemaster Imperator's harem.

Meanwhile, Tomas was just an ugly fisherman from a provincial island. He forced a friendly smile. "So, Antonius, what's the latest news of the Teleri advance?"

Antonius smirked. "Trying to squeeze out every last fish sale before they come and you flee back to Twins Island?"

"Of course not," Tomas said. "I just wanted to know. Last I heard, they'd encircled Mykos."

"Encircled? It's called a siege." Antonius puffed out his chest, his eyes flitting sidelong toward Sofia.

Sofia just blinked her long lashes at him.

Tomas' gut knotted even more. "Right, a siege. It's just two days' march from here."

Antonius snorted. "Stick to Divining, and leave soldiering to soldiers. They have to capture Mykos first, or leave their supply lines exposed. Mykos can hold out indefinitely, because the Teleri's dumb Bovyan brutes lack the siege engines to breach the city walls. On top of that, they have no means to deny Mykos access to the Inland Sea and trade with the Serikothi." He lifted his chin toward one of the crimson-uniformed rowers at the tanner's.

Tomas cocked his head. That didn't make sense, because... "Couldn't the Teleri leave soldiers back to protect their supply lines? Or send cavalry ahead?"

Gasping, Sofia covered her mouth. "Is that what Diviner's Sight is telling you?"

Antonius' bellowing laugh just about shook the stall over. "If it is, I'd tell him to get a new eye. Teleri Bovyans might be able to overwhelm anyone in the open field, but there's no way they'd risk sending troops here without first securing—"

Shouts and screams erupted from the west end of town and grew louder. Here in the marketplace, the merchants all pointed and chattered among themselves.

"What's going on?" Sofia came out from behind her stall and peered toward the commotion.

Hand on his sword hilt, Antonius straightened. "I'll go see. I think—"

A tide of townspeople rushed into the square, first from the main road, then from the four side streets. Some tried to head toward the docks, only to turn back.

The press of humanity surged like a wave, taking Sofia with them. Tomas snatched her hand, only to be pulled along. Antonius waded through to reach her, until another surge of people crashed in from the other side.

"Sofia!" her father yelled, hand outstretched from the stall several paces away.

Above the stutter of desperate feet came clopping hooves. Tomas looked to Sofia to make sure she was alright, then to Antonius. "Horses!"

"Where? Oh!" Antonius gawked.

Behind the flood of people from the main street trotted a column of enormous horses, ridden by enormous men. Chainmail jingling, they carried spears with black banners emblazoned with a nine-pointed gold sun.

"Bovyans..." Antonius gasped.

Bovyans! Tomas could only shrink back. Descended from the mortal son of the Sun God, Solaris, they'd once been noble protectors of a land torn apart by the Hellstorm. Originally a source of hope and order to replace the Runemaster Imperator who'd abandoned his sundered empire, they'd since transformed into the barbaric rulers of the Teleri Empire. Until now, he'd never seen one.

Let alone dozens.

Most had dark hair, though there were a handful of blonds. With their fair to olive skin tones, the majority could be mistaken for any of the three indigenous ethnicities of the North. A handful had darker complexions, ranging from bronze to light brown. Their main difference from other humans was sheer size. Ranks of Bovyans now blocked the six entrances into the marketplace, preventing anyone from leaving.

Tomas' forehead scrunched up. Something didn't make sense. Bovyans were nothing if efficient. If Antonius was right, that they wouldn't risk attacking Lorium without first taking Mykos, why were they here now?

"Eldaeri from Serikoth." A Bovyan pointed at a small, crimson-uniformed officer not ten feet from Tomas. He lowered his spear and dug his heels into the horse's flanks.

Townsfolk jostled and made way as the Serikothi drew his naval sword. It looked flimsy compared to the Bovyans' arming swords. Indeed, the officer himself looked flimsy compared to the behemoth bearing down on him.

Hooves thundered across the ground. People screamed and pushed. Shielding Sofia with outstretched arms, Tomas found himself on the edge of the panicked circle, so close that the rush of air and smell of the horse battered him as it charged by.

The Serikothi officer stood frozen in place, his eyes rounded. The spear punched through his chest with a sickening thud, and he let out a strangled cry. His broken body crumpled to the ground as the horse slowed and wheeled. A pool of blood spread under him.

Bile rising, Tomas shielded Sofia's eyes with one hand and covered his mouth with the other. She pushed his hand aside, and gasped.

"Serikothi!" a voice boomed across the square.

Why were the Bovyans targeting the Serikothi? Tomas craned to get a better view.

Horse hooves thundered. Swords rasped from scabbards. Bovyans rode among the running and screaming people, cutting down unseen victims.

"I surrender," a voice pleaded somewhere nearby.

"A galley!" yelled another Bovyan. "Secure the docks!"

The docks. Tomas' heart joined the bile in his throat. If the Bovyans swarmed the docks, there'd be no escape. He had to get there first. Rumor had it that horrible things happened to the women in the Teleri Empire. He took Sofia's trembling hand. "We need to escape the town."

Face sickly pale, she gave a tentative nod.

Tomas closed his eyes and envisioned Lorium's layout as if he were a bird flying above. With the Bovyans attacking the Serikothi galley on the west end of the docks, they might be able to sneak to his boat on the east. He pulled her along, working through the terrified throng. More people emptied into the square from the six entrances. Several Bovyans circled the area, but none patrolled the space between him and the small alley between two shops on the east side.

"Sofia! Tomas!" Antonius' voice carried over the people. "Come back!"

Tomas hazarded a glance back. In the arc of his vision, at least three Bovyans met his gaze. He froze. From their positions, their plan was clear: the invaders were herding people into the square. Now, the sobbing townsfolk had mostly stilled.

With just a handful of constables armed with rapiers, and only a few knives among the locals, there was no resisting. Not after the Teleri shocktroopers had made short work of the Serikothi officers.

Tomas tucked his slingshot deeper into the back of his pants. His village was famous for its sharpshooters, but he wasn't one of them, and a couple of rocks would do nothing against so many armored men.

A hush fell over the townspeople as one of the Bovyans rode forward. He was a head taller than the others, the squared shoulders of his black tabard giving him the look of a demigod. When he spoke, his voice boomed. His accent sounded so...official, as was to be expected from a people originating in the Sundered Empire's heartland. "Captain, bring the Serikothi forward."

Bovyans pushed through, prodding a dozen of the crimson-clad rowers and two of the shorter Eldaeri officers into the space before the leader, and pushing them to their knees.

"I am Governor Keris." He loomed over them like a storm cloud over a tiny boat. "I will soon be in possession of your galley, and I need a crew. You will be paid a gold *draka* per month with bonuses for good work. If you agree, rise."

Tomas exchanged glances with Sofia. The Serikothi didn't even pay that much to ship crews. Their Eldaeri rulers were also famous for their harsh treatment of their Arkothi subjects.

One officer and all but one of the rowers stood, heads bowed.

Keris pointed to the kneeling rower. "You do not wish to join?"

The man raised his head. "Begging your pardon, Governor, but I have a family in Serikoth. If word got back that I served the Teleri...well..." his meaningful glance fell on the officer at his side.

"I understand. Surrender your weapons, swear on Solaris you will never take up arms against the Teleri Empire, and you may return home."

What? So easy? Tomas scanned the townsfolk's faces.

The rower's eyes widened, and a murmur went through their ranks. The crowd, too, chattered at this development. Two of his compatriots returned to their knees.

Keris motioned to one of his underlings. "Take these recruits and record them into your register."

The henchman thumped his chest with a fist, and gestured for the rowers to rise and follow him.

"Not you." Keris set his spear in the path of the Serikothi officer. "The Eldaeri race has falsely claimed to be the Chosen People of my ancestor's divine father. This is an insult to the gods. Captain, execute him, and the other."

A collective gasp just about sucked the air out of the square. Eyes panicked, the Eldaeri turned and started to run, only to meet the thrust of a Bovyan sword. The other officer scrambled to his feet, but two Bovyans dispatched him with brutal efficiency. Blood pooled where their bodies fell.

The people cried out again. A sour taste rose in Tomas' throat. Before today, he'd never seen a murder; now he'd witnessed three brutal ones. And there were other slain Eldaeri Serikothi elsewhere in the marketplace. The Bovyans were ruthless.

Governor Keris pounded his fist to his chest. "Now that we've gotten that ugly business out of the way... People of Lorium. You are now under the protection of the Teleri Empire."

Protection? Occupation was more like it. Tomas had to sneak to his boat with Sofia and row back to his village. It might be within sight of Lorium, but the Teleri would have to find someone who could get them past the Jaws first.

If these invaders could reach the island, though, the governor looked like he could conquer it all by himself. His gaze raked over the locals. "Our protection comes with a price, but it is a fair one. We shall buy your surplus grain and fish directly from the farmers and fishermen at market prices, and we will never take more than the town can spare."

A handful of groans broke out from the middlemen like Mauritizio, and the tax collectors from Mykos, the seat of government.

Keris scowled, quieting the throng. He pointed north across the water to Lydath's Golden Bowl, gleaming atop the mountain that overlooked Tomas' village. "I also need someone who can take us to Twins Island."

A pit sank in Tomas' stomach.

His home. The Bovyans wanted his home.

CHAPTER 2:

Escape Plans

Tomas had daydreamed of holding Sofia's hand, though he never imagined it would be as they edged back toward her father's stall, ducking beneath the watchful eyes of Bovyan shocktroopers. Whether his palm was clammy from her sweat or his own, he wasn't sure. More concerning was the fact that Governor Keris wanted to go to the island where Tomas lived.

The small fishing village welcomed all kinds of visitors. Treasure hunters came with hope, barren couples left with it. Bovyans, on the other hand… Tomas' heart sank. "Do something," he hissed at Antonius, who was following them.

Antonius glared. "What would you have me do? There have to be at least two hundred of them. On horseback."

"Now," Keris said, voice booming over the square, "our scribes will be taking a census. All females must report to our tattooists."

The crowd broke out in protest, with many women wailing.

Tomas shuddered as they reached Sofia's stall. Reports out of other occupied territories were hazy at best, but rumor had it that women suffered the most vicious exploitation at the hands of the Bovyans.

Sofia's grip tightened, and he found her in the corner of his vision. If she was fair-skinned before, she was pale as a ghost now. Her hands trembled. At fifteen, she'd join the other young women. Now she'd definitely not want the vial he'd brought her.

He leaned over and whispered in her ear. "I know a way out of the square. I'll take you to my village."

Her eyes found him. A look of recognition bloomed on her pretty face. She turned to her father.

Julius nodded. "Go, keep her safe. Please."

Slinking low through the back of a stall, hand clasping his slingshot, Tomas guided Sofia to the smithy, just a few steps away. Heat rose off the forge, but the blacksmith had stopped what he was doing to listen to the occupiers. He ignored them as they passed through to a rear alley.

Holding Sofia back, Tomas looked left and right. No one was around. He looked over his shoulder, and his heart sank.

Antonius was still following them. Three would be more easily seen than two.

"Stay back," Tomas hissed. "I need to get Sofia to safety."

"I'm coming with you. You'll need someone who can fight." Antonius patted his sword.

Tomas kept himself from scoffing. Antonius had already confessed to not standing a chance against a Bovyan. Still, there was nothing Tomas could do...except use his reputation as a Diviner and lie. He pointed to a random patch of the sky. "Kor, the Hunter, is rising. If you come with us, they'll catch you."

Antonius blanched. He glanced back through the smithy, but then shook his head. "I'll take that risk. Go."

In the marketplace, the sound of Bovyans barking orders rose above the murmurs of compliant townsfolk. They weren't resisting at all.

Tears glistened in Sofia's eyes.

With one group of Bovyans moving to secure the docks, time was running out. Tomas took her hand again and guided her through the alley, along the rear of the shops facing the market square. His straw shoes left tracks in the packed dirt, but the Bovyans were probably too busy to realize they were escaping.

While many of the buildings were connected, the occasional gap offered direct line of sight into the square. Tomas paused and peeked around; for now, it didn't seem like anyone else thought to escape. The townsfolk were all forming lines.

At the end of the row, they came to the shoreline road. The sea's waters lapped up against the beach that lined the road's far end. His island appeared an indistinct blob in the distance, though Lydath's Golden Bowl glittered like a coin above it from the mountain's summit.

Home! Just half a league away. It would probably be several days before the Teleri bothered to cross the strait, and even then they'd need someone to guide them through the line of underwater rocks which made the approach treacherous. Maybe someone would betray them, but by then he could get his family and Sofia into the marshes.

Tomas's gaze shifted back to the boats. He cursed under his breath.

Thirty paces away, a Bovyan sat high on a horse, guarding access to the docks. Watching over all the boats. Beyond him at the far end, his comrades had secured the Serikothi bireme, and looked to be putting all of its Eldaeri officers to the sword.

Shaking their cries out of his mind, Tomas focused on the task at hand: for now, the soldier's back was to them. Tomas took a step—

The Bovyan wheeled the horse around.

Heart racing, Tomas jumped back behind the corner of the building, out of the Bovyan's line of sight. Curse Antonius for slowing them down. They might've reached the docks first if not for the delay. There had to be another way. He scanned the sea.

Old Gian was still out there in his boat, looking back toward shore, though in the wrong direction. Still, he was close, closer than the docks. They could probably reach the water before the Bovyan rode them down.

With frantic waves, Tomas tried to draw the old fisherman's attention.

Old Gian's head turned, locking on the Bovyan, but he showed no sign of seeing them.

Snarling, Tomas waved again.

Their gazes met.

Thank all the stars in heaven! Tomas pointed to himself, then Sofia. He pantomimed swimming out, then toward his home island.

Gian's head cocked for a few seconds, but then he looked from the Bovyan on the dock and back. He beckoned.

Tomas blew out a sigh and turned back to Sofia. "Can you swim?"

Tears trickling down her cheeks, she nodded.

Good. Despite Lorium being on the Inland Sea, not everyone could. He squeezed her hand. "Old Gian will take us to my island, but we need to swim to him. There's a mounted Bovyan, though, so we need to wait for him to look the other way, keep low, and hurry across."

He peeked around the corner.

The cavalryman reached the near end of the docks and looked to be turning his horse around.

The window of opportunity would open as soon as he started in the opposite direction. If they were fast and quiet, they could make it. Tomas looked back at his companions. "On three. One. T— "

Antonius snatched Sofia's hand and burst past. He sprinted across the road and jumped over the seawall to the beach. The Bovyan's head jerked toward them.

The rotten dung beetle! Tomas broke into run, just as the Bovyan snapped his reins and spurred his horse. The hooves thundered toward him on the hard-packed road, covering half the distance before Tomas made it halfway across. His legs locked up, refusing to move. He looked first at the warrior, then at Sofia.

She and Antonius sloshed through the shallows and dived forward into the water.

Tomas looked back to find the horse even closer.

He fumbled for his slingshot, but his shaking fingers wouldn't work. Willing his feet to move, he resumed his flight. He leaped over the seawall. Landing in the sand, he dashed toward the water.

His heart thudded in his ears; or maybe it was the pounding of hooves coming closer. Sofia had outpaced Antonius and was holding onto the boat, eyes on Tomas, and beckoning.

He hazarded a glance over his shoulder.

The Teleri bore down on him, spear in hand.

Tomas' eyes widened. This was it. His death. Just like the Serikothi in the square. All because that coward Antonius couldn't wait just two seconds for the Bovyan to turn his head around.

The haft struck him in the temple. White stars filled his vision, followed by dark splotches. Tomas collapsed to his knees as the horse passed, kicking up water and mud.

His last image, before all went dark, was that of crimson-uniformed Eldaeri officers being thrown off the Serikothi ship.

CHAPTER 3:

Death Wish

Each time Prince Koryn of Serikoth had tried to get himself killed in some brazen cavalry charge, he'd not only survived—his fame as the Lion of Serikoth had only grown. Astride his faithful chestnut stallion, he stared at the blockwood gatehouse on the other end of the stone bridge, certain he'd finally succeed this time.

The realm might consider him a living legend, never knowing he was living a lie.

Several lies. All would be memorialized with his glorious death this afternoon. He looked over his shoulder. His cavaliers sat straight in their saddles, burnished cuirasses glinting in the afternoon sun, crimson capes and helmet plumes fluttering in the breeze. Victory after victory against Bovyan incursions had inflated their sense of invulnerability, and now they thirsted for war and glory against a different rival.

An older one.

All the fault of his accidental successes.

Instead of ending his miserable existence, Koryn had instead deluded the realm into thinking they could defeat a sleeping giant. He shifted his gaze to the ten dead guards in his own gatehouse, now reverently draped in crimson cloth. Usually, the only barbs hurled across the river were verbal in nature, but these men had been cut down by crossbow bolts.

He'd be the next casualty. Let his death today be a cautionary tale, and hopefully smother the realm's zeal for reigniting a war against kin. It had ended in treaty a century before, but still simmered in the people's hearts.

Pain flared across his lower back, an old injury exacerbated by weeks at sea, followed immediately by a full day in the saddle. It would all be over soon. He took several deep breaths. No one else would need to die today. "Cavaliers of Serikoth. Hold your position here. I will cross into Tarkoth and demand an explanation."

The thirty men stamped their spear butts into the bridge's flagstones in approval, not knowing his true intention. No one ever did, not even the secret lover he could never be with.

At his side, Damaryn crossed his fists over his chest and bowed his head, sending his golden hair rippling in the afternoon sun. The color was a rarity among their race; perhaps an aberrant manifestation of elf blood flowing in Eldaeri veins from millennia ago. He looked up, concern etched in his face. "Your Highness, might I suggest a flag of parlay? Crossing will be seen as an act of war."

"Captain Damaryn, the mongrels have already unleashed the first salvo." He gestured at the deceased behind them, many shot in the back.

Before Damaryn could answer, Koryn squared his shoulders and tapped his heels twice into Bronze's flanks. It was sad to have to sacrifice an old friend, but the men needed to see that despite their beliefs, a cavalier *could* die in the saddle. His heart squeezed as he patted Bronze's neck. "Good boy."

Bronze broke into a trot. His horseshoes clopped over the bridge's old stones. It was one of the last bridges between what were once one people: the Eldaeri, Solaris' Chosen. There'd once been dozens of these structures up and down the Valeri River, some spanning several hundred meters long. Here in the north, this one was only twenty meters, yet the emotional gulf might as well have been twenty kilometers. Perhaps it was time this bridge, too, came down.

Up ahead, nobody from the Tarkothi side had raised a challenge. Maybe this was their strategy: cowards that they were, perhaps they just planned to send a crossbow bolt through his eye, leaving his sickly, but more judicious and intelligent brother to inherit the throne.

He was now just ten meters away, halfway between identical gatehouses that stood like sentinels on either side of the river. The only difference was the color of the banners: crimson for his Serikoth, green for Tarkoth, both emblazoned with the same silver, nine-pointed sun. A symbol of one people, now divided.

Eight meters. This was a bad idea. Koryn's stomach knotted. Any second now, one of the Tarkothi would pop up from behind the barricades or guard tower and point a repeater at him. This was it. For him. Hopefully not Bronze. But it had to be done.

Four meters. No movement. No sound, though the rustling of the river and the pounding of Bronze's horseshoes on stone might drown out Tarkothi activity. At this distance, a blind orc could shoot him through the eye.

Like every other time he'd consigned himself to death, his resolve all but vanished. Even with the king's ultimatum to find a bride, Koryn could still keep his inappropriate lover a secret. After all, they'd been together for years with no one knowing. He glanced over his shoulder.

Faithful Damaryn was there, against orders, riding stiffly in the saddle a meter behind him.

In Koryn's single-minded focus, he hadn't noticed. He tapped his heels into Bronze's flanks, bringing the horse to a stop. He hissed through gritted teeth. "I told you to stay back."

"It looks deserted," Damaryn said.

Koryn peered ahead. He was so close, and no one stirred. Surely they would've hailed him by now. He pitched his voice to carry. "Soldiers of Tarkoth, I am Koryn Vardamcar, Crown Prince of Serikoth. We demand you open the doors."

No answer came, nor did it sound like anyone was on guard. All the resolve drained out of him. Koryn motioned to Damaryn. "Open the gate, Captain."

Crossing his fists over his chest, Damaryn dismounted, marched past, and inspected the heavy double doors.

Like the rest of the gatehouse, and its twin on his side of the bridge, they were made from dense, fireproof blockwood. Koryn's ancestors had brought the saplings across the sea when they'd returned to Tivaralan three centuries before. One people, united in the Sun God's mandate: Solaris' Chosen would restore order after the Hellstorm and Long Winter had sundered a sprawling, decadent empire into dozens of starving warlord holdings.

Damaryn looked back. "The doors aren't barred, Your Highness."

"Open them."

Damaryn pulled one side open.

A man in a leather cuirass and green Tarkothi surcoat tumbled out.

Koryn whipped his sword out and trotted forward to protect Damaryn.

The enemy fell face-forward to the ground, a crossbow bolt lodged in his back. Already dead. From the stench, and the ashen hands, possibly for a day or more.

Damaryn jumped back, eyes wide, then looked up and exchanged glances with him.

"It looks like our men didn't go down without a fight," Koryn said. Small solace for their families.

Damaryn shook his head and traced a finger from their side of the bridge to the dead man. "How would our soldiers be able to hit him in the back, behind the gate?"

Though both his Serikothi and the rival Tarkothi prided themselves on their marksmanship with the repeating crossbow, this was indeed an impossible shot. On second thought, some of their own men had died in a similar fashion. Beckoning the rest of the column over, Koryn encouraged Bronze through the gates.

On the other side, five more Tarkothi laid dead, flies buzzing about their bloated corpses. Like the one at the gate, their thin frames, beige skin, and dark hair marked them as his distant kindred: pure-blooded Eldaeri. Had they not met a violent end, Solaris' grace might've blessed them with another century of good health.

Koryn sighed. Enemy or not, they were still Solaris' Chosen. There were too few of them left in the world.

"Only six?" Damaryn asked. "By terms of the treaty, we are both allowed ten at these border crossings."

"The Tarkothi have diluted their bloodlines and even let their Arkothi subjects serve in their armies. Their cowardly, non-Eldaeri comrades must've fled." Koryn motioned to the cavalier at the head of his approaching column. "They may be rivals, but they share our blood. Have their bodies respectfully laid and covered, then rejoin us."

The cavalier crossed his fists over his chest and bowed his head.

With a jerk of his hand, Koryn motioned the rest forward.

Deeper into Tarkoth.

"Are you sure this is wise, Your Highness?" Damaryn asked.

Koryn snorted. "Probably not. Still, there can't be more than a hundred Tarkothi infantry this far north. They'll be no match for cavaliers."

"It only takes one shot," Damaryn muttered as he walked back to his horse.

Koryn buried a snort. If only it were so easy. He gestured down the hard-packed road, which ran along the riverbank to a village a hundred meters away. It probably quartered the rest of the enemy garrison, and they would have answers. As they passed, ethnic Arkothi farmers looked up from green fields of sprouting wheat and muttered among themselves.

Children darted among the several dozen wooden structures with thatched roofs. His gaze locked on the largest, a barracks made of blockwood.

"Villagers," he said, "clear the road. Return to your homes."

Though the Serikothi had no jurisdiction in Tarkoth, unarmed peasants wouldn't disobey mounted, armed men. Scowling mothers pulled children into their houses, while other Tarkothi pressed up against the closest buildings.

He gestured toward the blockwood barracks. "Cavaliers, secure the premises."

The men drew their bows and notched arrows. The horses fanned out with the precision of a dwarf-made clock, surrounding the structure. Koryn's chest swelled with pride. Serikothi cavaliers drew from the best cavalrymen in the realm, and no fighting force in Tivaralan could match their discipline.

With a perimeter formed, and arrows trained on windows, several of the men dismounted and stormed through the door with naked sabers. "Hands up! Hands up!"

A minute later, one came out, crossed his fists over his chest and bowed his head. "Your Highness, the barracks are secure. There are three injured soldiers and a woman tending to them here."

Koryn exchanged glances with Damaryn, then dismounted. He marched to the barracks. Damaryn fell in a step behind him. No sooner had he entered than a young woman with thick black hair rushed at him.

She flailed against his chest with her bare hands. "You animal!"

His men pulled their bowstrings, by Koryn motioned them down. He seized her wrists before she hurt herself on his armor.

She struggled in his firm grip. "Murderer!"

Deeper in the room, three soldiers in Tarkoth's green lay bandaged on cots. Like her, they were fair-skinned, with heights and builds too large to be Eldaeri. Their coarser features suggested they were full-blooded Arkothi.

"You killed Meryn," she wailed. Tears streaked her plump cheeks.

Meryn was an Eldaeri name. Was this girl a lover? Or even a wife? It wouldn't be a surprise, given the Tarkothi Eldaeri's penchant for mixing races. Lips pursed, Koryn scanned her wrist and found the woven bracelet that marked marriage. "We killed no one."

Eyes wide, she shook her head. "Liar!"

Damaryn strode forward with a scowl. "Watch your tongue, woman. This is Crown Prince Koryn—"

Koryn held a hand up, and Damaryn fell into silence.

"It was your men," one of the injured soldiers said. "They attacked us from behind at dusk."

"They killed the headman," the woman said, tears glistening in her eyes. "And stole all the messenger birds. They said if we touched the bodies, they'd come back and kill us all."

Koryn exchanged glances with Damaryn, then back to the Tarkothi. "We do not resort to such dishonorable tactics."

"I saw you," said another soldier. "Serikothi crimson."

"Your Highness." A cavalier appeared at the door. "Five Tarkothi riders are approaching. Two kilometers away.

"Captain Damaryn," Koryn said, "find out what you can here."

"What about you?" Damaryn's forehead creased.

"We're going to greet the Tarkothi. If you do not hear from me in two phases, send word to the king." Koryn marched out and traced a circle in the air. "Cavaliers, on me, single rank."

Those who'd dismounted returned to their horses. Koryn swung into the saddle. Tapping his heels, he urged Bronze into a gallop. Behind him, the cavaliers streamed out of the village and fanned into one rank on the verdant farmland.

Far in the distance, Tarkothi riders approached at a trot. It was hard to tell how they were armored, but the diminishing dirt cloud indicated they'd come to a stop. The cavalrymen on the flanks broke off, one to the north and the other to the south, while the other three reared, turned, and broke into a hard gallop back the way they'd come. One on one, no Tarkothi knight would stand a chance against a Serikothi cavalier; now, the Serikothi enjoyed a four-to-one advantage.

Koryn raised an arm and signaled his orders. The cavaliers responded with clockwork precision. Three men on either wing split off in pursuit of the two outriders. The rest of his cavaliers followed him in giving chase to the three. The ground rumbled with the charge, and clouds of dirt kicked up behind them.

The enemy had a kilometer lead, but if Serikothi cavaliers were twice as good as Tarkothi knights, Serikothi chargers were ten times better than their Tarkothi counterparts. Descended from the magnificent horses bred by the ruddy-skinned Kanin in the continent's central plains, they were faster, hardier, and more intelligent...and Bronze was the best.

Koryn withdrew his bow from its case in the saddle and strung it. Perhaps a quarter phase of the Iridescent Moon had passed before they came within range. Hills rose into mountains in the distance, marking the border between Tarkoth and the Bovyan's Teleri Empire. He fit the arrow and took aim. It was against the Serikothi code to target horses unless absolutely necessary, and it would only be a moment before he could hit the rear guard's back.

He drew back the string and—

Koryn let off the tension, held up the hand signal to halt, and reined Bronze in.

Up ahead on a ridge stood ranks of Tarkothi, their green banners hanging limp. Two or three thousand. They held positions on two hills to the north and south, as well.

Koryn's cavalier line slowed to a stop. They were probably just outside of crossbow range from the troops deployed on the north and south hills. They'd almost been drawn into a trap, one which would have surely fulfilled his death wish, but also claimed the rest of the unit. By Solaris' grace, he'd spotted it before all his men entered.

Now he could die, without risking the rest of his cavaliers.

CHAPTER 4:

Enemies on All Sides

With his line of cavaliers deployed behind him, Koryn evaluated the trap he'd almost guided them into. It was one thing to die, and something completely different getting all the men under his command killed. The Tarkothi occupied the high ground above a basin surrounded by three hills. The only cover was a solitary farmhouse.

From here, though, it looked and sounded like the Tarkothi were already loosing volleys at a target obscured by one of the hills. Pulling a dwarf-made spyglass from his saddle, he guided his horse parallel to the opening into the basin.

He sucked in a breath. Over a hundred unarmored soldiers marched up the far hill's slopes, toward the Tarkothi center and into the barrage of crossbow bolts. Several dozen had already fallen, while some continued forward on all fours, and others used spears to limp along. But who?

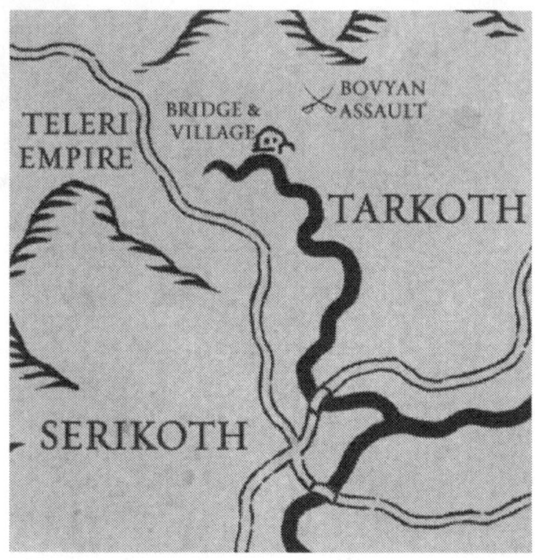

They wore neither Serikothi crimson nor Tarkothi green. No, waving above their orderly ranks were black banners embroidered with the gold sun of the Teleri Empire. Their lack of fear in the face of certain death identified them as Bovyan shocktroopers.

What were *they* doing this far east? Up to now, all of Koryn's victories had come against the Bovyans along the Serikothi border to the west. Their tactics had been limited to forming up a line of shields and spears, and relying on their sheer size and training to overwhelm opponents. It didn't work well against his cavaliers, and wasn't working now against Tarkothi crossbow volleys.

A white glint flashed at the top of the hill. Koryn shifted the scope to focus on it, and had to draw another sharp breath.

The Light of Solaris.

A gift from Solaris to his Chosen, it held a spark of the god's divinity. No Eldaeri army with the Light shining at its head had ever lost a battle. After the civil war split the empire, Tarkoth retained the Light. For it to be here meant...

A member of the Tarkothi royal family led their troops.

Koryn focused on the man carrying the Light. A green cloak draped over his shoulders, partially obscuring a glinting cuirass. The silver circlet over his long brown hair marked him as a prince, and the thin, high-bridged nose, dark eyes, and strong jaw could've made him a sibling. He gestured into the basin.

Following with his spyglass, Koryn found what the Tarkothi prince was pointing at: a single Bovyan had broken away from his decimated lines, and was retreating toward the farmhouse. Yellow flashed in its window. Koryn trained the scope on it.

Huddled inside were two blonde girls, probably no older than eight. They likely weren't of Solaris' Chosen, given their hair color, but their safety was still the responsibility of the ruling Eldaeri.

At the top of the hill, the Tarkothi prince passed the Light to a general and spurred his horse. He charged down the slope through a gap in the enemy lines. Brave, but irresponsible. Bordering on insanity.

Something Koryn would do, too.

Still, the Tarkothi prince wouldn't reach the Bovyan in time to help the girls. Not on a Tarkothi horse.

A Serikothi stallion, however... Snapping his spyglass shut and shoving it into his saddlebag, Koryn spurred Bronze into a gallop. Now who was irresponsible and insane?

"Your Highness!" a cavalier yelled.

Koryn ignored him, instead fitting an arrow to his bowstring. Bronze's hooves pounded in the dirt, eating up the distance to the Bovyan. By Solaris, the brute would reach the farmhouse before Koryn could take a good shot. He loosed the arrow anyway.

It just missed, lodging into the doorframe. The Bovyan looked over, then ducked through the entrance. Little screams pierced the air.

Koryn covered the ground in a few seconds. Before Bronze slowed to a stop, he swung out of the saddle. He drew his sword and charged in.

The two girls clung to each other by a burnt-out hearth. Sobs wracked their tiny bodies. They looked all the tinier given the size of the Teleri soldier. Koryn had never seen a Bovyan so close.

Descended from the mortal son of Solaris, the monster stood at least a head and shoulders taller than Koryn, and was nearly twice as broad. Their race might've once been noble and honorable, but now they were nothing more than marauding thugs. Ignoring the wails of the girls, the Bovyan fumbled with his bag. A chainmail tunic jingled beneath his black cape.

Sweaty palms compromised Koryn's grip as he cocked his sword back and prepared to run the enemy through. There was no honor in stabbing a man in the back, but he didn't otherwise stand a chance against such a humongous warrior.

The Bovyan swung around, his blade sweeping in a broad arc.

Koryn lifted his own weapon. Made from a falling star, Sunblade absorbed some of the shock as it stopped the blow inches from his throat. Still, his teeth rattled. Heart pounding in his ears, he disengaged and circled, putting himself between the enemy and the children.

"Your hands tremble, Eldaeri." The Bovyan pointed his sword. "Your race is weak, too weak to claim yourself the Chosen of Solaris. You don't deserve to share this world."

Koryn pursed his lips. The traces of elf-blood that flowed through his people's veins might make them smaller than the average human, but gave them long life and health.

And speed.

The Bovyan lifted his blade.

Koryn drove forward. The sword punched through chainmail, flesh, and bone. Another blade burst out from the other direction, sending a spray of blood into Koryn's face.

Gurgling, the Bovyan crumpled to his knees, revealing the wide-eyed Tarkothi prince behind him. His complexion looked almost green.

The Bovyan dropped his weapon and gripped Koryn's blade. He stared at it with wide eyes. "Eldaeri…royal sword. It is…my honor…to be killed by a prince of Serikoth." He collapsed in a jingle of armor.

Blood poured from the wound as Koryn pulled Sunblade free. The smooth metal, further slickened by fluids and innards, allowed it to slip out with ease.

On the other side of the hulk, the Tarkothi folded over. He held himself up by his sword, which might've been a twin of Koryn's own. Was he injured? It didn't look like he'd—

The Tarkothi prince vomited onto the dirt floor.

A first kill, perhaps. Koryn shuffled on his feet, remembering his own. It had been at sea, when he was just a teenager, on a hunt for the Pirate Queen's marauders. Still, this prince was a man grown. Perhaps Tarkothi royalty rarely bloodied their own hands.

A large Tarkothi with blond hair and a square jaw burst through the door, sword in hand and green-garbed guards in tow. The markings on his surcoat indicated his rank as a lieutenant. His eyes fell on the prince. "Prince Elrayn! Are you all right?"

Koryn stared. Elrayn? Tarkoth's Crown Prince *was* getting his hands bloody. To save two girls… He turned to find the children huddled together, lips trembling. Every instinct said to comfort them, but they were Elrayn's subjects, not his.

The pathetic man was wiping his mouth and trying to hide it, and doing nothing for the two.

Koryn went over and knelt by them. "Are you all right?"

The girls tentatively nodded. One of them smiled.

And to think, his lover said he would never be good with children. "Where are your parents?"

The older of the two pointed out the door. "On the other side of the hill."

It provided the perfect excuse to get out of here. Koryn took their hands. "Come."

"Wait." The large lieutenant studied the fallen Bovyan with dispassionate eyes. He knelt down and retrieved a blood-stained sheet of paper.

"What is it, Tharos?" Elrayn stretched a hand out.

Tharos proffered the page.

Elrayn's eyes roved over it, then widened. He looked up and glared at Koryn. "Your sword. You're a Serikothi Prince. Given the rumors of one of them being sickly, I would guess you are the healthy one. Crown Prince Koryn Vardamcar, the legendary Lion of Serikoth."

Koryn crossed his fists over his chest and bowed his head. "Well met, Prince Elrayn."

"We can dispense with the pleasantries. I know why you are here." Elrayn flung the bloodied sheet at him.

Koryn caught the paper and scanned it.

Our alliance with Serikoth is ratified. Their assassins will capture the North Bridge. Attack Esterios to draw the Tarkothi armies north. First Consul Geros Bovyan XLIII

Koryn's brows furrowed, and he checked the wax seal. It was embossed with the Teleri's nine-pointed sun crest.

This wasn't possible. His Serikoth didn't even use assassins, and certainly wouldn't ally with the rapists and murderers of the Teleri Empire. He shook his head. "I know nothing of this."

"Yet you are here," the aide said, "near the North Bridge."

"Your men attacked our outpost," Koryn growled.

Elrayn jabbed a finger at Koryn. "I still can't believe this. Civil war tore our grand empire apart. It is the greatest taint on our people's glorious past, a folly of arrogance and stubbornness. Now, you would ally with the disgraced ancestors of Solaris' mortal son, against your own brethren."

"Are you still our brethren?" Koryn gestured to the two girls behind him. "It is Solaris' mandate to protect lesser humans, not intermingle with them."

Elrayn's face flushed an ugly shade of red.

Koryn chewed on the inside of his cheek. He'd said too much, and they were outnumbered in enemy territory. He whipped out the message that had brought him here, and held it up. "This arrived by messenger bird yesterday morning. It says Tarkoth ambushed our garrison on the North Bridge."

Elrayn shook his head. "A survivor from your brazen attack on the North Bridge substantiates the Teleri message about assassins."

"A lie," Koryn snarled.

"You are our prisoner," Elrayn said, "until we figure this all out."

Prisoner! Then again, it had been a risk ever since they set hoof in Tarkoth. Koryn turned his sword around and held the hilt toward the enemy prince.

Elrayn waved his hand. "Out of courtesy, you may keep Sunblade. If you initiate hostilities, however, we will claim it as a spoil of war."

"You wouldn't." Koryn lowered the blade. Just one of six, the swords were all heirlooms of the Eldaeri people.

"Yes, I would. And we would kill your cavaliers."

"Let them go, and kill me instead," Koryn said. Better to die in battle than old and bitter over lost love.

Elrayn shook his head. "This is a sign from Solaris. You see, I've already made arrangements with the Queen of Korynth to have your sister, Alaena, wed my brother, Aryn. Now that you are here, I want you to marry my sister, Karyna."

Koryn's head spun at the implications. Elrayn was arranging marriages, this one at swordpoint, to bind three rivals through alliances. To... "You want to reunite the Eldaeri Empire."

"To stand as one against the threat of the Teleri Empire. To restore our former glory." Excitement rose in Elrayn's voice.

Koryn snorted. "To position yourself as the future ruler of it all."

"If Solaris wills it." Elrayn's enthusiasm left little doubt of his faith in the gods' will.

Reunifying the empire.

How had Koryn not heard of Tarkoth and Korynth negotiating a marriage alliance? For his sister Alaena, adopted by the Queen of Korynth, that meant marrying Tarkoth's Prince Aryn. Koryn had met the aloof prince in Cathay a month before. He'd come off as something of a philanderer, the way his eyes roved over his pet half-elf.

For Koryn, being a pawn in this game was worse than Father's ultimatum to get married. At least in the latter, he had a choice in who, even if it could never be his beloved.

were bred to fly from relay stations to a home ship, no matter where it was. There were eight birds roosting in wall nooks in this smaller room, along with a writing table for correspondence. The system far surpassed the speed, cost, and efficiency of the horse relays used by the rest of the world, including Jie's homeland.

She flipped the quill—such a strange writing instrument—in her fingers as she approached the newly arrived bird. She froze. The bird beside it had a darker shade of grey in its feathers. It had never roosted on this ship, at least not since she'd come aboard, while all the others had come and gone and returned at least twice each.

Still eyeing this new friend, she loosened the tube around the—

Heavy footsteps clopped across the deck toward the door. A key thunked into the lock.

Jie pocketed her light, plunging the room in darkness. Still, there was no hiding place, no time to return the quill and either retie the tube or fish the message out. Whoever was at the door would wonder why it was unlocked, and the bird tampered with.

She leaped up to the board above the open window, then swung through, feet first. Turning around halfway out, she caught the bottom edge of the window's outside frame with her fingers. Her legs dangled. If her grip failed, she might not survive the plunge into the sea, and certainly wouldn't last long in the frigid waters.

Light flashed in the window.

"Guards!" someone yelled.

Jie took a deep breath. The minutes she'd wasted savoring Aryn's touch had cost her the time to read the missive. Now she had to get back. Giving herself a swing, she lunged for the porthole one deck down and three *chi* over. It was half her body length, and the hull sloped inwards, but she managed to catch hold with one hand. Toes finding purchase on a decorative ridge running along the ship's hull, below the row of portholes, she hauled herself up. She peeked in.

Aryn still slept, his back now to the wall.

Her slender body was just small enough to squeeze through. She landed lightly on the floor. On deck, garbled voices grew louder. There was no chance of getting back to the cabin she shared with the Aksumi Mystic. So much for keeping her relationship with the prince secret: Aryn would be the best one to vouch for her whereabouts right now.

She stripped off her stealth suit, underwear and all, and covered them with the dress on the floor.

The blankets rustled ever so quietly, but they might've been a New Year's fireworks display for all the sound her elf ears picked up. She looked back.

Prince Aryn's eyes roved over her.

A well-bred Cathayi lady would have covered herself. Jie was not well-bred, and it was kind of nice for a man—royalty, no less—to appreciate her flat body. Unlike a certain clan brother. Flashing him a grin, she sashayed what hips she had, a trick she'd never learned well in her previous life as a courtesan-in-training.

Aryn reached for her. "Come back to bed, Jyeh."

The way his tongue mangled her name was so...enchanting. Her heart buzzed like a dragonfly's wings. It would've been child's play to avoid his hand, but she let him capture her wrist and pull her close.

"Your Highness," she said, dipping her chin. "There seems to be some commotion outside. I want to get back to my cabin before my presence with you besmirches your name."

Laughing, he spun her around and sat her down on the edge of the bunk. His fingers walked up her back, sending a symphony of tingles down her spine. "I have another idea. Will you be my princess?"

Jie nearly choked as she stifled a shudder. The last princess in her life was far from the perfect specimen of grace and beauty. In fact, if any woman could challenge Jie for a flatter body, it would be her homeland's own awkward princess. She spun around and arranged her expression into detached nonchalance.

Aryn raised an eyebrow. "You don't seem pleased."

Heavens, where'd her ability to hide emotions flee to? Some spy she was. "Your Highness, I don't think I'm an appropriate match for a prince."

He flashed a devilish grin that rivaled the one she could conjure if the situation required. "I'm a second son. It doesn't really matter who I marry. We'll make beautiful quarter-elves."

And quarter Cathayi. If the Tarkothi royal courtiers were as shallow as Cathay's, they'd look down on yellow babies with slanted eyes. And considering her no-good father of an elf had abandoned her as a wailing babe, perhaps her yellow half was the better half.

Not to mention, there was always the clan to consider. The master had adopted her, raised her as his own. Now there was the pressing mission to track the assassin, find out why Serikoth had allied with a now-deceased rebel lord back home, and then continue into the Teleri heartland to root out the clan traitor. No, Aryn was just a pleasant diversion.

Or was he? If she kept having to remind herself...

A sharp series of raps thudded on the door. It opened smoothly for the first eight inches where she'd oiled the hinges, then creaked the rest of the way.

"Your Highness," called the grating voice that could only belong to Peris. As Aryn's childhood friend and aide-de-camp, he was the only one onboard who'd barge in without waiting to be acknowledged.

He also had little affection for her, his attitude much like a jilted lover. He'd yet to catch her here, but now she needed to be seen to allay suspicions of a different kind of monkey business. With a twist of her wrist, she slipped out of Aryn's grasp. She snatched up the sheet and covered herself. A surreptitious tug of her foot drew her dress—and the stealth suit beneath—closer to the bunk.

Peris clomped in. He held a book bound not in leather like most of the Northerners' tomes, but rather the heavy paper cross-stitch that her homeland had used three centuries ago. His humongous hand obscured the wavy script. The book didn't look familiar, but how would a

Tarkothi aide get ahold of it? And why did he bring it to Aryn's cabin?

His eyebrows clashed together like angry caterpillars as his sharp gaze locked on her. He thrust the book into the fold of his green officer's coat. Standing taller and broader than the average human, and much larger than the Eldaeri prince of Tarkoth, he lumbered like a bull on his way to breeding. Stopping at the foot of the bunk, he crossed both wrists over his chest.

Aryn rested his chin on her shoulder. His voice tickled her ear. "Peris, I'm a little busy."

"Your High—" Peris cleared his throat as he looked past her. "Your Highness. There were some...irregularities in the rookery."

Jie sucked on her lower lip. Back home, legends spoke of Black Fist spies being in two places at once; here, they wouldn't suspect her. For all anyone knew, she was just an orphan they'd found on the streets of a major port city.

"What kind of irregularities?" Aryn asked.

Peris glared at her again. "I don't think—"

Aryn waved a hand. "It's okay. Just say it."

"The door was left unlocked, and a bird's message tube opened." Peris held up a small scroll, its broken wax seal embossed with Tarkoth's royal crest: a nine-pointed sun, representing the Eldaeri belief that their Sun God had given them some divine mandate. If they looked under her dress and found one of the many hidden pockets in her stealth suit, they'd find the clay copy she'd made from the imprint.

"It must've come loose in flight, or maybe the bird was intercepted."

"Or someone on this ship broke in." Peris' eyes never left her.

Jie leaned into Aryn and brought one of his hands to her thigh.

Aryn yawned. "None of our men would do such a thing."

"Remember," Peris said, stare locked on her, "an assassin shot a crossbow bolt from this ship, killing a Cathayi noble."

Jie nodded. "He's right." It was part of the reason for her trip, after all.

"*And* we have passengers." Peris' glare bored into her.

"Well, Jie was clearly here. What about her friends?"

'Friends' was a loose term, given Jie had just met her three travelling companions. She shook her head. "A Paladin wouldn't do such a thing, and between a Mystic and Diviner, they could magic up whatever the message said." Though the Diviner was more of a conman, and all he was magicking up these days were the Mystic's moans.

"They were in their cabin?" Aryn asked.

Lips pursed, Peris nodded.

"Good. Well, what does it say?" Eyeing the scroll, Aryn stretched his arms out and yawned. His sheet slipped, causing Jie to grit her teeth, but he caught it.

Peris' face flushed an interesting color of red. "It's from the king. You, uh, are engaged."

Jie's heart might have stopped. Apparently, someone *did* care about second sons.

"What? To whom?" Clasping the blanket around his waist, Aryn bolted up, leaving Jie to cling to the end to keep herself covered.

"Princess Alaena of Korynth."

It shouldn't matter, but Jie hated this Princess Alaena of Korynth already.

But that wasn't important as the book in Peris' coat.

CHAPTER 6:

Elements of Surprise

HOUSE MYRANAR
ROYAL FAMILY OF KORYNTH

QUEEN SELAYNA MYRANAR

PRINCESS NADYA
(PRESUMED DEAD)

ALAENA VARDAMCAR

Adopted from Serikoth

Although she was the princess of one nation and the heir to another, the only thing Alaena wanted to rule over right now was the gorgeous elf beneath her. She resisted as he tried to push her off, responding by pulling his luscious golden hair back and exposing his smooth neck so she could lavish kisses there. His fragrance was intoxicating.

Delicately slender but calloused fingers interposed themselves between his neck and her lips.

"Shhh!" His voice was barely audible.

No sooner did she start to sit up, pouting, than he pulled her back down on top of him; an unexpected but not unwelcome surprise. Her curly red locks formed a curtain around their faces. She leaned in, only to have him shake his head. A frown contorted her cheeks.

His violet eyes locked with hers, apologetic. His mouth didn't move, yet his melodious voice sounded clear in her head. *Listen. Do you hear it?*

Alaena forgot about her wounded pride and listened.

Nothing, except the chirping of birds and the rustling of the river in the distance. She might as well have been deaf compared to an elf.

What is it? she mouthed. She looked around, but the canopy of brush in which they had concealed themselves allowed only a few blades of afternoon sun.

His voice was clear in her mind, as if he were orating in the palace's audience chamber. *Several people approaching in boots and chainmail, near the river.*

Near the river! That was almost a kilometer away. Fanaya's tits. His hearing might even rival that of the small Madaeri people. She brushed her hair behind her ear with a coy smile, rearranged her tunic, and eased herself off of him. "It's probably just the queen's men out looking for me," she whispered. "They won't find us."

The queen, bless her foolish old heart, should've learned this lesson by now. Alaena would be found when she was damn well ready. Which wasn't right now; not with a pretty elf to subjugate.

Still, with the soldiers so close, and the possibility of roc riders searching from above, it was time to move deeper into the woods.

She took up her pack in one hand and her bow in the other. Even though she was a decent shot with the famed Eldaeri repeating crossbow, she preferred the bow for its relative quiet and elegance. She turned to the elf. "Come on Thielas, let's get behind them."

Without waiting for him, she pushed out of the canopy. Through the thin branches, she found first the Blue Moon, then the Iridescent Moon. Always seated in the same spot in the heavens to the west-southwest, it now waxed to half. Close to eighteen hundred hours, leaving only an hour of sunlight before dusk.

With the setting sun at her back, she worked her way through the thin-branched trees toward the rustling of the river. The woods were sparse here, much less dense than the lush blockwood and sablewood forests of her home in Serikoth. They provided fewer hiding places.

And sparked that empty hollow in her chest. Homesickness, some would call it.

It'd been over twenty years since Alaena had last seen those majestic trees and breathed in their invigorating scents. Damn her own decision to come here, made when she was too young to understand what leaving home meant. Sure, her adopted queen was much kinder than her father, and the Korynthians weren't nearly as uptight as her own people. Still, the minute traces of elf blood in her veins yearned for lush forests that Korynth's stony coastal plains didn't support. With the river in sight, she brushed a limb out of her path and stopped. A partial bootprint made the faintest impression in the soft ground near the bank.

She turned her head to find Thielas just a few paces behind her, moving as silently as always.

Alaena knelt by the print. "Heading north. Either very large or not very skilled." Which definitely described the queen's men in the woods.

Thielas simply nodded, but raised an eyebrow, prodding her to continue her analysis. He'd taught her so much about woodcraft, starting back when she was an unruly brat running free in Serikoth's forests.

"It lacks a tread pattern, so it's not one of ours," she added. "Very recent. Most likely male, from the size of the heel."

"And armored." Grinning, Thielas held his hand to his ear, mocking her poor hearing compared to his.

"Bastard." Alaena snorted at him. Her people had intermingled with elves in millennia past, giving them long, healthy lives, but not their exceptional senses, nor a talent for magic. His exaggerated sniffing punctuated his playful taunt.

There it was—a sweet, pungent scent. Alaena scanned the area. A wet mash of red fibers, partially hidden by a barberry bush, caught her eye.

Thielas wrinkled his nose and made a face. "Pickled coffee fruit."

Alaena stuck out her tongue. The neighboring Levastyan Empire had flooded the eastern markets with the beans, and the nasty drink they made was all the rage at court. If it tasted anything like it smelled, it would be like licking a bunghole—a fetish she hadn't worked up the bravery to try.

Thielas chuckled. "You're missing my point."

"No, I'm not, ass." A nice ass, at that. "Coffee fruit is rare around here."

"Not only that, but Levastyans use it the same way your people smoke gooseweed —"

Alaena shook her head. "There's no way Levastyans could get so deep into Korynth without our roc riders spotting them."

"—and Altivorcs eat it, because it gives them a quick energy boost."

Altivorcs! The short, stocky humanoids had once enslaved all of mankind, but since their defeat in the War of Ancient Gods a thousand years before, they were no more than roving bands of mercenaries. How and why would they be in Korynth?

Thielas' ears twitched, and he held up a hand.

The sound was loud enough that she could hear it, too: the jingling of mail, mixing in with the river's rolling waters. The only ones who should be in armor would be the queen's men, looking for her; but she and Thielas had already established these weren't the queen's men.

"Follow the river north, quietly." Alaena knew what his response would be, waited for it.

"You're going closer?" The elf's tone sounded incredulous.

Alaena grinned and flashed her most sultry smile. Elves rarely showed much interest in humans, but she could mold this one like clay in her hands. Without another word, she slipped north, moving soundlessly along the low ridge overlooking the riverbank.

Thielas froze in place, grabbing Alaena's arm and yanking her back.

Before she could protest, an arrow zipped right through where she would've walked. She looked away from the river, in the direction from which the cowardly attack had come. A shape ducked behind a tree trunk.

Thielas pulled her down, off the ridge and onto the riverbank, just as a few more arrows whizzed over their heads. One ricocheted off a tree trunk and fell harmlessly near her feet. She snatched it up as he pulled her along, behind the cover of a large boulder.

Alaena studied the arrow. The fletching was matte black, belonging to no local bird. The metal head, too, was long and sleek.

"There are at least four of them. Shall I whisk us away to safety?" Thielas' eyes were narrowed, his voice urgent as he pressed his back against the boulder.

She shook her head. "I want to know who is attacking us."

"Alright then, cover me," Thielas offered her a grim smile. He closed his eyes and began to sing in the musical words of elf magic.

Alaena's eyes darted from side to side, looking for threats for about fifteen seconds, fighting off the lulling effect of the elf's beautiful voice.

A low hum pulsed out from the boulder, followed just a second later by another.

Thielas opened his eyes. "Five of them. Four closing in, moving tree to tree, another running north." With nonchalant grace, he unslung his bow and nocked an arrow. Then he ducked out from behind their cover, shot, and jumped back.

A sharp cry pierced the air, but Thielas ignored it. "One is coming low around the other side of the rock."

Alaena pulled the bowstring taut and turned the corner. Creeping low to the ground was a bipedal figure with turquoise skin and scraggly black hair, a serrated broadsword in one hand. It was the first Altivorc she'd ever seen.

He wore chainmail over a glossy black tunic that stood out like a damn bride at a royal wedding. His eyes widened, but she gave him little time to do anything else as she loosed the arrow into his neck. A sound gurgled in his throat as he clawed at wound. She nocked another arrow.

Another cried out from a dozen feet away, her view obscured by the boulder.

Not waiting, she turned around the rock to see someone throw himself behind a tree about ten meters away. Two others lay in pools of black blood, shot through the eye by the elf. "Come out," she yelled. "You're cornered."

"I don't think he speaks your language." Thielas trained his arrow at the spot.

"Well, why don't *you* tell him?"

Thielas shrugged, his apologetic smile more annoying than charming for a change. "I don't speak the Altivorc language, beyond a few important words."

"Like?"

"'Die.'"

Alaena snorted. "You've hunted them for *how* long and haven't had time to learn it? Why don't you just magic up a translation?"

"Because that would take too much time, and the other one who is running away will bring his friends back." Thielas' amused smile made his cool logic all the more infuriating.

"Fine, I'll handle this one, you chase the other down." It wasn't worth admitting it, but Thielas was a far better woodsman and could run faster through the brush.

He flashed another smile and bolted down the path.

Alaena turned her attention back to her hapless target. His heavy breathing behind the tree made it sound like he was doing something inappropriate, but more likely he was just nervous. "Come on, you're not going to escape. Let's make this easier on both of us."

A curved dagger, a bow, and a quiver of arrows were tossed out from behind the tree in succession, each landing with a thud in the brush a few feet away. An arm appeared from behind the tree, empty and lifted in surrender.

"The sword, too," Alaena prompted. Maybe he understood, maybe he had a sword. It was hard to tell from here.

He ducked out from behind cover and hurled his broadsword toward her, answering her uncertainties.

Still, he lobbed it like an Estomari merchant princess, with no chance of it finding its mark. She loosed the arrow. He groaned as it thudded into his shoulder. He turned to run, but the injured arm hobbled his pace. Alaena caught up to him with little effort. Sword in hand, she swung at his legs with the flat of her blade. He tumbled face-first to the ground with a yelp.

Alaena shook her head as she sheathed her sword, disappointed that her arrow had snapped. Withdrawing a length of rope from her pack, she knelt on the Altivorc's head and bound his hands behind his back. When she rolled him over, she sucked in her breath.

He was young. Not yet a man. His black eyes were wide, and his breathing rapid.

"Stay still," she said. She tried to make her voice as soothing as she could—which was not at all. "I won't hurt you, unless you try something stupid." She pointed to the broken arrow shaft lodged in his shoulder and withdrew her knife. The leather sheath she stuffed into his mouth did little to muffle his screams as she worked the arrowhead out.

Thielas' presence loomed over her shoulder. Without looking back, she asked, "Did you get the fifth?"

"Yes. He surrendered when the underbrush came up and ensnared him. I have him here."

Arrowhead removed, Alaena withdrew a small vial and sprinkled a few drops of pungent liquid over the wound. The boy shrieked through gritted teeth, and Alaena patted him reassuringly. She looked back at Thielas. Behind him, an older Altivorc with dozens of small scrapes lay bound in vines. Even after a decade, Thielas' magic never ceased to amaze her.

"So, how about that magic translation?" she prompted.

Snorting, Thielas chanted again in the language of elf magic. "All right, speak."

The boy's eyes widened. "You can speak my language?"

"Sure, kid," Alaena said. "Now tell me, what's your name?"

"Frkt."

Alaena tasted the name. Maybe her tongue wouldn't be able to make the sound. "So, Frkt, where are you from?"

"Klz."

No place she'd ever heard of. At the side, the other Altivorc struggled at the vines and grunted. Scowling, he shook his head at the boy.

Alaena grinned. It was always better to start with easy questions, which someone wouldn't lie about. It was time to probe some more. "How long have you been in Korynth?"

"Five days."

"What are you doing here?"

The runt's lips twitched. "Hunting."

Alaena looked at Thielas. "Can you make him tell the truth?"

Thielas snorted. "If I had that kind of magic, I would use it on you."

"Then can I cut him?" She grinned and turned back. "Look, nobody hunts in armor. If you don't tell me why you are really here, I'm going to open that wound back up and let you bleed out."

The boy shook his head so hard it might've fallen off. "We were hunting...you."

Alaena's stomach squeezed. "Me? Why?"

"To keep you from marrying the Prince Aryn of Tarkoth."

Thielas coughed.

Alaena's stomach leaped from her chest to her throat. Marriage? To a Tarkothi prince? While Korynth and Tarkoth weren't on bad terms, her homeland of Serikoth still harbored animosity from the civil war which had torn the Eldaeri Empire apart, a hundred and twenty-some years ago. She put the dagger at the kid's throat. "What are you talking about? I'm not getting married."

The boy's eyes shifted to his companion's, then back to hers.

"Explain yourself." It couldn't be right. She'd snuck out of the capital days ago. Certainly the queen wouldn't have decided so suddenly, and without consulting her first.

Tears trickled down his cheeks. "I don't know. I just do what I'm told."

Alaena whirled on the other captive and flipped her dagger through her fingers. "I'm not going to torture a boy, but an adult..."

The older Altivorc squirmed through the vines, putting a few extra inches between them.

She was upon him in a split-second, and set her dagger tip to his groin. "Your young friend's memory has failed him, but I think yours is just fine. Who sent you?"

He closed his eyes, his lips forming incomprehensible movements.

Though maybe not incomprehensible for Thielas. She turned to him. "What's he muttering?"

"I'd guess a prayer to his gods."

She nodded. "What's the head of their pantheon called?"

"Tivar."

Of course. All humans—save for her own Eldaeri ancestors, who'd escaped the mainland when the Altivorcs had conquered it millennia ago—had once renounced the true gods and worshipped Tivar. She turned back to the soldier and applied a little pressure with the dagger. "When I'm done with you, you won't be fit to serve Tivar. But I hear the Emperor of Cathay hires eunuchs."

Thielas shook his head. "They haven't employed eunuchs since their last dynasty."

She winked at him before turning back to the man. "You *will* talk. Either now, or in a few minutes, with your voice a few octaves higher."

"All right."

She looked over her shoulder. "What happens to followers of Tivar who break an oath?"

"Their soul will pull Tivar's flaming chariot for all of eternity," Thielas said.

"Doesn't sound like fun." Alaena gave a fake shudder. "Swear on Tivar you will tell the truth."

His lips pursed.

She shredded across his inseam.

"I swear!" His eyes widened.

"Good man. Now, let's try again. Who sent you?"

"Our king," the man said.

An honest but useless answer. "Why did he send you?"

The Altivorc chewed on his lip. "I wasn't told all the details, but we're acting on behalf of the Teleri Empire."

Alaena sucked in a breath. It made sense. The Teleri Empire might be too busy conquering its neighbors now, but their Bovyan rulers wanted nothing less than the eradication of the Eldaeri race. Her race. The one which had brought peace and prosperity to the people suffering after the Hellstorm and Long Winter.

"It sounds urgent," Thielas said. "Shall I whisk you back home?"

She grinned. One of the perks of sleeping with a descendant of the Elf Angel Aralas was never having to walk anywhere if she didn't want to.

Still, something didn't add up. Though the country was small, it was strange that these Altivorcs could track her down, when she could elude Korynth's rangers and roc riders. “I want to know how these men found us.”

He shrugged, mirth dancing in his eyes. “I can find out.”

She turned and headed to where the boy’s broadsword lay on the ground. She picked it up and looked back. “You do that. I’m going to walk home.”

“That will take days.”

“I am happy to make them wait.” The queen had been more of a mother than Alaena’s real mother, and confronting her might break the old woman’s heart.

CHAPTER 7:

Illusions

Aelward Niromar had joined the Tarkothi Royal Navy because a ship was one of the few places where nobody cared he was the king's illegitimate son. Sailors used the term *bastard* so often, it might as well have been a term of endearment. It was far better than the pretty honorifics delivered by courtiers, whose fake smiles hid derision.

Here, leaning against the *Sea Dragon's* black forecastle rail, Aelward served in anonymity and rose in rank through his own toil. He tugged at the sleeves of his stiff green coat. This current fool's errand—to fetch some princess and press her into a political marriage—would put him just a little too close to court intrigue.

And too close to his idealistic half-brother's fish-brained schemes. Crown Prince Elrayn was nothing if not ambitious. More surprisingly, the king had agreed. Neither had both oars in the water.

Aelward turned and looked out to sea. Far ahead, another ship bobbed, its sails down.

"Oi, Ignatius." He beckoned a young sailor in a loose white shirt and baggy pantaloons.

The man stared at him with rounded eyes, then approached and leaned in. "You are no longer one of us," he whispered. He raised his voice. "Sir." He crossed his fists in front of his chest.

Aelward shivered, and not from the salty breeze whipping through his hair. Since receiving a field commission to command crew, he had to reacquaint himself with honorary addresses and salutes. At least it was sincere this time. Of course, he had to get used to speaking like a stuffed shirt, at least among the stodgy officers. He pointed out to sea. "Mister Rogin, find out the disposition of that ship and bring me a scope."

"Very good, sir." Ignatius crossed his fists and then hustled down to the main deck.

Aelward squinted at the ship. At this distance, it was impossible to make out the flag. Still, the morning reports, garnered from the admiralty's central bird roost and sent to every vessel in the fleet, made no mention of other ships in the general area.

Ignatius huffed up and presented the dwarf-made looking glass. "The crow's nest reports it's a galleon flying the Pirate Queen's flag, three kilometers ahead, stationary."

"What's it doing?" Drawing the scope out, Aelward zeroed in on the ship. Sure enough, a three-master faced directly at them. A white-clad boarding crew armed with cutlasses stood in orderly ranks on the deck. The Pirate Queen's blood-red standard, with its white nine-petaled rose, blossomed out as a crosswind caught it.

His forehead scrunched. The Pirate Queen had become more aggressive in the last year, ever since replacing the old white-on-black skull flag.

Still, a galleon didn't stand a chance against the Tarkothi flagship, with its four cannons.

The Pirate Queen was no fool. Nor did she parley. So what was her intention?

Aelward found the Iridescent Moon to the west-southwest, two hundred-fifty degrees, always in its reliable seat in the sky. He snapped the curved grills over the lens to gauge the time. Fourteen-hundred hours, fifteen minutes. Removing the grills, he panned out the focus and scanned the surroundings. A trio of volcanic islands jutted out of the waves to the west-northwest, three hundred degrees. An uncharacteristic mist shrouded their bases.

His jaw tightened. While one or even five galleons didn't pose much of a threat, that fog could hide a dozen ships. With the *Sea Dragon's* sudden change in orders, they weren't supposed to pick up a cruiser escort until they reached Korynth. He snapped the scope shut and turned to Ignatius. "Keep an eye on the islands, Mr. Rogin. Report to helm if you see any ships there."

"Very good, sir." Ignatius crossed his fists. Aelward climbed down from the forecastle and then hurried across the main deck along the windward side. Sailors with both hands free crossed their fists as he passed, while those with only one free hand placed it over their chest.

He climbed the steps to the helm, where he found Captain Sorin, a stuffy old man who'd spent decades at sea. First Officer Laron stood at his side, his posture a study in stoic professionalism. The helmsman worked the wheel.

"Captain." Forming fists, Aelward crossed his arms and bowed his head.

"Aelward, my boy. How's the view from the bow?" The captain examined his perfect cuticles.

Aelward pointed to where the galleon now stood out to the naked eye. "One of the Pirate Queen's ships up ahead."

"We saw it." The First Officer harrumphed. "Looks dead in the water. One of the Pirate Queen's, eh?"

"Looks like they want trouble." Aelward offered the scope, which the First Officer refused.

Captain Sorin laughed. "She's been more daring lately, ever since they started flying that red flag. If not for the urgency of our mission, I'd sink it. Order the bow gunnery to fire when we come within range. They'll move out of the way."

Aelward gestured toward the islands. "At our current course, those islands will be on our port flank at time of intercept. The fog could hide more enemies. Might I suggest we chart a course to the leeward side?"

The captain snorted. "The *Sea Dragon* could take on the Pirate Queen's entire fleet of toy boats. We'll have to remind them that a Tarkothi warship is not a coastal barge. Your father sank, or captured and scuttled, all the pirates' best ships three decades ago."

Aelward gritted his teeth. Though the captain's tone spoke of nostalgia, it was a reminder of a past Aelward had hoped to leave behind when he joined the navy. Everyone in Tarkoth knew the king had taken some lowborn wench to bed during the year-long campaign to clear the trade routes through the Estomar, and then brought back a certain bastard.

That was neither here nor there, even if that certain bastard was here. Aelward peered at the islands and fog. "Should we mobilize the marines, just in case?"

The first officer cleared his throat. "The captain gave you an order, Lieutenant."

Keeping his gaze on Aelward, Sorin waved a hand. "There's no need for dramatics, Mister Loran. Lieutenant, this vessel wouldn't have survived three hundred years if it couldn't overpower or outrun anything the Pirate Queen can float. Now, go relay my orders to the bow gunnery."

"Very good, sir." Even if it wasn't very good. Crossing his fists, Aelward bowed his head, more to hide his frown than to show deference. Even if Captain Sorin wanted to relive the old days, he shouldn't be risking the fleet's flagship while it was on a diplomatic mission. He worked his way toward the bow, sneaking glances back to helm. Each time, the first officer's eyes remained locked on him.

At the forecastle, Aelward scanned the galleon. It didn't look inclined to move out of the way. They were now close enough to make the size disparity with the *Sea Dragon* clear. The uniformity of the enemy's clothes and weapons were obvious to the naked eye now, though the waves muffled their jeers.

Sheer madness. Aelward looked toward the islands, now much closer, yet still obscured by fog. He gestured at the gunnery sergeant. "Mr. Luis, fire on the ship once we are in range."

"Very good, sir." Sergeant Luis crossed his fists. "Oi, men, guns at the ready!"

The gunnery squad snapped to work, unlocking the dwarf-made mount which bolted the Cathayi cannon to the deck. They'd been added to all *Intimidator*-class ships over a hundred years before, during the Eldaeri Civil War. The yellow-skinned Cathayi sold the cannon and firepowder to the highest bidder.

Thank Lunasti that didn't include the pirates, because even though cannon would unbalance their little ships, coastal batteries could muck up the shipping lanes.

Sergeant Luis lowered his targeting scope. "Ten degrees down, three degrees port."

At both guns, two members of the crew turned two different cranks, adjusting the angle of the barrels. Another member packed the firepowder charge, followed by a fourth man heaving the cannonball down the barrel. Lastly, with the help of internal springs, the entire team slid the cannon forward along the bearings in its mount. The efficiency was a thing of beauty.

Aelward unfolded his scope and focused on the enemy ship. Neither it nor its crew had moved.

"On my mark," Sergeant Luis said. "Starboard gun, fire!"

The gunner pulled the cannon's gunlock. The discharge roared in Aelward's ears. The gun glided back in the mount and eased to a stop on springs.

Aelward watched the cannonball hurtle through the air. It struck the galleon in the hull. An excellent shot from this range, but...it seemed to pass through nothing. No sound of splintering wood or screaming men. Cocking his head, he lowered the scope. "Direct hit, but..."

The team started the reloading process.

"Port gun, fire!"

The port cannon unleashed another round. Aelward raised the scope again, just in time to see the ball pass through the ship. Its crew had not reacted at all, still standing in orderly ranks. "Hold your fire, Mister Luis."

He turned to Ignatius. "Go tell the captain that something is wrong. We need to change course."

Ignatius crossed his fists, and then took the forecastle stairs two at a time before dashing across the deck.

Aelward turned back to the enemy ship, closing by the moment. He looked through the scope again. The crew stood stationary. Not only that, their skin tone, clothes, weaponry, everything, looked exactly the same. Even their facial features and expressions were like rows of identical twin statues.

"Sorcery," he muttered under his breath. The Pirate Queen's men came from nearly every race in Tivaralan, each with its own magic, and he'd never seen such uniformity among them.

An illusion.

But why? He turned back to the islands.

A gust blasted out of nowhere, filling the *Sea Dragon's* sails and pitching it to the leeward side. Aelward lurched into the windlass, catching at ropes to keep from falling.

Other sailors were not so lucky. A few of the starboard gunners slammed into the rail, and one went overboard with a shout. The sergeant fell to the deck. A sailor screamed as he fell from the crow's nest, while others clung to the rigging.

The ship righted itself and Aelward searched the helm. Captain Sorin was nowhere to be seen; the first officer was picking himself up. The helmsman clutched the wheel. On deck, sailors clambered to their feet, though one lay motionless in a pool of blood.

Aelward looked forward. The galleon was gone.

Disappeared.

Sucking in a sharp breath, he looked to port. Six pirate ships, whose single masts barely reached the main deck of the *Sea Dragon*, streaked toward them on a steady gale. They might have been flies harassing a horse given the size difference; but an *Intimidator*-class vessel hung back behind them, a twin to the *Sea Dragon* save for the flashing crimson flag of Serikoth. Which one was it? The *Invincible?* The *Intrepid?* Its two bow cannon pointed forward.

Right at the *Sea Dragon*'s flank.

An explosion erupted at the helm. Aelward's neck would ache for all the turning of his head, the—

He gasped. His men ran about like living torches, their features indistinguishable through the flames. Rigging and rear sails also burned in orange and red hues. Had the enemy ship even fired? There'd been no roar of cannons.

Some soldiers and sailors ran about the deck, but most stood frozen, looking around.

Waiting on orders.

Orders that would never come, if both the captain and first officer were dead or incapacitated.

"Men!" Aelward's voice caught in his throat. He cleared it and yelled again. "Oi! Men of Tarkoth, to me! No *Intimidator*-class ship has ever been lost; your *Sea Dragon* will not be the first!"

Eyes locked on him. He slid down the stair bannisters to the main deck and drew his sword. He worked his way toward helm, pointing. "Eris, Lonan, organize your teams to put out the fires! Captain Gio, deploy your marines on a firing line along the port side! Repel anyone who tries to board!"

"Very good, sir!"

"Aye!"

Men scrambled to obey his orders, which came out in the language of the sea instead of stuffy officer-speak. He grabbed Ignatius, who was wavering on his feet, and dragged him toward helm. Reaching the top of the steps, he scanned the high deck. The captain and first officer lay charred on the weathered planks. The helmsman was missing.

Aelward's stomach churned. This was awful. He looked to the port. Thank Lunasti that the Serikothi ship still hung back, its guns silent despite being in range. The six pirate ships couldn't be much more than a few minutes to boarding range, though how in hell they'd reach the deck given the height disparity was beyond him.

Curse the cannon mounts! Ingenious as the swivel design was, it could only rotate so much, and the enemy ships stayed single file, in the safe zone between the *Sea Dragon's* stern and bow port guns. Too bad that even *Intimidator*-class ships, as large as they were, couldn't handle more cannons without being unbalanced.

That was it. Maybe. It would either be the most brilliant maneuver in nautical history, or it would consign them all to a watery grave. He jumped to the wheel. "Stern starboard gunners, aim ninety degrees to starboard; bow port gunners, aim ninety degrees to port. Double the powder charge and lock the recoil dampeners. Fire on me command."

"Sir?" Ignatius' face looked as if he'd sucked a lemon. The entire crew froze in place, staring at him.

"Just do it, damn it! All ye salt dogs, grab hold of something." Because this would either give them an escape route, or send the *Sea Dragon* to the bottom of the ocean.

The sailors and soldiers snapped back to life and hurried to carry out his orders. His heart swelled.

"On me command..." He took a deep breath and swung the wheel hard to starboard. "Fire!"

The cannons roared. The ship pitched. It was all Aelward could do to hold on to the wheel. Many of the crew stumbled to the deck. The timbers creaked. It hadn't turned the *Sea Dragon* much, but it was enough that the wind filled its sails. More importantly, the attackers were now about sixty degrees to the aft, just in range of the stern port cannon.

"Stern gunners," he yelled again. "Unlock the dampeners and target the lead ship! Chain-shot in their sails and rigging next. Marines, shoot!"

The cannon fired. The ball careened across the lead ship's deck, splintering wood and felling screaming pirates. From the *Sea Dragon*, the marines peppered the enemy with repeating crossbows. The crew worked efficiently, from the riggers to the gunnery squad.

Aelward wiped sweat from his brow and looked through the scope again. The lead pursuer floundered, while the next scraped hulls despite its attempt to veer away. The other ships took evasive maneuvers. Their sails went limp, suggesting the gale had blown itself out just as quickly as it had picked up. For now, they were safe.

He looked to the captain and first mate, whose bodies lay charred and unmoving. Whatever hit them hadn't been a cannonball. He turned to Ignatius. "Who is next in command?"

Ignatius made a show of counting on his fingers. "The captain of the marines is the highest rank, but he doesn't know how to sail a ship. I would think it is...you?"

Aelward's heart sank. He'd hoped to make captain one day, maybe after years of experience. He raised his voice. "Oi, men. If ye don't object, I'm taking command of the *Sea Dragon* till we reach port. Hold our course. Have damage and casualty reports to me in a phase."

He looked aft and up to the Iridescent Moon, now at its mid-waxing crescent.

A phase later, the lead carpenter climbed to helm and crossed his fists over his chest. "Bow port cannon has warped, the mounting bolts have splintered the decks. The stern starboard cannon is ruined. The third mast has a large crack."

Aelward nodded. It was as he'd predicted. He'd bought time with the cannon. As long as the Serikothi and pirates had no more surprises in store for them, it was worth the sacrifice. Except... "Casualties?"

The ship's doctor crossed his fists. "Two men went overboard, one sailor died from his fall from the crow's nest. The captain and first mate are dead."

Aelward's jaw clenched. Had it been the right choice? Undoubtedly, they would have lost more if not for his insane maneuver. Though now, other questions arose. Why had the Serikothi allied with the Pirate Queen?

For now, he was in command on a mission to pick up some floozy who was princess of Serikoth by birth, heir to Korynth by adoption, and betrothed to his half-brother Aryn.

All for Elrayn's ambitions.

CHAPTER 8:

Deceptions

Koryn followed Prince Elrayn out of the farmhouse, with Tarkothi guards flanking him. They were Arkothi stock, taller and broader than him, though not as large as their prince's aide Tharos, and certainly much smaller than the Bovyan leader they'd slain. As non-Eldaeri, they wouldn't have been allowed to bear arms, let alone serve in armies, back home in Serikoth.

Outside, several dozen Tarkothi soldiers—both full-blooded Eldaeri and Arkothi, as well as a few that looked like mongrels—encircled his cavaliers, training their repeating crossbows on the horses. Despite the impossible odds, his cavaliers took aim with their bows.

Koryn's chest swelled. They'd sacrifice themselves to the last man, if ordered. He pushed past his captors. "Cavaliers, stand down."

With dips of their chins, they lowered their bows. Though they'd obeyed with the efficiency of dwarf gears, the hard looks they gave him said they weren't happy about the command.

Koryn turned to Prince Elrayn. "Your Highness, you have me. Let my men go."

"They will guarantee your good behavior."

Koryn unbuckled his scabbard and held up Sunblade. "I swear on the swords of our fathers and the Light of Solaris that I will come peaceably with you."

"Will you marry my sister?"

Koryn chewed on the inside of his cheek. He wouldn't be able to marry his beloved, anyway. In his head, a voice that sounded suspiciously like Damaryn pointed out that though an enemy, Elrayn's family descended from the emperors of the Eldaeri Empire. The bloodline was as pure as any noblewoman in Serikoth. Still, to do so would make him a pawn in Elrayn's ploy to control all the Eldaeri kingdoms.

"Your answer?" Elrayn's eyes searched his.

Death was better than being a pawn. Koryn drew his sword.

Around him blades rasped from sheathes and crossbows cocked. The cavaliers raised their bows with the synchronicity of an orchestra. The large lieutenant, Tharos, interposed himself between him and Elrayn.

Elrayn's sword trembled in his hands as he stepped back out of reach. "Sharpshooters, take aim at the prince's legs. He does not have to walk to get married."

Smirking, Koryn set his weapon to his own throat. "Let my men go, or I will order them to charge through your ranks and kill as many of you as they can before dying themselves. I'll kill myself before I blindly agree to marriage."

Blindly, Elrayn mouthed. His eyes roved from the line of horses to his own crossbowmen and back to Koryn. "You are bluffing."

If only he knew.

"Cavaliers, on my signal, loose, then charge." Koryn raised a hand and stared at Elrayn. "I welcome an honorable death."

The Tarkothi looked to their prince and among one another.

"Three seconds," Koryn said. "One."

Bowstrings creaked. Tarkothi men's grips loosened and tightened on their weapons.

Maybe this was really it, a fulfillment of his death wish. "Two."

Sweat glistened on foreheads. The stallions scuffed their feet in the dirt.

It hadn't been a wonderful life, but in between duty and honor, there had been those sparkling moments with his lover. This was it. He started to sweep his hand down. "Thr—"

"Wait." Snarling, Elrayn held raised a staying hand. "Men, stand down."

The tension eased as men on both sides lowered their weapons.

Koryn let an audible groan escape him. That had been close.

Elrayn cleared his throat. "Prince Koryn, if you write and sign an oath, your cavaliers may go in peace. Of course, they must leave their sabers and arrows, and return directly to Serikoth."

To the Eldaeri, a written oath was a bond of honor, not to be taken lightly. To sign would mean he'd have no choice but to comply. Still, Koryn nodded, to save his men.

Elrayn gestured Tharos over. "Provide the prince an ink and quill."

Lips pursed, the large man produced a leather-bound folder with a sheet of paper attached. Inking a quill, he proffered it.

Koryn received it. Cradling the board under his right hand, he took the quill and wrote in the Eldaeri language: *On my honor, I peaceably surrender to Prince Elrayn of Tarkoth, in exchange for the release of all Serikothi cavaliers. Prince Koryn Vardamcar.*

He held it up to Elrayn. "Here."

The Tarkothi prince's eyes roved over the words. "I want you to add the words *with me* after *cavaliers.* Specifics are important, after all."

With a snort, Koryn did as instructed. *In my company* would've been more formal.

"Please add *bequeath jwz* in the postscript," Elrayn said in an apologetic tone. "*Jus Wit Zurit*, by my hand. It's an old Arkothi standard which we have adopted in Tarkoth."

Koryn rolled his eyes. The Tarkothi had let themselves be influenced by the customs of the decadent Sundered Empire, which had destroyed itself with rune magic gone awry. He complied anyway and held it up.

Tharos snatched it from his hand and scanned the letter. With the Arkothi sharing the same alphabet, but with different words, it would be gibberish to a non-Eldaeri.

"Very well," Elrayn said. "Your men may leave."

Koryn turned to the line of horses. "Cavaliers, leave your quivers and sabers, and return to Serikoth. Have Captain Damaryn send a bird to the capital with word of my capture."

Crossing their fists over their chests, the cavaliers did as instructed. The Tarkothi received their weapons with bowed heads.

Marching over to Bronze, Koryn pressed his forehead to the horse's. They'd been through so much, and they'd just been reunited after his journey to Cathay. As much as he'd like to ride on him now, Koryn couldn't let a magnificent Serikothi charger fall into the hands of the faithless Tarkothi. Chest squeezing, he took the reins and handed them to one of the cavaliers.

"I'll take him to the captain." The cavalier crossed his fists and bowed his head, then spurred his own mount on.

The horses peeled off in perfect synchronicity. Chest filling with both pride and despair, Koryn watched as they galloped back the way they'd come, until their dust cloud settled. Sheathing Sunblade and buckling the scabbard, he turned to Elrayn. "Why do you want these marriages so badly?"

"Follow me." Elrayn gestured toward the hill where he'd been entrenched.

A thousand Teleri bodies littered the basin. To a man, they appeared to be in their early thirties—close to the age when they'd inevitably die from the Bovyan Curse. Crossbow bolts peppered their unarmored bodies. Some appeared to have taken their own lives with the sharpened saplings they used as spears. The stench of voided bowels and bladders hung in the air.

Prince Elrayn covered his quivering lips. His complexion bordered on green. He swallowed hard enough for everyone to hear. So pathetic.

A Tarkothi aide jogged up to Elrayn and crossed his fists over his chest. "Congratulations, Your Highness. We only lost ten men and three horses. A brilliant victory."

Koryn snorted. "You outnumbered the Teleri ten to one, held a stronger position, and used repeating crossbows to slaughter unarmored men. And of course, you held the Light of Solaris, under which no Eldaeri army has lost in the three centuries. Did you bring me here to show off?"

Tharos lumbered forward with a raised fist. "Insolent. Our prince drew them into this valley and—"

"Peace, Tharos." Elrayn held up a hand, then turned to Koryn. "We have fortresses blocking every mountain pass between here and the Teleri Empire. Over the last several months, Bovyan units like this one have risked treacherous high paths and attacked towns and villages near the border. They execute every Eldaeri they come across, and spare all others."

Koryn suppressed a shudder. As descendants of Solaris' mortal son, who'd lived three hundred years before, the Bovyans resented the much older Chosen People of Solaris. While the Bovyans had once been honorable guardians of Central Arkoth in the immediate aftermath of the Hellstorm, they'd since devolved into brutal conquerors.

Kneeling by one of the corpses, Koryn examined the makeshift spear in his lifeless fingers. "Only the officer I killed had a sword and armor."

"*We* killed," Elrayn said. "You and me. Tarkothi and Serikothi, separated by hundred-year-old grudges. Now, only together can we repel our mortal enemy and save our race."

The excitement in the prince's voice needed quelling. Koryn gestured at the field of bodies. "It looks like they cannot even afford to properly arm their soldiers."

Elrayn shook his head. "Make no mistake. The Teleri Empire controls vast amounts of land and resources. They have the largest army and the strongest, best-trained men. These, and the platoons that invaded before, are just the vanguard sent to pluck low-hanging fruit while they concentrate their efforts elsewhere around the Inland Sea."

"These Bovyans would soon die from the curse, anyway. They—" Koryn's jaw slackened. The Bovyans' progenitor had been tricked by Solaris' nemesis, Tivar, and his descendants had all been cursed with an early death at age thirty-three. Their warrior culture glorified death in battle. These men had willingly sacrificed themselves, without wasting resources for the Teleri war machine.

Elrayn searched his eyes. “You understand now. Against this kind of resolve, our individual nations will not survive alone once the Teleri focus their full attention on us. This is why the Queen of Korynth agreed to marry your sister to my brother. This is why I hope the message we took from the Bovyan officer, about your alliance with them, is a lie.”

Koryn nodded in slow bobs. It was too much to fathom in such a short time. “I swear on our ancestors’ sword, and on the Light, Serikoth has not allied with the Teleri Empire against you.”

“We cannot trust them.” Tharos gestured at the Teleri’s damning message. “The Serikothi nobles betrayed the Chosen People of Solaris once before. Treachery runs in their veins.”

Koryn glared at the large aide. Who was he to speak?

Drawing up to his full height, Tharos squared his shoulders. He might not be as large as the Bovyans, but he did cast a long, dark shadow.

A chill ran up Koryn’s spine. His hand strayed to his sword.

Tharos...smirked? He reached for his own weapon.

Elrayn held up a hand. “Lieutenant Tharos, send a messenger bird to the capital with details of this battle, along with my...proposal.” He looked sidelong at Koryn.

The wedding proposal, arranged not by formal letters of introduction, but at the point of a sword.

Expression clouded, Tharos crossed his fists and bowed, then tromped up the hill toward the Tarkothi command tent.

Elrayn turned to him. "Tharos grew up on a disputed island in the Valeri River. His parents were killed by a Serikothi attack."

Koryn shook his head. The Treaty of Elbahia, which had ended the civil war, had demarcated the Valeri River as border between Tarkoth and Serikoth, but subsequent floods and earthquakes had created new islands with disputed statuses. There'd been skirmishes over the century—he'd led several—but... "I've never heard of serious casualties, at least not in many years, and never of non-combatants."

"Would you even care about Arkothi farmers?"

Koryn chewed on his inner cheek as they continued up the slope. How to address that veiled accusation? "Of course. It is the Chosen's duty to govern and protect lesser humans."

"And yet, you couldn't envision them serving in your military. When your soldiers orphaned Tharos and his brother, Peris, they were able to survive by joining our army. Tarkoth benefits, because not only are the brothers talented swordsmen, they also have an affinity for training messenger birds. Serikoth would've never recognized and cultivated their talents."

Koryn snorted. "If you give the Arkothi swords, one day they will be pointed at you. Even if the Chosen have made their lives better, do you doubt they pine for the days when an Arkothi sat on the Imperial Throne of Arkos? Even now, they whisper hopes of the Runemaster Imperator returning with the lost crown."

"Funny you should mention the crown..." Elrayn's lips twitched into a grin before he shook whatever ridiculous thoughts he held out of head. He gestured at the Tarkothi soldiers, made up mostly of Arkothi, who were preparing to march. "It may have been three hundred years, but they won't soon forget the Last Runemaster Imperator's arrogance bringing the Hellstorm down on the world. No, the Arkothi are content with our rule, and would far prefer us to the Bovyans."

In this, Koryn couldn't disagree. Because of Tivar's curse, Bovyans could only sire male children, and women of other races would miscarry a second Bovyan pregnancy. They procreated through a vile breeding program, which institutionalized the gang rape of every fertile girl in their vast territory. After giving birth, a new mother would never even hold her own baby. He'd be taken away, so that the empire was the only mother he'd ever know. Meanwhile, the young woman would serve as a wet nurse for a different lot of boys before being sent back to her life. To marry an Arkothi man, and give birth to more girls. To continue the cruel cycle for the next generation of Bovyan shocktroopers.

Without breaking stride, Elrayn searched his eyes. "You understand, don't you? Our own people are slow to reproduce. We need the Arkothi to brace against the rising Bovyan tide. More importantly, we need each other."

"And yet, I am your prisoner," he said as they neared the crest of the hill. Up ahead, full-blooded Eldaeri were breaking down the command camp around Lieutenant Tharos, who looked to be writing at a desk.

"It does not have to be that way." Elrayn pointed east. "A thousand kilometers away and three hundred years ago, our ancestors arrived on the blackships, with sablewood and blockwood saplings, messenger birds, rocs, and the repeating crossbow. Men and women of Solaris' Chosen, all working together to defeat tyrannical warlords and bandit princes who preyed on the survivors of the Hellstorm and Long Winter. We ushered in an era of peace and prosperity. Together, we can protect our race and fulfil Solaris' mandate."

Stopping, Koryn studied his counterpart. Elrayn looked sincere and sounded motivated by high ideals. Still, there was nothing noble about forcing a marriage. And when it came down to it, he was positioning himself at the top of the royal heap. "Alliances can be forged without nuptials."

"And yet, marriage is one of the strongest bonds between nations." Elrayn gestured.

Tarkothi guards prodded Koryn in the back.

Resuming his stride, he glared back at them. Such insolence was to be expected of non-Eldaeri. He took long strides to catch up. "You won't gain my father's trust by keeping me as a hostage."

"You are technically a trespasser and prisoner of war. Write a letter to your father. Tell him that you assent to a marriage to our Karyna. You won't be disappointed. She's a beautiful, pliant young woman."

Maybe it was worth it. Koryn wouldn't love whomever he married, anyway. Damaryn would be quick to point out that if she was *pliant*, they could turn the tables on Tarkoth through her. Still, it was better to negotiate from a position of strength. "And if I refuse?"

"Look," Elrayn said, pointing.

They came to a stop next to Tharos. Koryn looked over the man's hulking frame at the missive. Like the oath he'd signed before, it was written in the Eldaeri language.

Latest Teleri incursion repelled. Possible Teleri alliance with Serikoth. Serikothi Crown Prince captured. Marriage to Karyna?

Koryn looked up at Elrayn and scowled. "How could you teach our language to a non-Eldaeri?"

Elrayn snorted. "He has other talents, too. Tharos, have you studied Prince Koryn's handwriting?"

The aide looked over his shoulder and sneered. He held up the oath Koryn had written and signed. "It is the weak, feminine style of someone who keeps secrets."

It was Koryn's turn to snort.

"Were you able to forge a new message?"

Koryn's snort turned into a sharp breath.

"Yes. With the nonsensical additions you tricked him into including, I was able to get a sample of the entire alphabet, and his signature." Tharos flashed a smug grin.

Koryn's eyes widened. A brilliant deception, one he'd fallen for.

Tharos slid out another letter from below the first.

Koryn gasped. It looked just like his handwriting.

Father, I've met Princess Karyna of Tarkoth and we have fallen in love. In the interest of bringing our great houses together, I wish to marry her. Please bless this union.

The trickery! Still... "Quite a talent, but how do you plan on getting official correspondence to my father? Even now, my men are sending word about my kidnapping."

Elrayn grinned. "I did tell you Tharos' talents include training messenger birds? We've intercepted correspondence before, and even have a copy of your signet ring."

Koryn lunged for the forgery.

Standing and spinning, Tharos shoved him back with a meaty paw.

It took all of Koryn's effort not to fall on his ass. He reached for Sunblade, but the other guards restrained him.

Elrayn shook his head. "It looks like Prince Koryn isn't as peaceable as his written word. Tie him up."

Struggling with his captors as they led him away, Koryn looked over his shoulder. "Bastard!"

"That would be my half-brother, Aelward. Maybe I'll have him marry one of your cousins." Waving, Elrayn turned to Tharos. "Any news from Lorium?"

CHAPTER 9:

Eye for an Eye

When Tomas opened his eyes, it felt as if the blacksmith had hammered his head against an anvil. He was lying in the sand. Considering how dark it was, night must be close to falling.

No, not night. Thick storm clouds, blotting out the sun. Not clouds...dark shapes. He had to blink several time to clear his vision. Shadowy forms coalesced into armed men, all towering above him.

"He had this," one of the Bovyans said.

Tomas shook the cobwebs out of his head and squinted.

One of the warriors was holding up his slingshot.

"A deadly weapon," said another.

Deadly? The stretchweed from his island did make the sling especially strong and elastic, and Tomas was a reasonably good shot; but not good enough to hit these monsters' unarmored faces. His gaze dropped to the first's feet. The vial of berry juice Sofia had asked for lay crushed under his boot.

"And look." The Bovyan pointed at him with the slingshot's handle. "His eyes."

"You're right, sergeant," said their leader...Keris, was it? His accent was so crisp, especially compared to the locals. "One blue eye, one green...and an ugly bastard, to boot. Take him to the town square."

Another spoke. "What about the ones who escaped?"

"They're headed to the island," said another.

Keris turned to the island, pausing for a moment as his head lifted up toward the Golden Bowl of Lydath. Then he looked back. "That is our primary objective, anyway. We'll get them in time."

Whether it was from the blow to the head or fear, Tomas' stomach twisted. Just what did the Bovyans want with the island? Did they plan to be the latest expedition to fail to reach the Golden Bowl? Was that why they'd risked attacking Lorium?

"In the meantime," Keris said, "we need to make an example of this one."

An example! What were they going to do? Tomas bolted upright. A new wave of pain surged through his head. He'd soiled his pants, too.

His stomach roiled. He leaned over and heaved once. Twice. With the third, his breakfast poured into the sand, its sour stench mingling with the crisp sea air.

Strong arms hauled him to his feet. "Come on, boy."

He blinked several more times. There were at least four Bovyans, who towered heads and shoulders above him. Each was easily twice as wide, even though their faces didn't look that much older than his. Any one of them could've snapped him in half.

One foot in front of the other, he half-walked, half-floated in their clutches. The brutes marched with such precision, like the old dwarven clocks Julius sold. His head spun, and his stomach lurched again, but nothing came out.

They passed the buildings lining Lorium's market square. Townsfolk made way, pointing and muttering and shaking their heads.

At the center of the square, they stopped. Tomas' feet found solid ground, though it did little help his dizziness. Around him, the crowds fell silent.

"People of Lorium." Keris' voice boomed over the square. "This young man tried to escape his duties to the Teleri Empire. For that, he would normally be flogged."

Wails rose among the hundreds of people.

Tomas' head was spinning, but flogging he understood. As if getting smashed in the head by a spear haft wasn't punishment enough! Still, even though it would leave scars across his back, the pain was only temporary. It was a small price to pay for helping Sofia escape. For—

Keris held up a hand, quieting them. "Let it be known that anyone who tries to flee their responsibilities to the empire shall suffer that fate, here in the square, with everyone watching. Man, woman, child, it doesn't matter. With no order, there can be no peace and prosperity."

Gritting his teeth, Tomas tried to focus his thoughts. Concentrate, block out the pain. He could do that. He wouldn't scream out. He wouldn't cry. It couldn't be much worse than Father whipping him with a belt.

"However," Keris said. "There are extenuating circumstances."

Extenuating. Tomas tasted the strange word in his mouth. Was this a good or a bad thing?

"His eyes."

More murmurs erupted, all sharing the same sentiment: different colored eyes were a sign of the Diviners. A rare gift. One that would spare him flogging.

Tomas blew out a sigh. Maybe the Teleri would find a valuable use for him. Surely he could outsmart a bunch of thick-necked, walnut-brained warriors with some generic predictions about future victories.

Keris silenced everyone with a horizontal slash with his finger. "It's the mark of the Runemasters."

The collective gasp might've sucked all the air from the square. Or at least, that was how it felt in his head. In the immediate aftermath of the Hellstorm, for which they were blamed, most Runemasters had been hunted down and killed. Angry mobs had smashed their rune-inscribed artifacts and burned texts explaining rune magic. In the intervening years, the few Runemasters who'd escaped the purge had made themselves useful by inscribing glyphs into trinkets, but their more devastating magics were lost.

"Begging your pardon, Governor," a farmer said. "Tomas is no Runemaster. He's a Diviner. He's Estomari you see, not Arkothi like us, and that was his gift. The one which the elves taught them, so that mankind could help overthrow our orc slave masters so many centuries ago. His people divined the ideal time to attack Lydath's Golden Bowl, on the island yonder. The one Tomas is from. We—"

"Silence, or you will be flogged." Keris grabbed Tomas by the hair, sending flares of pain through his scalp.

Surely the Bovyans knew the ancient history, knew of the Diviners' contribution. Of course, Tomas was no true Diviner. He had no real magic, other than his smarts.

"Divination is a lie," Keris said. "Meant to make magic sound harmless. No, the only magic of this world comes from channeling the power of demons. Whether it is channeling their power through runes, or communing with them to divine the future."

What? These foreigners had it all wrong. Tomas struggled in his captor's grasp, but to no avail.

"Never forget, the Runemaster Imperator of Arkoth brought the Hellstorm down on the world, tearing the land asunder and throwing your ancestors into the Long Winter. It was only our progenitor, Geros Bovyan, who vanquished the last of the powerful Runemasters and brought peace and prosperity to the Sundered Empire. It is your duty to bring all with their mark to us, so that we may pluck their eye and quell their evil power."

"Wait, wait." If Tomas felt dizzy before, the blood now rushed from his head. Bile rose in his throat. His eye. They were going to take his eye.

Again, the townspeople all gasped in unison, protests on their lips.

No, not his eye. He squirmed, but powerful hands forced him down to his knees. A child could have done the same to him, given how faint he was feeling.

His voice croaked. "I can take you to the island. I know the way past the Jaws."

"The knife." Keris extended his hand. Someone handed him a dagger, whose blade glowed white-hot.

Tomas' heart pounded in his ears. No, this couldn't be happening. Fighting to no avail, he squeezed his eyes shut.

"He's just a boy," someone yelled, and many other voices echoed the sentiment.

Yes, he was just a boy. Tears flooded Tomas' eyes.

Keris' voice boomed over the crowd. "Even the Runemaster Imperator of Arkoth was a boy once. Once he reached adulthood, his cabal unleashed the Hellstorm. Even a child may grow into a monster."

"Please," someone else said. "Have mercy."

"This is merciful. In the years after the Hellstorm, we would have slain him and condemned his soul to Tivar, the Corruptor. Now, we simply excise the evil, so that his soul might be saved."

A thumb pulled his right eyelid open, even as it fluttered to stay closed. Just inches away, waves of heat pulsed against his face. Around them people wailed and cried. Keris was saying something, but the words were impossible to make out through his panic.

The tip gouged into his eye. Agony seared into him. Fluid boiled up and sizzled. Tomas screamed. His body convulsed in spasms. Yellows, oranges, reds, and white filled his vision; then darkness.

CHAPTER 10:

Pieces of a Puzzle

With Aryn now standing, and Peris looming over them, Jie squirmed to keep the blanket covering her flat body. Having been naked in front of friend and foe alike more times than she could count, it was all for a show of modesty: really, she was far more intrigued by the antique book from her homeland that Peris had squirreled away in his coat.

Aryn's face scrunched up in the adorable way it always did when he was confused. "So I am supposed to marry Princess Alaena of Korynth. Isn't she old enough to be my mother?"

Jie's heart sunk to her stomach. Her Aryn, married to an ancient hag. Apparently, in these foreign lands, her language's proverb about old cows eating tender grass applied to women, as well.

"No," Peris said, shaking his head. "You are thinking of the former princess of Korynth. The one who's been missing for thirty-some years."

Brows furrowing, Aryn cocked his head. "Then who's this Alaena?"

"Vardamcar."

Jie decided she already hated this Alaena Vardamcar, whether she was missing—a princess' best state of being—or not. Still, the name Vardamcar was the same as the prince of—

"Wait," Aryn said. "If she is princess of Korynth, why does she have the surname of Serikoth's ruling family?"

If Peris' tone had been any more patient, she'd have thought he was waiting for the orc gods to return in their flaming chariots. "She was the princess of Serikoth until the Queen of Korynth adopted her as her heir."

Jie sucked on her lower lip. As much information as the clan gathered, these foreign royal family relationships were not included. It didn't help that the belligerent prince of Serikoth, Koryn, who might've conspired against Cathay's throne, shared such a similar name to a rival kingdom that his sister was apparently heir of.

With one eyebrow raised, Aryn cocked his head. "I'm surprised Father didn't offer Karyna to Korynth."

Karyna, Koryn, Korynth. Jie buried a snort. It was almost as bad as *Intimidator* and *Indomitable*. No matter how superior the Chosen People of Solaris considered themselves, they weren't blessed with creativity in names. A lesser spy might have a hard time sorting it all out.

"He *did*," Peris said. "The Queen of Korynth was looking for someone more...spirited."

Aryn yawned. "Elrayn is behind this. Father filled him with grand dreams of reunifying the Eldaeri Empire. It's a fool's errand. I'll have no part in it."

"You don't have a choice. The Queen of Korynth and your father have agreed." He proffered the scroll. "The orders are strange: it says we are to alter course for Elbahia so you can meet her."

He stared at the paper. "Why is that strange?"

Sometimes, Jie wondered if Aryn just pretended to be dim, or really wasn't the sharpest throwing star in the armory. Of course, they didn't know their real orders, since they had been following her forged ones.

"Because we don't have to alter our course. The *Intimidator* was headed that way. We were never going to catch it, anyway, not after you insisted on taking that half-elf whore to Bella Isla."

"I'm right here," she muttered.

Aryn scowled. "She's not a whore. And we had to refill our fresh water supplies."

Jie smiled at his defense. And it had been a pretty island. Not to mention the things he'd done to her...

"Only because we went to Bella Isla in the first place, and had the run-in with the Pirate Queen's ships."

Aryn shrugged. "Details."

"There's more." Peris proffered the missive again, which Aryn took this time. "Your brother captured

Serikoth's crown prince, Koryn, at the border with the Teleri Empire."

Jie ran calculations in her mind. How was that even possible? Crown Prince Koryn had been aboard the *Intimidator.* How could he have gone so far inland in what...a day?

"Oh." Aryn rolled his eyes. "He's the one we met in Cathay. Such a pompous bunghole. What does Elrayn plan to do with him?"

"Marry Princess Karyna to him."

Karyna, the princess, not the nation, nor the Serikothi Prince. Or was that the ship name? Jie frowned.

"It wouldn't be the first time someone was forced to marry at swordpoint." Aryn drew lines in the air with his finger, so reminiscent of the clueless spy back home. "Me to Alaena, Karyna to Koryn—they'll no doubt have pretty children with similar names. Of course, Elrayn's leaving himself out of it. I'm sorry, Jie, it doesn't like there are quarter-elves in our future."

Jie's heart sunk into her stomach. The right decision had been made for her, but that didn't mean she had to like it.

"There's more." Peris stabbed an emphatic glare at her.

Aryn turned the scroll over and back, then held it up. "Where?"

If Peris' jaw tightened any more, he could smash walnuts. "About your mission."

"To get married?"

"No, the one you tasked me with." Peris pointed at her with two darts of his eyes. Did it have to do with her? Had he figured out she was a spy?

"Oh." Understanding bloomed on Aryn's face. "Not here."

Jie scrutinized his distraught expression. Whatever he and Peris planned to discuss might hold yet more clues related to her mission.

He leaned down, cupped her chin, and pecked his soft lips against hers. "Jyeh, love, I have some business to discuss with Peris. We are going to the bridge; why don't you get dressed and see yourself out?"

She bowed her head. "Yes, Your Highness."

He released the blanket into her care, exposing himself. She clasped it around her, and feigned a shy glance at Peris, who ignored both his prince's nakedness and her bare shoulders.

As Aryn hopped on one leg, tugging on his pants, Jie plotted a path back to the bridge. By the time he'd finally dressed, looking sharp in his naval uniform, she'd decided. He flashed a smile and beckoned Peris to follow.

As soon as they marched out and closed the door behind them, Jie snatched up her stealth suit and slipped into it. She squeezed through the porthole and, using it as a foothold, timed the gentle rocking of the waves.

On an upswell, she sprung up to catch the outer sill of the bridge's windows. Then she pulled herself up. It was quite simple really, though it carried greater risk of death than going along the inside of the ship from the deck.

If they were hurrying, it would take Aryn and Peris another thirty to forty seconds to reach the bridge. She looked through the crack between the shutters, and found the chamber dark. Enough time to slip in and hide. Safer than remaining outside, where one pitch of the ship could send her for a permanent swim. On the other hand, inside would leave no escape route. Balancing on the ledge, she crouched and held on to the window frame, letting her knees absorb the rise and fall of the ship.

Sounds muffled slightly by the shutters, the lock to the bridge door clicked, and the door creaked open.

Jie pressed her ear to the crack.

"Have you finished translating it?" Aryn whispered.

Translating? If he was referring to the ancient book, that meant Peris could read and speak the motherland's tongue. No telling how many conversations he'd been privy to back home, with everyone assuming they could speak freely. It also meant that Aryn's obtuse demeanor might all be an act. Jie's heart squeezed.

"It's an older version of their written language," Peris said, voice low. "The symbols are the same, but they don't follow the spoken grammar."

"Were you able to understand any of it?" Aryn's tone carried more boredom than interest. It was a relief, really, to think what he showed on the surface reflected his true being.

"After the Hellstorm, the last Runemaster Imperator went to the mountain of Lydath's Golden Dish."

Jie closed her eyes and matched history with geography. The Hellstorm, when the heavens rained fire, had ravaged the world three centuries before, tearing open seas and lakes where there had once been dry land. A millennium before that, Lydath's Golden Dish had been a monument to the banished orc gods, abandoned and inaccessible since mankind overthrew their orc slave masters during the War of Ancient Gods. It was somewhere in the North, but where?

Thank the heavens Aryn asked. "Where is that?"

As always, Peris spoke like a patient mother explaining the obvious to a bored child. "It's on Twins Island in the Inland Sea, near the Arkothi free city of Mykos. The closest town is Lorium."

Jie only knew of Mykos because her intended path into the Bovyan-ruled Teleri Empire passed through there. Once a center of farming for the Sundered Empire, it was now a free port on the Inland Sea, where one might hitch a galley ride into the Teleri heartland. *This* ship lurched, forcing her to break her concentration on details so as to avoid a watery grave.

"Any mention of..." Aryn's brow was probably furrowing in that cute way "...what was my oh-so overly ambitious brother in search of?"

"The Crown of Arkos."

Aryn harrumphed. "What could he possibly want with some sorcerous artifact? Our people can't use magic."

Despite his sigh, Peris still sounded patient. "It's a symbol of legitimacy. The Arkothi people pine for the return of the Runemaster Imperator and his crown, despite the fact his cabal unleashed the Hellstorm."

"So my brother wants to be an emperor...sometimes I can't believe we share the same parents."

"It seems fitting that a king of Solaris' Chosen People would wear the crown."

Jie would've scratched her head if that didn't mean letting go of the window frame and increasing the chance of a fall and swim. Somehow, a book written by one of her countrymen three hundred years ago had information about the last emperor of Arkoth. The Runemaster Imperator himself.

Aryn snorted again. "So does the book mention the crown?"

"I don't know the Cathayi symbol for crown, so I couldn't tell."

"We can ask Jyeh." No matter how many times Aryn mangled her name, it never failed to set her heart aflutter.

"She's a street urchin." Peris scoffed. "Almost certainly illiterate."

Jie pursed her lips. The comment stung, but it was also a sign that Peris believed the disguise.

"It's worth a try."

"She's a subject of Cathay. Even if she can read, she would ask questions about how we got ahold of this book, which would lead to questions about our secret mission in her homeland."

Jie's lips relaxed, only so she could suck on the lower one. A secret mission meant that these Tarkothi had had ulterior motives for attending the imperial wedding back home. And just how did they get ahold of this book?

Aryn yawned. "You're an expert liar, I'm sure you can fabricate a plausible story."

"If you command it, I will ask. However, let me see if she can write their symbol for *crown* first." An unlikely combination of mirth, doubt, and disdain hung in Peris' tone.

"Brilliant. Now, who else knows about this book?"

"That we have it? Only you, Prince Elrayn, and my brother, who translated the encoded message I sent through the admiralty. I was waiting to find out about the crown before I sent another message."

"All right. Go find Jie and bring her here. She dresses slowly, so she's probably still in my cabin."

"As you command."

The door opened and closed.

Jie reached down and grasped the ledge, then eased herself off. The straight drop was easier than when she'd swung over from the rookery. She caught the porthole, landed with her toes on the decorative ridge, and then jumped back up and through the opening.

Outside Aryn's cabin, the clopping of Peris' boots grew louder.

Darting to the bunk, she tore off her stealth suit, stashed it in its hiding place under the bed, and took her time slipping into the pink dress.

The door swung open. Peris tromped in, his eyes sweeping the cabin before settling on her.

Jie pulled the dress tighter around her shoulders, pretending embarrassment. "You should knock."

"You should leave. At our next port." He neared, setting his height looming over her. He fixed her with a glare, but then produced a gold coin, which he pressed into her palm. "You're Prince Aryn's passing fancy. He'll tire of you, and look for the next exotic girl."

Feigning intimidation—or perhaps it wasn't feigned, given how large his shadow loomed over her—she hunched her shoulders and stumbled back. Her chest squeezed. "I…"

What was wrong with her? It wasn't usually this hard to come up with some glib response. Was it fear? No, she'd been strung up naked before a rebel torturer, and still won a duel of words. No, it was her uncharacteristic insecurities, usually buried deep, bubbling to the surface. The fact she was just Aryn's plaything.

She shook the silly notion out of her head. *He* was *her* plaything, *her* passing fancy, a distraction until she could continue with her real mission.

With a snort, Peris turned on his heel and stormed out. Apparently he wouldn't be asking about the book or crowns, or if she could read.

She chuckled to herself. Now, her open-ended mission might include an ancient book from back home. Which might reveal the location of a missing magical artifact, last seen near Lydath's Golden Bowl, near a town called Lorium, which wasn't important enough to appear on any map she'd seen.

CHAPTER 11:

One-Eyed Boy in the World of the Blind

Every joint ached, and even though Tomas burned inside, cold sweat stuck to his clothes. Still, that was nothing compared to the throbbing in his right eye or the weight of his head. He was lying on a straw pallet, and kicked off what felt to be a wool blanket. A flowery scent hung in the air, and indistinct voices whispered nearby.

He opened his eyes. At least, he tried to. The right side felt strange, and the act of opening it caused the pain to intensify. Only half his world appeared in front of his face, and everything looked...flat.

Oh, this had to be a nightmare. Please let it be a nightmare. He lifted his hand, only to find a strip of smelly cloth covering where his eye had been.

Tivar take him, it hadn't been a dream. The memory of Keris running a white-hot dagger through his eye made his stomach roil all over again. Only, that image had had depth and width. Now he could only see half of a flat world.

How had this happened? If only he hadn't come to Lorium today. If only he had sold his catch and left. If only Antonius had waited two seconds before making a break for Gian's boat, this would've never happened.

He turned his head right, then left, to get his bearings. Two people stood nearby, or at least they felt nearby. It was hard to tell with only one eye. He was in a small room with plain wood walls. Dry lavender hung in the only window, and sunlight and the occasional voice came in through it.

"He's awake!" said a male voice. A familiar voice.

Tomas squinted his good eye toward the source.

Sofia's father, Julius.

"Where am I?" He tried to sit up.

Small, gnarled hands eased him down, and a woman spoke in a gravelly voice. "Easy, Tomas. I've applied a poultice to your eye, and given you a draught of herbs to ease your fever. You've been asleep for two days, but you still need to rest."

He studied the wizened old woman for a moment, before realizing she was the town healer. "Where am I?"

"Sofia's room," Julius said. "I claimed you when the Teleri asked about your family, and brought you here."

"Thank you." Tomas gave him a grateful nod. To think, the Bovyans could've left him there in the square, all alone and helpless.

"It's the least I could do, for sacrificing yourself for Sofia."

"Oh, Tomas." The healer patted him on the shoulder. "Most of the townsfolk would've done the same for you. You've always been so helpful."

Then again, maybe death would've been better. He was ugly enough with two eyes.

Julius lowered his voice. "And, of course, I had an empty bed to offer."

Heart pattering, Tomas struggled to sit up. This was Sofia's room. He'd been outside the window before, but never seen inside. "Is Sofia all right?"

Julius gave a tentative nod. "I assume she made it to your village with Old Gian and Antonius. The Teleri let fisherman go out again today. At least, the ones with families in town to guarantee their return. I asked Cyprian to visit your village and find out how Sofia was doing."

Tomas gave a slow nod. Cyprian had grown up in the village, and knew the safe path through the Jaws.

"I've been so worried," Julius said. "I can't wait for Cyprian to return. Can you can still see the future?"

Tomas' hand strayed to his eye.

"Don't touch," the healer said.

Tomas lay back down. It wasn't like he had ever been a true Diviner in the first place. Still, what Julius reported was reassuring. At least for now, Sofia was safe.

Father, Mother, and Maria, too. As for Antonius, he could rot at the bottom of the Inland Sea for all Tomas cared. "What's been happening here?"

Julius pointed out the window. "A wagon full of their scribes and tattooists arrived this morning. They are counting heads and recording them in their books."

Books…there weren't many in town. Hardly anyone who could read, Tomas included.

The healer shook her head. "The marketplace is quiet. Nobody wants to go out. The Teleri bought all the surplus food, and hired the townsfolk to transport it to their siege on Mykos."

Julius sighed. "They confiscated all my runewares. The light baubles, too. Said they were lit by demons trapped inside."

Poor Julius. Even more so than the rune-inscribed artifacts, dealing in light baubles created by Aksumi Mystics had made him wealthy. There must've been thousands upon thousands of those lights throughout the world. All powered by demons? It didn't seem possible. "What are they going to do with them?"

"They said they will be taken back to their capital in Telesite. Their priests can smash the baubles and destroy the demons without letting them escape."

From the next room came a rapping on a door.

Julius straightened and looked over his shoulder. "It's the Bovyans. It's my time to register with the census." He turned and walked out of the room, closing the door between them.

Census? The word sounded foreign.

The healer held up her right wrist, revealing the Teleri Empire's nine-pointed sun, rendered in a unique shade of brown. Somewhere between soil after a rainstorm, and Levanthi coffee. She harrumphed. "You'd think they wouldn't need to mark a woman my age."

"What is it for?" He sat up and studied the design as best he could with one eye.

"All females in the Teleri Empire get one, usually at age two. Or later in life, if their homeland is conquered, like ours."

Tomas closed his eye. To think, if Sofia hadn't escaped they would've tattooed her, too. "Why just females?"

Her eyes searched his. "The Bovyans don't have women of their own. They need other races to bear their next generation of boys. The tattoos..." She shuddered. "Well, you'll see it on the younger women outside. It's a special dye. Before a girl comes of age, it is blue, but then it changes to red. If she's ever had a baby, it turns brown. You'll never see a girl with a red tattoo walking on any street in the Teleri Empire."

"What happens to women after they give birth?"

Sighing, the healer shook her head. "They can go back to their homes, get married, and have more children. More girls, to make more soldiers."

Though Tomas' head wasn't spinning like when he'd gotten smashed by the spear butt, the sheer barbarism sent thoughts flying through his mind. Apparently, these brutes just used women's wombs to breed yet more brutes, and then discarded them. Sofia and Maria would suffer that fate. Unless... "Why don't women get brown tattoos?"

The healer shook her head. "Whoever can copy that exact shade of brown would be both rich and hunted."

Tomas' gut churned. He had to get back to his island. Take Sofia and Maria into the marshes where the Bovyans could never follow. Maybe Sofia would even marry him, protecting her from rape at the hands of the Teleri.

He sat up. Ignoring the healer's protests, he went to the door, which led into the main room. He opened it a crack and peeked through.

At the front door, Julius, his wife Cornellia, a Bovyan, and another foreign man spoke. Julius' head hung in cowed submission.

So absorbed were they in conversation, it would be easy to sneak out the back door. Opening the door just wide enough, Tomas slipped through and started tiptoeing toward the back.

"Take down that painting," the Bovyan boomed. "The Runemaster Imperator is never coming back."

Tomas looked over his shoulder, only to remember that eye was gone. He turned and looked the other way, and locked eyes on the offending artwork.

It was a stylized painting of the Last Emperor, a young man with handsome features framed by brown hair. The Crown of Arkos adorned his head, the bluish grey accentuating his fair skin. A starburst jewel—an artifact from the war between elves and orcs thousands of years ago—sparkled on his brow. Only the wealthy could afford these oil paintings, but many households had printed versions from the presses in Mykos.

"You!"

Tomas turned his head more to find the Bovyan pointing at him.

You're the Demon-Eyed." The Bovyan turned from him to Julius. "He is your son?"

Julius opened and closed his hands. His forehead glistened. "Yes. Yes, he is. My only child. That is his room."

The third man looked down at a leather-bound tome and scribbled something with a quill. He looked up at Cornelia. "You will have to report to the tattooist."

Covering her right wrist, she gave a tentative nod.

Sofia and Maria, too, would get that tattoo if Tomas couldn't hide them. He squared his shoulders and started across the room...

...and paused.

It was too hard to tell just how far the furniture was away from him, and he seemed to be walking in a curve instead of a straight line. He put one hand in front of him and worked his way toward the kitchens and the back door.

The healer burst out after him and took his arm. "You need to get some rest."

He shook his head and glared at her with his single eye.

Her grip loosened.

"Please, just take me to the door."

"You need to rest."

He needed to get back home. He started toward the back door.

With a sigh, the healer accompanied him, her hand on his arm gently guiding the way.

Julius called out from the front. "Where are you going...son?"

Tomas turned his head to the right, but his limited vision didn't reach Sofia's father. He turned back the other way. "I need some sea air."

Julius gave a tentative nod, and turned back to the Teleri.

Pushing through the door, Tomas emerged into an alley. The healer led him back out to the main stretch, east of the market.

The street was nearly deserted, save for the occupiers going door-to-door. On occasion, a Bovyan would take a young woman from her house and down the road toward the marketplace.

Tomas tried not to shudder as his own path had him following a pair of sobbing sisters, led by a particularly large soldier. Inside the square, four queues of females—from girls barely old enough to walk, to young women—formed at two stalls. With his one eye, he peered to the front of one of the lines.

A girl no older than twelve sat on a chair, right arm resting on the counter, gritting her teeth while an olive-skinned Arkothi man tattooed her wrist. Governor Keris loomed over them, arms folded in front of his barrel chest.

Tomas' fists tightened. He needed to get Sofia and Maria to safety. He pulled free of the healer. "Thank you, but I can make it the rest of the way."

Could he? He stared down the street, between the row of houses, trying to process the scene. He'd walked down this road at least once a week for the last ten years, but it looked all wrong. Flat. His head ached, and his eye socket burned. Shaking free of the healer's grasp, he took several tentative steps and stumbled out to the shoreline road. The thudding of a drum drew his single eye to the Serikothi bireme, now flying the Teleri's black standard, lurching through the Inland Sea.

He shuddered. It was just around the bend into the road that that bastard Antonius had betrayed him, leading to his capture... And the loss of his eye.

And just like that day, there on the road that ran along the head of the docks, a Bovyan sat on a horse. He was turning away a fisherman with his heavily cloaked friend. A woman no doubt, trying to get away from the town, probably to the next village over...

Ah, Tivar take every last Bovyan. Tomas opened and closed his hands. Though his own boat was still tied down to the wharf, the sentry blocked the way. Even if they hadn't taken his slingshot, it would be useless against them; not to mention, he needed both eyes to aim. Trying to sneak past would get him flogged, or even worse, they might take his other eye. He shuddered again. There had to be some way to get back home.

He closed his eye—eye—and envisioned the island's shore. It appeared in his imagination, painted in width and depth, even if he'd never see it that way for real again. There...that was the solution. He turned around and headed back to the marketplace as quickly as his muddled head would allow.

Keris had moved from the first stall, and now hovered over the tattooist in the second.

Tomas took cautious steps to the front of the line of girls. Some were crying, while others hugged themselves or each other. Most stopped and whispered and pointed as he passed.

Up close, Keris looked even huger and more intimidating than the other day. He tugged at the collar of his black surcoat, undoubtedly hot in the midday sun. And he wore chainmail beneath. And heavy leather boots.

All keys to the plan.

If Tomas could summon the courage to go through with it.

He swallowed hard. He could do this. For Sofia and Maria, he had to. He stepped up to the girl now getting a tattoo. "Excuse me, Governor."

Keris turned, his jaw set rigidly for a second before relaxing. "You. Now that we've excised the demon from your soul, you should be resting. You'll need to be in full health so that we can pay you for honest work."

"I feel much better." Tomas nodded, even though his limbs felt heavy and languid, and it was hard to form a coherent thought.

"Good. For now, we really don't need you. We—"

Tomas pointed toward the Inland Sea. "My sister needs to get her tattoo, too."

The women in line gasped.

Keris afforded him a raised eyebrow. "You know what the tattoo is for, right?"

Tomas nodded. "It is a mark of loyalty to the Teleri Empire."

"Yes. There is no more patriotic a service a woman can perform than giving birth to the next generation of the realm's protectors."

"Well, there are many women who live on my island, and the underwater rocks make the approach treacherous." Tomas bowed. "I would be happy to prove my own loyalty by showing you the way."

If the girls had gasped before, they were now muttering. No doubt, they thought he was either a collaborator or just plain stupid.

He'd live with that, if only to get back home. Tomas channeled the look of a faithful village dog into his own expression, and met the governor's gaze. It was only after a moment that he realized he'd turned his head, like a bird, to get a better view with his one eye.

Keris studied him for a few seconds, before his head turned to the mountain that rose above the village. He raised a hand and beckoned one of his henchmen.

The soldier marched over, his chainmail jingling, and pounded his fists to his chest on arrival. Like most of the other Bovyans, he had olive-toned skin, with dark hair cropped close to his head.

"Go find Sathis and Fethos. They are to take the boy back to his island. Oh, and a scribe and tattooist."

"Yes, sir." The soldier pounded his fist to his chest and marched off.

Keris turned back to Tomas. "So you're from the village. What can you tell me about it?"

"It's surrounded by the Jaws, a ring of rocks which—"

"No." Keris frowned.

Maybe he wanted to know more about the number of women. "There are twenty-seven families—"

"With twins?"

Tomas favored the governor with his one eye. It would be dangerous to lie, but even more disastrous to reveal the whole truth. "Yes."

"And Lydath's Golden Bowl." A kind of hunger gleamed in Keris' eyes.

Tomas scrunched his forehead. Maybe the Teleri needed more gold for their war effort. Whether the Golden Bowl was actually made of gold, nobody knew, since no one had visited it since the War of Ancient Gods a thousand years ago. Its glint was visible from the town square, and he pointed. "It sits atop the Temple of Lydath, at the summit."

"I can see that."

Two Bovyans marched over. Like most of the others, they had olive skin and close-cropped dark hair.

"Ah, Sathis, Fethos. I believe Consul Haros had a mission for you. His envoy will arrive in two days, once this town is fully secured. In the meantime, this boy will guide you to the island."

If only Keris would come along, as well.

If only the Chosen People of Solaris in the East would launch an attack. Because someone had to fight back against these Bovyans. Well, if the Eldaeri of Serikoth, Tarkoth, or Korynth didn't, Tomas would.

CHAPTER 12:

Happily, There's No Place Like Home

Alaena stormed through the throne room, past the crowd of lords and generals dressed in royal blue and silver livery. While most were shorter, slenderer Eldaeri like herself, a handful were ethnic Estomari with fair skin and a wide range of hair colors. Mutters erupted among both as they opened a path for her. Royal guards in polished steel cuirasses stepped to block her way, crossing their white lances before her, but then backed off. Whether it was out of respect for her station as heir, or the fact that she stank so badly from the weeklong trek back, it was hard to know.

No doubt her hair, red and unruly on the best of days, looked like a family of chipmunks had nested in it. She might've been the first person to ever drag mud across the chamber's marble floors, pack still strapped to her back.

"Alaena, welcome home." Dressed in a dark blue gown with silver embroidery, Queen Selayna sat straight and regal on Korynth's throne, which was nearly identical to the throne of her homeland, Serikoth; itself a supposed copy of erstwhile enemy Tarkoth's.

Alaena could definitively say Korynth's throne—made of laminated blockwood and sablewood—resembled Serikoth's. In fact, the entire throne room, with its circular shape and four stories of encircling mezzanines, might've been an exact copy of Father's audience chamber. The Gold Ring, hung from silken threads off the fourth-floor mezzanine, sparkling in the sunlight which filtered through the translucent quartz dome. Supposedly, Tarkoth's palace layout was the same, all three built by dwarves and modelled on the old capital of Elbahia.

If she had anything to say about this marriage proposal to Tarkoth's Prince Aryn, she'd never get a firsthand view of Tarkoth's throne room, where the Light of Solaris hung. In her birthplace of Serikoth, the White Staff was displayed in the same way. All parts of the Scepter of Solaris at one time; now separated, like their kingdoms.

She unslung her pack and untied the Altivorc broadsword. Everyone gasped when she tossed it on the floor with a clang. "Altivorcs tried to kill me."

The hall burst into chatter. Courtiers and soldiers pointed at the weapon, while ministers leaned and whispered in each other's ears. General Myra, commander of the roc riders, tossed brown hair over her shoulder and scoffed.

If the queen was surprised, the thin lines that crinkled in her forehead were the only sign. Though she was past seventy, Eldaeri blood kept her skin otherwise smooth. Her large, dark eyes seemed to see everything. Straight and dignified, she was the embodiment of a Korynthi queen.

So unlike Alaena, who would one day sit on that throne. She afforded the murmuring courtiers a contemptuous glance. "How surprised I was to find out from my would-be captors that I was engaged to wed a Tarkothi prince. Those worthless, backstabbing—"

The queen cleared her throat and gave a subtle point of her chin. "Alaena, we have guests."

Alaena followed the motion.

Standing to the right were three full-blooded Eldaeri men dressed in the dark green uniforms of Tarkoth's navy, looking very much out of place. In the woods, she would've spotted anything out of the ordinary; in the palace, out of her element, she'd missed them. Naval swords hung at their sides. If they shared the same insignias as Serikoth's navy—very likely, given they were once one nation—then the highest-ranking officer they'd deigned to send was the lieutenant standing between two ensigns.

He was handsome enough, with a sun-kissed bronze complexion and long brown hair tied into a ponytail. Like all Eldaeri, he had no facial hair, and probably none on his chest, arms, or legs, either. His large, dark eyes and thin, high-bridged nose bore a striking resemblance to Queen Selayna. Since Tarkoth's navy gave commissions to the noble families like sailors spread venereal diseases, perhaps he shared a common ancestor with her.

Despite his good looks, he swayed in place as if he were still standing on a ship. Sweat collected on his brow, and the way his jaws moved resembled the bison eating grass on Serikoth's plains. When he crossed his wrists and bowed, he was as stiff as a blockwood tree. His mere existence disproved the universal nature of Eldaeri grace. "Oy, Lass—"

Gasps broke out through the audience chamber, and hands shot to mouths.

Alaena stared at the boor. Lass? Did he think she was a wench on one of the Pirate Queen's ships, spreading her legs for coin? Not to mention, Eldaeri women had played a vital role as sharpshooters and roc riders during the establishment of the empire, and the first Korynthi queen had seized the throne from an incompetent king.

The local lords might not like Alaena, but now even they muttered at the Tarkothi officer. His aides elbowed him, and he flushed the shade of oak leaves in fall.

"My apologies. I meant..." His eyes stared up into his head, and his lips moved in silence before he straightened and met her gaze. When he spoke again, his tone was as stiff as his posture, the words as rote as child learning to read. "Greetings, Your Highness. I am Aelward Niromar, currently in command of the Tarkothi Royal Ship the *Sea Dragon.* We have the honor of conveying you to Elbahia, where you will meet your future husband, Prince Aryn."

Alaena glared at him, and he looked back like a startled deer. She released him from her gaze and turned to the queen. "Your Majesty, I am not marrying Prince Aryn."

Despite the public impudence, which would rile the most patient lords, the queen hid her emotions well. It was never possible to know what Queen Selayna was thinking. She spoke as in a measured tone. "Alaena, you will show Lieutenant Aelward the gardens."

That was it? No mention of marriage to a faithless enemy? Alaena opened her mouth to say something.

Though subtle, the queen's eyes glinted with warning. Though kind behind closed doors, she would not tolerate any more outbursts in public.

Alaena snatched up her pack and slung it over her shoulder. She met the navy man's gaze and jerked her head. "Follow me."

He looked to Queen Selayna, crossed his arms, and bowed his head. He waved his men back, and stumbled after her like a fawn taking its first steps. If Tarkoth's ships were manned by such maladroits, it was a wonder they still controlled the eastern seas.

The courtiers all chit-chattered as she left the throne room, Aelward staggering after her, nearly tripping down the flared marble steps into the entry hall. Several of the royal guards followed in lockstep behind him, through the cavernous gallery. The sounds of Aelward's boots fell further behind, and slowed to a stop.

She glanced over her shoulder.

He spun in a slow circle, mouth agape as he looked up at the marble columns. He seemed to pause at each banner of the Korynthi noble houses hanging from the second-floor mezzanine. His wide-eyed innocence was almost adorable. No doubt he was a country boy by birth. The Tarkothi navy must've trained their rural bumpkins and rubes exceptionally well to maintain its reputation for professionalism.

All except this one. Clearing her throat, Alaena pointed back the way they came, to the first-floor central hallway that passed under the throne room. "While you're at it, would you like a tour of the administrative offices?"

His eyes lifted to hers, and then he hurried to catch up.

Without waiting, she turned and headed to the double doors. Royal guards crossed their fists and bowed their heads as she passed through into the grassy yard. Up above, a dozen rocs circled and dived, the female riders shooting arrows at unseen targets in the field on the other side of the palace.

Alaena shuddered. They'd tried to train her to ride a roc when she'd come to Korynth, to keep up the longstanding tradition of Korynthi princesses. Fear of heights had ended that before it even started; still, watching the graceful birds swoop and wheel was mesmerizing. As long as she was on the ground.

She tore her gaze away and stopped by the apple trees, their branches now bedecked in white flowers, waiting for Aelward to catch up. Bees buzzed from bloom to bloom. The queen hadn't specified which garden, so maybe a trip to the royal apiaries would be fun. The klutz might careen into one of the hives and suffer too many stings to command his pretty ship.

Outside, he straightened, and his anxious expression calmed. Loosening his high collar, he blew out a long breath. He muttered to himself, but it was just loud enough for her to hear. "Thank Sargasso we're outta that infernal den of loose-lipped sycophants, backstabbers, and..."

She stared wide-eyed at him. Maybe he wasn't that bad after all.

"Sorry, lass. I mean, my apologies, Your Highness." He met her gaze and squared his shoulders. His lips moved again, eyes staring up into his head like a young prince trying to remember heraldic symbols. "I didn't mean to besmirch—"

"Yes, you did." She flashed a smile. He'd been trying to draw on formal language, yet his instinct was to fall back to sailor-speak. "You get used to the sycophants and backstabbers, though."

He shook his head and opened his mouth, but then said nothing.

"Speak."

Eyes wide, he waved his hands. It was almost as adorkable as his gawking in the central hall. "Nay, lass. *Loose lips sink ships*, we say on the open seas."

She held up a finger. "Around here, we say *When in Arkos, do as the Arkothi do.* Speak."

"Speak?" He arched an eyebrow, looking nothing like the lost puppy from before, and speaking easily in the tongue of sailors. "Arkothi are less known for lip flapping, and more famous for drinking wine, eating cheese, and buggering goats."

A proper lady would've blanched. Maybe that was his intention. Alaena just chuckled. Two could play at this. "It sounds like the kind of place a sailor would enjoy."

"I've yet to meet a sailor who'd sip from a glass of wine before downing a frothy mug of ale."

"But you have to admit, the goat is quite enticing." She mimicked the arch of his eyebrow.

"Only when trussed up to a spit and—"

"I forgot, sailors are experts with knots." She held her arms above her head and crossed her wrists. "Leave out the goat, and I might sign up for the navy."

He let out a guffaw. "Aye, lass. Tarkoth let me into the navy, so the standards can't be but so high."

His laugh was so genuine, so unlike courtiers. Perhaps this Aelward wasn't so bad after all. For now, she'd even forgive the *lass*. She drew closer and whispered. "Let me share a secret: I've been to Arkos before."

He backed away, eyes even wider. "How? It's in the heart of the Teleri Empire."

She nodded. "And despite jokes about old Arkothi habits, the Bovyans don't allow much luxury or any depravities. No goats for you."

"Arkos was never high on me list of places to visit."

"Isn't that why people join the navy? To visit new places?"

His expression darkened. "Some people, maybe."

"But not you. Let me guess, to prove yourself."

He shrugged.

"Family, then."

His head bobbed left and right, not exactly shaking nor nodding, more like the Ayuri diplomat who'd once come to court, head constantly bobbling.

"Then...what word did you use? There's *a lass* back home who fancies a *lad* in uniform?"

Aelward choked. "No, no lasses back home."

"A goat, then?"

"Only tied to a spit, and roasting over a fire."

He was evading the question, but she'd find out in due time. There were many ways to unsettle a man. She leaned in and let her lips brush against his ear as she whispered, "Just how good are you with knots?"

Face flushing red as a virgin's on her wedding night, he stepped back and ran into a tree.

"Avast." Grinning, she advanced, claiming the ground he gave up.

He coughed, reached up and took a branch between his fingers. "As far as I can tell, this palace is identical to Tarkoth's in almost every way. But an orchard, that's different."

"Yes," Queen Selayna said.

Alaena had her breasts up against her prey and made no move to back away, despite the arrival of the queen. She did, however, look over her shoulder to find the queen gliding across the grass.

Flanked by six royal guards, she held the sheathed Altivorc broadsword in her hands. "Lieutenant, I trust Princess Alaena has been a good host."

He straightened, crossed his fists, and bowed stiffly. "Yes, sir. I mean, yes, Your Majesty."

The queen gestured to the orchard. "The first queen of Korynth was farsighted. She planted fruit trees and vineyards, and established beehives. She claimed it was a symbol of Korynth's value as the Eldaeri nations' breadbasket; but there's more."

"It represents fertility." Alaena rubbed up against him, and his body went rigid as blockwood planks. If his face could get any more distraught...

The queen's lips pursed just enough to convey her disapproval. "When Korynth broke away from Serikoth, we were always worried about a siege. Having these trees not only added beauty to the grounds, but also provided a source of food in times of war, and source of revenue in times of peace."

"A lass with a good head on 'er shoulders." Aelward said, squirming away and bowing. "I mean, a farsighted woman."

Alaena bit back laughter.

"Indeed. Beauty and strength. It is also symbolic of Korynthi Eldaeri. We've always cultivated our princesses to think for themselves. Though sometimes…" the queen's eyes settled on Alaena. "…that leads to a free spirit."

"Aye," muttered Aelward under his breath.

Alaena threw her hair over her shoulder. "None more free-spirted than the queen's own daughter, who ran away, never to return."

The queen's placid expression contorted for a split second before returning to normal. She waved to the guards. "Leave us."

The royal guards all crossed their fists and bowed, then turned on a heel and moved to the edge of the garden.

The queen watched them go, then turned back. "Alaena, your marriage to Prince Aryn has already been agreed on. We have suspected an alliance between the Teleri and Altivorcs for quite a while, and this weapon lends more evidence." She pulled the broadsword from its scabbard and studied the blade.

Alaena gestured northwest. "The Altivorcs aren't a threat. They're nothing more than roving bands of mercenaries. Even if they came together, they couldn't move an army through the mountains, because we control the main passes."

"The Altivorcs aren't our only worry. Their alliance suggests the Teleri will finally move against Solaris' Chosen. They've been sending raiding parties into Tarkoth for several months." The queen swept the broadsword in precise circles, an impressive feat given her age. "Now, it looks like they want to keep you from marrying Prince Aryn."

"Then they share a common interest with me."

If the queen's sigh could sound any more exasperated, Alaena had never heard it. "By wedding to a prince of Tarkoth, you will bring the Houses of Corivar and Myranar closer."

Alaena scowled. "What about House Vardamcar? The blood of Serikoth runs in my veins, and House Corivar is our enemy. I will not marry one of them."

Shuffling on his feet, Aelward coughed.

Queen Selayna held up a staying hand. "The choice was never yours. Even if you were born Serikothi, you are heir to Korynth."

"I was never really given a choice about that, either. You and my father tricked a child too young to know what she was doing. You, so you could have your heir, him..." because sacrificing a daughter he never really cared about could increase his influence in Korynth. There was no point in saying what everyone knew.

"I..." Aelward's mouth open and closed, and he edged away.

"And as for being the heir? None of those..." Alaena looked at Aelward and waved back toward the palace. "What did you call them, loose-lipped sycophants and backstabbers?"

Heading shake so violently it might wobble off, Aelward waved his hands. "Oi, lass, leave me out of this."

Alaena turned back to the queen. "None of them accept me as heir. They want one of your blood and theirs, a true daughter to House Myranar. Once you are gone, there will be civil war again."

The queen shook her head. "It doesn't have to be that way. Prove yourself a capable leader, worthy of the Myranar name."

"And once ye wed Prince Aryn," Aelward said, "ye will have Tarkoth as an ally."

The queen looked to him and back, then nodded. "But you must be able to show that he is subordinate to you."

"Should be easy enough," Aelward muttered under his breath.

Both Alaena and Queen Selayna jerked their heads to him. Did he, a minor naval officer, know something about the prince?

His eyes rounded, and he waved his hands again. "Sorry lass. Loose lips. I mean, my apologies, Your Majesty, Your Highness. I have no doubt our prince will make a fine, supportive husband."

The queen's eyes narrowed. "Excuse me, Lieutenant, while I have a word with the princess."

Aelward crossed his fists and bowed.

The queen glided a few meters away to a grove of peach trees. They were certainly still within earshot of him. Eyeing him, she switched from Arkothi to the Eldaeri language, which most pureblooded Eldaeri could read, but only the royal families actually spoke. "I wouldn't expect the lieutenant to know much about the prince, but he will certainly know more than we in Korynth do. His ship sustained damage in an attack by the Pirate Queen. It is undergoing repairs and waiting for an escort of cruisers. You will have two days to guide him around the city, and learn more about your future husband. Then, you will go to Elbahia to meet Prince Aryn."

Alaena crossed her fists and bowed. She tried to keep her expression as impassive as the queen's.

Let her believe she'd go quietly. She had other plans. After all, an Eldaeri man, least of all a prince of Tarkoth, would never be able to bear the shame of his betrothed caught with her legs wrapped around a minor naval officer.

And handsome Aelward was adorable enough to make it a fun little tryst.

CHAPTER 13:

Siren

Two more days. A few hours in Korynth had already been too long. Aelward stood alone by the window of his guest chambers in the Korynthi palace, gazing out into the harbor below. Light from all three moons danced in the waves, spotlighting the *Sea Dragon.* Though there were a dozen docks dating back to when this region was the southernmost stronghold of the Eldaeri Empire, Korynth, without easy access to sablewood trees, had never developed a navy.

Two more days, and the *Sea Dragon's* repairs would be finished. He'd be back to open skies, salt air, and the expanse of water, and out of this stifling palace. It was too much like the one in Tarkoth, from the exact same interior layout, to the stuffed shirts that whispered and pointed when he, the king's bastard, passed. Loose-lipped sycophants and backstabbers, all.

Alaena, on the other hand...

Aelward pulled at his collar. The lass was exploding firepowder, spirit as red-hot as her fiery red hair, which curled like knots of seaweed. Her eyes, green as the ocean. So few Eldaeri had that color hair and eyes, and even fewer had that kind of spirit: like a tempest blown by Sargasso himself.

There was no taming it.

What an adventure it would be to try. It would be like captaining a dinghy in a typhoon, to be tossed and battered, before an inevitable trip to the bottom of the sea. And that girl was no unexplored ocean. No doubt, many a man had tried to navigate those fjords, and been shattered upon the rocks. She was likely cause of many a shipwreck.

His stomach twisted like the impossible knot. On his honor as an officer, Alaena was as forbidden as cursed pirate treasure. It wouldn't be him, no, but his half-brother Aryn who'd be thrown into the storm. Who, out of his three royal half-siblings, he resented the least. Aryn had never been unpleasant to him, the bastard get of their royal father's affair.

The blockwood door creaked open. The din from the throne room filtered in.

He swung around.

The light behind her made it impossible to make out Alaena's face, but the windswept curls could only belong to her. She leaned against the doorframe. Gone were the pungent tunic and pants, replaced by a diaphanous gown which bared toned arms. The light from the central hall filtered through the fine cloth, silhouetting her full curves. From the shape, it didn't look like she was wearing undergarments.

He swallowed hard. Tides and tempests, she was like Sargasso's sirens, luring men to their death; only here, giving into temptation would be treason, not to mention the cuckolding of his own marginally favorite half-brother, with his future half-sister-in-law.

Tides and tempests, his head spun. Aelward crossed his wrists and bowed his head. "Lass."

She chuckled.

He cringed as soon as the word left his mouth. All this polite, diplomatic speech would be the death of him. He rehearsed the words a few times in his head before saying, "I mean, good evening, Your Highness."

"Good evening, Lieutenant Aelward Niromar, commander of the *Sea Dragon*, binder of goats. Aren't you going to invite me in?"

All the gods in heaven and hell, nothing good would come of this. He draped his formal coat over his shoulders and walked toward her. "How about if I join ye out yonder? It's dinnertime, isn't it?"

She thrust a hand out, pushing him in the chest. "There's nothing but...what did you call them? Loose-lipped sycophants and backstabbers out there. I had a different meal in mind."

Her hand was hot as it worked its way inside his lapels and onto his bare skin. Her eyes were inviting as a trade wind on a becalmed day.

Aelward swallowed hard again. He took her hand.

And almost jerked back.

It wasn't soft and smooth like a pampered lady's. No, it was rough and calloused, like a sailor's.

So perfect.

He shook the idea out of his head, removed her hand, and pushed past her, out into the mezzanine balustrade overlooking the throne room.

Hells, it had been hot in his room, at least since Sargasso's Siren had arrived. He gulped in the cool air and looked over the balcony. Down below, platters of food were laid out on long tables. Lords and ladies milled about in their finery, blabbering about gods knew what.

Actually, he had a good idea about what. The Tarkothi prince who would move to Korynth. And his wild bride, who would one day sit on the throne.

The one who now came up behind him. She pressed her ample bosom into his back. "I see you are wearing a clean uniform. It's quite striking."

He turned and nodded his thanks.

"It would look better on the floor by your bed." She tilted her head back to the room.

Tempests! The lass was nothing like the demure Eldaeri girls back home, and even more wanton than the Arkothi wenches trawling the waterfronts. In the bright light, her nipples poked out from the gown, dangerous like shoals exposed at low tide. He drew his eyes up. "Lass, I don't think that'd be appropriate."

Her pout sent his heart racing. "Am I not beautiful?"

He swallowed hard again. "Nay, you're one of the most beautiful lasses I've ever laid eyes on. Sargasso take me to the bottom of the sea if I'm lying."

"Then why?"

"You're to marry me b—prince. If he found out..."

Her lips quirked up on one side. "He need not find out."

"Castles have eyes and ears."

She raised a suggestive eyebrow. "They also have secret passages."

If Korynth's palace was the same as Tarkoth's, he probably knew some of them. The escape routes, the shortcuts for servants, the dwarf-made secret doors. There was a spot, not far from here, where they could rock the ship. Nobody need know.

No, it was too risky. "I'm starving. How about we make our way to the kitchen, and avoid the loose-lipped sycophants and backstabbers?"

Looking up from her lashes, Alaena beckoned. Maelstroms and mastheads, she was so enticing. He followed her around the mezzanine to the main stairwell. She crossed one leg in front of the other, the sashay of her hips rolling like the tides. Her gown clung to her, showing the v-shaped divot defining the waterline between her stern and keel. To think, hours ago she'd been filthy, all those luscious curves covered by sweaty, thick wool.

Royal guards all saluted with crossed fists, yet even with their otherwise stoic expressions, their eyes roved over her. So did the lords, all bedecked in high-collared shirts.

Sweat gathered at Aelward's brow. Not from the seductress in his midst, but from all the memories of court life.

She looked over her shoulder. "I swear, inside the castle you walk like a bride the day after her wedding. Or a newborn fawn. Do you not like the indoors?"

No. But secret scars from childhood visits to the Tarkothi court would remain secrets. For now, let her believe it was claustrophobia. "Yes. I prefer to be on the open seas, with a wind at me back and a course set ahead of me."

"Sailing through tight straits, I bet." With a wicked grin, she stopped at a bare spot on a back wall on the first floor. The Tarkothi castle had a secret door here, where a passage led outside. Out to where she planned Sargasso knew what.

"I thought we were going to the kitchens." He gestured down the hall which wrapped around the palace, under the throne room, to where chefs would be preparing a feast.

She raised an eyebrow. "You know where the kitchens are?"

Hells, he'd slipped. Or maybe she'd tricked him, like a selkie. "Yes, a sailor won't miss the smell of roasting meat."

Brow furrowed, she sniffed at the air. "I don't smell anything."

"You're not a sailor, lass."

Her eyes twinkled with mischief. Grabbing his sleeve with one hand, she pressed a spot on the wall. The secret door slid open without a sound, letting the fresh air rush in. She pulled him out into the starry night.

If the night really was cool, Aelward could barely tell. Heat rushed to his face, and he loosened his collar, as if fresh air could settle him.

Oh yes, the night was cool. Her skin erupted in goosebumps, and her nipples...

He blinked several times and lifted his gaze to the heavens. The heavens above, that was.

She shoved him up against the granite walls, calloused hands sliding between the buttons of his uniform to his chest.

"Oy lass, what are ye doing?"

"When I see what I like, I take it." She leaned in, her hot lips brushing against his neck.

A jolt of excitement went up his spine. He started to reach around, to wrap her in an embrace...but then stopped. "Lass, you'll get me court-martialed, maybe even hung."

"Then you'll die happy," she whispered in his ear.

He pushed back on her shoulders. "Nay, lass. This is wrong. Ye are to marry Prince Aryn."

"I imagine he's in the warm embrace of some woman now."

Probably more than one, from what he'd heard. "But he's..."

"...A man?" She smirked. "What's good for the buck is good for the doe."

He snorted. "If the does were as capable as the bucks, they'd be sailing our ships."

Her eyebrow arched. "What about the Pirate Queen?"

After the Tarkothi navy had shattered the pirate lords' hold on the Estomar nearly three decades before, the mysterious Pirate Queen had risen. How, nobody in Eldaeri lands knew, but she'd united a few dozen pirate bands, expanding their reach and influence to heights not enjoyed since the first Pirate King three centuries ago. Still... "An exception, not the rule."

She harrumphed. "Our people used to see men and women as equals. We fought alongside men during the Eldaeri pacification of coastal Arkoth. It wasn't until we let Arkothi culture dilute ours that women became the so-called *fairer sex.*"

Aelward nodded slowly, like a buoy at low tide. The history was not just written in the annals of the empire, but also recounted in songs. Outnumbered by the local warlords, Eldaeri men and women all contributed to bringing peace to the land. The ships, the crossbows, the trees, the messenger birds and—

A shadow flashed across the white moon, casting them in darkness. A roc, wings outspread, banked around the palace's southeast tower, the angle exposing its lithe rider.

Aelward sucked in a breath. It was a woman. Of course it was a woman. For roc riders, it had always been the pragmatic tradition, given a woman's lighter weight. In the era of pacification, they'd scouted out enemy positions and rained arrows on opposing armies from the skies. At the time of the civil war, the roc riders were stationed and trained in the plains and farmland of the west. Now, there were none left in Tarkoth. Supposedly none in Serikoth, either.

She followed his gaze up and grinned. "See? A job a man can't do."

Her words, along with the sight of a female roc rider effortlessly navigating the vast night sky, nagged at his mind. He couldn't refute her argument about the equality of sexes. By Sargasso, he was a fool. The fire in his cheeks burned brighter, not from lust, but from shame.

"I see, lass," he said, leaning back against the wall. "I also see that had ye stayed in Serikoth, ye'd like as not be trussed up and pretty. A proper, demure Eldaeri princess, like Princess Karyna in Tarkoth. By coming to Korynth, ye blossomed."

In more ways than one. She now angled her shoulders so that the neck of her dress puffed out, providing a view of the trench between her breasts. "How cruel it is, then, to be given wings to fly, only to be caged by marriage."

A marriage that was all part of Elrayn's fish-brained scheme to reunite the Eldaeri Empire. "There, there, lass. Prince Aryn is quite the amiable bloke. Capable, but he'd never presume to captain yer ship of state ahead of ye."

"You know him?" Her expression brightened.

Aelward muttered a silent curse. Had it been silent? Or had he said it aloud? The last thing he needed was Alaena swabbing out all his secrets. He shook his head. "His reputation is well-known in Tarkoth. He always defers to the Crown Prince, always gives the Crown Prince the glory. I imagine he'd do the same for ye."

Her face, radiant enough to rival the moons a second ago, darkened. The pout, which had been flirtatious before in his room, sagged in despair. She was like the ocean, becalmed by Lunasti's grace one moment, only to rage with Sargasso's fury the next.

If Alaena's fiery spirit had ignited lust in his loins, this new vulnerability sent an ache into his heart. There might be no such thing as perfection, but she was close. Aryn would never appreciate such a complete woman. Philandering prince that he was, he didn't deserve her.

Aelward might not either, but at least he understood. Hells, forget duty. Nobody would ever have to find out. He leaned forward to claim her lips.

Twirling on her heel, she threw her back against the wall beside him and sighed. "I don't want to rule."

And just like that, the moment was lost. Aelward frowned. "Didn't ye make that choice?"

She sank down to the ground. "What does a five-year-old know? My father, who wanted to influence Korynth, made it sound like it would be fun. He didn't say it meant tearing me away from my mother and coming to a foreign land."

As delightful as it would be to strip away her gown, he shrugged off his formal coat and draped it over her shoulders. He plopped down beside her. "Ye know, lass, I never knew me mother."

She turned to him, eyes searching his. "No?"

He bobbed his chin. "Me da took part in the campaigns against the pirate lords. Though married with children, he fell in love with a local girl. With circumstances at home, he couldn't bring her back, but he brought me."

It was the truth, just not the whole truth. Perhaps it would be enough to put wind in her sails. Maybe she was still up for…

"I'd guessed your father was a farmer, not a sailor. Is that why you joined the navy?"

His father wasn't a sailor, and that was exactly why Aelward had joined the navy. Still, he wanted no lies between them. Half-truths would have to do. "As a bastard, I wanted to get away from home, and make a name for myself. No better place than Tarkoth's navy."

"Maybe I'll join the navy." Her grin was infectious.

Aelward's lips twitched. "But as I said, there be no does on our ships."

"I'll dress up like a man." She thrust her arms through his jacket sleeves and crossed her fists like a good navy man.

It only plumped up her cleavage. With a curvaceous body like that, there would be no mistaking her for a man. He laughed, but her expression gave him pause.

Her face was as serious as a lifeboat taking on water. "You're in command of the *Sea Dragon*; take me aboard as a boy to clean the decks."

To imagine Alaena in that uniform, on all fours, swabbing the deck. Aelward shook the musing out of his head. "Your hair will give you away."

"I'll shave it off."

If he shook his head any more violently, he might stir up a storm on his own. He took a frizzy red lock between his fingers. "It's what makes ye...ye."

"I'll give it up, just as quickly as I'll give up the throne of Korynth."

"Maybe ye can, but I can't disobey me orders. It's me duty to take ye to Elbahia."

"And you will be." The mischievous expression had returned. "Just not as a betrothed princess."

His heart pounded again.

She looked up through her lashes. "What can a girl do to convince a ship captain to let her onboard?"

His mouth opened and closed, but no words came out.

She jumped to her feet and offered him a hand. "On your feet, sailor. We shall set off for the kitchens, for I am hungry now."

He took her hand and pulled himself up. The moment was lost, but maybe there would be another chance before they made it to Elbahia and her inevitable meeting with Prince Aryn.

CHAPTER 14:

New Places, Old Clues

As Jie rode in the open carriage with Prince Aryn and Peris through the streets of Elbahia Island, she considered the old adage: travel enriched life, if it didn't kill you first. The architecture lining the cobbled streets was much like she'd seen in Tokahia, one of the recent stops on their sea voyage. Two- and three-story rowhouses boasted decorative columns and gently pitched roofs; moving glass panes covered the windows. Unlike the concrete and tile buildings of the Estomar, however, these were built from Eldaeri blockwood.

The *Indomitable* had docked at Elbahia's seaport in the south, where the Serikothi's *Intimidator* was still moored. With minimal activity onboard, it didn't look to be going anywhere soon, so there was still a chance to sneak aboard and dig up traces of the assassin she was tracking. Whether that would be before or after a visit to Cathay's trade office—and the small Black Lotus cell that operated there—would depend on timing and circumstance.

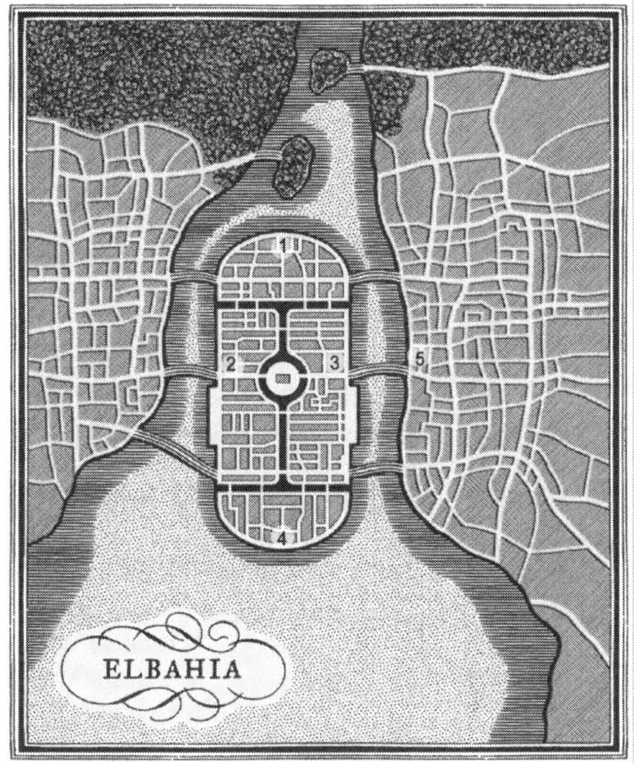

1. Korynthi Palace
2. Serikothi Palace
3. Tarkothi Palace
4. Main Docks
5. Tarkothi Guest Villa

For now, though, the carriage travelled up a road along the east side of the island. On a map, it looked like a perfect oval in a natural harbor on the Valeri River, about one *li* wide and three *li* long. She converted the measurements to the Eldaeri standards so as not to sound like a fool around Prince Aryn and Peris. "Elbahia Island is such an exact oval, half a kilometer wide, a kilometer and a half long, and it couldn't naturally form on this part of a river. Did your ancestors shape it with magic?"

"I didn't realize Jyeh was an Aksumi Geomancer." Aryn laughed as he looked to Peris. He swung an arm over her shoulder. "No, my love. Despite our traces of elf blood, none of Solaris' Chosen seem to have an affinity for magic. However, thousands of years ago, before the Altivorcs conquered the world, an elf city supposedly thrived here. Perhaps it was their wizardry which created this island."

With plenty of elf blood coursing through her veins, Jie didn't have any magic, either. She nodded, scanning the surroundings. Though a handful of Tarkoth's green banners hung from some buildings, the majority of flags were white with a gold, nine-pointed sun, fluttering in the mid-morning light.

"The flag of the old Eldaeri Empire," Aryn said, following her gaze. "Elbahia was the old capital. For our seafaring ancestors, it was a perfect location: near the center of our lands, as far inland as sea-going ships could travel. Since the civil war, it has been neutral ground."

Historical archives back home recounted how the Hellstorm had sundered the Arkothi Empire, leading to the Bovyans controlling the north, and the Eldaeri conquering the east. Her homeland's historians speculated on the civil war which had split the Eldaeri Empire in three, but from her visit to Tokahia, Jie had learned that history was truly *his story*, and no doubt the Tarkothi had their own spin. She feigned total ignorance. "What happened to your empire?"

Aryn yawned. "Arrogance. Ambition. Stupidity."

The same could be said about the fall of Cathay's previous dynasty, whose emperor had arrogantly broken vows sealed by Heaven, leading to the Hellstorm and Long Winter. Perhaps arrogance, ambition, and stupidity contributed to the fall of every ruling house. She raised an eyebrow, prodding him to continue.

Scratching his head, Aryn turned to Peris. "What was the name of the last emperor?"

Peris glared at Jie for a moment. "Emperor Bolryn."

"Right." Aryn nodded. "Emperor Bolryn, despite being married twice, never had children. Some say his seed had run dry, but rumor had it..."

Neither Aryn nor Peris said anything, but the aide's lips twitched.

"He preferred the company of men?" Jie supplied. It wasn't unheard of back home, though past emperors had dutifully produced heirs, regardless of their preferences.

"Boys. Who knows, it was a hundred and twenty years ago. In any case, he adopted two of his second cousins: Valeryn Vardamcar and Darwyn Corivar. One from the

East, another from the West. He brought them as children here to Elbahia." He pointed toward the center of the island.

Sitting on a hill was a white granite palace unlike any Jie had ever seen. Unlike the hard edges found in most fortresses and castles throughout Tivara, the old palace adopted smooth lines reminiscent of elf architecture, combined with the spires and columns favored by the ancient Arkothi. A central dome of sparkling quartz vaulted high above the city, even taller than the four spired towers at its corners. Jie feigned amazement, while she considered how hard it would be to sneak in.

"Anyway," Aryn said, "At the time, my people had started mingling with the local Arkothi and Estomari. Some conservative lords felt that as the Chosen of Solaris, we had to maintain racial purity. They championed Valeryn, who shared their beliefs."

Jie nodded. People tended to be tribal, to their own detriment. "And Darwyn?"

"He was Bolryn's heir. He supported the loosening of social strictures. Then there was some foreigner, an Ayuri like your Paladin friend, who became chancellor. It was very odd for a Southerner to rise so high. What was his name, Peris?"

The big man shook his head. "For his crimes, his name was expunged from our historical records."

"They must have been significant crimes," Jie said.

If Aryn nodded any more violently, his head might fall off. "He instigated the civil war, stoking the passions on both sides. Valeryn took control of the west. Our ships and armies faced off against each other."

Jie shuddered. To think her own homeland had recently averted a civil war. Thanks to her, of course.

"In the end, the chancellor negotiated the Treaty of Elbahia, which split the empire into two kingdoms at the Valeri River." Aryn waved toward the riverbank. "Tarkoth took the Light of Solaris, while Serikoth took the White Staff upon which the Light sat in battle. We designated this island as neutral ground."

Jie pictured a map of the region in her head. "But there are three Eldaeri Kingdoms."

"Right. Korynth is in the Estomar. The great lords there broke away from Serikoth, and claimed the Gold Ring."

"Gold Ring?"

"It was part of the Scepter of Solaris. It affixed the Light to the White Staff." Aryn held a thumb and finger in the shape of a circle, and thrust a finger through it. He grinned suggestively.

Heat flushed to the tips of Jie's elf ears, and she looked sidelong at Peris.

The way his lips pursed, he'd no doubt picked up on the prince's not-so-subtle motion.

Jie cleared her throat. "So the precious heirloom of the Eldaeri was separated into three."

"All because of the foreign chancellor's appeasement."

"And Serikoth just let Korynth go?"

Aryn nodded. "They were depleted after two years of civil war, and Tarkoth supplied Korynth's rebels with arms and supplies. In any case, Estomari and Arkothi culture are different enough that Serikoth probably realized it would be more of a headache to keep."

Jie cocked her head. Estomari and Arkothi people were both fair-skinned, though perhaps the Arkothi were a shade more olive. Culturally...she looked out onto the street.

Where the Estomari people in Tokahia dressed in blinding, headache-inducing colors, the Arkothi people here embraced a more subdued palette. Men in high-collared tunics mingled with women in undecorated long dresses and stockings as they hustled from craft shops to grocers, from fishmongers to artisans' studios. Unlike the Estomari, they didn't interact with gesticulations exaggerated enough to shame an opera singer. Most stopped and bowed as the royal carriage passed. Aryn greeted them with broad smiles, but then frowned when he looked down at the missive in his lap.

"Is it about your bride-to-be, Alaena?" Jie asked, the name bitter on her tongue.

Peris snorted.

With a shake of his head, Aryn looked from his large aide to her. "There is no word of Princess Alaena. No, these tidings are graver. One of our outposts up north was ambushed, and survivors claim it was the Serikothi. We are going to a funeral barge now."

Jie sucked on her lower lip. Back home, she'd witnessed firsthand how the Serikothi and Tarkothi—

once one people—disliked each other. They'd nearly come to fists on the docks. Still, it was hard to imagine they'd engage in armed conflict, especially with the Teleri Empire's Bovyans waiting to pounce on them both.

The carriage trundled to a stop near some wharfs along the eastern side of the island, where several river barges were moored. A steady stream of dockworkers carted crates to warehouses along the main road.

The driver jumped off the front seat and came to open the side door.

"I need to pay respects to the dead before we return their bodies to their families," Aryn said, stepping down. "I think you will want wait here."

Jie shook her head. The dead often held clues for those who knew to find them, and if there was a war brewing between Serikoth and Tarkoth, this would be the first place to look. "I will pay respects with you."

"Why?" Peris studied her.

Aryn waved a hand at him. "It's all right. She can come."

They walked deeper into the island, to a warehouse smaller than the rest. Tarkothi soldiers at the door crossed their fists and bowed their heads as Aryn approached.

No sooner did they open the door than a blast of cold air sent goosebumps prickling over Jie's exposed shoulders and arms. She followed the prince in.

Partially shuttered baubles shed a dim light over a room that looked much more cavernous on the inside than the outside. Steps immediately descended into concrete depths. Rows of crates alternated with rows of… "Ice?"

Aryn's grim expression relaxed for a second. "Yes, there are small lakes in the mountains, where we harvest ice."

Jie's head bobbed in slow nods. Though mountainous, only the northernmost range of her homeland was covered in snow during the winter. She followed him down the steps, teeth chattering.

Peris smirked at her. "This is no place for a woman."

Ignoring him, Jie trailed after the prince through the maze of crates. Some were marked as fish and other meats. There was nothing like this cold storage back home, and most foodstuffs were salted, smoked, pickled, or fermented to make them last. Her stomach grumbled at the memory of fermented soybeans. To have some now…

She shook the craving out of her head as they came to two bodies on biers, covered in green shrouds.

Aryn crossed his fists over his chest and bowed his head. "May Solaris choose you to serve at his side."

Peris joined in the salute, and Jie followed their lead with a local curtsey.

When Aryn raised his head, he sighed. "I can't believe Serikoth would attack us."

"They are treacherous," Peris said. "They shot our men in the back. If I were in your place, I wouldn't marry Alaena Vardamcar."

Gazing at Jie, Aryn said, "I don't want to, but she's the heir of Korynth. We could put pressure on Serikoth from both sides, like when Korynth first split from Serikoth."

Jie took note: it was rare for him to makes such an astute observation.

Peris spoke through gritted teeth. "She's still Serikothi by birth."

While the two men debated the merits of marriage to this hussy, Jie ventured closer to the bier. If only she had her toolkit! It was hidden with her stealth suit and magic knife in the false bottom of her travel chest. On Aryn's command, it had been packed on a cart at the docks and sent to the Tarkothi royal villa. She'd have to rely on her own observation skills. She lifted the sheet and looked.

Their lithe frames and shorter stature indicated the victims were full-blooded Eldaeri. Bruises marred their necks.

Aryn gasped. He put a hand over her eyes. "My lotus blossom, you don't want to see something so horrible."

If he only knew just what kind of atrocities she'd seen before. With a raise of her hand and a bend in her knees, she ducked under him and came back up. "How did you say these men were killed? Shot in the back?"

"With a repeater," Aryn said.

That wasn't how this one died. If only she'd been able to visit the scene of the attack. With a heave, Jie rolled the soldier onto his side. Blood stained his tunic, right between his shoulder blades. She eyed the entry wound, and then inserted her finger in.

"What are you doing?" Aryn's tone sounded aghast.

"Are you insane?" Peris asked, voice more suspicious than disgusted or surprised.

The wound went deeper than the reach of her finger, between two bones and into the lung. Still... "He was shot after he was already dead."

Aryn sidled over. "Are you sure?"

She pointed to the bruises around his neck. "He died of asphyxiation. The crossbow bolt came later."

"How can you tell?" Aryn's voice was one of wonderment.

"Yes, how can you tell?" Peris said, voice quite suspicious.

"There isn't much blood around the wound. He likely died standing, and his heart wasn't pumping when he was shot."

Peris snorted. "Speculation. His heart wasn't pumping because he was hit in the heart."

"No," she said. "The bolt penetrated the lining of his lungs, and not the heart. Had he been breathing at the time, the lung lining would be torn by the rise and fall of his chest."

Peris tromped over. "How can you tell all of this?"

It would've been better to check the bodies after the two had left. Instead, a glib excuse would have to suffice. "My father embalmed the dead and taught me anatomy."

"You have that custom in Cathay?" Aryn asked.

No, but he didn't have to know that. And Master Yan *had* taught her quite a bit about anatomy. She nodded. "Do you have the bolt that killed him?"

Aryn exchanged glances with Peris, then shook his head. "I doubt they kept it. What about the other one?"

If only she'd been able to see the undisturbed scene and the murder weapon. Jie went to the other body and lifted the sheet, pausing at the muffled voices and footsteps from the entrance. Crates blocked her view of the door, so she returned to her examination.

This soldier had been shot in the eye. Like the other, he had bruises around his neck and very little blood around the entry wound. However, the hair on the back of his head was matted. She probed with a finger in that spot and found the exit wound, a small hole in the skull.

"Well?" Peris' put his hands on his hips. "Shot through the eye."

"Yes, but like the other victim, he was choked to death." Ears perking as footsteps neared, she pointed at the bruises around his neck. "Afterwards, they shot him at very close range, close enough that the bolt went all the way through his brain and out the other side."

Nodding, Aryn smiled at her. "You have many talents."

"Yes." Peris' eyes narrowed.

"Brother." A new voice spoke from down the row.

Jie fought the instinct to reach for the magic knife that was usually strapped to her inner thigh, but which was currently on some cart, and looked up.

Two green-cloaked men approached, bringing with them a whiff of musk. One was short and thin like Aryn; the other, robust like Peris. With his delicate features, dark hair, and resemblance to Aryn, the smaller was likely Crown Prince Elrayn. The other had blond hair and a prominent jaw. Given his size, he might have Nothori blood. Those hardy people from Tivaralan's northwest had all been subjects of the Arkothi Empire, and perhaps some had emigrated to this region in centuries past.

Both Aryn and Peris crossed fists over their chests and bowed their heads. Jie curtseyed.

"Your Highness," Peris said. When he raised his head, he smiled broadly and clasped wrists with the other large man in Arkothi fashion. It was the first sign of human warmth he'd shown up to now, disproving Jie's unspoken theory that he was actually a Biomancer's zombie or Artificer's golem.

Aryn leaned in and whispered to her, "Peris' brother, Tharos."

Besides their large size, the two didn't look that similar; though, these Northerners did seem to have a wider variety of features than the people back home.

Prince Elrayn laughed. "You can let go of each other now."

With sheepish grins, both Peris and Tharos stepped back and crossed their fists over their chest.

The Crown Prince turned to Aryn. "I'm glad I found you here. I just arrived in Elbahia with some interesting cargo." His eyes strayed to Jie, and then he pulled Aryn all the way to the end of the row.

Peris and Tharos now both looked at her. Without Black Lotus training, she might've shied away, given their significant size and how they loomed over her. Still, she puffed her chest out and flashed her most insolent smile. In the meantime, she angled her head to see if she could eavesdrop on the princes.

Their whispers reached her elf ears, but the language might as well have been gibberish. Still, Aryn's scowl, and the jerking waves of his hand, suggested he was not pleased. Elrayn's body language was placating. No doubt they were talking about that Alaena Vardamcar—

"No," Aryn said in Arkothi. "You can't just keep him as a hostage. Or force him to marry Karyna."

His voice echoed in the warehouse. Tharos must've already known whoever this hostage was, because he continued studying her without the least amount of interest in the princes; even Peris seemed more motivated to stare her down.

"Just who are you?" Peris took a step forward.

Jie held her ground. "I haven't changed since you met me in Cathay. I'm just an orphan."

Harrumphing, Peris pointed two fingers at his eyes, then one at her. "I don't know what your designs on Prince Aryn are, but I'm keeping my eye on you."

"I'm just his honored guest."

Blond Tharos laughed. "Guest in his bed, I bet. Don't expect it to last long. He will be marrying Princess Alaena soon enough."

Her again. Jie shrugged. It's not like she had ever hoped to have a future with Aryn. Or had she? Really, she should be more concerned with her mission of tracking down the clan traitor. Of course, there were also the suspicious deaths of these soldiers, and whatever the book Peris acquired said about the last Runemaster

Imperator and his crown, perhaps lost near the town of Lorium in the shadow of Lydath's Golden Bowl.

CHAPTER 15:

Lore of the Land

Tomas' boat could hold up to six normal-sized people, but the Bovyans—Sathis and Fethos—might've counted for two each. Their broad shoulders barely fit within the width of the hull. With the scribe and tattooist on board as well, there was barely enough room for Tomas to squeeze in.

"You need me," he had said, when the Bovyans suggested otherwise. "There are underwater rocks, and if you don't know where they are, you better hope you can swim in your armor."

He hoped they couldn't. With all the uncertainties, he struggled to take a breath, and his eye socket still burned.

The Bovyans had grumbled, but grudgingly conceded his point. Now, flustered by his slow progress across the straits to his island, they sat in the back, rowing. He'd cast them an apologetic grin before surrendering his oars. He was just conserving his energy, and the two of them, with their gigantic arms, thrashed through the water much faster than he could if he were by himself.

Of course, they were better warriors than rowers, which was likely why they'd hired the crew of the Serikothi bireme they'd captured. That vessel's drums thudded somewhere in the distance, even as his own boat lurched through the waters.

Like him, the tattooist and scribe gripped the bulwarks, knuckles white. Whether it was sweat or mist off the lake collecting on their brows, it was impossible to tell. If they knew what he was planning, it would definitely be sweat.

Up ahead, his island grew larger, until it took up a quarter of his new, narrower visual field.

The scribe gasped and pointed. "Lydath's Golden Bowl!"

Tomas nodded. It had been just an indistinct blob from the town's shore, but it now took shape as they grew closer. The tilt made it look like a moon's waning gibbous. For the islanders, it was a landmark for the safe approach.

"How come your village folk haven't taken the gold?" The tattooist's eyes gleamed with greed.

Besides the orc gods' curse... "It's impossible to reach. Even in ancient times, before the water level rose, the orc priests could only get there by using their fell magic."

The tattooist prodded the scribe. "Water level? What's this bumpkin talking about?"

The scribe swept his hand from one end of the sea to the other. It stretched farther than the eye could see, save for the mountains looming above the island. "Millennia before even the War of Ancient Gods, this entire region was above water. There was a great dwarf city beneath the mountain, and their underground network of mines and towns extended for hundreds of leagues."

Tomas stared at him. His family had lived on the island for generations, and nobody had ever mentioned dwarves. "You're wrong. There was a human city in a basin, and during the Hellstorm—"

The scribe shook his head. "The Hellstorm was three hundred years ago. This tale goes back thousands. When the elves, dwarves, and humans allied against the orcs, the orcs invoked the wrath of their gods and collapsed the tunnels. It wiped out most of the dwarves, and left an enormous gash in the earth. Only the mountain remained, and the orcs enslaved the survivors."

Tomas gaped. How come none of the locals knew of this?

The scribe afforded him a smug glance. "The orcs built the Temple of Lydath on the summit. Where Lorium and the Barrows sit now, at the edge of the crater, was a human city with a single bridge running to a holy city high on the mountainside."

"*Unholy* city," Tomas said, even though his village now occupied the same spot. "It's where our ancestors delivered sacrifices to the Temple of Lydath. Even today, you can sometimes hear the wail of the ghosts of the people murdered there."

As if in confirmation, a low howl keened from the mountaintop.

Tomas shivered.

The scribe just shrugged. "In any case, during the War of Ancient Gods, our ancestors, along with elves and dwarves, fought their way to the foot of the Temple of Lydath, and called on Solaris' divine might to topple the Golden Dish. Arkothi humans settled the canyon, and over the ensuing centuries, the small village grew into a grand city. The orc's holy city on the mountain became the Runemaster Imperator's summer villa."

The tattooist snorted. "All I see is water."

The scribe glared. "When the Runemaster Imperator unleashed the Hellstorm on the Ayuri Empire, from that very spot, they retaliated with magic of their own. A star fell from the heavens, rocking the earth and changing the course of rivers."

Tomas nodded. This much, they agreed on. He'd searched for the fallen star in the swamps, to no avail.

"So?" the tattooist said.

The scribe swept his hand from east to west again. "Rivers inundated the canyon, forming the Inland Sea."

Inundate… Tomas had never heard the word before, but assumed it referred to the flooding. It had left the Runemaster Imperator's villa submerged, save for the tops of the dozens of towers which made up his village. "There are treasures from the Drowned City scattered across the lake floor. Our village women dive for them in the shallows, but the best stuff is a hundred *pedes* below."

The tattooist laughed. "For all that wealth, I'd train to hold my breath longer."

Tomas harrumphed. "There's also ghosts. Both from the people who died in the Hellstorm, and the human sacrifices of the ancient orc priests."

The tattooist spat into the lake. "Superstition."

Tomas shook his head, though his neck ached from having to hold his head at an angle. "Our divers sometimes see them. Sometimes, they never come back."

The scribe blanched.

Now the wooden platforms and bridgeways surrounding the glinting domes of Tomas' village were taking shape. He gestured to the Bovyans. "Paddle to the right."

"But your village is straight ahead," the closest, brown-haired one said.

"If we go that way, we'll crash against the Jaws." Tomas scanned the waters for the bireme, though the distant thud of the drums suggested it was nowhere nearby. "Paddle to the right. Left oars out of the water."

The Bovyans complied, and the boat veered right.

Tomas pointed to a line of rocks that the bobbing waves occasionally exposed. "Those are the Jaws. They almost completely ring the island."

The scribe's forehead scrunched up. "How did they form in a lake?"

"They were the walls around the Temple of Lydath," Tomas said.

The village drifted farther behind, and up ahead, the line of the Tooth jutted thousands of *pedes* across the water.

The tattooist pointed at it. "Is that part of the Jaws?"

Tomas shook his head. "That's the Tooth. It's what remains of the bridge that once connected the mountain to the basin, where the Barrows are today."

The village disappeared around the Tooth, and they soon came upon the Egg: a smooth, enormous boulder sitting on a ridge some fifty *pedes* above the waterline.

After a quarter of a phase, they'd almost reached the spot. Tomas' stomach twisted like one of his complicated knots. Maybe the Bovyans deserved what was coming to them. They'd taken his eye, after all, and would rape every last unmarried girl in town. Still, the tattooist and scribe weren't Bovyan, they were just collaborators. Or perhaps they'd been forced into this awful work.

Unfortunately, this was the only way to get back to the island without the Bovyans. The only way to protect Sofia and Maria.

Tomas pointed to a rock which disappeared under a wave, only to reappear a second later. "See that rock? It's a marker for the only safe way in."

The Bovyans both nodded.

"Now, you two have been trashing like a fish out of water. We need to build up speed if we are to make it through the gap. Row together, on my call." Tomas clapped his hands together, creating a fast beat.

Like the gears of a dwarf clock, the Bovyans rowed in perfect unison. Their strokes became sleek and smooth, and despite their chainmail, despite all the weight in the boat, they glided through the water like a fish.

By the Divine Fisherman, they'd picked up the skill quickly. They were travelling thrice as fast as he could manage by himself. The perfect speed.

"A little to the right of the rock," Tomas said. Every muscle tensed, coiled, ready to move. Any second now...

The boat smashed into the underwater rocks. The hull splintered and lurched.

Tomas leaped from the boat, just avoiding another ridge of rocks, and dove into the frigid waters of the lagoon formed by the Jaws and the island.

His eye socket seared, and it was even harder to gauge distances underwater than usual. He kept his hand to the side, running along the rocks until he surfaced. He turned and looked.

Only part of the boat remained above water. How far behind, it was impossible to tell with his single eye. At its side, the scribe and tattooist floundered with wild swings of their arms. They couldn't swim.

Guilt formed a pit in Tomas' gut. He treaded water and waved them toward the rock. "Grab ahold of that!"

It would keep them from drowning, but not from freezing, and there was no help coming, not to the windward side of the island.

He looked around. The Bovyans were nowhere to be seen. As he'd planned, their drenched tunics, bulky chainmail, and heavy boots must've dragged them down. Two more ghosts to add to the Inland Sea.

Guilt squeezed his chest. By the Divine Fisherman, he'd just led two men to their drowning deaths, and two more would soon join them soon.

Like one of his bobbers, one of the Bovyan's heads popped above water with a splash, followed soon by the other. Blood trickled from a gash on the second's forehead. They were on the far side of the boat, though how far was impossible to tell, and they looked to have no trouble treading water in their armor.

All guilt fled, replaced by any icy sensation running up his back. This wasn't how his plan was supposed to work. What would it take to drown these brutes?

Thank the Fisher, he had a backup plan. Eye socket stinging, Tomas resumed his swim toward shore. It was only a few hundred *pedes* away, a swim he'd made as a child hunting for oysters along the Jaws.

The Bovyans shouted something, but it was unintelligible over the splash of his arms through the water.

He swam with smooth strokes, breathing steadily as he crossed the distance to the island. After a few minutes, he shifted to his side and looked over his shoulder.

The Bovyans were swimming after him. Tivar take the bastards for the loss of an eye! It was impossible to tell if they were gaining or losing ground on him.

He continued, aiming toward the gorge between two crags. If they caught him, he could reasonably claim it had been an accident. Hopefully, it wouldn't come to that.

His limbs found purchase on the ground and he scrambled to his feet, sloshing through the gritty shallows until he reached the entrance to the gorge.

Now, at high tide, water flooded the entire floor, forming a swamp. His bare feet sank into the cold mud. Ash and maple branches stretched skyward, their canopies filtering the sunlight. He had to step over many a large root curling out of the water, and with the new limitations on his vision, he tripped on more than one occasion.

Birds chirped and frogs croaked, and streams babbled from the mountaintops down into the gorge. The sounds would help mask his escape, even as he could hear his pursuer's jingling armor. His heart raced as he worked his way deeper into the ravine, and at the fork, went north, further into the island. He plucked some stretchweed along the way, so he could make a makeshift slingshot later.

"Boy! Where are you?" one of the Bovyans—Sathis? It had been easier not to name them, given the plan to drown them— called from far behind, his voice distant and echoing off the cliff walls.

Tomas froze, pressing his back against the gnarly bark of an ash tree. His eye socket burned so much, it was hard to concentrate.

"The little bastard did this on purpose," said the other, Fethos.

"If you don't answer, we'll assume you intentionally tried to get us killed."

Silence.

Maybe it would be better to reveal himself, pretend that he hadn't tried to escape. They'd be lenient, because they needed him. No, he could lose them in the swamp.

He had several hours until the tide receded, which gave him time to move without leaving tracks.

Their voices muttered, the only intelligible word being something about a crown.

The first Bovyan spoke again. "You go this way, I'll go that way. As long as we head west, we'll come to the miserable runt's village."

Let him think that. The network of gulches and ravines created a maze, and the only one that led to the village veered eastward first. A bird's-eye image of it appeared in Tomas' mind. He could lead the Bovyans far away, and strand them there; or he could wait and let them bypass him, then head home where he could eat—

His stomach rumbled.

He hadn't eaten for two days, and his last meal had ended up on Lorium's beach. Now that he'd stopped, his arms and legs felt like a boat weighed down by anchors. Meanwhile, with full bellies, the Bovyans could take long, loping steps.

He pressed on, moving from tree to tree and stopping to listen for jingling mail. There was only one now, and from the sound of it, he'd stripped off his tunic. He was close now.

Body trembling, Tomas pressed against a thick silver maple, and rounded it, keeping it between him and the sound of the Bovyan's clinking armor. His ankles sloshed in the water, but the black-haired Bovyan, Fethos, was even louder as he muttered and slogged through the morass.

When the sounds disappeared in the distance, Tomas let out a long sigh. The Teleri thug was between him and home now. Hopefully, the soldier would take a wrong turn at one of the gorge's many forks and branches.

For now, though, every muscle screamed for him to rest, while his stomach insisted he eat something. He treaded over to a stand of watercress, pulled some out, and chewed it. Never before in his life had their bitter leaves tasted so good. He collected some elderberries and devoured them, as well. Unfortunately, none of the fallen branches were the right size or shape to make a good slingshot.

With his energy trickling back, he resumed his trek, keeping the sound of Fethos' chainmail well ahead of him.

Tomas stubbed his toe on a submerged root, and tumbled face-first into a tree.

The bird chirps fell silent. The clinking of armor stopped.

Damn! Tomas froze. His toe hurt, his face stung, and now he'd given away his position. He peered through the tree trunks, trying to get a good view of the monster.

A sliver of mail flashed in the dappled sunlight, and the sloshing resumed, back toward him. A sword rasped as it was pulled from a scabbard.

Tomas' heart raced. He bent over, his hand closed around fallen branch. It wouldn't do him much good against a real weapon, but it was better than just throwing himself on the Bovyan's sword.

The Teleri was coming closer, perhaps no farther than ten paces away.

Tomas fought the urge to look around the tree. His makeshift club would be useless against the killing machine. Maybe he'd just surrender.

They'd make him lead them back to the village. It would be better to die here.

The Bovyan swung around the tree. "You!"

CHAPTER 16:

Travel Broadens the Mind... If You Survive

With her trunk yet to arrive from the *Indomitable*, Jie rummaged through a wardrobe in a second-floor guest room in the Tarkothi royal villa in Elbahia. Fine clothes made of local satin or silk imported from Cathay were neatly organized: frilly dresses for ladies; pants and tunics for men, all with the muted color palettes favored by the Arkothi. At last, she found pants, a shirt, and a tunic her size, most likely meant for a young lord. Her own cloth shoes—a necessity for scaling walls—didn't match, and she covered her head and pointed ear tips with a scarf. The clothes might stand out on the streets, but it was just a temporary measure to slip out and not have her dress hem get caught on who-knew-what.

She peeked out a window, which provided a view of the paved walkway from the central residence to the wrought iron gates. Aryn walked with Crown Prince Elrayn, Tharos, and several guards in tow, to where a carriage waited outside. Usually unflappable, Aryn jabbed a finger at his brother. His furrowed brow and hard-set jaw made him look even more handsome.

Though she couldn't read lips speaking Arkothi, his fierce expression suggested they were probably talking about Aryn's betrothed, Alaena. When the Crown Prince had met Jie, he'd been quite dismissive, and whatever he'd said about her in the Eldaeri royal language had elicited a frown from Aryn.

They climbed into the carriage, which set off to the north.

Not straight to the west. That was where the old palace of Elbahia's dome and four spires loomed high above the rest of the island city.

Aryn had lied, unless his older brother had deceived him. He'd said they were expected at a meeting with the Serikothi at the palace, and had bid her rest here.

Not like she had time to rest, ever since an assassin had killed a lord back home. Wherever Aryn and Elrayn were going, along with Peris and his Cathayi book, it gave her time to get away and investigate the *Intimidator.* There might be enough time to report in to the Black Lotus cell operating out of the Cathayi trade office, but only afterward.

For now, she'd be without her lockpicks, throwing stars, or the magic knife she'd acquired in Tokahia. She was armed only with a bladed hairpin, and guided by the hunch that the Serikothi had helped the assassin. Opening the door, she slunk through the bauble-lit hallway as it wrapped around the second floor. The thick red carpet, made of Ayuri wool, made it easy to walk without sound.

Coming to a door on the east side, she paused and listened. Satisfied the room was empty, she slipped in. Like her own guest chamber, this room also had a bed with a carved wooden frame. Indirect sunlight trickled in from the curtained window. Jie crept over and looked.

As in all the buildings she'd visited in the north, the window had sliding glass panes instead of wood shutters like back home. Here, at the back of the mansion, it opened up onto a sheer, twenty-foot drop to the east branch of the Valeri river. Buildings flying Tarkoth's flag lined the opposite bank, some three hundred feet away. Weak human eyes, if they just happened to look across the river from there, probably wouldn't pick her out on the shaded side of the mansion.

Waiting until a fisherman's boat passed down below, she eased the window open and climbed out. The hand and footholds were easy to find between the granite blocks, though mist from the river made the stone slippery, a minor challenge. She edged down and to the south, where the villa's outer wall met the side of the building. A peek into the compound revealed several gardeners hard at work, and there was always a chance that someone would look out one of the mansion's windows; so after resting her fingers, she descended lower, using the exterior wall as a blind.

Clearing the villa walls, she dropped down to the streets of Elbahia and started toward the seaport. The roads were paved in white stone, and sprawling blockwood villas lined the streets. The few passersby looked to be wealthy, from the fine cut of their tunics and dresses, and the handful of soldiers all wore Tarkothi green.

Before long, the mansions thinned, giving way to rowhouses, and after that a mix of first-floor shops with residences above. The crowds thickened, and now, soldiers in Korynthi blue and Serikothi crimson mingled with the Tarkothi green. Despite being ostensible enemies, no hostilities broke out. None even afforded her headscarf or mismatched shoes a second glance.

It was odd. Having been stationed in Cathay's most bustling port, and having recently visited the busy docks of Tokahia, she noticed Elbahia was missing something: the dregs of society. In Cathay, it'd been thugs and orphans; in Tokahia, a mafia infestation. But here, no ruffians, no vagrants, no...poverty. And very few non-Eldaeri. Her hope of finding a street urchin to trade clothes with before trying to sneak aboard the *Intimidator* were diminishing like the afternoon sunlight.

Just as it seemed a lost cause, she skidded to a halt on a side street, at the opening of an alley between blockwood rowhouses. Six young men jabbered as they tossed knives at a round target. Copper coins exchanged hands, while some laughed and others groaned. All were dressed in nice, but not fine, clothes, most likely Levastyan linen or cotton. They might not be the dregs, but neither were they productive members of society.

Among them was a young teen, the only Eldaeri among them. He was just a little taller than her, and wore a grey tunic over black pants. Not a perfect fit, but it wouldn't stand out as much as her borrowed silk finery. Certainly, they would trade for it. She turned into the alley.

They paused their game and favored her with grins.

"Hey boy," the oldest one said. He had a mop of brown hair, dark eyes, and smooth skin that suggested he'd never done a day of hard work in his life. "Nice clothes, but what's with the scarf on your head? Are you pretending to be a Levanthi nomad?"

She deepened her voice to sound like boy on the border of puberty. "Yes."

The boys all laughed.

"No camels for you to bugger here," said one.

"And there's a toll to walk down this street." The first tossed a knife in the air and caught it by the blade, then flashed a grin.

The others mimicked his expression and crowded around.

Hair pricked at the back of her neck, and instincts kicked in. The leader—Mop Head—was the largest, the biggest threat. Shrimp, with the clothes she wanted, held back, while Cleft Chin, Troll Hands, Crooked Tooth, and Weasel Eyes encircled her.

Jie was feeling magnanimous today, and as long as they didn't resort to violence, they wouldn't suffer a broken bone or dislocated joint. She brushed the sleeve of her silk tunic. "I want to trade. This beautiful tunic for yours."

"What's to keep us from taking it from you?" Mop Head tossed his knife in the air again.

She darted in and swiped at it, catching the handle before he could. She set the blade to his throat.

All of them stared at her, wide-eyed.

"I could just take it from you, but I'd prefer to play fair." Not like she ever played fair. "Let's play a game. If I hit your target dead center, I get the kid's tunic and pants. If I miss, he gets mine."

Shrimp shook his head. "But..."

"It's okay, nobody can hit it dead center." Mop Head turned from Shrimp and spat on the ground. "You'll get to walk around looking like a prince. At least until we sell the clothes."

"Then we are agreed?" Jie hefted the knife, getting a feel for its weight distribution.

Shrimp started to shake his head.

"Yes," Mop Head said, with too much confidence for someone about to lose a bet.

It didn't matter where she was or where her missions led her. Whether she was in Cathay or Elbahia, one thing remained the same: men and their inflated egos. Without looking at the target again, she flung the blade across her body. It hit dead center with a *thunk*.

All heads turned, disbelief written on their faces. Jie, however, locked her gaze on Mop Head. Fear flashed across his ugly mug, while the rest of his body went stiff as a corpse, as if resisting the instinct to flee. If he were smart, he would.

Jie used the moment of shock to slip out of their circle, close to Shrimp. She wiggled her fingers at him. "Your clothes. Give them to me."

"This is your fault," he snarled at Mop Head. Grumbling, he pulled his tunic off and shimmied out of his pants, leaving him only with a thin undershirt and underpants. His friends all laughed.

"You can have mine, if you give me your knife." Jie held out her hand.

He curled his lip, and tossed the blade in a gentle arc.

Jie caught the tip on her index fingertip and balanced it for a second. Then, backing a little further away, she flipped it up and caught it between her teeth. That show of dexterity would keep them from trying anything. Pinching his pants between her knees, she eased off the silk tunic so as not to cut it on the knife or dislodge her headscarf, and threw it to Shrimp.

"Wow, he's skinny," said Weasel Eyes.

With her now wearing only a thin, short-sleeved shirt, the cool air sent her forearms erupting into goosebumps. She lifted his tunic over her head, with equal care to avoid jarring the knife and perhaps widening her lips like a mime's she'd seen in Tokahia.

"Now!" Mop Head yelled.

Jie's heart leaped into her throat. She yanked down the tunic, shredding its neckline; but now, Troll Hands had seized her in a bear hug from behind, around her elbows, and lifted her off the ground.

Shrimp snatched ahold of her pant legs and tugged them off.

The young men all froze, some of them gasping.

And she knew why. The lacy undergarment Aryn had bought her in Tokahia.

Crooked Tooth pointed. "It's...it's a girl."

Now, a very angry girl.

So much for magnanimity. Jie pushed the knife out with her tongue and caught it with her hand. She slammed her heel into Shrimp. The force of the blow sent him onto his butt, and Troll Hands stumbling back two steps. It was enough to loosen his grip, allowing her to bend an elbow. With a twist of her wrist, she cut his arm.

He yelped and dropped her, and she landed in a crouch, again encircled.

While Troll Hands cursed and Shrimp coughed, the other four held their knives out.

Jie turned to Mop Head. "I suggest you call off your friends and let me pass, or some of you might not be going home to momma tonight."

"Stupid girl, there are six of us."

Jie darted forward at him, in the same motion kicking Shrimp's pants backward into Weasel Eyes' face. Using zigzagging slashes, she severed Mop Head's palmar tendons. As the knife slipped out of his fingers, she caught it and sidestepped Crooked Tooth's lunging stab. With a sweep of her foot, she tripped him, and elbowed him in the jaw as he fell past her. He'd survive, and the tooth she dislodged would probably allow him to straighten the rest of his teeth.

Mop Head gawked at his wrist, while Crooked Tooth lay flat on his face. Shrimp had yet to stand, and Troll Hands nursed the gash in his arm. Weasel Eyes struggled to get the pants out of his face.

Jie turned to Cleft Chin. "Now, let me go, or I will widen the gap in your jaw."

Cleft Chin stepped aside and lowered his head.

"The pants." She held her hand out to Weasel Eyes.

Hands trembling, the last of the ruffians bowed his head and proffered the pants.

She snatched them and whipped them out. Backing away from her vanquished foes, she jumped up into the air and thrust her feet through the pant legs as she came down. She cinched the drawstring to keep them from slipping off her hips. Once she reached the road, she turned and ran toward the ocean docks.

On occasion, she had to duck behind people to avoid members of the *Indomitable's* crew. Still, it only took a few minutes to reach the concrete quays, which reached like fingers into Elbahia's harbor. The old capital had been established where seagoing vessels could no longer navigate the Valeri River, and now, three enormous Eldaeri blackships were moored there. Tarkoth's *Indomitable* occupied the easternmost dock, while two ships flying Serikoth's crimson flag were docked on the west. The *Intimidator* was the larger of the two, and might've been a twin to the *Indomitable.* It looked like sailors were provisioning the smaller.

Again, those similar names. Snorting, Jie veered westward, away from the lines of workers carting crates from the *Indomitable*, and toward the *Intimidator's* nearly abandoned wharf. Two Serikothi marines, cutlasses hanging at their side, stood guard by its gangplank.

There were no moving people to hide behind, no way to get closer without being seen. If only there'd been time to visit the Cathayi trade office, she could've secured the perfect disguise.

Even dressed like this, the idea might still work. It was the only chance of getting aboard.

The guards stepped together and blocked access to the gangplank as she approached. "What do you want, boy?" one asked.

On careful examination, they were the same two she'd seen back home over a month ago, who'd mocked the way she waddled after riding a horse all night. She'd been wearing the cute pink dress Aryn gave her, so it was doubtful a soldier would now recognize her dressed as a boy. She bowed like a proper Cathayi gentleman. "Kind sir, I would like to have a word with the quartermaster."

They favored her with narrowed eyes. "On what business?" the first asked.

With her half-Cathayi looks, and with the assumption that Serikothi and Tarkothi naval procedures were the same, she'd already formulated a lie. She produced a letter written in Cathay's wavy script. "My father is an official trade representative from Cathay. Here's a list requisitioned from your quartermaster."

The other chuckled. "And he can't afford to dress you in clothes that fit?"

"Government salaries." She shrugged. "As my father says, buy today, reap benefits tomorrow. I'll grow into these soon enough."

"Don't your people dress in long silk robes?" The first asked.

"*When in Arkos...*" she grinned.

"This one is full of proverbs." The marine snorted. He took the paper.

Jie blinked innocently at him. Hopefully, it would work.

His eyes roved over it. He then turned to his companion. "Do you understand this?"

The second shook his head.

The first sighed. "Take him to see the quartermaster."

"Follow me," the second marine said.

She trailed him as he clopped up the gangplank, which pitched steeply up thirty-some feet to the main deck.

"When will the *Intimidator* set sail?" she asked halfway up.

"Whenever Princess Alaena is ready to return to Korynth with her new husband." The venom in the Serikothi's tone was unmistakable.

Alaena, again. Jie's stomach knotted. To the Serikothi, Aryn was an enemy; and that woman was daughter of the Serikothi king, even if she was heir to Korynth. "When will that be?

The marine paused, and pointed south, downriver. "There's a ship approaching."

Jie followed the gesture. Not far in the distance, three ships flying the dark green flag of Tarkoth sailed upriver.

"One of those is the *Sea Dragon*. Princess Alaena is on that ship. How long she stays here, that's up to the royals to decide. We don't sail until they say so. Now, come along."

On the *Intimidator's* main deck, everything looked familiar. Identical to the *Indomitable*, from the number of cannons to the distance between each of the five masts.

Aryn had said something about the two ships belonging to the same class, whatever that meant. There were six more, all at least two hundred years old. With the exception of Tarkoth's flagship, the *Sea Dragon*, they shared names starting with *In-*, and implying invincibility. It was all so confusing, and if it were up to her, she'd just call each and every one *Insufferable*.

Still, the Tarkothi sailors spoke of all the ships, even the Serikothi ones, with hushed awe. If Aryn's worshipful tone in describing it was any indication, the youngest, but most storied was named the *Invincible*. While her homeland of Cathay might dominate the western seas, its ships seemed like dinghies by comparison.

She followed him to the aft toward the sterncastle, the gentle rocking of the boat easy to adjust to after all the time at sea. Only a handful of sailors were around, repairing ropes or doing other maintenance work. They'd be easy to sneak past later.

As on the *Indomitable*, whose layout she'd learned well on the voyage over, the quartermaster's cabin was located at the rear of the quarterdeck, next to the captain's and the royal suites. Her gaze lifted to the upper deck, to the rookery and bridge. There'd be far more information there.

The marine pointed to the quartermaster's cabin. "He's in there."

"Thank you." She put her fist in her palm and bowed, Cathayi style.

He turned and marched back toward the gangplank.

Jie headed over and pretended to knock. When she felt the marine's eyes on her, she turned and waved, and he continued down to his guard post.

She made a quick evaluation of the sailors. None were looking in her direction.

With the sun low in the west, the bulwarks cast shadows eastward. Taking advantage of her dark clothing, she hugged the bulwark as she moved soundlessly to the steps and climbed to the quarterdeck. She continued toward the aft, to the next set of steps which took her to the bridge.

The position gave her a good view of the rest of the *Intimidator.* With the sailors too busy to look in her direction, she listened to make sure nobody was inside the bridge, then crept inside. Like the *Indomitable's* bridge, banks of windows lined the three walls, and were now unshuttered to let in the breeze and sunlight. It also had the same large central table, carved to resemble a map of Tivaralan.

The blocks representing friend and enemy ships had moved since the last time she'd checked the *Indomitable's* map. She scanned the three ships in the harbor, visible from the stern windows, with their icons. According to the blocks, they were named *Sea Dragon*, *Windlance*, and *Elf Arrow*. All Tarkothi. A fourth ship, the *Wave Dancer,* was not more than a few kilometers behind.

She crept to the captain's leather-bound logbooks, neatly arranged on a set of shelves built into the wall. If the Serikothi had collaborated with the mysterious assassin, there might be clues within. She pulled the most recent one. Skimming through it, she paused on the entries around the *Intimidator's* visit to Cathay. It looked as if they had been in a race with the *Indomitable* to reach Cathay first. Still, weather, ports of call, crew disposition...nothing seemed out of the ordinary.

Her eyes shifted to the ship's manifests, a shelf below the captain's logs. A copy of the manifests had never been filed with the trade office in Cathay, because of *Intimidator's* quick departure. Their hasty retreat was the main reason for the clan to suspect Serikoth as an accessory to the assassination. A certain clueless spy back home would be in Heaven to get ahold of these manifests. She flipped through the pages, looking at the cargo and passengers the *Intimidator* had picked up and delivered to and from its trip to Cathay.

Nothing screamed *assassin*. Then again, if the killer had been trained in Black Lotus Clan ways, there would be nothing obvious. The aforementioned clueless spy would see the patterns, though. She stuffed the book into her shirt, to deliver to the trade office later.

A commotion grew louder outside. No doubt they were wondering where the Cathayi representative's son had disappeared to. It was time to make an escape. Jumping into the water would ruin the manifest, and it also increased the risk of getting caught. She looked out the windows. To the south, the Tarkothi *Sea Dragon*, yet another twin of the *Indomitable* and *Intimidator*, had entered the harbor with its escort. To the east was the dock she'd boarded from, where a few more marines had gathered and were now pointing at the *Intimidator*. To the west, the smaller Serikothi ship *Solaris' Spear* was moored, its deck some twenty feet away and a little over ten feet down. Sailors and dockworkers looked to be provisioning it.

The footsteps came closer to the door.

Jie dashed to the east end, turned around, and sprinted toward the west window.

The door creaked open.

She vaulted from the window frame and soared through the air. The air gushed by her. The *Solaris' Spear's* deck rushed up to meet her.

Heavens, she was going to come up short.

No, she wasn't. She barely cleared the bulwark, and dove into a forward roll. Sailors startled, staring at her with wide eyes, then turning their heads, probably wondering when it had started raining half-elves.

Jie crouched below the bulwark and peeked back at the *Intimidator.* The large windows provided a view of two marines searching, but none looked this way.

Staying below their line of sight, she crept toward the gangplank.

"You!" boomed a voice from the *Solaris' Spear's* sterncastle.

Jie looked back.

The captain stood there with his hands on his hips. "Who are you? Where did you come from?"

Jie glanced back to the *Intimidator.* For now, the captain's impressive voice hadn't drawn their attention. Still bending over, she scampered faster.

"Men, stop him!"

Sailors jumped up from what they were doing. One lunged at her, but she stopped short, letting him careen into the bulwark with an *oomph*, before continuing. Despite her shorter legs, she would reach the—

Two marines came up the gangplank. The first grabbed at her, but she twisted out of his reach, only to be wrapped up from behind by the other. She seized the side of his pants leg, sidestepped, slid her leg behind his knees, and twisted. His pants ripped as he toppled over. He released her to stop his fall. She turned and sprinted down the gangplank, sidestepping surprised workers who were carrying crates up.

She picked her way through the people on the quay, the Cathayi trade office her next destination.

Two docks past where the *Intimidator* was moored, dockworkers grunted and pulled the *Sea Dragon* in with heavy ropes. Corded muscles rippled under the strain. Several people gathered around, watching the ship come in. Among them stood Korynthi soldiers in polished steel cuirasses, their blue capes and white helmet plumes identifying them as royal guards.

She paused behind a cart and peeked around. The *Sea Dragon* flew not only Tarkoth's flag with its nine-pointed emblem, but also a flag with a gold circle emblem. The symbol of House Myranar, ruling family of Korynth. Royalty was aboard. Jie's gut twisted. Princess Alaena, of course.

And in the crowd was a large man, heavily cloaked, head hooded. Despite his size, he moved with the dexterity of a cat, head in locked on the ship even as he slid through the crowd with nonchalant grace. Had he been shorter and thinner, she might've mistaken him for a certain clueless spy by the way he walked. His head turned.

Peris.

Jie ducked back behind the cart. Why wasn't he with Aryn? And why was he skulking in the background? Jie looked back from where she'd come. At least for now, her pursuers were looking in the wrong direction. That gave her time to wait and evaluate.

There, in the throng, three men in dark hooded cloaks were watching Peris, doing a bad job of trying not to be noticed. Peris' body language was that of someone wanting to be seen. He was baiting whoever his tail was.

A royal carriage emblazoned in Korynthi blue trundled over. Dockworkers tied the *Sea Dragon* down and pushed a gangplank up. The royal guards all snapped to attention. At the exact same time, when they blocked his tails' line of sight, Peris flicked a folded sheet of paper into the carriage.

She had to find out what the note said, but she couldn't help but wonder where Aryn and Elrayn were.

CHAPTER 17:

Strategic Moves

Pulling at the fine linen tunic they'd give him, Koryn leaned back in his cushioned chair and looked out the arched window at the Light of Solaris. As was always the case when the twelve-faceted crystal was in Elbahia, it sparkled in the cupola atop the palace dome.

The palace loomed in the distance, above the green-flagged Tarkothi eastern district of Elbahia Island, across the eastern branch of the Valeri River. Though they'd blindfolded him when the barge had approached the old capital, it was clear they were keeping him on the Tarkothi side of the river. The room's fine furnishings and expensive decorations made it fit for a nobleman's guest house, but it was still a prison, and he was bound by his written oath not to resist.

"Your move."

Koryn looked back across the long sablewood table, where the Tarkothi guard had just moved his king out of check. Though of Arkothi stock from his size, skin tone, and features, the guard wasn't bad at chess.

But not particularly good, either. Koryn moved his queen. "Checkmate."

Around them, the other guards threw their hands up and groaned. Some stomped on the blockwood floors of the great hall, the beautiful brown planks absorbing the sound.

His opponent slapped two silver crowns down onto the checkered board. Not even the clink echoed in the vaulted hall. "By Solaris' Spear, again! I can't count the times you've beaten us."

Even with the lack of sleep since his capture. Even while drinking the valerian root tea they'd provided to help him sleep. Grinning, Koryn shrugged. "I can't count the times you all have beaten me."

"But we haven't," said one.

Koryn raised an eyebrow. "Technically, you can't count zero."

They all broke out in laughter.

It was fun, actually, collecting a mound of Tarkothi-stamped copper and silver coins, which he could never spend. To feel a sense of companionship with commoners, even if it was enforced at the point of a sword.

No burden of responsibility. No worrying about hiding a secret love affair, which would be near-impossible to keep hidden once he married. Not thinking about that future every hour of the day made life almost bearable.

His lover would be laughing at his whimsical thoughts of abandoning duty, because he knew Koryn would sooner die in a reckless cavalry charge.

Koryn blew out a breath. "All right, whose money am I taking next? No wager is too small."

The men started clamoring to be next, but then snapped to attention.

"Your Highness," they all said in unison, crossing their fists over their chests and bowing their heads.

Koryn turned to look.

Prince Elrayn had returned, with his large aide Tharos flanking him. A familiar young man stood on the other side. He would've looked princely with the way he carried himself, except for the non-diplomatic scowl.

Among their newly arrived complement of Tarkothi royal guards were two dark-skinned Aksumi men.

Koryn studied them. Their hair coiled tight to their heads, with some white peppering the black. Dark eyes accentuated their prominent noses and strong chins. Plain grey robes hung on their shoulders. It was strange to see their race so far north, so preoccupied their kind was with advancing sorcery in their homeland to the far south. A crystal teardrop hung from one's neck, glowing blue.

Elrayn's smile was as contrived as an artificer's golem. "I trust my men have made your stay comfortable?"

Koryn smirked. "I almost forgot I was your prisoner."

"Such an ugly word. You are our honored guest."

"Indeed," Koryn said.

The other man at his side muttered something unintelligible, but his dour expression wasn't hard to read. "Prince Koryn," he said through his teeth. "We meet again."

Again. Koryn studied his features and regal bearing. An Eldaeri sword, twin to his own, hung at his side. His eyes widened. "Prince Aryn."

Aryn nodded. "Indeed. I beat you to Cathay."

Their ships had raced to the far west, ostensibly to attend an imperial wedding in Cathay. In reality, both had hoped to secure an exclusive firepowder agreement with Cathay's court. Koryn had cut their trip short when the Cathayi had all but accused him of harboring an assassin. They'd only made two stops on the way back, in Sodorol, the *de facto* capital of Aksumiland, and Tokahia. Perhaps Aryn had picked up the Aksumi men in the former. "I reached Elbahia first."

"Yes," Elrayn said, "Quick enough for you to trespass into Tarkoth, leading to your joyous nuptial agreement."

Aryn glared at his elder brother, and Elrayn scowled back. There was an unspoken argument there. Maybe Aryn objected to wedding Alaena as much as Koryn wanted to avoid marrying their sister, Karyna.

A wedge that might be exploitable? Still, Koryn's jaw tightened. "My father will never acquiesce to a forced marriage. I would not doubt that he's mustered an army to free me."

Aryn's eyes widened, and he scowled again at Elrayn.

In the background, a mysterious expression passed between Tharos and the Aksumi men.

Elrayn tilted his head toward his aide. "Tharos has written many letters for you, letting your father know not only how beneficial the merging of our houses would be, but also how *in love* you are with Karyna."

A woman he hadn't even met. Father wouldn't believe the lies. Damaryn had to have sent word of his kidnapping, and would certainly suspect forgery or coercion. If Karyna was like typical Serikothi Eldaeri women, she'd be nothing like his lover. Koryn nearly choked on his laugh. "And you've received correspondence from my father?"

Elrayn held out a hand to Tharos.

The aide opened a leather-bound document folder with his meaty hand and removed two sheets. From where Koryn sat, it was easy to see the Serikothi royal seal imprinted in the wax. If they were real. Tharos passed the pages over.

With Aryn craning over his shoulder, eyes roving back and forth, Elrayn received the letters. With a nod, he passed them to Koryn.

Koryn swiped the papers away. He read the first, even as Aryn came around and now looked over his shoulder. It was written in the royal language, in Father's bold, confident hand.

My Son, how overjoyed I am to hear that not only have you finally found a woman of proper standing, but that it is none other than Karyna Corivar. A union of our two houses will rebuild bridges at a time when it is sorely needed.

Koryn's face contorted. If this wasn't one of Tharos' forgeries, even Father was falling into Elrayn's trap.

Perhaps Damaryn hadn't been able to send word. Maybe his cavaliers hadn't made it back to the border to report his capture. Or, perhaps Father was so bent on arranging a marriage he believed this nonsense. He tossed the page away and read the next.

My Son, Solaris' blessing is upon you. It is not often that men of our station find actual love. Karyna is rumored to be a classic Eldaeri beauty. It comes as no surprise that she has won your heart.

As if beauty mattered! No doubt, Karyna was a pampered, vapid girl, with little activity between her ears. She'd never understand him like his lover. Koryn closed his eyes and imagined running one hand through silken gold locks, another down a slim waist to a soft, rounded bottom.

"So, everyone is in agreement." Elrayn grinned. He gave a knowing nod to Tharos. "At least, on paper."

Tharos crossed his wrists. "Karyna arrives in Elbahia this evening."

This evening! Koryn schooled his expression into impassiveness. How many days had he been here? Three? Four? No matter what Elrayn was saying, Serikoth had to be looking for him. Threading his fingers behind his head, he leaned back in his chair. "I have to applaud your trickery. However, there is a glaring flaw in your plan."

Elrayn raised an eyebrow. "And what is that?"

"How are you going to get me to speak my marriage vows?"

Elrayn's smile reached the side of his eyes. He gestured over to Tharos.

Koryn's jaw tightened. While these Tarkothi mongrels exhibited varying levels of incompetence in chess, Crown Prince Elrayn was a master strategist. Not only that, no amount of goading would get him to reveal his plans. A worthy adversary. Perhaps a more skilled opponent. If only Damaryn, a brilliant tactician himself, were here to help. What did Elrayn have planned?

Tharos, in turn, brought the Aksumi men over. Their grey robes swished as they approached. Both bowed in the Arkothi style, one stiffer than the other. Were they Mystics?

One spoke, his accent as stiff as his bow had been. "Your Highness, the Serikothi prince has weak willpower, and will be quite...malleable."

Koryn's gut knotted. They were going to influence him with magic, perhaps make him fall in love with Karyna, and forget all about his lover. Oh no, he wouldn't make it that easy, not in the face of such a dastardly plot. He lunged forward, hands ready to strangle the life out of Elrayn.

Two Tarkothi men restrained his arms, even as he struggled in their grasp.

Koryn's eyes darted to Aryn, whose lips were curled in disgust.

"Don't be upset," Elrayn said, a hint of smugness in his tone. "This is good for all Eldaeri. Together, we can stand against the Teleri threat. My father and the Queen of Korynth, in their foresight, approved the wedding of Aryn and your sister, Alaena. Our three nations will be joined again."

Giving up his struggle, Koryn's eyes darted to Aryn.

The younger prince's lips were pursed. Perhaps he objected to his own upcoming nuptials. Koryn would be equally concerned about marrying someone as free-spirted and stubborn as his sister, Alaena.

Perhaps it would be another wedge to exploit. Koryn shrugged. "I would imagine Alaena is just as enthusiastic as Aryn."

If Aryn's jaw clenched any tighter, he could bite through steel. His glare settled on Elrayn.

Koryn watched the silent exchange between the two. Up to now, Elrayn had outmaneuvered him, but perhaps there would be a way to turn brother on brother—just like had happened during the Eldaeri Civil War, only with him splitting a family instead of a traitorous chancellor dividing nations.

Either that, or escape. But no, he'd sworn, in writing...

What had he written, exactly? To peaceably surrender? It said nothing about not trying to escape, and the Tarkothi must've violated terms by preventing his cavaliers from returning home. Had to have, because they certainly would've told Damaryn to send word of his surrender. Now, they planned to use magic on him.

He scanned all the soldiers. He had his sword, and in single combat, he could defeat any of them. However, there were too many right now, and Tharos alone was huge. And who knew what the Mystics could do?

Both Aksumi men waved their hands and grunted out syllables that sounded like an Altivorc curse. One sidled over beside Koryn, and the other pointed at him.

Koryn braced against the fell magic. Nothing seemed to happen.

"There," the sorcerer said. "It is done. The Serikothi prince is under my charm. He will say his vows tomorrow."

Would he? Koryn didn't feel any different.

"Show me a demonstration," Elrayn said.

The Aksumi who had pointed at him nodded.

Maybe the magic had worked...but if it hadn't, Elrayn would play along so as to make them think he was under their control.

"Touch your toes," the Aksumi said.

Nothing compelled Koryn to obey, but he bent over and touched his toes. In the corner of his eye, he caught the second Askumi curling his index finger. Perhaps that was the gesture meant to control him?

"Amazing!" Elrayn said. "Excellent job putting us in contact with these Mystics, Tharos."

The first Mystic bowed. "When the time comes, I will be able to control him like a puppet master, without even words. However, I must conserve my energy for the other subject."

Another subject?

Elrayn crossed his fists and bowed his head. "Well, Aryn and I must take our leave to go greet your future wife. You'll be a married man by tomorrow."

Schooling his expression into stupid compliance, Koryn returned the salute.

"Please, enjoy your stay. Take a bath, scent and oil your hair. You have a big day tomorrow. I'll have a courtesan sent to give you a massage, and provide other services if you so desire... Do save your seed, though. You've kept your father waiting for a new generation of heirs long enough."

Koryn suppressed a shudder. He watched the two princes and their entourage head down the stairwell. The two Aksumi followed a few steps after them.

The last of the retinue disappeared down the steps. Koryn hadn't seen the first floor, and the sound-absorbing quality of the blockwood floors prevented even their bootsteps from revealing how far it was to the entrance.

All of this information would be necessary if he was to succeed in his escape. At least for now, they thought him affected by magic, which would make his escape that much easier.

CHAPTER 18:

Nostalgia

Despite the old adage about saltwater running through Eldaeri veins, Alaena hated the sea. Salt and grime clung to her travelling shirt and pants, likely making her fireproof to even the Last Dragon Avarax's flames. Her stomach churned, as it had for the entire journey. The only time a person should rock like the waves was while copulating. Now, standing at the prow of the *Sea Dragon*, she watched as the spires and dome of Elbahia's palace grew closer. The sooner she was on dry land, the better.

"Men, prepare for docking!" Aelward's booming, confident voice carried across the water from his position on the quarterdeck.

She turned to look at him. If she'd been attracted to the adorable sailor back home, she lusted after him now. The clumsy, awkward, and ill-trained lout on land had transformed into a gallant and dashing commander at sea. He now glided across the deck with the dexterity of a feline, looking as comfortable as a fish in water. Enthusiastic sailors and officers were quick to carry out his orders.

To think, she'd planned on using him in Korynth. If he'd been caught sleeping with her, she would've played the inexperienced maiden for the all the Tarkothi to see. No doubt, Prince Aryn would've called the wedding off, not wanting to be second to a lowly lieutenant in their vaunted navy.

More like sixteenth. Or was it seventeenth? Who was counting, anyway?

The way Lieutenant Aelward carried himself on a ship, she would've made him sixteen or seventeenth. Not out of machination or trickery, but for the way his pure masculinity sent shivers up her spine and made heat flare in other places. Fanaya's tits! A man in uniform...

...was disciplined.

At least, Aelward was. She'd stuck to him like a wet leaf on the voyage over, and he'd resisted all attempts to rock the boat some more.

She let out a long sigh, and turned back to the concrete wharfs. Three other ships were already moored: two Serikothi vessels to the west and one Tarkothi to the east. Once the *Sea Dragon* and its two escort frigates docked, the Tarkothi could easily block the harbor to prevent a Serikothi ship from escaping.

Of course, she had no intention of escaping by sea.

No, once her feet were on dry land, she was only a footbridge away from disappearing into the lush forests of Serikoth. Forever. Like Queen Selayna's own daughter, she'd abdicate her position as heir to Korynth's throne. It was doubtful that anyone, save for Thielas himself, could find her once she went to ground.

Her heart picked up a beat. How long it had been since she'd been among the dense expanses of blockwoods and sablewoods? The three Eldaeri kingdoms didn't need her anyway. Surely they could arrange marriages between other princes, princesses, and noble families.

Sailors threw out ropes to dockworkers, and they started to pull the *Sea Dragon* into port. Down below, at the head of the quays, a Korynthi honor guard formed up around a royal carriage. Behind them, crowds pointed in their direction.

"Your Highness."

Alaena's heart thumped. She turned.

Wearing a long green coat, Aelward was bowing, wrists crossed in front of his chest. Had there been a hint of sadness in his voice?

He straightened and pulled the wrinkles out of his dress uniform. "They will extend the gangplank soon, and it is my duty as commanding officer of the *Sea Dragon* to guide you down to the dock with an escort of my marines. We will back away, and the Korynthi honor guard will receive you."

"Predictably," she said, winking, "just the opposite of when we boarded in Korynth."

His face flushed an adorable pink. "Aye, lass. I mean, yes, Your Highness."

No doubt, he would transform into the newborn fawn again, wobbling on his knees and tripping over his own boots. She shook the image out of her head. Now, she needed to plan her escape. The carriage was likely to convey her to the Korynthi royal villa on the north end of the island. Somewhere along the way, when the opportunity presented itself, she could jump out and run. None of the honor guard would be likely to keep up with her.

Aelward extended an open hand, guiding her toward the gangplank. At the top, he bent his elbow.

She slipped her hand in, and tingles ran up and down her spine. Fanaya's voluptuous tits, a man hadn't set off this intense a Cathayi firework show in her in a long time. Marines in dress uniform deployed behind them, drawing their cutlasses and holding them ceremonially against their right shoulders.

They descended and marched across the dock toward land. As predicted, Aelward lost all air of command, his step out of sync with his men and looking for all intents and purposes like a drunkard. The firework show inside her guttered to a few fizzles. It was *her* hand in his elbow that stabilized him.

Reaching land, the marines and Korynthi guard snapped to attention with clockwork precision. Aelward was a split second behind, enough that it drew giggles from the crowds. There didn't seem to be any Tarkothi green or Serikothi crimson among them.

Supported by a cane with a bejeweled handle, an older man in Korynthi blue livery hobbled forth and bowed. He raised his eyes. "Welcome to Elbahia, Your Highness."

Alaena smiled.

It was Lucius, a Korynthi duke of Estomari stock. He was as nice a son-of-a-bitch as the Estomari could get, and had always been kind to her in court. It'd been years since they'd last meant, and time affected non-Eldaeri much faster. More wisps of grey now streaked his black hair, and lines of wisdom crinkled at his eyes.

"Thank you for your warm welcome." She gave a slight curtsey, though her sea-stinking pants weren't quite appropriate for the motion. They were quite appropriate for sprinting, however. She gestured to Aelward. "This is Lieutenant Aelward, commander of the *Sea Dragon*."

Lucius raised an eyebrow. "A lieutenant, already with his own command?"

Aelward bowed. "Aye, but only until today. I took command in an emergency. Now that we are in Elbahia, a captain will be assigned to us."

"I see," Lucius said with little interest. He turned to her, extending an open hand to the carriage. "As much as I would enjoy discussing matters with the lieutenant, we must make haste, Your Highness. We are to meet Prince Aryn at the palace at the waxing half."

Alaena looked up and to the southwest, past the elongated Blue Moon to where the Iridescent Moon hung in its reliable seat in the heavens. It now waxed toward its fourth crescent. That only left two hours for her to reach the Korynthi villa, take a bath, change into a formal dress, and travel to the palace. Even if she truly planned to play along, there would be plenty of excuses for being late.

Still, it was time to throw things into chaos. She leaned into Aelward's shoulder. "I want the lieutenant to accompany me. I still need to ask him about Tarkothi customs." Even if they were pretty much the same in all the Eldaeri kingdoms.

Around them, the marines' and honor guard's stoic expressions all slipped in unison.

Staring at them, Lucius raised an eyebrow again. "You didn't ask on the journey over?"

"I don't think our customs are much different, anyway," Aelward said. "And I'm not sure it would be appropriate— "

"Don't you want to meet your prince?"

Aelward's complexion drained of blood. "That...that..."

"So it's settled." Alaena pulled him toward the carriage.

"I must protest." Aelward stumbled after her, despite his supposed protest. He looked back to his second-in-command and made some naval gesture.

Hundreds of pairs of eyes followed them. It was working better than expected.

A servant opened the carriage door. Despite his clumsiness, Aelward bowed and held her hand as she climbed the steps. With her tug, he clambered in and took a seat across from her. Count Lucius climbed in last and sat next to Aelward. His nose wrinkled.

Alaena reached across and pulled Aelward over to her side. His shocked expression was too adorable.

She scooted over to make space for him, but something crinkled between her and side of the carriage. Tilting her weight over, she looked.

A folded sheet of paper, with her name written on it, lay scrunched next to her hip.

A letter. No wax seal.

Who could it be from? None of her fifteen—or was it sixteen?—previous bedfellows lived in Elbahia, and none would have a way of knowing she was coming here. Considering how most had begged her to stay with them, maybe that was for the better.

Flashing an apologetic smile at Lucius and Aelward, she leaned to the side and twisted to shield the letter from them. She unfolded it and read.

Dear Alaena,

I know of your reticence to wed Prince Aryn. He feels the same way. Part of the tri-party agreement is a yet-to-be announced marriage between Crown Prince Koryn and Tarkothi Princess Karyna, and Karyna has as much enthusiasm for him as you do for Aryn. She is arriving on the Tarkothi ship Wave Dancer this afternoon. Meet me behind the bathhouse at your villa at the waxing fifth crescent, and let me tell you our plans. There is a way out of this.

Peris, Aide to Prince Aryn.

Alaena's head spun. How dare Prince Aryn not want her! It was her who didn't want him first. Well, at least this letter confirmed the planned marriage between her eldest brother and the Tarkothi princess. But why wouldn't they announce it? Not only that, Koryn's hatred for Tarkoth was well known, even as far away as in the Korynthi court. He probably begrudged this ridiculous swapping of princes and princesses as well. Alaena was doing everyone a favor by running away.

She searched the crowds of people. Who was this Peris, anyway? It was hard to believe an aide would know so much. Though of course, it wouldn't be appropriate for Aryn to meet her in person with his plans to get out of this. He must've decided to send an underling instead.

Refolding the letter and stashing it in her belt, she turned to Aelward. "Besides my wedding to Aryn, have you heard of any other royal matches?"

Aelward cocked his head. "Nay, lass."

Either this Peris was lying, or the wedding was the best kept royal secret. "I received word that Princess Karyna will be marrying my brother, Crown Prince Koryn."

"Nay..." Aelward shook his head.

"She's arriving on the *Wave Dancer* today."

"The admiralty would've let us know. How did ye find out about this?" His expression was one of bewilderment. Clearly, he didn't know much regarding these royal plans.

"Do you know of a Peris, aide to Prince Aryn?"

"Um...nay, lass." Aelward looked to Lucius and back to her, and tugged at his uniform collar. It was a telltale sign he was nervous.

Ignoring Lucius' stare, she placed a hand on Aelward's thigh and leaned into him. She let her lips brush against his ear, as if it would make the next lie more true. "You can tell me. The sailors were all talking about him."

"There are rumors.... All unsubstantiated." Sighing, Aelward shifted in his seat. "He grew up in the palace, friend to Prince Aryn, and perhaps a close confidante of Princess Karyna. She is fond of him, for sure, but the rumors on sailors' lips might be exaggerated."

Alaena threw her hair over her shoulder and pondered the situation. Her betrothed, Prince Aryn, had an aide, Peris, who might or might not have an extra interest in Princess Karyna, who was secretly arranged to marry Alaena's brother, Crown Prince Koryn. Her head spun at the bizarre web of interconnections.

No, not a web, but a tower of tarot cards, ready to topple.

His head tilted to where the letter had been. "Why do ye ask, lass?"

Each time he used *lass*, Lucius scowled. "*Your Highness*," he said with extra emphasis on the title, "You are to meet your future husband. I'm not sure if..." His eyes locked on Aelward.

Aelward pulled at his collar again.

Alaena leaned in and claimed Aelward's lips.

His entire body stiffened for a second, but then relaxed into her. The muscles of his chest and arms felt toned and firm beneath her hands. She probed at his lips with her tongue.

He refused her entry. He pulled back, gawking.

A low rumble rolled in her throat, unbidden. Fanaya's ass, he was ruining the reputation of sailors everywhere. It'd only been a show for Lucius, but now, the rejection stung. She searched his eyes. "You've never kissed a girl, have you?"

He opened and closed his mouth, but no words came out. He looked out the opposite window.

Lucius cleared his throat. "Princesses shouldn't be kissing men on the eve of their wedding. They—"

Alaena shot him a glare. "I will kiss who I please, when it pleases me." She turned and looked out her window.

The carriage settled into awkward silence, the only sound the wheels whirring over the stone-paved street. It'd been years since she'd been here, but outside it looked much the same as Korynth. Blockwood rowhouses rolled by, with the occasional white flag of the old Eldaeri Empire. Men in tunics, women in dresses, not a single tree. Her soul felt caged. Her hand strayed to Peris' letter.

The carriage slowed to a stop, inside the Korynthi royal villa at the north end of the island. If memory served her well, there was wooded island just to the north. A means of escape. But first, she'd see what Peris had to say.

The double doors opened. A servant bowed low as she hopped out. The mansion looked the same as it had twenty-some years ago, save for the hedge in front of its white stone walls having grown thicker.

She beckoned to Aelward. "Lieutenant, come in and have Cathayi tea or Levastyan coffee. Or whatever they have. You will attend me when I meet my future husband at the palace."

His complexion turned a little green, as if he were seasick on dry land. Had the carriage ride been that uncomfortable?

She grinned. "It's your chance to meet the princes of your nation. I'll give my personal endorsement for a promotion."

Aelward pressed himself as far away from the carriage door as possible, but tumbled out when a servant opened his side. He fell to the ground with a thump.

Alaena gasped, and hurried over to help him. Fanaya's tits, she must really like him, because she would've laughed at any other man.

Face red, he refused her hand and climbed to his feet.

"Are you okay?"

He waved a hand. "No harm done, lass, save a bruised ego. I should be going."

"No, stay. I'll join you after I take a bath and change." Gesturing to the chamberlain, she looked up through her lashes. "Unless you'd like to join me in the bath."

Aelward's jaw might've reached the floor.

"Your Highness!" Lucius jabbed his cane into the pebbled path. "Absolutely not."

She flashed a smile, then turned to the chamberlain. "Please take the lieutenant to the hearth room."

With a tight frown, the chamberlain bowed.

She turned on her heel and strode through the granite mansion's double doors.

A maid barely dipped into a curtsey before hurrying after her. "To your right, Your Highness. Your bath is ready, and we will have a dress from your baggage brought to you."

"The brown one," Alaena said over her shoulder. It certainly wasn't the prettiest, but it would be the easiest one to run in. "And bring me my slingshot."

"Slingshot?" the maid ventured.

"Just do it."

When the maid hurried off, Alaena strode through the indicated side door and into a yard with trees. The first trees she'd since arriving. She placed a hand on one's trunk, and looked to the wooden bathhouse. She looked toward the Iridescent Moon, now waxing just past the fifth crescent. After a quick glance around, she went to the back.

"You're late," a deep voice said.

Alaena looked left and right. The voice had come from near the wall, but nobody was around. "Show yourself."

"I am Peris." The voice now came from the small bathhouse window.

She turned, expecting to see a face leering there, but no. "Where are you?"

"That's not important. What is important is that we can help each other." The voice seemed to come from nowhere and everywhere. If Aelward had not said Peris was a real man, she would've suspected him to be a ghost.

She scanned the ground.

Though slight, gravel was displaced in several small indentations, over a meter apart. The distance indicated someone with long legs, though the depth suggested light weight. The tracks ran from the garden wall to a hedge of evergreen with thick spindly needles. Brow furrowing, she looked from there to the directions the voices had come from, and back.

A large, hooded man stood up from behind the hedge. To have such left faint tracks, he had to be skilled. "I'm impressed, Your Highness."

"Peris, I presume."

"Yes."

"Are you here on Aryn's behalf?" she asked.

"And my own. Princess Karyna and I are in love. She doesn't want to marry Prince Koryn."

So the rumors were true. She nodded.

"I have a solution to all our problems."

CHAPTER 19:

Eye for an Eye

Tomas' heart lurched into his throat. How had the Bovyan made it around the tree so quietly? Gripping the branch in two hands, he used all his might to swing the heavier, fatter end at the beast's head.

The Bovyan raised his sword into the path of the swing. Tomas' hands rang as the blade bit deep into makeshift club. With a twist of his wrist, the Bovyan wrenched at the branch, and Tomas held on for dear life. He yanked it back and stared at the remains of his weapon.

A *pede* of the branch's length hung from a strip of torn wood. A clean line dug three-quarters deep into its girth.

Turning it over in his hands, Tomas struck again.

The Bovyan went to parry, but the dangling end curved around the deflection and slammed into the side of his bare head. He staggered back a step and crashed into a tree.

Tomas gaped. He'd just vanquished one of the deadliest warriors in the world, with little more than a—

The Bovyan shook his head back and forth, scowling. With a glare he took several purposeful steps forward, sword pointed. "You little, one-eyed runt."

Gritting his teeth, Tomas swung a third time. The Bovyan stepped back, and this time, the hanging end of the branch went flying off from the haft. The sudden loss threw Tomas' balance off, nearly sending him to the squishy ground. Now, he had only a two-*pede* stick. He backed away, only to find his path blocked by a tree.

A sword point pressed at his throat. Tomas' heart pounded in his ears. This was it. There was no way the warrior would forgive the attack.

The Bovyan cast a broad shadow over him. "I thought you were only good for trickery, but you show heart. More than any of the constables in Lorium. Now, no more games. Take me to your village."

Just a second ago, Tomas had been resigned to death. Now, faced with it, he wanted nothing more than to live. To marry Sofia and raise a family. He sighed. "All right. But I'm hungry and tired. I can't go much farther."

The Bovyan's eyes searched his, but then he nodded. He sheathed his sword, but drew a dagger. "Well, thanks to your plan, our food ended up feeding the fish."

"That wasn't what I intended," Tomas lied.

"No tricks. Move."

"Wait, let me collect some food."

The Bovyan's forehead scrunched up for a moment, but then he nodded. He yelled. "Sathis! I found him."

His voice echoed through the ravine, but probably wouldn't reach Sathis' ears. All for the better, since escaping one Bovyan would be easier than two.

Tomas searched around and picked more watercress, wild onion bulbs, and berries. What he didn't eat, he wrapped in a strip of cloth torn from his shirt. He didn't offer any to Fethos, nor did the Bovyan ask for any, or make any move to harvest food himself. He'd get hungry, making it easier to escape later.

That thought melted away as quickly as it had come.

"Fethos!" The other Bovyan's voice echoed in from the way they'd come. Soon, the brown-haired Bovyan appeared. "I hit a dead end, and doubled back."

Fethos shoved Tomas forward a few steps. "I found the little rat. He scrounged up the courage to attack me."

"Not bad, kid." Sathis chuckled. "Left a good cut there."

Fethos touched the wound and looked at the blood on his fingers. "I've gotten worse."

Sathis nodded. "What now?"

"He was headed in this direction, so this should be the way to his village." Fethos pointed west. Correct for now, but they'd have to take a fork east later.

"What about the scribe and tattooist?"

Tomas stomach twisted. They didn't stand a chance. Either the cold or thirst would claim them, and it was his fault.

"Nothing we can do about them." Fethos shrugged.

"We'll need to get new ones. When we get to his village, we'll order the villagers to ferry us back across the straits to that pathetic little town."

Fethos gave a nod, then prodded Tomas. "Hurry now."

Tomas bowed his head and continued the slog. They marched for a couple of hours, taking twists and turns at the forks in the path, before approaching the trail that would wind back around the mountain to the village.

Children would often come this way. Every villager, at some time in their youth, had tried to find the path to Lydath's Golden Bowl. If some happened to be playing in this area now...

Sweat clinging to his brow, Tomas held his breath. Was that a flash of the blue-dyed clothes the villagers liked? Or just a colorful bird? Laughter? Not looking in that direction, trying to keep his breathing even, he took the Bovyans past, deeper into the gulch.

No children appeared. Still, even as his own energy guttered the further they went, their stamina showed no sign of flagging. Now, too, the tide was going out, leaving muddy spots where footprints would ruin any chance of escape.

He painted the image of the ravine network in his head. They were reaching the end of this section, leaving only a few paths that headed higher into the mountains. Places where goats ventured, but no sane human would dare. He'd certainly never gone this way, even when he'd searched for a way to Lydath's Golden Bowl or the legendary fallen star as a child. It was just too dangerous.

Now, it would provide an opportunity for these lumbering Bovyan hulks to slip and fall to their deaths...if his limited vision didn't get him killed first.

At least his death would keep the village safe.

Tomas shook the idea out of his head. It would be a temporary solution, only. Once Governor Keris had finished in Lorium, he'd send more of his minions over. Sofia and Maria would suffer at the Bovyans' hands.

Gritting his teeth, Tomas veered east along an unfamiliar ridge that sloped upwards. The way was even harder to see with the sun below the crags.

"Are you sure you know where you are going?" Sathis asked.

Tomas turned his head and found the Bovyans in his vision. He nodded. "Yes, you have to go up before you go down. The village is due east of here."

At least the last part was true, enough that the Bovyans could only nod and follow.

Tomas had to climb in many places, seizing outcroppings with his aching fingers, and finding purchase in nooks and crannies with his toes. If not for the Bovyans prodding him, he would've given up several times.

Shrubs jutted from the rocks in places, providing hand and footholds on occasion. At least the berries and watercress had replenished a little of his energy; otherwise he would've taken a fatal tumble long ago. They paused to drink water from natural pools. In some places, goats looked on from higher vantage points, expressions smug as they gloated at the humans' lack of climbing skill.

Still, the Bovyans kept pace. Despite their bulk, they proved to be proficient climbers. Each time they asked how much further, he could only reply that it wasn't far now.

With dusk's approach, his single eye made it impossible to continue. They were high on the mountain now, almost three-quarters of the way to the Golden Bowl, at a greater altitude than he'd ever gone before. Perhaps this really was the way to the ancient temple of the orc goddess.

Even his flat vision provided a spectacular view of the gorge below, and the Inland Sea beyond. The Blue and White moons had already risen in the east. Their light danced in the rippling waters below, but did little to illuminate the path. Meanwhile, the mountainside blocked the view of the Iridescent Moon to the southwest. He stopped on a broad ridge and waited for his captors to catch up.

"We need to stop for the night," Tomas said, "or we'll break our neck."

Sathis afforded him a suspicious eye. "Surely there is an easier way to reach your village."

"Not from the place where we landed." Tomas shrugged with fake apology.

Sathis nodded to his comrade. "Well, I'm hungry. Let's see if we can kill one of those goats."

"Fine." Scowling, Fethos prodded him. "You go find some water and firewood."

Apparently, they didn't expect him to escape. How could he? Not with one eye and night about to fall over a treacherous mountain path. He set about looking for wood and pools of water. Hopefully, he'd also find a perfectly-shaped branch to make a slingshot.

Rounding an outcrop, he froze.

Where the next cliff face met the saddleback ridge, skullcaps and oyster mushrooms competed for space along a strange rock formation. He bent over to collect some. They looked similar enough to an untrained eye. He'd eat the oyster mushrooms, while giving the skullcaps to the Bovyans. Eating them would lead to diarrhea, vomiting, chills, and eventually death.

While he collected them, careful to keep them separate, he noticed lichen attached to their stem base. Where they pulled free, the rock surface shone in the moonlight. He ran his hand over the spot. It was smooth, metallic.

He scanned it again. The object was cylindrical, its entire length larger than a man, and formed a basin for dirt. Thick grasses, the type with edible tubers, sprawled from it in a haphazard fashion. It looked to be partially lodged into the rock. Was it a planter of some sorts? Part of the Temple of Lydath which had tumbled down the mountain long ago?

He yanked some of the grasses, revealing the finger-length, fleshy tubers. Something flashed in the moonlight before the soil fell back from the hole. How strange. Perhaps it was an artifact from the temple, maybe something that could help him.

Setting the tubers down, he brushed away the soil...and then, with a startled gasp, he jumped back.

A yellowing skull grinned back at him. In one of its sockets was a single glass eye with a brown iris, staring back at his own remaining eye.

A laugh broke out behind him.

His heart just about jumped out of his chest. He spun around.

Fethos stood there, a broad smile on his face. "Never seen a skull before?"

Tomas shook his head so fast, it might've fallen off. Ancient bones from the Hellstorm had washed up on the beaches, but never a skull.

"It can't hurt you." Fethos spat. "You should take that eye. It would make you a lot easier to look at."

Tomas shuddered. Sure, he was ugly with two eyes, and even worse than with just one, but the thought of taking something that was in a dead body was disgusting. Not to mention, he'd have two different-colored eyes again. Who was to say the next batch of Teleri to ride through wouldn't pluck his real eye out, leaving him completely blind?

Fethos laughed, and beckoned into the darkness. "Sathis, come look at this."

"What is...oh." Sathis sidled up and plucked the glass eye out of the skull. "This must've been here for hundreds of years. I wonder it how it got here."

Tomas looked up the cliff again, and the two followed his gaze.

“Maybe it’s a coffin,” Sathis said. “That fell from the old temple.”

It had lodged into the cliff face at a strange angle for it to have fallen straight down. Perhaps an earthquake had shifted it years after it had fallen. Was that an orc body inside? Or a human sacrifice? He looked at the skull again and recoiled.

“The fisher boy needs to face his fears,” Fethos said. “That’s the only way he can grow. Plus, it would make him easier to look at.”

Sathis snorted. “I guess.”

Tomas hit the ground with a thud that knocked his breath away. An oppressive weight bore down on his chest. He looked up to find Fethos.

“This is for your own good.” Fethos stretched his hand back. “Give me the eye.”

They were going to shove the glass eye—from a dead body, no less—into his socket. Tomas squirmed and flailed and swung his fists, all to no avail.

“Is that really necessary?” Sathis asked.

No. It wasn’t. Tomas pounded on Fethos’ stomach, but did little more than bruise his hand on the chainmail.

Fethos batted the futile attacks away. “Only when he faces his fears will he be a man.”

They wouldn’t even consider this if they hadn’t taken his real eye. Tomas’ ears buzzed as he struggled to get away, but Fethos was just too heavy.

“Give me the eye, Corporal. That’s an order.” Fethos’ voice was nearly a growl.

Sathis sighed. "Let me clean it a little first, so his eye socket doesn't fester."

Tomas' heart throbbed erratically in his chest. Squeezing his eye shut, he turned his head to the side, but Fethos' iron grip under his chin forced it back. With a thumb, he pulled Tomas' eyelid open. Tomas screamed and struggled, clawing at his captor. It didn't do any good.

The glass pushed past his lids and popped into his eye socket.

Pain seared through his head, much more than it should have. It felt as if ants were crawling from his eye socket into his brain, biting and stinging as they went. Tears filled his good eye. How could a simple glass eye cause so much agony?

His brain felt like it was trying to burst out of his skull. Unintelligible sounds echoed in his mind. Then, unconsciousness claimed him.

CHAPTER 20:

Unwelcome Reunions

Aelward sat on the soft couch in the Korynthi villa's antechamber, tugging at his collar. Exquisite porcelain from Cathay sat atop carved blockwood side tables. An oil painting above the hearth depicted the first Queen of Korynth, the one who'd seized power from her husband.

He pushed his feet into the plush Ayuri carpet. What had he been thinking, coming here? He was supposed to be greeting the new captain of the *Sea Dragon*, instead of chasing some floozy like a ship trying to catch a feather blown on Sargasso's zephyrs.

Mauls and Maelstroms.

That wasn't the worst. If he couldn't get out of the trip to the palace and the meeting with Elrayn and Aryn, then Alaena would find out he was their bastard half-brother. And if she did, she'd probably lose all interest in him. The delicate handle to the teacup snapped in his grip. Pain bit into his thumb. He looked down at the blood.

What had he been thinking, indeed. He knew damn well.

If Alaena had gotten into the Korynthi carriage at the docks without him, he'd never see her again. At least, not up close, unless he somehow got promoted to admiral one day and had to present himself at the Tarkothi palace.

No, she would be at the Korynthi palace, ruling as queen. The docks would have been goodbye forever.

Until he got into carriage with her, damn fool that he was. He was like the fabled Captain Noor, tricked by sirens into smashing his ship on the rocks.

Had it been worth it? To feel her lips on his? Tides and Tempests, if only he'd let himself relax and enjoy it. Oh, how he'd wanted to wrap her in an embrace. To claim her like an uncharted island, right there in the carriage.

Yet, with Count Lucius watching, how could he? It would ruin his career in the navy. Hells, he was ruining it by waiting here.

He let out a long sigh and stood. It'd been what, a full phase already? Women and their long baths! He had to get back to the *Sea Dragon*. Forget a final farewell, which would likely break his resolve. He'd just tell Count Lucius to pass his regards on to her, that he had to go. It had been an ill-fated voyage.

One that would end now. It didn't matter what the chamberlain said, Aelward headed for the door.

A commotion of frantic whispers erupted from the foyer.

He set a hand on his saber and looked through the arched doorway.

Servants in Korynthi blue livery were scurrying about until the chamberlain strode down the central hall. With a gesture, he silenced everyone, and two men opened the double doors.

Elrayn and Aryn stood there, in green formal tunics, Eldaeri heirloom swords hanging at their sides. Several Tarkothi royal guards in steel cuirasses stood steps behind.

They weren't supposed to be here. Lurching back, Aelward knocked over a vase. He reached for it, but it crashed to the floor, shattering even on the plush carpet.

Both princes looked through the archway and met his eyes. Elrayn beamed with his usual fake smile, while the darkness that clouded Aryn's expression lifted.

Aelward cast his eyes down.

"Well, well," Elrayn said. "Look what flotsam the tide washed in."

"Welcome, Your Highnesses." The chamberlain bowed low. "Princess Alaena is preparing for her meeting with you at Elbahia Palace as we speak."

Elrayn put a hand to his chest. "We heard she arrived late, and feared she would not make it to the palace in time. We took the liberty to visit. Please forgive us for not sending notice, but my brother is most excited to meet his future bride."

If Aryn's expression had eased earlier, it now darkened again.

"Of course," the chamberlain said. "Please, let me get you some tea." The chamberlain bowed low and motioned them to the waiting room.

To join Aelward. A taut line hitch knotted in his gut.

With a wave of Elrayn's hand, the Tarkothi royal guards snapped to attention and retreated off the stoop. Elrayn marched into the waiting room, Aryn a few steps behind him.

Aelward crossed his fists and bowed his head as military protocol demanded. "Your Highnesses."

Elrayn studied him. "Lieutenant, what are you doing here?"

Aelward recited the formal language in his head a few times before speaking. "Your Highness, I was forced to take command of the *Sea*—"

"Yes, yes." Elrayn snorted. "I read the reports from the admiralty."

Pulling at his collar, Aelward gritted his teeth.

Elrayn looked up at the dwarf-made water clock. "You, in command. It explains why the *Sea Dragon* arrived so late today, bottling up the mouth to the harbor, no less."

Aryn's eyebrows clashed like waves curling over a beach. He elbowed Elrayn.

"What?" Elrayn shrugged. "He's a junior officer, after all. I wouldn't expect him to be as experienced as a captain."

Aryn's lips pursed.

Aelward had been shuffling toward the foyer, and now stole a glance around the corner, down the hall where Alaena had disappeared. If she came back now, she'd find out.

Elrayn turned back, fixing him in place. "In any case, I know why you are in *Elbahia*. Why are you *here*?"

"I..." The words caught in Aelward's throat, and he had to clear it. "Princes Alaena asked me to accompany her."

"Oh, did she?" Elrayn looked sidelong at Aryn. "Whatever for?"

It seemed she thought she was doing him a favor, introducing him to royalty. Or maybe she'd really hoped to take a bath with him. The awkward memory of her lips on his flitted through his mind, and he shrugged. "I think she came to...trust me...during the voyage here."

"Maybe she knew who you were," Aryn said.

It'd been so many years since Aelward had heard his half-brother's voice, he'd almost forgotten what it sounded like. He shrugged again. "She showed no sign of it."

Elrayn waved a dismissive hand. "So tell me, my bastard half-brother, what is the princess' disposition to taking Aryn as a husband?"

Shuffling on his feet, Aelward shot a glance around the corner again. She'd be coming down the hall any second now. "She seemed...ah..."

"Out with it, now." Elrayn glared.

Aelward clenched his fists. How satisfying it would be to clock Elrayn in the face. He loosened his hands. "She seemed excited." At least as excited Aryn, who fidgeted with his sleeves.

"There," Elrayn said triumphantly to Aryn. "No doubt, she sees the importance of the Eldaeri coming together to face the Bovyan threat. Forget about the mysterious half-elf."

Half-elf? There were so very few in the world, since elves rarely ventured out of their secluded realms. Aelward started to speak, but then sealed his lips.

Elrayn nodded, as if he'd read Aelward's mind. "Yes, Aryn here picked up some stray half-elf on his trip to Cathay."

Cathay! Aelward had hoped to be assigned to the *Indomitable* for that voyage, but a friend in the admiralty let him know that Elrayn had intervened to kill any hope of that.

"He has wild ideas about marrying her." Elrayn fixed his gaze on Aelward. "You, of all people, should tell your half-brother the folly of royalty mingling with strange women."

Aelward's jaw clenched. If this wasn't the Crown Prince... "What about Karyna?" he asked. "I heard she was going to marry Tarkoth's crown prince."

Gawking, Elrayn exchanged glances with Aryn before turning back. "How did you know about that? How could you possibly know?"

"Princess Alaena mentioned it."

"How would she know?" Elrayn's voice rose. He turned to look at Aryn. "Did you tell her about it? Or the crown?"

The crown? Did the king not know about this? Just what was Elrayn planning?

Aryn only shrugged in his typical nonchalance. "Of course not."

So how did Alaena know? Aelward thought back. There was that... "Crinkled piece of paper."

Both of the princes turned to him.

"What?" Elrayn demanded. "Paper?"

"There was a piece of paper in the carriage. She mentioned the marriage right after she looked at it."

"Only eight people know about this." Elrayn turned to Aryn. "You've been against it from the start. You didn't pass the information to Princess Alaena, did you?"

Laughing, Aryn pointed to himself. "I just found out about it today. I've been with you ever since. I don't even know what my future bride looks like, how would I get a message to her?"

Aelward looked from brother to brother, the raging tempest blustering around the eye within. While they were distracted, the exit looked quite enticing.

Elrayn's brow furrowed. He counted on his fingers. "Tharos wouldn't have had a chance, he is greeting Karyna right about now. Your half-elf...she didn't know."

"Peris," Aryn droned.

Elrayn's lips twisted into a snarl. "You told him to end that affair, didn't you?"

"Of course. I thought the separation on the trip to Cathay would be good for him."

Aelward's head spun like a whirlpool. So, the rumors about Karyna and Peris were true. Loose lips were sinking this ship.

In any case, for now, the brothers looked to have forgotten all about him. Here was his chance to escape before Alaena came back and learned who he really was. He started to the door.

Elrayn's gaze fixed him in place like a becalmed ship. "Where are you going, Lieutenant?"

"I must be reporting back to the *Sea Dragon*." Aelward crossed his fists and bowed his head.

"You should have thought about that before coming here." Elrayn shook his head. "No, half-brother, you have been privy to state secrets. I order you to stay with us. As annoying as that shall be."

Rapid footsteps shuffled across the marble floors in the hallway, getting louder by the second. The chamberlain turned the corner, panting. "Your Highnesses, horrible news! Princess Alaena is missing. We fear she has been kidnapped!"

"Kidnapped?" Elrayn's voice sounded incredulous.

Kidnapped! Aelward's heart lurched into his throat like the recoil of cannon. "Where was she last?"

"In the bathhouse, we thought. Come." The chamberlain beckoned them to follow.

Aelward and the two princes brushed past the breathless chamberlain and went down the hall, past several archways into rooms. He turned into a side hall lined with doors, which ended in a heavy blockwood door. He pushed through.

Outside, the sun hung low on the horizon, casting long shadows. He marched up the white gravel path to the bathhouse, past a couple of trees. Steeling himself, he threw open the door.

Nobody was there. Just a bath, and rising steam. The towel was unused, though Alaena's travelling clothes lay on the bench.

"Our bastard brother...I mean, baby brother...was in a hurry," Elrayn said to Aryn as they caught up, suspicion in his tone.

Aelward swung around, marched out, and jabbed a finger at the chamberlain. "Did anyone come by 'ere?"

"The maid." The chamberlain pulled a distraught brown-haired girl of Arkothi stock from behind him.

Tears pooled glossy in her eyes, and she shook her head. "I'm sorry, kind sirs, but she told me to leave her. I only came back when I heard her scream, and nobody was here."

A page in Tarkothi livery burst through the door from the main residence and bowed low. "Your Highness...back at the guest house...your guest...."

CHAPTER 21:

Unpleasant Pleasures

Koryn stood up from the table and walked over to the window of the Tarkothi guest house. Earlier, Prince Elrayn and Prince Aryn had climbed into a Tarkothi carriage. Several of their royal guards mounted up on horses around them. Tharos remained behind with his two Aksumi sorcerers, but then got into a second royal carriage that pulled up.

That'd been half a phase ago. Now, he blew out a breath. Elrayn's plan made sense: Tharos and the Aksumi were going to get Princess Karyna now, and charm her with sorcery as well. The poor girl—Elrayn's sister, no less. No doubt, he expected the both of them, under the influence of the Aksumi Mystics, to swear their nuptial vows tomorrow.

The sorcery hadn't affected him, though. A wry smile tugged at Koryn's lips. Maybe that would've been better, to be blissfully ignorant. To be magically in love with an appropriate wife, instead of living the lie that tore his soul apart.

But no. He had all his faculties, and he'd use those to get out of this situation. He turned to the guards. "I'm sorry boys, but no more chess tonight. I think I'll take your Crown Prince's advice and take a bath. Have that courtesan sent. I'm feeling like a voluptuous brunette tonight. An Arkothi."

To keep up the act, he swept his gaze over the men and winked. "I trust your discretion."

"Of course." The guards all bowed.

"Good. Draw the bath with lavender, and bring some wine. A Tokahia red, if you have it, Korynthi white if you don't."

One of the guards crossed his fists and bowed, then turned to go downstairs.

"With a good woman," Koryn said, faking a grin, "I don't think I'll need the valerian root tea to help me sleep tonight."

Predictably, the soldiers all laughed and whooped.

"On second thought, have the tea brought to the bathhouse, for after I'm done with her. I need to make sure I do get some sleep for my big day tomorrow."

Another of the guards bowed and followed the first downstairs.

With the remaining men all watching, Koryn made a show of studying the chessboard, drawing his finger as if tracking moves. Presently, one of the guards returned.

The man bowed his head, and held up a cloth. "I'm sorry, Your Highness, but we must blindfold you to take you downstairs."

"Of course." Koryn shrugged. Once he was in the bathhouse, he would already be most of the way out.

They covered his eyes and cinched the blindfold behind his head. One helped him to his feet with the utmost politeness, and guided him across the hall to the steps.

"Be careful," the soldier said. "We are going down the steps."

They descended sixteen steps in all. Right seven paces, left fifteen paces. A door creaked opened and a cool wind prickled his skin. The men's boots crunched on gravel, nine more paces until another door opened. Warm, steamy air poofed into him, carrying it with a scent of lavender.

"Here we are, Your Highness. We'll close the door behind you, and you may take off the blindfold."

"Thank you." Koryn nodded in the soldier's direction, then went inside. When the door closed, he uncovered his eyes.

Steam billowed off a large wooden tub which was set into the floor of a small room, perhaps only two meters by three. The walls were made of sablewood, perfect for humid conditions. A single window, much too small to fit through, let in muted light from above a bench built into the wall opposite the door.

He sat down on the bench, next to a bottle of red wine, two wineglasses, and a cup of tea. He kicked off the embroidered shoes and waited.

Outside, it sounded like two guards were chatting in muffled voices, but the wood made their words hard to discern.

In his head, he went over the plan. The prostitute would come in, and he'd invite her into the lavender bath, plying her with wine and valerian root tea. With practiced hands, he'd bring her to bliss so that her moans would maintain the act. If she didn't fall asleep from the wine, tea, lavender, and orgasm, he'd unfortunately have to choke her into unconsciousness; hopefully it wouldn't come to that. Then he'd don her dress, and the cloak meant to hide her identity from prying eyes, and escape.

A dress! How humiliating it would be to run around Elbahia in one. But desperate times called for desperate measures. The plan hinged, of course, on an Arkothi woman being a similar enough size for him to deceive the guards.

Outside, the men stopped chatting. The door opened again, revealing a cloaked woman. The muted light was angled too low to make out much more than her large form.

"Welcome." Koryn leaned back and flashed his most alluring smile, one that had wooed many a girl. Inside, he cursed himself. When he said *buxom*, the guards must've thought he meant an ox. She was larger than most Arkothi men, even. Underneath her cloak, this prostitute's dress might be so big as to slip off of Koryn once he donned it, and perhaps trip him up if he had to run. How had they even found her? How could she possibly make a living?

"Turn around," she said, voice soprano and sweet, "and allow me undress you."

He shook his head. "I had something else in mind."

"Oh? I didn't think the Prince of Serikoth so naughty."

So the guards had even revealed his identity. Koryn snorted at the lack of professionalism. "Yes, I want you to dance as you remove your clothes, and get into the bath."

"The prince *is* naughty."

"Have some wine." Koryn turned to his side to retrieve the bottle.

Cloth rustled.

A knife thunked into the wood beside him.

By sheer luck, Koryn had twisted just in time to avoid the stab. Eyes wide, he slammed the bottle into the woman's head. He leaped to his feet and used his other hand to jab an elbow into her temple. He thrust the shattered bottle into her side.

With a deep, decidedly unfeminine groan, she staggered.

Koryn reached into her hood, seized her hair, and slammed her head into the bench.

She fell face-first to the floor, but still struggled. By Solaris, she was tough.

Tossing the remains of the bottle to the side, he sat on top of her and pummeled her over and over with his fists. At last, her body went limp.

Due to her size, it took no small amount of effort to flip her over. The hood slid as her head lolled to the side.

He gasped. His would-be assassin was a man. Despite the caked layers of foundation and rouge, it was clear, now that his face was uncovered and resting in the brittle light. No wonder his cry of pain had been so...deep, even if he'd somehow managed to lilt his voice so high. They'd sent a man to do a woman's job.

A very large man, at that. Bigger than most Arkothi, but too small for a Bovyan. He was about the same size as Tharos, but this wasn't Tharos, unless the make-up had done that good of a job. No matter what, he didn't look familiar. Maybe it was the twin brother Elrayn had mentioned when this mess had all started. Peris, was it?

And who were the *they* who'd sent him?

Elrayn needed him alive to cement the marriage...unless part of his plan was to use a double. No, that didn't make sense, unless those dark-skinned Aksumi who'd accompanied him were sorcerers who could create illusions. Supposedly, they'd mastered that magic in the distant past, which had allowed them to infiltrate the Runemaster Imperator's court during the Hundred Years of War.

Though what about his voice? Enough people knew it too well. Then again, this man had mimicked a woman's voice well enough. Yes, the Tarkothi had planned to kill him, and it had only been by coincidence that he'd survived. To think, some imposter, a pawn of Elrayn using magic, had almost become Crown Prince of Serikoth.

Retrieving the assassin's knife, he looked up at the door. The guards must've heard the commotion, even through the sablewood walls. They'd be coming in any second now.

No, it was quiet outside. They were waiting for this man to come out. They'd been so kind to him, lulling him into a false sense of security. Maybe they'd been commanded to be nice.

As quickly as he could, Koryn stripped the cloak off the body and draped it over his own shoulders. He pulled the hood up. Knife in hand, he came out, ready to take the men by surprise.

He threw the door open. Afternoon sun blinded him.

Shit! He swept the knife in tight arcs, as if that would deter anyone with a sword.

No attack came. No weapons rasped from scabbards.

He blinked several times to clear his vision.

Both guards stood limp to either side of the door, propped up against the wall. It looked as if their own daggers had been used to pin their collars into the wood, to keep them standing.

It didn't make sense. If the assassin had gone to the trouble to pretend to be a woman to get past the guards, why would he kill them, too?

Unless maybe he needed them to appear to be on guard, so that anyone looking from the windows would assume nothing was amiss. Or maybe the assassin would've let them fall later, and make it look like a failed attempt to escape.

Koryn raked his gaze left to right. No one else was around. A white gravel path, flanked by wispy trees and shrubs, wound from the bathhouse to the side door to of a three-story blockwood building. From the position of the tall, arched windows, the great hall probably took up the top two stories. For now, no one was visible from the windows.

Koryn slipped back into the bathhouse. Pushing, pulling, and tugging, he worked the dress off the assassin. When he donned it, it hung loosely around his shoulders and pooled on the ground. He tied a knot toward the front to keep it up.

Damaryn would split his sides laughing. How humiliating to be seen in public like this. But still, as the captain would point out, it was a necessary measure if he wanted to work his way through the Tarkothi city and cross one of the bridges onto neutral Elbahia Island.

In any case, somebody wanted him dead, and it was clear now that that somebody wasn't Elrayn: he would've just ordered it, instead of sending some hired knife.

CHAPTER 22:

The Demon Eye

The scent of roasting meat sent Tomas' stomach rumbling, while some melody echoed in his mind. Head pounding, he sat straight up and opened his eyes.

Night had fallen, but the ridge was lit by the dancing flames several *pedes* away. They cast Fethos' face in a flickering reddish hue as he turned over a goat mounted to a spit above the fire. Sathis lay on his side, head propped up as he chewed on one of the tubers. The skullcaps and oyster mushrooms were mixed in a pile nearby.

Tomas blinked a few more times. The scene around the fire was so clear for nighttime, and the details so distinct. It would normally be impossible to distinguish the mushrooms from each other at this distance, even in bright daylight. Not only that, his vision was three-dimensional again.

He stifled a gasp, lest he give away that he'd awoken. He was still lying by the cliff, where Fethos had violated his body with that glass eye.

A glass eye that shouldn't be able to see. This couldn't be right. He closed his good eye.

And had to bury a gasp again.

The acuity came from the glass eye.

Impossible.

He opened his good eye, while closing the other. Not only was the scene darker, it also wasn't as sharp. He switched eyes again, just to make sure he wasn't imagining it all.

No, the glass eye gave him clearer, brighter vision. Even with the good eye closed, it provided good sense of depth. Perhaps even a better sense of depth, given the low light. And a wider visual field to the right. He blinked it three times.

Strange sounds echoed in his mind, just like before he'd fainted, and again when he'd just awoken.

His soul just about jumped out of his body. He let out a little squeal. What was happening to him? Was he dreaming? Or going mad? He pinched himself, just to make sure he was awake.

He was. And the skewed difference between eyes was making him a little dizzy.

"You're awake." Fethos beckoned him over. "If you're done bawling like a baby, the meat is good. Come have some."

Tomas nodded. For now, he'd hide his miraculous cure, let them believe he could only see from one eye He pushed himself up and walked over. "How did you kill a goat?"

"With this." Sathis flipped his dagger through his fingers.

"It let you get close?"

"Didn't need to." Laughing, Sathis flung the dagger.

Lines and runes flashed in Tomas' vision, sending him stumbling back in surprise.

The dagger's flight followed one of the lines in his vision.

Tomas blinked his eye a few times.

The sounds rang out in his mind yet again. This time, there was a clear cadence. Syllables. Intonation. It was a ghostly female voice. Now that he thought about it, that was the sound that had woken him up just now. "Did you hear that?"

Fethos and Sathis exchanged confused glances.

"Hear what?" Fethos said, eyes narrowed.

Heavens above. Like the Aksumi light baubles, the eye must be magic. Runes had flashed in his visual field, after all. And what Governor Keris said about rune magic must be true: a demon was trapped inside. A succubus, perhaps, speaking some demonic language. Just what had Fethos done when he shoved it into Tomas' eye socket?

"Are you all right?" Sathis favored him with an arched eyebrow. The Bovyan's bewildered expression shouldn't have been so evident in the low firelight.

Tomas wasn't all right. Not with some demon lodged in his eye socket, spreading its accursed tentacles through his mind. With a tentative nod, he took each step like a fish investigating a coral formation, and made his way over to the fire.

Fethos offered him a slice of goat meat.

Tomas rarely ate red meat. They could get chickens in town, but generally the townsfolk and villagers subsisted on fish. Curious, and stomach rumbling, he took a bite. It was a unique texture and flavor, as foreign as the demon's voice in his head, which was thankfully silent for now. Quite delicious, actually, and he chewed more.

The Bovyans laughed.

"He's hungry," Fethos said.

"But look at his eye." Sathis leaned in, pointing. "How come the glass eye is moving?"

Moving? Was it roving, pointing in the wrong direction, acting with the demon's will? Tomas hand shot up to the demon eye. His field of vision hadn't changed at all. "What's wrong with it?"

Fethos now leaned in, too. "A glass eye shouldn't move with the good eye, but yours is."

Tomas glared at the Bovyan, who stared back as if Tomas was one of the curiosities from the travelling circus. It was his fault a demon was getting a grip on his soul.

Fethos shrugged. "Well, Solaris smiles upon you."

If anyone was smiling, it wasn't the benevolent God of the Sun. Not with a demon whispering in his mind. Tomas looked down at the mushrooms. The Bovyans had mixed them together, and the skullcaps and oyster mushrooms looked similar enough. He closed his good eye.

Even as the flicking firelight cast dancing shadows, the demon eye picked out the differences between the two. Maybe this unfortunate event wasn't so bad, after all. He'd just have to find a way to make use of the eye's powers, without endangering his soul. He picked out one of the oyster mushrooms, thrust a stick through it, and roasted it over the fire. He turned it over and over, under the dripping grease from the goat. The aroma wafted into the light breeze.

Tomas' mouth watered, but even more so, his hopes rose. Now, the Bovyans would just have to follow suit, and pick the skullcaps.

"His head isn't turned at an angle, either," Fethos said.

Tomas cursed to himself. With his vision back to normal...better than normal...It had been so natural to look straight ahead. He shrugged. "I'm getting used to it."

Sathis gave him a sharp nod. "In the end, you will appreciate the loss. Better to lose an eye than your soul."

If only they knew. At least for now, the demon was silent, no longer whispering whatever temptations it would use to lure his soul to pull Tivar's flaming chariot for all eternity.

Tomas took a bite of his mushroom and closed his eyes, exaggerating how much he savored it. "Mmmm, this is so good."

He opened the demon eye a slit.

The Bovyans were sifting through the mushrooms. Sathis picked a skullcap, while Fethos speared an oyster mushroom with a stick. They both cooked them beneath the roasting goat's drippings.

Tomas' heart picked up several beats. Even if just one of them died, it would be that much easier to escape.

Heavens. Were these evil thoughts the demon's influence? Making him think dooming the Bovyans to an agonizing death was morally justified? What would happen to his soul if he continued down this path?

His stomach knotted up again, killing his appetite. Sathis hadn't been that bad compared to Fethos, and he was the one about to eat the skullcap. And if Fethos didn't eat any skullcaps, he might suspect Tomas had poisoned Sathis on purpose.

Sathis pulled back his stick and sniffed at the mushroom.

If Tomas was going to give a warning, it was now or never. His soul was at stake.

No—even before the demon eye, he'd hoped to drown the Bovyans, and sacrifice the scribe and tattooist as well. He'd made this decision long before, in order to save Sofia and Maria from the barbarism that had already started in Lorium. Images of those poor girls lining up to get tattoos appeared in his mind's eye.

Sathis bit into the skullcap. His eyes rolled up into his head as a grin formed on his face. "By the Keepers, this is delicious."

At least the Bovyan would enjoy a last meal before ultimately suffering a grisly death.

Now, if only Fethos would eat a skullcap, too. On the other side of the dying fire, he gobbled down his mushroom. He shrugged, and made no move to eat any more of them.

"I'm going to get some sleep," Tomas said. With a bow of his head, he lay down on the hard rock.

"Me too," Fethos said, dashing all hope that he'd eat a skullcap. He turned to Sathis. "Keep an eye on the fire, and make sure he doesn't try to escape."

This was working out well. He just had to stay awake until Fethos fell asleep and Sathis died from the skullcap. It would be a perfect opportunity to flee. Maybe even slash Fethos' throat while he slept.

Tomas shuddered. That had to be the demon eye making that last suggestion.

Just where had this thing come from? He rolled over and studied the planter. No, coffin. Who was the person who'd been inside? Had it been a human? Or an orc? How did it come to have a demon eye?

The coffin had fallen from the Temple of Lydath, so the answer might be on the mountaintop. He was closer to it now than he'd ever been in his life, driven by the necessity of leading the Bovyans astray. Tomas tilted his head and looked up toward the Golden Bowl. Moonlight gleamed off its surface, several hundred *pedes* above.

If he ever found a way up there, maybe he could learn a way to exorcise the demon from his new eye. And if not, Julius had said something about the priests of Solaris in the Teleri Empire also being able to do that.

On the other side of the dying fire, Fethos lay still, his huge chest rising and falling gently. To the side, Sathis was staring into the embers. His face scrunched up as he rubbed his stomach. The skullcap must've started taking effect.

How long would it take? Their current position didn't provide a view of the Iridescent Moon, but at least a phase had to have passed since Sathis ate it.

Sathis' torso heaved. He flipped over onto all fours and crawled to the edge of the ridge. He leaned over and vomited. Once, then twice, until nothing came out except a pitiful moan.

Tomas shuddered. It was his fault. He shifted his head and studied Fethos. The man didn't so much as stir, despite the all the noise, and Sathis didn't make any move to ask for help.

Instead, he crouched low, head hanging over the cliff. He didn't look like much of a threat. A little longer, and he might pass out.

Or, Tomas could push him off the side. It would be the merciful thing to do. With Fethos sleeping so soundly, there should be a good opportunity to escape.

Tomas eased himself up. Tiptoeing over the rock, he worked his way around the fire to where Sathis suffered. Yes, he was as good as dead, and the skullcap would make the death miserable. A quick, painless death was the humane thing to do. Tomas took a deep breath and got ready to push.

Sathis turned around. His voice sounded weak. "What are you doing?"

"Your vomiting woke me up." The lie came too easily to his lips; no doubt the demon in the eye twisting him. "I was coming to check on you. Are you all right?"

"Just an upset stomach. Maybe the goat meat was too raw."

So he didn't suspect the mushrooms.

"All right. Let me know if you need any help. I'll stay up a little longer..." If only to see if Sathis deteriorated enough to make an escape easier.

Tomas backed away and headed to the coffin. Stories from before the Hellstorm glorified the entombment of the Arkothi Runemaster Imperators, how they were buried with countless treasures. Perhaps there might be other artifacts buried in the dirt which would tell more about who it was, and how or why he'd obtained a demon eye. There probably wouldn't be another chance.

Even with just the moonlight, the demon eye cast the night in shades of green and grey, like the legends of elf vision. The disparity between it and his real eye added dizziness to the receding headache. Closing his real eye, he pulled more of the tubers and other vegetation. He probed into the soil with his fingers, pulling handfuls out to clear it.

His hand brushed against something long and hard, and he pulled it out, revealing a bone as long as his forearm. Likely, one of the bones from the body's arm. Nearly dropping it, he shuddered. He was no better than the grave robbers who'd plundered the tombs of the Arkothi Imperators after the Hellstorm.

According to legend, they'd been buried clasping swords on their chest. If this one was the same, maybe it would have a weapon. With reverence appropriate for the honored dead, Tomas set the bone down and worked at clearing the dirt where the body's chest would be, being careful not to cut himself on a potential blade. There were only more bones, ribs from the shape of them, and no weapons. Only a square piece of metal that was probably a belt buckle. The rest of the belt must've rotted away over the centuries. He pocketed the buckle.

Perhaps there was a dagger at the body's hip. Tomas continued his excavation on its left side, finding nothing, and then to the right. His fingers hit up against metal cylinder. His heart skipped a beat. A dagger hilt? To acquire a weapon, without trying to steal one from the Bovyans, would be too lucky, given all of his bad luck so far.

He dug away at the dirt, which was much denser here, until there was plenty of space around the hilt. He wrapped his hand around it.

Lights flashed in his vision. The female voice spoke in his head again, words undecipherable.

Gasping, he released the hilt and nearly fell back on his butt. He looked over his shoulder, to where Sathis now lay on his side, his breath labored, and Fethos showed no sign of waking.

He stood back up. Heart racing, he reached for the handle again. He touched it with a finger and pulled back.

Nothing happened.

Tentatively, he wrapped his hand around the hilt.

The voice spoke again, in the same demonic language.

Letting go of the weapon, he whispered, "What do you want?"

Silence.

Still, he could guess. It wanted to twist his soul. To murder the Bovyans in cold blood with the dagger.

Gritting his teeth, he grasped the hilt.

The voice spoke again. It sounded like the same intonation pattern of thirteen syllables as the first two times.

Memorizing the sounds, he waited, and when the voice remained silent, he gave the hilt a good tug. It remained firmly stuck in the dense soil. Maintaining a firm grip, he shifted his position.

Red runes flashed across his vision. He released the hilt and nearly fell on his butt.

The demon was clearly trying to communicate with him, both through language and maybe even writing. Not that he could read Arkothi, let alone the magic runes that the demon wrote.

No matter, he wouldn't let it corrupt his soul. With a sigh, Tomas dug away the soil from around the skull. It wore an open-faced helm. Maybe it could protect him from a blow to the head, but the idea of putting on a helmet worn by the dead made his stomach roil.

He looked back to the fire, now not much more than glowing logs.

Sathis lay almost unmoving, save for the labored hitching of his breath. Asleep, just like Fethos.

Tomas considered the weapon again. How easy it would be to kill both of them. Fethos first, and if the noise woke Sathis, he would likely be too weak from the skullcap to fight back.

He shook the idea out of his head. That was the demon eye, tempting his soul, even if it hadn't spoken words that he could understand.

The question wasn't whether or not to kill them, but whether to go up, or down. If they believed him when he said they had to go higher before descending into the village, they—or rather, Fethos—would continue up. Down was the safer gamble.

Wrapping up some of the tubers, he looked at the goat on the spit. Some of the meat might've been a nice addition, but it was too risky to get so close and possibly wake the Bovyans.

He peered down the path they'd come up, his new eye penetrating the darkness with ease. If he travelled all night, he might be able to reach the village by dawn.

He took three steps, then paused.

He looked up to the Golden Bowl. So close. Here was an opportunity that might never come again. At the very least, he could boast of being the first person to reach the Temple of Lydath since its sacking over a thousand years ago. From the summit, he could probably see the entire Inland Sea: from the Arkothi city-states to the west, to the Teleri heartland to the north, to Serikoth in the east.

At best, he might even find a solution to his demon eye.

If he survived.

CHAPTER 23:

Trails of Conspiracy

Jie watched Prince Aryn, the Crown Prince, and the lieutenant hurry back into the Korynthi mansion, leaving the bathhouse courtyard empty, before returning to examine the scene. It was so clear now: Peris and Tharos, though not as large as Bovyan shocktroopers, were the same size as the several Bovyans she'd encountered in the past who'd been trained by the mysterious clan traitor. All this time she'd suspected the Serikothi had helped the assassin in her homeland, but in all likelihood, it had been Peris acting alone. He'd hidden right in the open, right under her nose on the *Indominable* for the last month.

Back at the docks, after having read the message he'd left for this Princess Alaena, Jie had decided to eavesdrop on Peris' intended meeting. Still, his legs were much longer, and he'd be trying to lose the three men stalking him. Thus alert, he would've certainly seen her had she tried to run after him to the Korynthi villa. Instead, she'd used the carriage's undercarriage luggage rack to cling to the bottom, riding right beneath Alaena and the Tarkothi navy lieutenant. Unfortunately, that meant shifting positions and waiting until the servants left before finding her way to the courtyard.

By then, Princess Alaena and Peris had fled. Given the acoustics of the courtyard, the scream everyone heard had probably come from the other side of the nine-foot wall. It'd also likely been fake—from what little Jie had made out from the conversation in the carriage, this princess was no screamer, except maybe between the sheets. Even now, her gut twisted at the thought of Aryn and… She shook the idea out of her head. There was work to do, and the fading daylight would make studying the evidence harder.

Peris' insertion was a thing of beauty. Only a highly trained eye would have even noticed the tracks from the wall to the hedge. However, Alaena's tracks were more obvious, indicating the path of egress on the north side of the west wall.

A commotion of men's shouts and horse neighs erupted toward the front of the mansion. Aryn was leaving, and the frantic mention of a *guest*, worded in a tone that meant anything but a guest, suggested there was a much larger problem at a villa across the east branch of the Valeri river, in Tarkoth. Track Alaena, or follow Aryn…

Jie dashed back to the front, running over the grass for quiet. At the corner of the building, she peered around the side.

Aryn, the Crown Prick, and the lieutenant were entering the carriage with the nine-pointed Tarkothi seal embossed on its doors. Tarkothi royal guards mounted up on horses outside the gates.

She looked back toward the bathhouse. With dusk approaching, even her elf vision wouldn't pick out the minute clues needed to track Peris and Alaena. On the other hand, the princes might lead her to Tharos, who was looking less like Peris' brother by blood, and more like a fellow Teleri Bovyan agent trained by the Black Lotus Clan traitor. *Nightblades*, a Teleri doctor in Tokahia had told her.

Creeping low behind the hedges in front of the mansion, she worked her way toward the carriage. When all heads were turned, she dashed the several feet of open space, under the vehicle to the luggage rack. With no bags to hide among, anyone happening to be at ground level would see her.

The driver snapped the reins, and the carriage set off through the gates. The Tarkothi royal guards, now mounted, formed up around it. It made studying the scenery next to impossible.

Somewhere in this part of town was the Cathay trade office. And in it, Black Lotus operatives who could help her. It would also be a place to deliver the *Intimidator*'s logbook, even if it now seemed unlikely that the Serikothi were involved in the assassination back home. For now, though, it would have to wait.

Thank the heavens for the well-maintained, paved roads of Elbahia! There were no bumps or jostles along the way, though the whirring wheels and horse clops made whatever conversation the princes were having near impossible to hear. Instead, Jie tried to keep her bearings: when the carriage turned, how far it travelled. It looked like it was heading east, most likely back to the Tarkothi royal villa. Tharos was supposed to bring Princess Karyna there, but more likely he would take her to Peris, or even kill her.

They had to be getting close to the villa now. Jie frowned. She'd have to get out from under the vehicle, into the mansion, and change, before Aryn came looking for her.

The sound of the wheels over the pavestones changed, as did sound of the horse hooves. There was more of an echo. Below, water rustled by. They were crossing a bridge.

Which meant they were crossing into Tarkoth, and not going to the Tarkothi royal villa on Elbahia Island.

Up ahead, metal gates creaked open. The carriage passed through the walls into another courtyard before coming to a stop.

From her hiding place, Jie could only see up to knee-height. Now night, pools of soft white light from the carriage's bauble lamps crept across the courtyard's white pavestones. The driver dismounted and came over the doors, while a pair of slippered feet descended a set of stone steps and hurried over to the carriage.

"Your Highness," the newcomer said, "Prince Koryn has escaped!"

So that was the mysterious guest. Jie sucked on her lower lip. She'd met the insufferable Prince Koryn in Cathay, and he'd returned to Elbahia on the *Intimidator*, landing three days before her own arrival on Tarkoth's *Indomitable*. In those three days, Tarkoth had managed to capture him, only to lose him now.

"Escaped?" The anger in Crown Prick's voice would cow a seasoned warrior.

"I thought," Aryn said, "that you had him beguiled by the Aksumi magic."

"Magic?" the lieutenant sounded suspicious.

Jie's ears twitched. She'd been helping an Aksumi Mystic track down a rogue Illusionist and Enchanter, who were possible accessories to the assassination back home.

"Yes, he was charmed." The Crown Prick sounded incredulous. "So how did he escape?"

Slippered Feet's voice trembled. "The prostitute...well, not a prostitute...a large man pretending to be a prostitute..."

Large man pretending to be a prostitute. Probably a Bovyan Nightblade trained in Black Fist ways like Tharos and Peris. Possibly working with Aksumi deserters. Jie's head spun, trying to draw the connections.

Jumping down from the carriage, feet right in Jie's line of sight, Crown Prick snarled. "Just what was it, Adrian?"

This chamberlain gulped hard. "Prince Koryn killed the prostitute—who was really a man—and two of our guards, and then fled."

Aryn dropped down beside Elrayn. "I told you this was a horrible idea. If he gets back to Serikoth..."

"I know. All hopes of our alliance will fail."

Jie suppressed a snort. Did Crown Prick really think the consequences would be so mild?

"Nay, Your Highness," the lieutenant said from inside the carriage. "It'll be war."

At least someone had some sense, though none of these geniuses had yet bothered to ask how long ago it happened.

Elrayn harrumphed. "He doesn't know his way around here. Post guards on all bridges into Elbahia and every boat landing. Send out a search. We will find him."

"Yes, Your Highness," said another man with a deep voice.

More feet scurried about the courtyard as men went to carry out the prince's orders.

"This shouldn't be too hard," Elrayn said. "He's the only one in Serikothi crimson."

The chamberlain gulped again. "He took the prostitute's clothes."

Jie nodded appreciatively. This Koryn was apparently smarter than he'd appeared in Cathay.

Elrayn let out an exasperated sigh. "What was the prostitute wearing?"

The chamberlain fell silent.

"Does anyone know?"

The silence was damning. Jie stifled a chuckle. Not a single observant person among them.

"Take me to the bodies," Elrayn said.

"Yes, Your Highness."

The lieutenant jumped out, nearly tripping, and stumbling to join the princes' entourage as they headed toward the side of the building.

Jie crept out of the luggage rack and dropped to the paved driveway. She peeked out.

All the Tarkothi were mobilizing on the other side of the carriage, close to the gate. On the mansion side, everyone was striding around the corner.

Made of blockwood, the mansion rose three stories with exterior decorative columns. Given the height of its arching windows, the second floor likely took up the top two stories.

Sticking to the darkness between the lights, Jie hurried to the corner of the building and looked around. The two princes and the navy lieutenant, along with a group of three more soldiers, crunched across a white gravel path to a wood bathhouse. They were led by the chamberlain, his identity given away by his slippers. Fools that they were, they were disturbing any forensic evidence along the path.

Jie darted behind a nearby tree as the men stopped to look at the two bodies propped up outside the bathhouse door. On the one hand, Koryn was smart to keep them standing, so as not to draw suspicion from anyone looking from the window; on the other hand, it would've made more sense to take one of the Tarkothi soldier's uniforms than whatever the Bovyan had worn.

The men crowded into the bathhouse, and Jie crept over to get a closer look at the two dead soldiers. The first had been choked to death, the garrote still wrapped around his neck and tied to a dagger which kept him pinned to the side of the wall. His sword was missing. The two furrows running from where he stood to around the bathhouse indicated he'd been partially carried, partially dragged to this spot. The assassin had either been too weak to carry the body, or had used the man's dangling feet to cover his own tracks. If it was indeed a larger Bovyan, Jie's bet was on the second. Not that he'd needed to, since these Tarkothi weren't studying the tracks.

Peeking in at the men crowding the bathhouse, pointing and arguing, she darted across the doorway to examine the other body.

He was similarly mounted to the wall, though the bloodstains from the top of his shoulder, trickling in a thinner line down his back, suggested a punctured subclavian artery as means of death. There were no visible tracks, save for the ones he'd made when walking to his post. After drawing the first guard to the side of the bathhouse, the assassin must've come around and murdered the second.

Then gone into the bathhouse. Jie listened to the bickering men.

"This is your fault," Aryn was saying. "Your hare-brained plan is going to start another Eldaeri Civil War."

Elrayn snarled. "Someone else knew. Someone who didn't want this marriage to happen."

That was a pretty long list, it seemed, including both sets of brides and grooms. Jie buried a snort.

"And someone who'd kill for it not to happen," the awkward lieutenant said.

Someone who didn't want the Eldaeri to unite. The Teleri Empire. If that body was a Bovyan... Jie peeked in, but couldn't get a good view of the corpse behind all the arguing men.

Aryn clenched his fists. "Karyna should be arriving at the villa in Elbahia soon. We need to make sure she's protected. Let's go."

Jie silently agreed. If the Teleri Empire had used Bovyans to try and kill Serikoth's Koryn, Tharos might be targeting Tarkoth's Karyna. Who, from what Aryn had said in the past, couldn't swing a sword and wouldn't know the sharp end of a dagger from the hilt.

"I need to report back to the *Sea Dragon*." The lieutenant sounded quite desperate.

"No, Aelward," the Crown Prick said. "You know too much. Useless as you are, you are going to help us."

Jie only had a view of this Aelward's side profile. On the voyage over, Aryn had mentioned him as the king of Tarkoth's bastard son. In her mind, she drew up a family tree of the Eldaeri royal houses, at least as she'd learned on this trip: Karyna, Elrayn, Aryn, and Aelward of Tarkoth. Koryn, Odryn, and Alaena of Serikoth, with the latter adopted as heir of Korynth. All, save for Odryn—who was supposedly a bookish weakling—were here in

Elbahia through Elrayn's machinations. All possible targets for the Bovyans.

The men turned to leave, and Jie ducked back to the side. As they hurried out, she darted behind them and into the bathhouse.

The large body lay on its side, with multiple wounds to the head. Glass shards were scattered on the floor, along with a broken ceramic cup with some kind of pungent root. A smashed wine bottle looked to be one of the weapons Koryn had used. The victim himself was not as large as a typical Bovyan, but fit the size profile of Nightblades she'd seen. No blood trails left the bathhouse, suggesting Koryn had either bound any wounds, or had escaped unscathed.

The bathwater was tepid and scented with lavender. With no hairs or exfoliated skin floating in it, it was probable that nobody had entered the bath.

She took in the room with a second scan. Could the scene have been staged? If there was another Bovyan operative involved, they could've succeeded in killing Koryn and disposed of the body, making it look like he'd escaped. She walked around the bathhouse, looking for signs of a second Bovyan, but the remaining tracks suggested only one.

Returning to the interior, Jie made a last scan. Her eyes swept the room and locked on several red fibers lodged in the joint between the bench and tub. She swept them up with her finger and sniffed. They smelled of fragrant flowers, a woman's perfume. With no other clues, she would assume the assassin had worn a red dress. One which Koryn would perhaps be wearing now.

She dashed out of the bathhouse in an attempt to catch up with the princes. She rounded the corner of the mansion, just in time to catch the driver about to snap the carriage reins, and too many people in the courtyard who'd see her if she tried to hitch a ride. The chamberlain stood at the carriage doors, bowing.

They needed to know what Koryn was wearing, if only to prevent the Eldaeri nations from playing into Teleri hands and going to war. Modulating her voice, she used a *Mockingbird's Deception* technique to imitate the chamberlain's voice, and a *Ghost Echo* to throw it: "Prince Koryn is wearing a red dress!"

The chamberlain looked around, brows furrowed.

Jie ducked back.

The driver snapped the reins, and the carriage set off.

What to do now? Track Koryn? Or go back to the Tarkothi royal villa to try to protect Karyna, if she was still alive? That option would undoubtedly lead her one step closer to the Black Lotus traitor.

Jie's stomach twisted. Most likely, Tharos had already killed Karyna, and he'd be nowhere near the villa. She started back to the bathhouse to see if she could determine how Koryn escaped.

Outside the walls, shouts erupted. Horse hooves clopped in unison, making it impossible to tell just how many were approaching. Jie crept back toward the main gate.

A column of cavalry burst into the courtyard. Lantern light flashed off their steel cuirasses and across their crimson capes as they fanned out, bows nocked.

Serikothi cavaliers. Jie had seen them in Cathay, witnessed their deadly precision and efficiency.

The Tarkothi soldiers drew their swords.

One of the cavaliers came to the center, beautiful golden hair dancing in the wind. With a thin, high-bridged nose and large eyes, he was gorgeous, even as his eyebrows slanted in anger. "Release Prince Koryn!"

How did they know about Koryn being here? Jie studied the man. Captain Damaryn, who'd accompanied Prince Koryn to Cathay. Aryn had said something about him bedding half the noblewomen in Serikoth. Given how dashing and handsome he was, it wouldn't be a surprise.

Unarmed, the chamberlain held his arms up. "You are trespassing in Tarkoth. Leave now, or we will consider it an act of war."

Damaryn trotted up and pointed his saber. "You declared war when you kidnapped our Crown Prince. We know he is here."

"He is not." Expression resolute, the chamberlain shook his head.

"Then you will not object to us doing a careful search."

The chamberlain scowled. "You will do no such thing."

"You leave me no choice." Damaryn raised his hand.

Bows creaked as the Serikothi took aim at the Tarkothi soldiers.

It would be cousin killing cousin again, because the Bovyans were too smart. Against her better judgment, Jie ran into the light, hands waving. "Stop. Stop."

All eyes turned to her in shock. Then, Serikothi bows trained on her. One loosed.

Sidestepping, she reached across her body and caught the arrow. She held up her hands. "Stop! I have answers."

The archers looked among each other, hopefully not wanting to test if she could catch more than one at a time.

"Who are you?" the chamberlain gasped in disbelief.

"Yes," Damaryn said. "Who are you? Wait. You are Prince Aryn's pet half-elf."

Heat flushed to the tips of Jie's ears. In some way, he wasn't wrong. Still wearing the clothes she'd taken from the young ruffian, filthy from all of her hitched rides, she dipped into the local curtsey. "Yes, Captain. There's no time to waste. They did indeed have Prince Koryn in their custody, but he has since escaped."

"Lies!" the chamberlain said.

Jie turned to face him. "Which part? About you kidnapping the prince, or him escaping?"

"Yes... No... Neither!" The chamberlain's face flushed red enough that they might not need lights. "Guards! Take her!"

With naked blades, the Tarkothi men advanced on her. Serikothi bows shifted aim from her to the Tarkothi, freezing them in their tracks.

"Please, calm down." Jie waved her hands down and glared at the chamberlain. "You will prevent unnecessary bloodshed by confessing."

His lips tightened. The Tarkothi formed up, weapons pointed out.

This wouldn't end well. Jie turned to Damaryn. "I swear, your prince escaped. Follow me, and I will show you."

He studied her for a few seconds, before saying, "You clearly aren't a tool of the Tarkothi."

"No." She shook her head. "But I'm not their enemy, either. Nor yours."

He gave a quick nod, then gestured to his men. "Cavaliers. If any Tarkothi so much as tries to interfere, turn them into a pincushion."

The Tarkothi grumbled. The chamberlain just stared at her. Jie grinned back.

Damaryn swung out of his saddle with graceful ease. He straightened his surcoat and followed her back to the bathhouse.

"How did you find out they were holding Prince Koryn?" she asked.

"An informant came to our royal villa."

"How long ago?"

Damaryn looked up at the Iridescent Moon. "A little more than a phase ago."

Jie ran calculations in her head. The time it took for the messenger to come to the Korynthi villa to tell Elrayn, the time it took for the carriage to come back...the assassin must've attacked more than a phase ago, as well. Perhaps he also sent an informant to seed hostilities.

"Here we are." She pointed to the two dead guards. "An assassin tried to kill Prince Koryn— "

Damaryn sucked in a sharp breath. "An assassination attempt?"

She nodded. "It failed. The assassin started with the two guards here. He tried to make it look like they were still at their post."

"I see."

She opened the bathhouse door, revealing the dead man. "A Teleri operative, known as a *Nightblade*. I think Prince Koryn killed him, and escaped."

Damaryn beamed. "My prince is a formidable swordsman."

She wasn't going to ruin his worshipful expression by pointing out it had been a brawl involving a wine bottle. However... "I believe he is trying to find a way back to the Serikothi side...wearing a dress."

Damaryn's eyes widened, even as a grin tugged at his lips. He schooled his expression into professionalism. "Can you prove this?"

"No." She shrugged. "It's just a deductive hypothesis."

"Just who are you?"

"It doesn't matter. However, I have also deduced where you might find him."

He gave her a suspicious raise of his eyebrow. "Where?"

"I'd have to guide you." She looked past him at the horses. Heavens, not one of those beasties again. Nothing good ever came from her riding one.

Still, there was no other way.

CHAPTER 24:

Saber Rattling

Though the rocking of the carriage on smooth pavement wasn't as pronounced as a ship's on the sea, Aelward still drew on it for comfort. After all, he was about to see Princess Karyna for the first time in years. Of his half-siblings, two of which sat across from him, she was the one who'd despised him the most for their father's adultery. If Elrayn treated him like flotsam, Karyna considered him whale shit. As concerning at Alaena's disappearance was, at least she wouldn't see them all together.

Disorganized shouts pierced the night sky.

Torn from his brooding, he looked out the window.

They were approaching one of the bridges to Elbahia Island. Tarkothi soldiers were screaming and gesturing. Others rushed toward the span, carrying pikes.

Pikes, to prevent a single man from crossing a bridge? That was like using a harpoon to spear a minnow. Aelward tracked their motions.

Dark shapes lay on the bridge. When a cloud cleared the Blue Moon, the light shone on armed men. It was hard to tell in the blue-hued light, but they looked to be wearing Tarkothi green uniforms.

"Stop," Elrayn called to the driver.

The carriage slowed to a halt, along with the mounted royal guards around them.

Elrayn poked his head out and beckoned to a scrambling soldier. "You there, what's happening?"

The man skidded to a stop, his insignias marking him as a lieutenant. Wide-eyed, he crossed his fists and bowed his head. "Your Highness, Serikothi cavaliers broke through our checkpoint just fifteen minutes ago. We've suffered casualties."

Cavaliers! The Serikothi were bringing out their very best troops. No wonder these soldiers were reinforcing their position with pikes. Aelward muttered under his breath. "They must've found out about their prince. That means they are headed to the mansion. Where they won't find him."

"So it begins." Aryn's typically nonchalant expression contorted into worry.

Aelward pulled at his collar. Alaena was out there somewhere, just as hostilities were breaking out.

Elrayn shook his head. "The situation can still be salvaged. We just need to recapture Koryn and have him marry Karyna."

Pointing out the window and into the darkness, Aryn said, "He could be anywhere."

Aelward harrumphed. Elrayn was like a minnow trying to swallow a whale. Trusting Aksumi Mystics to charm a foreign prince. Too damn ambitious, too damn stubborn. Better to cut their losses, batten down the hatches, and fortify.

Elrayn motioned to the lieutenant. "Spare as many men as you can to search for an Eldaeri male wearing an oversized red dress."

Blinking a few times, the lieutenant crossed his fists, and started to run.

"Avast," Aelward said. "We need a backup plan, just in case we don't catch him. Send word to the admiralty, have our ships block the mouth of the harbor. Pull our citizens off of Elbahia Island and to the Tarkothi side of the river, and defend the bridges."

Eyeing him, Elrayn gave a hesitant nod, then conveyed those very orders to the lieutenant by the window. He removed his signet ring and gave it to the soldier as proof. "Return it to the royal villa when you can."

The man crossed his fists again and ran off.

"What now?" Aryn asked.

Elrayn nodded. "We continue to the villa, to secure Karyna."

Aelward's sense of foreboding returned. Now, on top of a reunion with a prissy princess, Elbahia was about to be turned into a battlefield.

The carriage continued over the bridge, escorted by the riders. Though skilled cavalrymen, they'd be outmatched if the vaunted Serikothi cavaliers attacked. Every strange sound had Aelward looking out the window. Outside, Tarkothi citizens scattered, many heading east toward the bridges and the safety of Tarkoth.

When they reached the royal villa, Aelward blew out a sigh of relief. Elrayn and Aryn hopped out of the carriage, and he followed a few steps behind.

Elrayn gestured to a page in green livery who was running out to greet them. "Has Princess Karyna arrived yet?"

The page bowed, fists crossed. "Yes, Your Highness. Her carriage arrived not long ago."

Elrayn's sigh was even more dramatic than Aelward's had been. "Take me to her."

At least this part of the Crown Prince's fish-brained scheme had worked.

The page turned around and shuffled through the thick rugs in the hall.

Aelward trailed after his half-brothers, taking in his surroundings. It'd been nearly two decades since he'd last been here. The framed oil paintings on the walls depicted famous land and sea battles from the pacification of the Arkothi warlords, three hundred years before. As a child, they were just fantastical tales, but now, he knew more about the tactics and strategies that had been used in each of these conflicts. How would future painters depict the upcoming war between the

Tarkothi and Serikothi? How would they see Elrayn? Or would he bury the real story, to make himself the hero?

They passed the grand dining hall, and his stomach sank. It'd been here that the three royal siblings had tricked him into making a fool of himself, humiliating him in front of the entire court. Karyna had been the one to plan it all.

Up the steps they went, heading toward the royal suites at the rear.

They turned the corner, just in time for Aelward to see a set of double doors fling open.

Karyna.

She ran out, smile wide, the blue satin dress' neckline low enough to reveal a crystal hanging from her neck just above her cleavage. Objectively, she'd filled out into a classic Eldaeri beauty. Skin smooth and as fair as an Eldaeri could get, she looked as if she'd never seen the sun or felt a sea breeze on her face. Her long brown hair was perfectly coifed.

Hanging back between his half-brothers, Aelward gritted his teeth. She wouldn't expect him to be here, and there was no telling what her reaction would be.

Her eyes went from Elrayn to Aryn.

"Elrayn," she said, voice clear as a ship's bell and as feminine as a siren. "Thank you for arranging this...meeting."

Thanks? Was she in favor of the marriage? Had the Aksumi used their black magic on her, like they were supposed to have done on Prince Koryn?

"And Aryn." She smiled. "It's been months since you were home. I trust your voyage to Cathay was enjoyable?"

Aryn bowed his head. "Yes, it was."

Her gaze finally settled on Aelward.

His stomach knotted. What barb would she try to lodge in him now?

"Lieutenant," she said with another gracious smile.

Lieutenant? Not *bastard*? Or *whore's get*? Perhaps she'd grown out of her grudge over the years. Aelward crossed his fists and bowed low. "Your Highness."

He looked back up, bracing for whatever insult she had planned.

None came.

She turned to Elrayn, expression bright. "When will I be meeting...you know?"

Aelward tugged at his collar. She was truly excited about the prospect of wedding the Serikothi crown prince. She'd never seemed interested in gaining power through marriage. Or maybe she was just doing her duty. Did she know Elrayn had tried to use magic to influence her groom-to-be?

Shifting his weight, Elrayn exchanged glances with Aryn. "Yes, uh...tomorrow. You will meet him tomorrow."

She clapped her hands together. Karyna had never been so girlish, even as a child. Could it be the effect of magic?

Narrowing his eyes, Aelward nudged Aryn and whispered, "Where are the Aksumi who charmed Koryn?"

Aryn leaned in. "I know, something is off."

"I told Tharos to keep guard over you." Elrayn gestured to the doors from which she emerged. "Is he in your room?"

Smiling, Karyna looked back.

"I'm here, Your Highness," a voice called from the room.

Elrayn's shoulders relaxed.

Aelward's too. His worst fears were melting away.

"What about the Aksumi?" Aryn asked.

"They rode..." Karyna's voice came out, sounding too much like the male voice that had come from the room. She cleared her throat. "They rode in the carriage, but asked to be let off."

Elrayn turned around and looked at them, brow furrowed. Then he pushed past her, toward the door.

She caught his wrist in a deft swipe. "It's all right. Tharos... Tharos is...naked."

Tharos? Aelward's brow crinkled. Rumors suggested she was involved with some soldier named Peris.

Elrayn stopped midstride, and looked back at her with rounded eyes.

"You sounded a lot like Tharos just now," Aryn said. He pulled his sword from its scabbard with a rasp. The dull grey metal, supposedly from a falling star, seemed to absorb all light.

Aelward drew his sword, as well. "And why would you be sharing a bed with Tharos? What's my name?"

"I know your name." She looked at him. "It's a very good name."

Still holding her wrist, Elrayn also drew his sword. A twin to Aryn's, its dull grey reflected no light.

With an expert motion, she twisted out of his hold and seized his wrist. She yanked him with abnormal strength, jerking him forward and sending his sword arm back. Changing the direction of her pull, she jammed the heel of her palm under Elrayn's jaw.

Sword spinning out of his grip, he flew back. His flailing hand caught the crystal around her neck and the neckline of her dress. The cloth ripped.

Aelward averted his eyes, looking down to where Elrayn tumbled to the floor.

It wasn't Elrayn, but Karyna, wearing Elrayn's dress uniform, now scuttling over toward Elrayn's sword.

What sorcery was this? He looked up at the first Karyna... No, it was hulking man, chiseled pectoral muscles exposed from where the shredded dress hung.

"Tharos!" Aryn said, lowering his sword.

Tharos? It had just been Karyna! Aelward's mind whirled like a typhoon. He, too, lowered his sword.

Smirking, Tharos hiked up his skirts and loped back toward the room he'd come from. His head start and long legs got him there before Aelward could even start to give chase. The doors slammed shut, and the lock clicked.

Aelward ran to the door, Aryn right behind him, and Karyna—no, Elrayn—picked himself up off the floor. As soon as his hand wrapped around the hilt of his sword, his image had shifted back to his normal, conniving self.

Suppressing a gawk at this strange magic, Aelward slammed himself into the threshold between the double doors as if he were ramming the side of a ship with the prow of his own. The doors buckled, but held. Inside the room, glass shattered. A second later, something crashed on the ground outside.

Aryn flung his shoulder into the doors, and the wood creaked.

"Together," Aelward said. "On three. One...two...three."

Aryn and Aelward charged together. The wood around the lock splintered and the doors burst open. Aelward just about crashed into the ground, but fought to keep his feet.

The spacious room was furnished with a four-poster bed, a make-up table, a wardrobe, and paintings. One of the windows was broken. Aelward ran over and looked out. There was no sign of this Tharos. With a second look, he saw some of the glass had blood on it, as well as a piece of the dress.

"Where is he?" Elrayn stomped into the room, Eldaeri sword in hand. "I'll behead the traitor myself."

"Escaped," Aelward said, looking out the window as Aryn came up beside him. Together, they scanned the darkness of the side courtyard.

Elrayn pushed by them and yelled into the courtyard. "Men! All men search for Tharos. He is wearing a torn blue dress."

"The more important question is," Aryn said, "where is Karyna?"

Aelward nodded. "I couldn't believe she was happy about marrying Koryn."

"The truth is," Aryn said, "she is in love with Peris."

"Who is this Peris?" Aelward looked from brother to brother. Up to now, Peris had just been a name and a rumor. Now, all these political marriages were as mangled as the cannons on the *Sea Dragon* after the fight with the pirates.

"Tharos' brother," Aryn said. "Our fool of a brother here had Tharos forge a letter in the name of his own brother, Peris. It was to Karyna, saying he wanted to run away with her, to trick her into coming to Elbahia. I'm beginning to think Tharos tricked Elrayn instead."

Hanging his head, Elrayn sheathed his sword. "After all we did for their family. I'm going to have both of them publicly hung."

Aryn let out a long sigh. "Peris has always been my trusted friend. I can't believe he'd do this to us."

"I don't know how he could do it," Elrayn said. "I had three of my spies trailing him all day, just in case he tried to make contact with Karyna."

"Just what did Peris do?" Aelward asked. "We need to piece together what happened, if we are to ever find Karyna." And Alaena, probably.

Elrayn nodded. "When we went to the Korynthi royal villa, Tharos went with the two Aksumi to meet Karyna. They were supposed to charm her and bring her back here."

"Instead, Tharos *became* her, using that necklace." Aelward pointed at the crystal in Elrayn's hand. "So that the real Karyna could go meet Peris, like *you* promised."

Elrayn's lip curled.

"Give it to me." Aelward eyed the magic crystal.

When Elrayn pulled it back, Aryn ripped it from his hands and gave it to Aelward. Both gasped.

Aelward went to the dressing mirror. He now looked like Karyna. "Magic. An illusion, which doesn't affect you when you hold the Eldaeri sword."

Both princes studied their weapons. Of course. Throughout history, the swords had protected their wielders from the remaining Runemasters.

It was all coming together now. "The attack on the *Sea Dragon* involved illusion and fire magic. I'd wager the same Aksumi sorcerers were involved."

Both princes gawked at him.

"Why didn't you tell us?" Elrayn jabbed a finger at him. "This is your fault! You should have told us."

Mauls and Maelstroms! Aelward gawked. "Every detail was in the report I sent to the admiralty."

Aryn pushed Elrayn's outstretched arm down. "He's right. This isn't Aelward's fault at all. Right now, we need to find out where Peris and Karyna ran off to."

"And find Alaena," Aelward added. He had a sinking feeling that she was somehow tied up in this catastrophe.

CHAPTER 25:

Rationalizations

Eyes closed, Alaena took in a deep draught of the forest air. The moist evergreen scent filled not just her lungs, but also her soul. It had been too long. She was home again. Well, maybe she hadn't made it into her homeland yet, but she was close enough: on a wooded island north of Elbahia, with a nearby bridge that would take her into Serikoth. Trails wound through the trees, providing a respite for the citizens of Elbahia who wanted to escape the urban jungle.

She opened her eyes.

Even in the late afternoon sun, it was easy to distinguish the smooth black trunks of sablewood trees from the brown gnarly bark of blockwoods. Both had been bred by her ancestors to grow rapidly; both had contributed to their conquest of coastal Arkoth, three hundred years before. Sablewood, for its ease and durability for building ships, and blockwood for constructing sturdy, fireproof buildings and fortifications.

To think, the very natural resources that made the Eldaeri so great were altered into unnatural forms like the palaces, villas, and ships back in Korynth and here in Elbahia. She took a deep breath again. Soon, very soon, she'd disappear into the woods of Serikoth, and nobody would be able to find her until she chose.

Except Thielas, of course. Then again, while the frivilous elf might be fun for the occasional tumble in the brush, he was just entertaining his human fetish. If only she'd had a chance to bring Aelward along. Whether he was a perfect specimen of manhood on ship who lit fire in her loins, or the awkward dolt on land who was just too adorable, and he was on the very short list of people she'd miss.

Patting her slingshot and knife, which she hopefully wouldn't need, Alaena tied up her skirts between her knees for more mobility. Unwieldy as the dress was, she'd changed out of her travelling clothes. They stank of the sea, which would make it easier for hounds or the little Madaeri to sniff her out. Now, she had to wait for the first part of Peris' plan to come to fruition.

At the moment, this was a perfect spot, providing a good view of the trail, and close to the bridge to make a quick escape. It would work, as long as Karyna Corivar hurried up and came. Wait any longer, and Koryn would get the bright idea of sending Madaeri trackers after her.

A twig snapped from down the path. At this late hour, it could only be her target. Alaena crept to the opposite side of a thick tree, one which provided a direct view of the path. She peeked around.

A cloaked figure pattered over the hard-packed trail, long green dress trailing behind her. Karyna Corivar, firstborn of Tarkoth's king. Coming with no guards, just as Peris had said.

Then again, he also said she was cautious and suspicious. To the contrary, in the moment, she clearly didn't care about avoiding dried twigs or leaves that would give away her position. Her happy humming was even more of a beacon for trouble. On occasion she'd look back over her shoulder, but her body language didn't suggest she was the least concerned.

She ought to be.

Alaena tugged on the sheep intestine gloves Peris had given her. His plan had sounded much too complicated when he'd told her. Still, his explanation made sense: he was under constant watch from Tarkothi spies and couldn't do it by himself. Alaena was famous throughout Eldaeri lands for regularly giving the Korynthians the slip in the woods. And Karyna didn't trust anyone with her forbidden relationship. This was the only way.

Something niggled at Alaena's admittedly selfish lack of morality. This wasn't right. There might be a better means of accomplishing the same goal. Still, this was here, now, and just about guaranteed: with Karyna out of the way, none of the marriage swaps would happen.

When Karyna passed through a gap in the tree canopies, blue moonlight shone on her. Her green dress's plunging neckline exposed much of her bosom, while the rest of the immodest style bared her arms. The lack of any muscle tone betrayed the pampered life of a Tarkothi princess. With skin pale for an ethnic Eldaeri, she'd probably never seen the sun. Not a single strand of her brown hair fell out of place.

And that smile! It was like the perpetual grin of a bobcat. The look of a woman in love.

Alaena would've vomited if it wouldn't give away her position. She'd almost thrown up when Peris waxed poetic about Karyna's beauty and sweetness. The things people did for silly notions of love. The silly things *she'd* done for love, when she first met Thielas. She ducked back behind the tree as Karyna came closer. She took the small glass vial Peris had given her and removed the cork stopper. A musky fragrance wafted out.

Don't let it touch you, Peris had said, though there hadn't been time to explain why before they had to escape the Korynthi villa. Maybe this wasn't a good idea, after all. If she just reasoned with Karyna, maybe she'd listen.

Or maybe not.

Peris had said Karyna knew how to raise a ruckus. Alaena dabbed the liquid onto a cloth.

Karyna passed.

Alaena slipped out behind her, careful to avoid the same dry twigs and leaves which Karyna snapped under foot. The crackling provided a way of hiding Alaena's own stealthy steps.

Was freedom worth betraying her homeland, and her adopted homeland? Alaena nodded to herself. This would be good for Karyna, too.

She reached around and pressed the cloth to Karyna's mouth and nose.

Without any struggle, Karyna's body went limp.

Amazing! Alaena fought the urge to examine the cloth, and instead caught the dainty princess before she crumpled to the ground. With no muscle tone, she was soft and light, and wouldn't be too heavy to carry. Alaena hauled her up onto her shoulder.

From further down the path came garbled conversations. A search party? Or a pair of lovers looking for a private place to romp? Either way, she couldn't afford to be seen with a woman draped over her shoulder.

She had to cross over into Serikoth to meet with Peris before anyone realized Karyna was missing.

CHAPTER 26:

Voice of The Demon

Against his better judgment, Tomas continued up along the ridge. During the day, it would've been treacherous; at night, it bordered on madness.

Still, the demon eye filtered his vision, showing the winding, rising path clearly between the cliff face and the deadly drop. It was getting easier and easier for it to work with his natural eye, and his dizziness had long since subsided. Indeed, the sense of fatigue and ickiness he'd felt since waking in Sofia's bedroom was gone.

After a while, the ledge straightened and widened. Continuing his hike, he looked back toward the camp. He had to be thousands of *pedes* away now, and he could just make out the Bovyans' lumpy forms. He closed his real eye and squinted with the right. The details around the campfire looked clearer, the soft red glow of dying embers distinguishable from the greyness around it. The two soldiers looked almost larger, as if he were half the actual distance away. They were still sleeping, though Sathis' body convulsed.

Was the demon helping him see better? Still walking, he blinked a few times to see Sathis better.

The disembodied female voice spoke again. Five syllables this time, the intonation suggestion a question.

What could it possibly be asking? Perhaps the evil spirit wondered why he hadn't killed the Bovyans?

Maybe because he wasn't a murderer, even after they'd shoved a demon into his eye socket. He gritted his teeth.

His vision flashed red. The voice spoke again, urgent this time.

His body froze of its own accord for a split second. When his limbs came back to life, he turned around.

Right in front of him was a gap where part of the ledge had fallen away.

Tomas heart lurched. Had he taken that step, he would have fallen to his death, far below.

Two syllables. The demon had warned him, and even stopped him in his tracks.

Why would it do so? Perhaps it needed to make sure his soul was corrupted completely before death. Or maybe it needed to be embedded in a living person to be alive itself. No matter the demon's reason, Tomas benefited: he wasn't tumbling down the mountain, screaming.

Now, though, he had to cross a ten-*pede* gap to the other ledge.

The space between was sheer cliff, though there looked to be plenty of hand and footholds. Tomas looked down and gulped. If his hands or feet slipped... Maybe it would be better to turn back, and return to the campsite before the Bovyans awoke.

He shook the idea out of his head and squinted with the demon eye. Just as it had provided a clear path on the ledge between the cliff and the chasm, it now painted a white contrast between foot and handholds against the dark cliff wall. It must be reading his intentions.

The voice spoke again. Six syllables.

More light-colored niches lit up against the dark backdrop, this time rising straight up from where he stood to another ledge up above. As he tracked the path the demon showed him, it continued rising. Up, to the left, up, to the right. Over and down a little, then back up.

All the way to the Golden Bowl.

Up, or forward.

Sanity said *forward*. It was dark, he was tired, and he had no gear for climbing.

Curiosity said *up*. Here was a chance to reach the Golden Bowl, maybe bring back enough treasure to make him rich.

Not to mention, with the demon eye showing him the way, he was taking an otherwise impossible path, one which Fethos couldn't follow. Wouldn't even consider possible.

All the gods in heaven, he was rationalizing. And it shouldn't have come as a surprise. Old legends spoke of demons serving the orc gods. The eye was likely drawing him back to its source, in Lydath's Temple. Showing Tomas a path, and altering the way he thought about things. That was the only way to explain him even considering this insanity. He'd never cared about wealth, and certainly would've never risked death to attain it.

Tomas took one last look at the campsite. With a deep breath, he reached for the first handhold. It felt cool and firm beneath his fingers. He foot fit neatly into a crevice. He continued this way, up several *pedes*. It wasn't that hard. Quite easy, really.

His vision flashed red, from up to down. The demon voice spoke again, in two syllables. He'd just set his right foot on an outcrop, and was about to transfer his weight, but now he froze. Like before, maybe not even of his own volition.

Up to now, every time his vision flashed like that, and the demon had spoken in those same two syllables, it had been a warning.

Maintaining his weight between his handholds and his left foot, he gave the outcrop a good shove with his right foot.

A veritable boulder broke free and tumbled down the cliff face.

He counted. One. Two. Three... At eight seconds, the rock splintered trees and thudded into the floor of the gorge with a resonant thud. Birds squawked in a flutter of echoing wings.

Enough to wake the Bovyans? Tomas craned his neck and squinted with the demon eye at the campsite far behind and below.

Again, the scene looked much closer than it should have been. Fethos rolled over onto his side. Sathis' breaths had become rapid, but he didn't otherwise move.

Tomas blew out a breath. They could probably sleep through another Hellstorm. Had they awoken and seen him, they would know how to follow. Not to mention, had he shifted his weight onto that rock, it would've been him impaled on tree branches, before splattering on the ground a thousand *pedes* below.

"Thank you, Demon Eye," he whispered under his breath. "Do you have a name?"

The succubus remained silent.

"Well, if we are going to be joined together like this for a while," but hopefully not too long, "I'm going to give you a name." It was a succubus, and the voice was rather sultry. It deserved a sensuous name. "I name you Sabine."

No response.

A grin came to his lips, unbidden. Silence was tantamount to acceptance. "Okay, Sabine, show me the way."

He looked up, and the safe path lit up before him, patches of white against the dark cliff. He continued up, with only a few detours as Sabine rerouted him around dangerous spots, or directed him into large crevices to avoid gusts of wind. He looked down on occasion, to check on the campsite, where neither Sathis nor Fethos stirred.

Without a view of the Iridescent Moon, it was hard to tell how long he'd climbed, but as he neared the summit, a band of midnight blue merged with the black near the horizon. His fingers, arms, hips, and knees ached, and even though he was on the leeward side of the island, cold winds now bit into him. Up above, the ghosts around Lydath's Temple wailed.

He should've listened to his own better judgement before embarking on this insanity. Just when he thought he couldn't climb any further, his outstretched hand reached the top. With his last bit of energy, he pulled himself up and collapsed face first onto the flat, cold rock surface. It felt like his chest and belly were freezing.

As much as he wanted to roll over, and maybe assess the surroundings, his muscles refused to act. Still, he'd made it. The first sentient being in a thousand years to do so, unless the Last Dragon Avarax had flown here since he'd awoken thirty years ago.

Tomas turned his head.

And looked right into the eye sockets of another skull.

His own eyes widened, and he would've jumped up if he had enough energy.

It had heavy brows and cheekbones, and tusks rose from its lower mandible.

A Tivari.

The rest of its skeleton lay sprawled and unconnected, long picked away by carrion birds and battered by the elements. Each of the bones looked thicker and heavier than the remains in the coffin below. Perhaps Sabine's original owner hadn't been Tivari.

Tomas looked past it, to Lydath's Golden Bowl.

From town, across the straits, the bowl looked large, and the view from the gorge below had hinted at its sheer enormity. That didn't prepare Tomas for the way it took up almost his entire field of vision up close. Now, at dawn, it looked like an inverted dome, the dull, lifeless yellow color of farmland in the winter. It was nothing special, beyond the beautiful gilded latticework that ran up and down along its surface, which was indiscernible when viewing from down below. Legends spoke of how the Tivari priests would keep the bowl filled with human blood, to appease their vile gods.

How many humans would it have taken? Fifty people lying head to foot might just about span its diameter. It was so deep that if twenty adults stood on each other's shoulders at its center, the topmost person might be able to see the top of the dish.

With several breaths, his flagging energy trickled back. He pushed his chest off the cold rock, brought his knees beneath him, and creaked up. A breeze blew through his hair and sent his skin prickling in goosebumps. Each time a gust swept through the bowl, it let out a low howl.

It sounded just like the ghosts they always heard from below.

Tomas laughed to himself. "Sabine, are any of your friends here?"

No answer.

He turned and looked down the way he'd come. It was so far to the ledge where he'd first decided to climb, and even further to the ravine floor. He followed the ledge backward to the campsite, where the Bovyans were now just little specks.

He kicked a stone over the side and counted until it smashed into the ground far below. Fifteen seconds. Over three thousand *pedes*.

He shivered. No wonder it was so cold.

He started to turn back, but froze. And gasped.

From this vantage point, the scene was a thing of beauty. The sun looked as if were rising out of the Inland Sea. Usually, from his village, the waters spread as far as the eye could see; from this height, he could see how the sea's south coast turned northward, right where a line of mountains rose and a river emerged. He squinted with the demon eye.

The grey splotch there enlarged and came into focus, revealing a towering fortress occupying the gap between the sea, river, and fort. Several biremes flying crimson flags were docked there.

What was the spot's name? Tomas' forehead wrinkled until it came to him. The Four Corners—where the lands of the Estomari City-States, the Arkothi Free Cities, the Teleri Empire, and the Eldaeri Kingdom of Serikoth met. Thundercloud Fortress protected both Serikoth and the Estomari City-States from the Teleri Empire, but left the Arkothi Free Cities in the west vulnerable to the Bovyans' increasing aggression.

His vision faded back as he followed the old highway from Thundercloud Fortress, through the plains of Southern Arkoth, to the town of Lorium, where he'd lost his eye. It looked like a brown patch in the green farmland around it. His gaze continued along the road west, across an ancient bridge over the Olkroy River, to Mykos, the lord city in the region. Even with the demon eye, he could only make out the city walls and the port.

Antonius had said the Teleri army had surrounded Mykos. From there, Governor Keris had pressed east along the highway to Lorium, but why? There were no walls, and the town would be impossible to defend. If the Free City of Lykos sent their fabled pikemen to relieve the siege on their allies in Mykos, they'd have to pass through Lorium first. As vaunted as the Bovyans were, two hundred wouldn't be able to hold off several thousand.

Tomas might not have a military mind, but if the Teleri wanted to defend a choke point, the bridge would be the spot. It was a monument to the rune magic and ingenuity of the Arkothi Empire, which had connected its southeast coastline on the Estomar to the rest of the realm—at least until the Hellstorm, when the formation of the Inland Sea had torn the empire in half.

He shivered. Despite the rising sun, it didn't seem to be getting any warmer up here. He tore his gaze away from the spectacular view, and swept across the mountaintop.

In addition to the skull at his feet, several more orc skeletons lay sprawled in a haphazard manner. There were at least thirty skulls.

Shuddering, Tomas studied the giant bowl.

It must've been level in ancient times, if it were to hold blood; now, it crushed what remained of the temple, and lay tipped on its side. A section of its rim touched the ground.

Tomas went over to that part, where the bowl's massive size blocked the gusts from the windward side of the island. As he suspected, water pooled in the concavity, and surely over the millennia any human blood must've been washed away... Even if the village told the rest of the world otherwise, in their attempt to sell fertility potions in Lorium's market. He cupped his hands and drank, then used some of the water to wash the tubers he'd carried all the way from the coffin.

Though they tasted better cooked, he gobbled them down. Once he was done, he worked his way back to the bowl's convex side, where the ruined temple lay.

It was less than half the size of the bowl, and only two stories tall. The main structure had probably been dome-shaped in ancient times, before collapsing under the bowl. Like the bowl, the entire temple looked like to be made of gold, from the crumpled walls and bent columns.

An elegant filigree, like the latticework of the bowl itself, ran in diagonal lines up and around the structure. There was nothing he could pull away or break off. The way some of the structure was discolored and warped, it must've been melted by fire. Really hot fire. Perhaps a legendary fireball from the Aksumi Pyromancers who'd helped storm it when humans had won their freedom from their Tivari overlords. Indeed, some of the bones nearby had a dark singe marks.

He walked around the circular building. More orc bones lay scattered around the flat mountaintop.

The entrance to the temple had collapsed when the bowl fell. The opening wasn't large enough for him to crawl through, but he could climb up to one of the windows.

Insanity! No telling what traps or evil spirits were in there.

Though now, it was clear the ghostly wails were no more than gusts of wind through the bowl. It was no more insane to enter than climbing all the way up here in the first place.

"What do you think, Sabine? Any of your friends in there?" Maybe a means of banishing her back to whatever underworld she belonged to?

No answer.

He'd come this far, and maybe there were some treasures he could take back. As if sensing his intentions, or perhaps prodding him on, Sabine outlined a way to the nearest window. Using the entrance's fallen transom as a step, he pushed himself up to where he could use the lattices as ladders. The curve of the temple sloped enough to make it an easy climb.

He reached the closest window and peered in.

Only a few thin lines of sunlight from the windows stabbed through the temple's darkness, making it impossible for Tomas to make out anything from his vantage point at the rim of the dome. He closed his left eye and blinked a few times.

Just as the demon eye worked in the black of the night, the temple's darkness shifted to greys. Columns stood at regular intervals along the walls. Mirrors were set into the walls between the columns, and perhaps at different times of the day, the blades of light from the window would shine in and light up the circular chamber.

Beneath the mirrors, a ledge protruded from the wall. Gemstones of varying shapes and sizes were encrusted into it. Just a handful of them would make him rich, and unless the orc gods ever returned on their flaming chariots, they wouldn't be able punish him for looting their long-abandoned sanctuary. The vast treasure must be why the Bovyans wanted to come to the island, though they had also said something about a crown.

Tomas shimmied through the window and used the diamond-shaped coffering in the columns to climb the dozen *pedes* down to the ledge. He jumped the last three *pedes*, his feet crunching onto the floor. He looked down.

He'd landed on a rib, which crumbled under his weight. It was part of a complete skeleton, whose thick bones clearly belonged to a long-dead Tivari. Several more lay against the walls, or bent over the ledge.

Tomas pushed one aside and studied the gems. They were embedded deeply, and impossible to pry out with his freezing, bare fingers. Maybe there was some kind of tool around here. A knife, to wedge underneath a stone.

Inside was just as cold as out. Teeth chattering, he worked his way around the walls, his feet leaving tracks in the thick dust on the tiled floor, until he reached a pair of double doors in an archway. It stood directly across from the collapsed entrance. He scratched his head. There was nothing on the outside of the temple to suggest these doors led anywhere.

He looked back to the front. A throne on a circular base rose in the center of the chamber, its back to him, blocking his view of the front. Tomas left a trail through the dust as he walked over and around, to look at the front of the throne.

An orc sat there, its eyes sparkling.

Tomas' heart leaped into his throat. He staggered back several steps and fell on his butt, then turned over, gained his feet, and sprinted to the entrance. He dropped to all fours. Try as he might, he couldn't squeeze through the little hole.

Surely the orc would be upon him by now, but all sounds were drowned out by the pounding of Tomas' heart in his ears.

Well, he hadn't escaped from Bovyans and climbed three thousand *pedes* up a cliff face in the dark, just to get killed by an orc. He turned around, ready to scratch, claw, punch, or do whatever he could.

The orc hadn't moved.

At all.

It might as well have been like the grand statues that supposedly lined the avenues of the oldest cities.

Tomas took a few tentative steps toward it. On second glance, the orc sat awkwardly on his throne, his head lolled at a slight angle. Whoever he'd been, he must've been important. Maybe the high priest, slain in the assault on the temple during the War of Ancient Gods. He was as wide as a Bovyan, though not nearly as tall.

Up close, the papery skin of its face looked desiccated and sallow. Its mouth hung open in a silent scream.

Unlike all the others he'd seen up to now, whose flesh and clothes had rotted away over the centuries, this one's open-faced robe looked to be made of some kind of leather. Its high collar covered the priest's neck, giving him a dapper appearance, like the ruddy-skinned Kanin scout who'd once ridden through Lorium. A thumb-width hole in the fabric opened right around its gut. An arrow wound, perhaps, from the epic attack on the temple a thousand years ago.

With a tentative hand, Tomas pulled the flap of the robe back. The Altivorc's undershirt must've shrunk over the ages, and now clung to its body. The hole from the jacket continued through the textured cloth, and looked burned around the edges. The arrowhead protruded a little way out.

Curious, he worked it free. A long oval crystal, it had veins of impurities running in intricate patterns through its body. There didn't seem to be any way to affix it to an arrow shaft.

Tomas withdrew his hand and looked into the Altivorc's eyes. He could've sworn they'd glittered before, and really, there was no way they could've survived intact all this time. He climbed up to the throne and studied them. No, they were glass, like his own demon eye, save with no pupils.

He let out a nervous chuckle. "Your friend, Sabine?"

The demon eye in his head remained silent.

Tomas extended a finger. He touched the left eye and jerked his hand back. Taking stock of himself, and finding himself still alive and unharmed, he touched it again. It was hard and cold, definitely not a real eye. Maybe this Tivari, important enough to sit on a throne, had used rune-inscribed eyes as well.

Which raised another question: Just who was the human from the coffin? Had he collaborated with the Altivorcs in order to get his eye?

Tomas started to pluck the orbs out, but then stayed his hand. By all the gods in heaven, what was he thinking? It had to be his own resident demon, tempting him to deface a body. Orc or not, it didn't deserve it.

However, it didn't need its robe as much as Tomas did. Wincing, he tugged and pulled at it. The corpse's arms and fingers proved to be stiff, the flesh of the hands firm to the point of rigidity. When he was done retrieving the garment, the body slumped over the throne's armrest.

With the corpse at this new angle, and its coat off, Tomas caught sight of its sheathed dagger. A smile came unbidden to his lips. At last, a useful tool! A sharp point, with which to dislodge the gems from the wall.

Tomas pulled the weapon from its sheath, only to find the blade's warped sides had curled into a tube, with no edge or point. Useless. With a sigh, he shrugged on his new robe. It hung down to his heels, and the loose sleeves dangled past his hands. Its collar rode up past his neck and flared out above his ears. Given its size, he probably looked more like a real Arkothi Runemaster than an orc priest.

Still, it provided much-needed warmth. Its weight also seemed uneven, from three large bulges strapped to both upper arms.

He withdrew one of the hard objects and examined it with two fingers.

The translucent crystal looked like a flattened egg, oval-shaped and clear. Maybe it was valuable. He'd get a better look at it outside, in the sun. For now, he returned it to the strap.

He caught sight of an inner pocket and opened it. The space inside looked larger than it should be. He probed around, and though it was empty, it was indeed much larger. More orc magic, perhaps.

All the wealth in here! Still, after a careful search around the circular chamber, he found nothing which could pry the gems from the wall. With a sigh, he crept over to the double doors. There were no handles to pull them open. The way they met their arching frame, it looked like they opened inward.

He pushed, but they didn't budge. There was certainly no way they could rise vertically, like portcullis, though maybe they could slide horizontally, like a Cathayi-style pocket door. He wedged his fingers into the crack and yanked.

They moved so easily he nearly flung them wide open, and had to catch them. He peered in.

His vision flashed red, and Sabine spoke again, the same two syllables of danger.

He jerked back, again, not entirely of his own will.

Nothing happened.

He pushed his head in once more, ignoring Sabine's warning. Like the central hall, this room was circular, no more than eight *pedes* across.

It had no floor.

Thank the heavens he hadn't stepped in, or he would have fallen... How far the shaft bored down into the mountain, it was impossible to tell with the dim light, even with the demon eye. A ladder carved into the walls provided the only means of descent, but perhaps it led into the depths of hell itself, where the orc gods tortured the souls of the wicked.

Where his soul would end up, if he didn't resist Sabine's temptations.

He shuddered. Perhaps the orc priests had cast bodies into this pit after draining their blood for the bowl.

Tomas laughed, the sound echoing off the walls. Maybe it was the legends of the ancient temple spooking him. The mountain rose at least three thousand *pedes* above the Inland Sea. This shaft would have to go much deeper if it were to reach the orc hells; and with a ladder, it was meant to go somewhere accessible by the orc priests. If what the scribe had said was true, the remains of dwarf city lay below here.

And maybe a treasure trove.

"What do you think, Sabine?"

She'd brought him to the temple, but now remained silent as to why, and what he should do next.

He pushed one door open to reach the ladder. The opposite door slid open as well, working like dwarf gears. Of course, the dwarves had also been slaves to orcs, and were masters of working underground, so they had probably constructed this shaft.

Raising the hem of the robe and tying it around his waist so he wouldn't trip over it, Tomas reached up for the handle which would help him negotiate the rim and reach the ladder.

No sooner did his arm rise than the gemstone he'd studied earlier slipped from its strap on his sleeve. He swiped at it, and pinned it between his hand and the wall. It flattened with a *click*, and light spilled from between his fingers.

Gems weren't supposed to flatten, not to mention shed light. It buzzed and whined, sending vibrations through his hand.

His vision flashed red. Sabine spoke those same two syllables.

Tomas jerked his hand back.

The stone's soft white light revealed more double doors as it plummeted down the shaft, and its wail grew louder. It echoed off the walls. No doubt there was demon trapped inside it as well, screaming as it returned to hell.

He counted, to get a feel of its depth.

At twelve seconds, the gem, now just a dot of white in the darkness, smashed into something solid.

Red flashed in his vision, and Sabine spoke the warning in his head again.

A glorious splash of yellows, oranges, and reds flared. Tomas' good eye went blind from the brightness, though the demon eye recovered almost instantaneously. A roar rumbled back up the shaft, shaking the ground.

Heart pounding, Tomas turned and bolted. The robe's hem came untied as he ran, nearly tangling around his feet. He reached the throne.

His vision flashed again, a red haze shifting from left to right toward the throne. Sabine spoke again, more syllables than he could keep track of.

Following the direction of the red haze, he rounded the throne.

Flames belched out of the doors with enough force to knock him face-first into the floor. They licked over him, singing the back of his hair and burning his scalp.

Tomas turned over and gasped. He palpated the back of his head. The burn wasn't bad, but he didn't have any hair left above the robe's collar line.

He sat up and looked. His own eye flared orange with the flames' afterimage. The demon eye, however, took in the chamber.

Almost all the orc bones had disintegrated to ash. The only ones left intact were those lying in a line between the throne and the entrance.

Thank all the gods in heaven he'd been in that path. Rather, thank Sabine. Even if her words didn't make any sense to him, at least she was trying to communicate by manipulating his vision.

He looked down his sleeve at the remaining gemstones strapped there, five in all. No, these weren't treasures. They were some come kind of weapon. Unholy ones, once wielded by the orc priests. Infused with the explosive power of demons.

Tomas shivered. A voice in is head, sounding suspiciously like Sofia's, implored him to leave the rest of the gemstones here. Another thought, no doubt Sabine twisting his conscience, pointed out that they might be useful.

Up above, the bowl groaned. The columns shifted, and the walls of the temple creaked.

CHAPTER 27:

Plans in the Night

With red skirts hiked up, and the cloak's hood covering his head, Koryn tried to mingle in with all the people in the dark streets. Elbahia lay just over the river; so close, yet so far away. Problem was, the Tarkothi citizens were mostly streaming in the opposite direction to this bank, many carrying lamps which bobbed in the darkness like fireflies. Soldiers, too, scurried every which way, and he had to turn around and go with the flow any time a patrol jogged by.

War was on everyone's hushed lips. Tarkoth and Serikoth teetered on the brink of reviving hostilities that had remained under the surface for over a century.

Why now? Certainly no one from Serikoth knew of his kidnapping, because of Tharos' forged letters. There had to be another reason. He had to find out. It'd been about two phases since his escape, and the first two bridges he'd tried to cross had been heavily guarded by Tarkothi soldiers. Boat landings, too, were crawling with the enemy, and trying to swim across at night would likely get him drowned.

On the other side of the river, the Light of Solaris illuminated the dome of Elbahia Palace, taunting him. He continued northward, though it didn't seem likely any of the bridges would be left unguarded. It might be he'd have to hunker down somewhere until the commotion died down.

"Over there!" a cry rang out from ahead.

Had they seen him? It didn't seem possible, given the darkness. Still, Koryn patted the sword he'd taken from one of the dead guards outside the bathhouse. It wasn't his Eldaeri heirloom, but it would have to do. He looked in the direction of the shouts.

Bauble lamps from the north were travelling parallel to the river, heading in his direction. It was hard to tell just how many soldiers there were. Behind him, another group looked to be coming this way. He turned onto a side street as the two squads approached.

"Report," said one of the group headed south. Given his smaller stature, he was likely an Eldaeri officer, leading ethnic Arkothi troops.

"Serikothi cavaliers! They've pushed through the Surian Bridge."

Koryn's heart soared. If it was the cavaliers on this side of the river, they must've found out about his kidnapping. But how? Maybe Damaryn's resourcefulness. Surely, he would have ordered infantry to hold the bridge they'd captured. He pictured the map in his head. The Surian Bridge was the southernmost.

"Where are you going?" asked the apparent leader of the southbound group to the other squad commander.

"To reinforce the Axern bridge, so that our cavalry can find and engage the Serikothi."

Tarkothi cavalry wouldn't stand a chance against Serikothi cavaliers, all things being equal; but it was night, and this was their home territory. He waited for the troops to head their own way, and then worked his way south. More shouts carried from across the river.

Koryn sighed. Elrayn wanted to unite their nations—a noble goal, if he wasn't using underhanded measures to secure power for himself—and now he'd widened the gulf between their people. The war hawks in Serikoth, emboldened by Koryn's own successes against Bovyan incursions, were chomping at the bit to renew open hostilities. They'd use this as an excuse.

And maybe a little part of Koryn needed it. The war effort might keep him from dwelling on forbidden lovers and marriage.

No. This kind of selfish thinking made him no better than Elrayn. Maybe worse, since Elrayn truly thought he had the best interests of Solaris' Chosen at heart. Like Koryn, he'd risked himself to save two children. For now, he needed to get back across to the Serikothi side and discuss the best course of action with councilors.

Before long, he came to the Drakon Bridge. Tarkothi soldiers had formed an infantry square in the middle, pikes pointing toward both sides. Koryn chewed on the inside of his cheek. Even his cavaliers might have a hard time breaking through the fortified bottleneck.

He continued south, occasionally ducking into side streets or joining groups of refugees to avoid patrols. Hopefully, Damaryn still held the Surian Bridge.

In the distance, a single set of thundering horse hooves grew louder. He turned in the direction and squinted into the darkness.

The horse drew closer. Cavaliers would travel in groups in enemy territory, so this rider must be Tarkothi. Probably searching for him.

Curse the damn dress. He should've taken one of the dead Tarkothi's uniforms. He hadn't wanted to waste the time trying to lower the body from where it was pinned to the wall, then stripping off its clothes. Now, though, it would've saved him time in getting across the bridge. He ran into a side street.

The rider turned to follow.

Damn it! Koryn drew his sword. It wasn't as well-balanced as Sunblade, which didn't bode well against a mounted warrior. He sank into his stance, and took the weapon in two hands. Though Serikothi rules of engagement didn't typically target horses, there wasn't much of a choice now. He cocked back, ready to jump to the side and hack at the beast's legs as it cantered by.

The rider reined in his mount a few feet away. It looked to be not one, but two people in the saddle.

One of them jumped off and approached. He was just a silhouette, but he didn't reach for a weapon. Koryn relaxed. Had the man wanted to attack, he would've stayed on the horse.

He squinted. Was that…?

"Your Highness!"

Damaryn's voice washed over him.

The tension fled from Koryn's shoulders. He lowered his blade.

Damaryn wrapped him in a warm embrace. The scent of his golden hair was so reassuring. "Bronze is at the stables."

Another wave of relief washed over Koryn. He looked up to see the other rider, who slipped off the horse, and appeared to be short. Not as short as a Madaeri or dwarf, but…

"You!" he said, disentangling himself from Damaryn's hug. "Prince Aryn's pet half-elf."

"Why does everyone keep calling me that?" The girl dipped into a curtsey. "My name is Jyeh."

"She helped me find you," Damaryn said. "She explained how, and I can't say it made sense…but here you are."

"I'd be curious to hear how." Koryn peered at her.

Jie's grin wasn't visible in the dark, but it carried in her tone. "All evidence I've seen suggests you are reckless, and that you don't think before acting. I figured you would try to get back to Elbahia immediately, instead of the smarter option of waiting for the Tarkothi to assume you'd made a clean escape. That would put you on this road, looking for a way to cross. The rest… Well, your dress has a distinct smell."

Frowning, Koryn started to speak.

Damaryn let out a laugh. “You look good in it, Your Highness.”

Heat rushed to his cheeks. Koryn studied the girl. In the dark, it was hard to see much more than her general shape. “Aren’t you on Tarkoth’s side?”

“No.” She shook her head. “I was just hitching a ride from Cathay on the *Indomitable*, and Prince Aryn made the trip enjoyable.”

Maybe she was trying to lull them into a false sense of security. Now that she’d found him, who knew what her intentions were? “Why? Where are you going?”

“Into the Teleri Empire.”

Koryn’s jaw dropped. “Whatever for?”

“I have my reasons.”

“Why are you helping us?” he asked.

“My reasons align with yours. Right now, the Teleri Empire is trying to bait your countries into war.”

Given the evidence at the outpost, it made sense. Maybe war would help Koryn ignore his miserable existence, but maybe that would just be falling into the Bovyans’ trap. He peered at her. “Just who are you?”

“It’s a long story, too long to tell now. You need to come with me.”

“Where?”

The half-elf pointed over the river. “To the Tarkothi royal villa.”

Koryn coughed. The half-elf was insane, or perhaps trying to trick him.

Damaryn interposed himself between them. "Absolutely not. The only place the prince is going is into Serikoth."

"Too much is at stake. Your sister, Princess Alaena, is missing. I think taken by Aryn's aide, Peris..."

Koryn's grip tightened on the sword hilt.

"Without Aryn's knowledge," Jie hastily added. "I'm sure Peris is a Teleri agent. I think his brother Tharos might've captured Princess Karyna, as well."

"They're both big, but too small to be Bovyans." Koryn shook his head. Tharos was a forger, not a shocktrooper.

"That's what I thought, too. But in the last month, I've seen a total of six similar operatives. That includes the one that tried to kill you, whose dress you wear now."

Koryn closed his eyes and thought back to the bathhouse. The man had been big, similar in size to Peris and Tharos. "Say you are right. What do I have to gain by going to the Tarkothi?"

"You can stop this war." Jie sucked on her lower lip, looking at him expectantly.

"It was Prince Elrayn who brought it on himself, by kidnapping me."

"And I helped find you. I could've left you alone, desperate and wandering. Eventually, the Tarkothi would've caught you." Jie snorted. "In a dress. Which makes you look fat."

Damaryn's lips quirked, but Koryn frowned.

Jie ignored both. "If not for peace, at least Serikoth and Tarkoth must work together to save both of their princesses."

Koryn looked to Damaryn, who was shaking his head. Koryn sighed. For the sake of both Korynth and Serikoth, they needed to rescue Alaena. And while Elrayn wanted to marry off Karyna, and Koryn had no interest in wedding her, he bore her no ill will for something that wasn't even her choice. For Solaris' sake, they'd even planned to use magic on her. On the both of them. They were both victims. He nodded to Damaryn. "I will think about it. If I go to the Tarkothi, it won't be without protection. Where are the rest of the cavaliers? Why aren't they with you?"

Damaryn gestured toward Jie. "She suggested we go alone, so as not to draw too much attention. I told Captain Floryn to hold the Surian Bridge."

The half-elf was proving to be smart and resourceful. It almost made her wild stories believable. Still, they only had one horse. Koryn nodded. "Ride ahead and tell them to prepare for my arrival. Send them to our barracks and have them deploy our soldiers around the Tarkothi royal villa."

"No!" Jie and Damaryn said in unison.

"Your Highness," Damaryn said. "You take the horse with Jie. We can't risk you falling into their hands. I'll find my way back."

Koryn shook his head. "I can't risk you, either."

"It's not far." Jie pointed south. "You can send a rider back for him."

"Go." Damaryn offered the reins. "Before I regret my words."

Koryn stared at them and shook his head.

Jie threw up her hands. "If you wait any longer, the orc gods are going to return on their flaming chariots."

"All right." Koryn took the reins and started to swing into the saddle.

"Wait." Jie held out a tunic and a pair of breeches. "This outfit is more complimentary of your figure."

Koryn smirked. He pulled the pants on, and with no fanfare, he pulled the dress over his head.

Jie *tsk*ed. "You'll wrinkle it that way."

"I planned on burning it." Korn donned the tunic and buttoned the front. Swinging into the saddle, he offered a hand to the half-elf. He could've sworn he heard her gulp, but she took his hand, and he pulled her up behind him. With a nod to Damaryn, he spurred the horse into a gallop.

"Heavens," she muttered, arms wrapped tight about him, her body stiff. "We're in a rush, but do we need to go this fast?"

Apparently, she wasn't good at everything. Koryn just snorted. They dashed past a group of yelling and gesticulating Tarkothi and soon reached the bridge. Bauble lamps lit the standoff in front of them: a line of Tarkothi foot soldiers had set pikes facing the cavaliers on the Elbahia side of the span. The cavaliers had their bows drawn. There didn't appear to be any crossbowmen on the Tarkothi side; at least not yet.

He looked over his shoulder. "Are you ready?"

She gulped again, but nodded.

Koryn spurred the horse. With the pikemen facing in the opposite direction, the horse crashed through their line with ease and galloped on. If the Tarkothi had tried to attack his back, they didn't seem to have hit anything. He looked over his shoulder again.

Jie was wringing her hand.

"What's wrong?"

"I just saved you from a spear in the back."

With her bare hand... She was either lying, or was far more than just Prince Aryn's bedmate. Koryn turned to face the gathered cavaliers. He slowed the horse to a stop.

"Your Highness!" the cavaliers said in unison.

Koryn cleared his throat and stood in his stirrups. "Cavaliers, send word to all soldiers in and around the area: I want squads of a hundred men to hold the bridges to prevent the Tarkothi from crossing. The cavaliers will disarm any Tarkothi soldiers on Elbahia Island. Neutralize any who resist, using whatever measures. The rest of our troops will converge on the Tarkothi royal villa. The rest of you, on me. We are going to disperse their position at the head of this bridge to open a path for Captain Damaryn. On my mark, two volleys, then charge."

The cavaliers all crossed their fists and drew their bows.

"Wait," Jie said, slipping off the horse as if her life depended on it. "What about coming with me to the Tarkothi royal villa?"

Koryn shook his head. "I said I will think about it, and only when I have it surrounded and can negotiate from a position of strength."

"We don't have time. Alaena doesn't have time."

"I don't trust Prince Elrayn."

Jie looked up at him with puppy dog eyes. "What about Prince Aryn?"

Koryn chewed on his inner cheek. Aryn had been more honorable than Elrayn, and seemed to object to the forced marriage, but he hadn't tried to stop his brother's machinations. Still… "I am going to recover Captain Damaryn, and I am going to follow through with my plan. However, I will consider meeting with Prince Aryn on a neutral site. Elbahia Palace."

"I need proof of your offer to parlay. Your signet ring." Jie held her little hand out.

"Why do I have a bad feeling about this?" He slid his ring off, leaned down, and pressed it into her palm. "I'll get you a horse."

In the soft white light of the bauble lanterns, Jie's honey-toned complexion paled. She shook her head. "That's okay. I'll just run." With that, she turned and slipped deftly through the ranks of cavaliers.

He looked toward Elbahia Palace, where he'd go after he retrieved Damaryn. Then he gasped. The Light of Solaris no longer shined atop its dome. Elrayn must've retrieved it, in preparation for war.

CHAPTER 28:

Misgivings

Jie sprinted as fast as her short legs would carry her. As tired as the run would leave her, she and horses didn't get along. The flood of Tarkothi refugees had slowed to a trickle, and the dark windows in all the rowhouses this early at night suggested many had already fled. If the island were to become a battleground, at least there wouldn't be many innocents caught in the crossfire.

Though it had been visible earlier from every part of the island she'd visited, the Light of Solaris no longer sparkled from its spot atop the dome of Elbahia Palace. With hostilities already flaring, no doubt the Tarkothi had retrieved it. What had Aryn said? That no Eldaeri army with the Light glowing at its head had ever lost a battle? Jie redoubled her pace.

After two turns, she had almost reached the Tarkothi royal villa. All the lights were on, and the compound was a beehive of activity as runners came and went. She skidded to a stop.

To catch her breath, of course. Not because she dreaded revealing her identity to Aryn. No, it was to catch her breath. A pit formed in her stomach.

Squaring her shoulders, she strode toward the main gates. Several soldiers hurried about the courtyard.

"Stop," a royal guard said, holding up his hand. "You aren't allowed here."

"I'm here to see Prince Aryn."

He afforded her a disdainful glance. "He is busy."

"I have information about the Serikothi Prince Koryn." She produced the signet ring.

He didn't even look. "Right, and I know where the Eye of Tivar is buried."

She held the ring up, but he looked past her.

Using a *Mockingbird's Deception* to imitate Prince Aryn, and a *Ghost Echo* to throw her voice behind him, she said, "Let her through."

Wide-eyed, the guard turned around.

Jie slipped behind him, then stayed in his blind spots as he twisted and turned, until he assumed she'd left and resumed his post. She glanced about the courtyard, where nobody else had seemed to have noticed her as they rushed to and from the mansion.

Using a messenger to shield herself from view, she went along to the side of the building, where she'd left a window open that afternoon. On the ground lay the twisted remains of a cushioned chair among shards of glass. She looked up.

Her window was now closed, but the one beside it had been shattered. She crept to a spot right under it, took off her shoes, and held them between her teeth. Rubbing her hands together, she started her ascent, her fingers and toes finding purchase along the uneven surface of the granite blocks. Not far up, she came to spikes lodged into the mortar, the kind used by the Black Lotus to aid in climbs or descents when there was time to prepare for a quick escape. They were spaced for someone much taller, held her weight with ease, and made the climb easy enough for a young Black Lotus novice to do with their eyes closed.

She paused to the side of the broken window. Smudges of coppery blood went all the way to the roof. What looked to be a dress for a large woman fluttered there, looking blue in the Blue Moon's light. With the spikes left in the wall as evidence, a Nightblade must've been here.

Nobody was inside the room. Taking her shoes, she brushed the glass shards off the windowsill, then gingerly worked her way inside.

In an otherwise sumptuous room fit for royalty, the double doors lay open, the lock mangled. Someone large had left an impression on the fluffy covers of the bed. A manly scent—Tharos' from before—clung to it. She looked under the bed, right under that spot, and pulled out a black utility suit like the Black Lotus would wear, only much larger.

Nightblade size.

She searched its hidden pockets, and came away with six throwing stars, a set of lockpicks, and a line of thin rope.

With that blue dress, the Nightblade must've been disguised as Princess Karyna, likely using an illusion bauble. He'd been in too much of a rush to change out of his dress when he fled. He'd thrown the chair through the window, then climbed up to the roof, so as not to be seen when his pursuers came to the window and invariably looked down. From there was anyone's guess, but he'd been gone long enough for his blood to have dried.

She crept to her guest room, and was happy to find her travelling trunk there. She picked the lock and opened it. Her own stealth suit and weapons were still inside the false bottom. Grinning in spite of herself, she retrieved her magically sharp knife and strapped its sheath to the inside of her thigh. Then she stashed the logbook from the *Intimidator* in the chest, though it now looked like it was no longer needed.

It was time to find Aryn. Swallowing hard, she crept toward the doors, the plush carpet making it easy to move silently, but froze in front of the make-up table's mirror.

Axle grease from the two carriage rides streaked her face and stuck to her hair. Dirt and grime covered her torn shirt and pants. No wonder the royal guard had turned her away. If Aryn saw her like this... She did her best to smooth her clothes out, but trying to rub the oil out of her face only smeared it more.

There was a whole wardrobe here, and probably even a vanity with a wash basin, but that would waste too much time. With a sigh, she headed toward the sound of Elrayn's voice of command, down in great dining hall. Aryn's voice, too, echoed.

She descended the grand staircase into the foyer. The messengers paid her no heed.

The chamberlain, however, stared at her, aghast. "You! What are you doing here?"

"I'm Jie. I came here with Prince Aryn, remember?" She dipped into a curtsey, even if the oversized pants made it awkward.

The chamberlain's lips rounded into a circle. "He had us looking all over for you. All we found was your dress. You are filthy! Where have you been?"

He wouldn't believe her, even if she told him the truth. "I would like a word with him, to let him know I am okay."

"As you can tell, he's busy." The chamberlain gestured to all the activity. "I'll let him know, though."

Jie strode past him, slipping out of his attempts to grab her.

"Stop!" He took off after her. "Someone, stop her!"

She made it to the arched entrance to the grand hallway, and paused. Telling what she knew would lead to questions, which in turn would inevitably lead to *the* question of her identity. The one thing she never wanted to let Aryn know, since he would think only the worst of her.

Instead, she could let things play out. A conflict between Tarkoth and Serikoth didn't concern her, or Cathay. In fact, as the prince of Cathay had told her, more hostilities would create a larger market for firepowder and cannons.

The chamberlain had just about caught up with her. All she had to do...

No. Nightblades were involved, and they were key to her mission. Maybe she could follow their trail. If only she could go to Cathay's trade office to recruit Black Lotus brothers and sisters to help—but there wasn't enough time. She avoided the chamberlain's grab again and strode into the room.

"Prince Aryn," she called.

Several sets of eyes turned to her, though the naval lieutenant wasn't among them.

Aryn's included. He beamed.

Jie's heart fluttered like butterfly wings. Heavens, when did she even start to think like that?

"I'm sorry, Your Highness," the chamberlain said, bowing several times, and still missing every attempt to seize her. "I couldn't stop her. She's quite slippery."

Waving a dismissive hand, Aryn stood and strode over, leaving Elrayn with a finger in the air and mouth agape.

The chamberlain gave up trying to contain her and shuffled back.

Every step brought him closer, and all her Black Fist skills melted away. She shrank bank. Everything they'd shared over the past month, she was about to throw to the wind.

Aryn smiled that oh-so-charming smile, the one which made her insides turn to jelly. "You're so...dirty. Where have you been?"

Banishing the butterflies in her gut, lest she lose all resolve, she straightened. "Prince Aryn, I need a word with you, in private."

"Oh?" His suggestive grin chipped away at her resolve. He looked back at Elrayn, hesitated, then took her hand.

His hand felt right in hers. She turned around and guided him back to the entry foyer, toward the grand staircase.

"I was just joking." His expression turned serious. He looked up to the second floor. "I really don't have time for that."

"No...there's something important I have to tell you. About Peris."

His brows furrowed. "You know?"

"Probably more than you. I'm guessing you think Peris and Karyna are running away together, with Tharos' help."

His mouth hung agape. "How did you find out?"

"It's what they want you to believe."

"That isn't the case?" Now his forehead scrunched up. It was just too cute.

She shook her head before her resolve faltered. "Follow me." She tugged him up the steps, to the room she'd entered.

He pointed to the Nightblade's utility suit on the bed. "Where did that come from?"

"It was under the bed."

"What possessed you to look under the bed?"

Several excuses almost came to her tongue, but instead, she motioned to the indentation in the blanket. "I would guess that Tharos sat there, and those clothes belong to him."

Aryn's eyes were wide with disbelief. "How could you know that?"

"The size of the indentation suggests a man of a two hundred *jin*...a hundred kilograms by your standards."

"How did you know it was Tharos? That could be anyone."

She nodded and guided him to the window. "If you look carefully down, you will see several spikes set at distances made for a large man. If you look up, you'll see blood stains leading to a dress. He was in a hurry to escape, and misled his pursuers by climbing up instead of down."

If her first deduction surprised him, now he looked to be in shock. "Still...how do you know it was Tharos?"

There was no way of explaining without revealing more of the truth. "I knew he was going to pick up Princess Karyna and bring her here. I would surmise that instead, he dropped her off to rendezvous with Peris."

Aryn's head bobbed in slow nods. "Go on."

"Tharos pretended to be Karyna, using some kind of magic bauble." Just like the one she'd used to impersonate her homeland's princess and infiltrate a rebel lord's compound. With Aksumi sorcerers involved, it could explain how so many people would confuse a hulking man like Tharos with an Eldaeri princess.

Aryn's eyes, wide until now, narrowed. "How can you possibly know all of this?"

Her next words would raise even more suspicions. She hung her head. "I overheard you. Both at the Korynthi villa, and then at the guest house on the Tarkothi side of the river, where Prince Elrayn was holding Prince Koryn." She looked up and searched his eyes.

His face paled. "It just isn't possible for you to be in those places, and to know all of this."

What she planned to say would raise yet more questions. "I saw Peris leave a letter for Princess Alaena in her carriage, right before she arrived. I hid among the undercarriage luggage back to the Korynthi villa. When I saw you there, I rode beneath your carriage back across the river to the guest house."

Now, Aryn's lips twisted into a snarl. "Who are you? Don't tell me your father worked on cadavers."

"Well, that part is true." She sucked on her lower lip, then let it go as his expression darkened more. "I work for the Emperor of Cathay. I've been sent here to track down those responsible for the assassination of two of our lords, as well as the traitor who trained them."

His shoulders slumped. "And me? Was I just part of your mission?"

No, she wanted to scream. She looked down at her feet. "The Teleri are trying to bait Tarkoth and Serikoth into war. That much is obvious. Peris could have killed you and Karyna, and Tharos could have killed Prince Elrayn at any time over the last decade. They only decided to kill Prince Koryn when the Mystic Illusionist arrived, to recreate his image and infuse a bauble with it. I suspect they will kill Princess Karyna, and blame it on Princess Alaena."

Expression tight, Aryn sat on the bed. Was that a tear in his eye? "Say all of this is true. How can we stop it?"

"Prince Koryn wishes to meet with you, and only you. I told him he can trust you." Jie produced Prince Koryn's signet ring and held it up.

He just stared at the ring, then at her. The silence bore down on her like a dwarf anvil.

"You found him?" he said at last, all warmth gone from his voice. His expression steeled.

She nodded. "Yes. I helped reunite him with his own people, but now they are preparing to assail this villa. If that happens, there is no avoiding an escalation into war. Let's meet with him, before it's too late for your nations. Before it is too late for Karyna and Alaena."

"How do I know you aren't working for an enemy?" Aryn's had strayed to his sword.

He wouldn't stand a chance, no matter how good a swordsman. Not with the throwing stars she'd recovered from Tharos' suit. Question was, could she really bring herself to harm him?

A pained expression crossed his face as his grip tightened on his sword.

CHAPTER 29:

Tides of War

Sword in one hand and bauble lantern in another, Aelward sprinted toward the docks with the dozen Tarkothi royal guards behind him. He'd finally convinced Elrayn to let him leave, to let him seize the Serikothi ships in port and get the *Sea Dragon* to blockade the mouth of the harbor.

Keeping to the Tarkothi side of Elbahia Island, they ran through the mostly deserted streets. About halfway to the quays, a group of about twenty soldiers passed in front of him at an intersection.

Aelward squinted, trying to make out the colors of their uniform in the full Blue Moon light. They looked green enough. Waving, he yelled, "Avast, men of Tarkoth. I am Lieutenant Aelward Niromar, of the Tarkothi Royal Navy. Under orders of Crown Prince Elrayn, ye are to join me in securing the docks."

The men slowed to a stop, peered through the darkness, and after a few seconds, crossed their fists and bowed their heads. They carried repeating crossbows and swords, which would help soften enemy lines. Still, what he really need were marines who knew about storming ships, especially if the Serikothi ship captains were also preparing for hostilities.

He clenched his jaw. Alaena was Serikothi by birth. Royalty. And now she was missing, no telling where she or her loyalties lay. No matter what, he hoped she was safe, and wouldn't be caught in the crossfire.

His makeshift battalion picked up three more squads of soldiers and a pair of cavalrymen by the time they reached the canal demarcating the neutral ground north of the port, swelling his numbers to almost a hundred. With him inexplicably in charge. Again. At least when he took command of the *Sea Dragon*, he'd been through the Tarkothi Royal Naval Academy, and knew ship tactics. Ground troops were another story, and they now looked at the bridges that crossed the canals with worried expressions.

Aelward sent one rider ahead to scout the docks, and the other to range onto the Serikothi side of the island. He then raised his sword and turned around to face his troops. "Soldiers of Tarkoth! We are about to cross into neutral ground. Make no mistake, the Serikothi have already done so. They know control of the shipping lanes to Elbahia is essential to victory."

The soldiers remained quiet, all eyes locked on him in rapt attention. A quarter were Eldaeri, and most were young and wide-eyed.

It felt dishonest to speculate with no proof, but these men didn't know him, didn't know if he was worth following. Maybe he wasn't. He swept his gaze over the entire group. "With that victory, the Serikothi would seek to impose their social order, where all are subservient to Solaris' Chosen. I tell you, we will not go back to those days. We fought a civil war to ensure that here, in Tarkoth, we value hard work and merit over circumstances of birth. Are you with me?"

The soldiers broke into cheers and thumped their fists to their chests, as the fabled legionnaires of the defunct Arkothi Empire would have. The way the Bovyans now did. Only, the former would've been armed with Rune-inscribed weapons and armor...

He gave a single nod, and they fell silent. "We come from different units, even different services. Indeed, I will need to break up our crossbowmen into three groups. But we will show the Serikothi how professional we are, show that even though we have never fought together before this night, we will still fight as one. Five fingers..." He raised an open hand and closed it into a fist.

The men cheered again.

"Stay with your squadrons as you cross the bridge. I will be waiting on the other side to divide you into new groups." Head high and shoulders squared, Aelward raised his sword and marched across the bridge, hoping he looked more confident than he felt.

On the other side, he turned around. The bridge was wide enough for eight to walk abreast, and they formed up in orderly ranks, spearmen in front and crossbowmen in back. He kept their groups together as best he could, but recruited twenty crossbowmen to join the royal guards. In the end, there were three small divisions of about thirty men. He assembled the officers around him.

One of the riders returned on galloping hooves. "Sir, all ships are still moored and anchored. At least fifty Serikothi marines have set up a perimeter around the *Intimidator* and *Solaris' Spear*.

Fifty. Aelward pictured the docks in his head. The Serikothi ships were at the two docks on the west end of the port. Marines would've formed an arc of two ranks, crossbowmen at the back, men with cutlasses at the front.

Still, a ship the *Intimidator's* size could carry a complement of two hundred marines; *Solaris' Spear* a hundred. Assuming as many as three-quarters were on shore leave, that left at least twenty to thirty more...and possibly up to another hundred. They probably had the same idea of capturing enemy ships.

Five Tarkothi ships, ripe for the plucking. Aelward looked back up at the rider. "Return to our side of the port. Go to each of our ships and have their marines defend the head of the docks and prepare to join us when we arrive, while the remaining sailors pull up the gangplanks. The *Indomitable's* cannon crews will target the aft portside gun at the *Intimidator*, and its stern portside gun at the Serikothi marines' position, and prepare to fire on my command. Other ships will point their prow guns at the harborside avenue and give any Serikothi threat a whiff of grapeshot. If none come, they will arc fire over the ships in front of them and into the Serikothi marine position."

The rider crossed his fists and bowed, then spurred his horse back toward the docks. If only the other rider scouting out Serikothi troop movements in the west had returned. Still, there was no time to waste.

A plan from a naval battle during the Pirate Wars came to mind, though he'd be executing it with men instead of ships. It might even be easier, since tides, currents, and wind wouldn't factor in. Aelward turned back to the assembled officers and motioned with his hands. "Alpha group will deploy to the center. On my command, all our crossbowmen will shoot into the enemy marines, to be joined by cannon fire from the *Indomitable*. Bravo Group, you will deploy north of the west side of the docks and hold off Serikothi reinforcements. If none come, your crossbow corps will join in the volley fire at enemy marines. The royal guard and any Tarkothi marines we recruit will march west up the harborside avenue. Any recommendations?"

"We don't usually fight in such small groups," an older captain said. "But I think this will work, given the size of the enemy."

"Brilliant idea, using the cannons." A royal guard lieutenant crossed his fists and bowed his head.

"Then we are in agreement." Aelward pointed his sword toward the port. "The *Indomitable's* first shot will be our signal to commence."

"Yes, sir!" the officers all shouted in unison.

Did they believe him? Did he believe in himself? He watched as Bravo group marched west, toward the Serikothi side of the island. Without a scouting report, he might very well be sending them into danger. Alpha group followed, though their task wouldn't be as risky. He raised his sword and signaled the royal guard into a march, with him at the head.

They encountered no resistance when they reached the Tarkothi side of the docks. Tarkothi marines from all four ships, perhaps forty strong, had formed an arcing line from the *Sea Dragon* at the east end to the *Indomitable* closer to the center. They all saluted with crossed fists as he passed, on his way to the *Indomitable*.

Its black hull loomed above, and even in the darkness the storied legacy of the five-masted beauty sent a chill up his spine. Just a few empty berths down, the *Intimidator* mirrored it. The epitome of shipbuilding, both vessels had led the Eldaeri conquest of coastal Arkoth nearly three hundred years before. Sailors and officers from both nations revered the *Intimidator*-class ships.

Now they might be firing on each other, for the first time since the civil war. If only dockworkers and tugs were around to help get the ships into the harbor where they could maneuver. Ordering the royal guards to halt, he climbed the *Indomitable's* gangplank to the deck, and up to the quarterdeck.

The famous Captain Suryn was peering through a scope at the *Intimidator.* Middle aged, with sea-wrinkled skin, he had a strong nose for an Eldaeri. He'd commanded the king's flagship during the Pirate Wars.

Aelward's heart raced. Though in command of this expeditionary force, he felt nothing but utter awe; and on a ship, he was subordinate to a captain anyway. He crossed his fists and bowed his head.

The captain turned and nodded, allowing Aelward out of his salute. "Lieutenant Aelward, is it? I heard about your maneuver to evade the pirates. Quite creative, even if it caused damage to your ship. Now, I hear you want me to fire on the *Intimidator*?"

Was that a compliment? Aelward bowed his head. His entire plan relied on the *Indomitable* firing on enemy marines. "Captain, by order of Crown Prince Elrayn, I've been put in command of the operation to control the port. I hope we won't come to blows."

"Look." The captain passed him the scope.

With a bow of his head, Aelward received it and peered at the Serikothi *Intimidator.* Its aft starboard cannon faced the *Indomitable*, while its prow starboard cannon was aimed at the massing Tarkothi royal guards and marines. Its own marines stood along the starboard, repeaters facing out. At least he hadn't lied when he told his soldiers that the Serikothi had taken up arms.

"It looks like someone in Serikoth had the same brilliant idea," Captain Suryn said.

Was that sarcasm? Aelward shifted the scope to scan the Serikothi marines on the ground. They'd shifted their formation to concentrate crossbow volleys forward. Unlike the fifty the rider reported, there looked to be over a hundred now. Both sides were evenly matched. He lowered the scope. To engage would lead to dozens, perhaps hundreds, of casualties. "What do you recommend?"

The captain offered a wry smile. "I see you wanted to translate the Battle of Bella Isla to the ground. A good idea, in theory, but reliant on a surprise attack on the enemy's rear."

Aelward nodded. There was his wild card. "I have two squads totaling sixty men, ready to fall on the Serikothi rear and flank."

"You have a good head on your shoulders, Lieutenant. Now, how about your heart? Are you willing to sacrifice men to control this port?"

Aelward tugged at his collar. A seasoned, celebrated veteran, Captain Suryn was famous for his bold decisions. Yet here, he was advising caution.

Images of the *Sea Dragon's* captain's charred remains after the pirate attack flashed in his memory. Of course, the stakes were too high, with little reward. Even if they managed to capture both Serikothi ships and control the port, Prince Elrayn's original goal was an alliance. If that came to fruition...even if they ended up in a position of greater strength, they'd probably have to return the ships. The men would've been sacrificed in vain. He let out a sigh. "We will execute my plan only if the enemy attacks f—"

A cannon roared from the *Intimidator.* A flash lit the night. The clicks and twangs of repeaters set a deadly rhythm. Yells and screams erupted. Aelward turned to look.

The shot had landed in the royal guard's position. Now, crossbow bolts were raining down. In the distance, from behind the Serikothi lines, Tarkoth's own crossbowmen started shooting. No doubt they'd heard the cannon shot.

"Fire stern cannon!" Aelward yelled.

The *Indomitable's* cannon crew stared, looking to the captain.

Captain Suryn nodded. "Fire stern cannon."

The gunner pulled the cannon's gunlock. The discharge roared. The gun jerked back in its mount.

The targeting officer lowered his scope. "A hit into the third rank of Serikothi marines. Two degrees down, one degree to port."

Two members of the crew turned two different cranks, adjusting the angle of the stern cannon barrel. Another member packed the firepowder charge, followed by a fourth man loading the cannonball. Lastly, with the help of internal springs, the entire team slid the cannon forward along the bearings in its mount.

Aelward crossed his fists and bowed his head. "Captain, I must take charge of the ground forces. Please focus fire toward the rear of the Serikothi position."

The captain nodded. "May the Light of Solaris guide you."

Waving smoke out of his eyes, Aelward rushed down the gangplank. Two royal guards joined him and helped clear a path on their way to the Tarkothi vanguard. All around him, men lay screaming, some crying for their mothers, most with crossbow bolts protruding from their bodies. At least one soldier had lost his leg, white bone sticking out just below his knee. His own crossbowmen were arcing shots over the front.

Blood slicked the pavement, and the coppery stench filled Aelward's nostrils. He gritted his teeth as he picked his way through wavering marines. His belly roiled, but he swallowed the gore down. Up ahead, it appeared as if the royal guards were pressing forward. The gap between them and the marines widened.

Another cannon roared from the *Intimidator*, and was answered by the *Indomitable.* For now, they weren't firing on each other, only into the soldiers on land. A series of bursts came from behind him, a salvo from the other Tarkothi ships on the far side of the docks. Unlike the larger *Intimidator*-class ships, the smaller vessels only had a single gun toward the front and back, but least they were able to participate in the bombardment.

"On me, marines of Tarkoth!" Aelward raised his sword, even as a crossbow bolt whizzed right by his head. Had he been just a foot to the left, it would have hit him in the face. He kept pushing through the retreating men toward the front. "Come on, sea dogs, don't let those scrawny royal guards win the day! On me, marines!"

A cheer rose up. Faltering marines halted in their retreat, turned, and pressed forward.

Where the front line had been, a dozen men, both Tarkothi royal guard and marines from both sides, lay unmoving. Blood-smeared pavestones were cracked where enemy cannonballs had skittered across them. Aelward pushed to the fore until he came to the rear of the royal guards. Up front, swords clashed. Though crossbows clicked and twanged from both the front and rear, no bolts rained down on the center.

"Men of Tarkoth, on me!" Aelward shoved his way to the front. A cutlass slashed at his head, but he sidestepped and ran his sword through a young, wide-eyed Serikothi marine. He snatched the man's cutlass away and wielded it in his left hand. More came, and he hacked and slashed, carving into their lines.

On his sides, royal guards, protected by steel helms and cuirasses, pressed back the Serikothi ranks. Tarkothi marines pushed through, taking advantage of the larger frames conferred by Arkothi blood over the smaller Serikothi Eldaeri. Out of breath, Aelward fell back and let the guards behind him take the lead. The sound of crossbows slowed.

Horns blared from the *Intimidator*.

"Fall back, fall back!" a Serikothi called.

The enemy's rear lines turned and ran, while the front lines backed away.

Aelward looked to his side, where his Alpha group cheered and saluted him as he passed.

"Onward," he yelled. "Push them back to their docks."

Cheering, men hurried to obey his commands. The battle was close to decided.

In the midst of the chaos, a Serikothi soldier ran forward through the onslaught, waving a flag of parley high.

Aelward raised a hand to call off the crossbowmen.

The enemy crossed his fists and bowed. "Sir, our captain wishes to discuss terms of surrender."

His own royal guards and marines broke out into a cheer, but Aelward silenced them. "I will meet with him."

The messenger bowed again, and ran back the way he'd come.

Aelward turned to one of his men. "Bring a chair."

With cross-fist salute, the soldier turned and ran through the Tarkothi ranks.

Presently, a Serikothi naval officer, insignias marking him as a captain, came forward with a retinue of marines surrounding him. His eyes flicked to the Tarkothi group, pausing on the non-Eldaeri. His lip turned into a curl.

Mauls and Maelstroms, such arrogance! Aelward strode forward, crossed his fists and bowed as naval discipline demanded.

The Serikothi captain looked past him at first, before meeting his eyes. "I demand to speak to your ranking officer."

"I'm Lieutenant Aelward. Tarkoth's Crown Prince Elrayn named me commander for this operation."

"Very well, Lieutenant. I am here to discuss the terms of your surrender."

Tides and Tempests, surrender? Heat flared in Aelward's head. "Captain, you don't seem to understand the circumstances. My men hold the field. Yours are holed up in your ships. I am here to receive your sword."

The captain smirked. "I guess news has not reached you yet. We have your Crown Prince surrounded at your royal villa. If you don't surrender, we'll burn it to the ground, with him inside."

Tempting, but.... Aelward laughed. "It's made of stone and blockwood. The only thing that will burn is some of the heinous artwork inside."

The captain's lips pursed for a second. "In any case, I am told our soldiers are ready to breach the villa walls. Send a messenger to the royal villa to confirm what I have said, and when you have heard the truth, be prepared to surrender your ships and swords."

Aelward turned to one of the royal guards. "Go find out if it is true."

With a cross-fist salute, the soldier ran north.

Aelward watched him go, but then his gaze locked on Elbahia Palace. Its dome gleamed in the moonlight, but... "The Light of Solaris... It's gone."

The enemy captain followed his gaze. His jaw dropped.

Had Elrayn sent someone to retrieve it? Or had the Serikothi stolen it? If held at the head of an army, they'd never lose. At least, that was what the legends said.

A suspicion sank in his stomach. Where had Tharos gone after his escape from the Tarkothi villa? To join Peris and Karyna? And where was Alaena?

CHAPTER 30:

Depths of Hell

With heat still blaring in the aftermath of the explosion, Tomas looked up at the dome. The rays of sunlight shifted as the windows warped under the groaning weight of the Golden Bowl outside. The gods only knew if the temple would collapse or not. Maybe a Diviner would know, too, but Tomas never was one, despite what he led others to believe.

His future would be cut short if he didn't get out, but how?

By the time he jumped back on the ledge, the window he was reaching for might be distorted too much for him to fit through. He looked to the entrance.

While the opening had been too small for him to fit through before, the shift of the bowl above had pulled some of the exterior metal columns away. Maybe he could squeeze through. He sprinted over, still blinking his eye to try to clear the afterimage.

The hole looked just large enough. Taking a deep breath, he got down on his stomach and started toward it.

A column groaned and fell.

Tomas' vision flashed red. Sabine issued a warning that made it through the pounding of his heart in his ears. He scuttled back. It crashed down outside, right where his head would've been had he wriggled through.

Pushing himself back to his feet, he looked around. Up above, the dome creaked, its concave shape bowing inward. The supporting columns on one side creaked as they warped. The temple was collapsing, with no way out.

Except for the shaft.

The one which had just belched fire, and might still be burning.

Still, with no other option, Tomas ran over and looked down.

The demon eye cast the shaft in dark greys, which faded to black not more than fifteen *pedes* down. Still, there'd been more doors down there. Above him, the dome flexed with a long, ear-piercing screech. All the jewels would be buried beneath the rubble.

Then again, a dead man couldn't enjoy his wealth. He raised the hem of the robe and tied it about his waist again. Careful not to dislodge another of the gems on his sleeve, he grasped the handle, stepped into the shaft, and shimmied along the rim to the ladder.

The creaks and groans in the main chamber grew louder. He started his climb down. Like the day before, when Sabine had helped him see a path up the mountain, she now contrasted the colors between the rungs and the wall. Maybe this would lead to another way out.

One foot after the other, he descended. The knotted hem of the robe started to loosen. If it came free and sank past his feet, he'd undoubtedly trip and plummet twelve seconds—two thousand *pedes*—to the bottom of the chute. Every now and then, he'd pass a set of double doors, but there wasn't enough space on the narrow ledge lining the walls to let go of the handles and pry them open.

Though easier than climbing up the cliff face, his arms and bare toes started to ache and his lungs burned. Made for the shorter, stockier orcs, the rungs were wider in width, but spaced closer than a human ladder would be. He paused after a few hundred and looked down. The rungs continued into darkness, but not far below was a set of double doors. Unlike the others he'd already passed, these stood partially open, warped outward. A set of handles allowed him to round the shaft along another rim.

He peered through the gap, but again, even the demon eye couldn't penetrate the darkness past a stone's throw. It wasn't wide enough to pass through, and it didn't budge when he tried to part them. He resumed his descent.

The lower he went, the larger the deformed cleft between the doors, leaving no doubt that the blast he'd caused had been more powerful at its source. Some thousand *pedes* below the temple, he came to a set of doors with enough space for him to squeeze through.

No matter what was on the other side, his body needed a rest. He slid-shifted around the narrow ledge to the doors, and, careful not to dislodge any more of the exploding gemstones on his sleeves, squeezed through the opening.

Emerging in a hallway wide enough for five men to walk abreast, he slumped down to the tile floors and leaned his back against a wall. The lines were smooth and perfect, as only dwarven engineers could accomplish underground. This must've been the start of the ancient dwarf city that the scribe had mentioned.

Not that he could appreciate it: even with the demon eye, it was darker here than in the shaft.

Sabine spoke in his mind, and his soul nearly jumped out of his body.

Twelve syllables in all, the tone had ended in a question.

If only he could understand. Maybe he should nod, just to see what would happen. What was the worst that could happen? Then again, it was a demon, so maybe not... Oh, what the hell. He nodded.

His vision shifted. Instead of the dark grey which faded to black along the edges, the walls, floors, and ceiling now appeared dark blue, with a clear line marking where each surface met. He could see further ahead, though in lighter shades of blue.

His hand, however, glowed red where it stuck out from the sleeves of the orc robe, and faded to orange, then yellow at his fingers.

He pushed himself off the wall. Where the back of his singed head had touched, a splotch of orange dimmed to yellow, then green, and finally blue.

He gasped. The eye could see heat, just like orcs supposedly could. Perhaps the human in the coffin had worked for the orcs, and needed to be able to see in darkness.

Blowing out a long breath, he shook out his fingers and wiggled his toes.

"What can you tell me about this place, Sabine?"

The demon eye remained silent; not that he would even understand her if she did answer. No doubt, the succubus inside was plotting her next move. She had probably set all his actions in motion, and was now leading him to where she had been originally trapped into the glass eye. Perhaps she knew of some way to break free.

Tomas shuddered. No telling what she would do to him, if that happened.

With nothing else to do while he rested, he pictured the temple in relation to the mountain. Based on how many rungs he'd descended, he was probably a good thousand *pedes* from the top. The hallway faced south.

Once he caught his breath, he rose and crept down the hall. Even with Sabine casting the hall in cold shades of blue, he couldn't see much more than six *pedes* in front of him; he'd have to rely on his other senses.

It smelled musty. There was a low hum, consistent in intensity no matter where he went.

No side corridors forked off of the main stretch. Up ahead, though, the dark blue of the walls gave way to a lighter blue. He picked up his pace, and the hallway opened up into a large cavern, some thousand paces from the central shaft. It was perhaps thrice the size of the temple above, and sunlight spilled in from where it opened to the outside. The air smelled fresh.

At last, a way out of this accursed temple!

He ran toward the opening. His vision shifted back to normal, though he had to squint with his good eye until it adjusted to the light.

More bones littered the floor, though they abruptly stopped at a crater in the middle of the cavern. At the bottom lay a huge set of charred ribs, as well as dozens of enormous scales. A dragon corpse? The Tivari had supposedly slain all but the great Avarax during the Dragonpurge. This one's remains had to be at least thirty *pedes* long.

Tomas edged along the crater rim. With one last look at the horrendous beast's remains, he hurried to the cave entrance.

His heart sank. It opened up onto a ledge, with no way down. Dirt had gathered here over the years, allowing evergreen shrubs to take root. He loped across to the edge and looked over.

A thousand *pedes* below the summit, the ledge provided a view of Lorium across the straits. He'd never seen the cave entrance from the town; he could picture that standing on the town's docks and looking up, the shrubs and jutting overhang would've made the cave opening blend in with the mountainside. From here, the view of his village was blocked by the curvature of the slopes. He looked back toward Lorium and squinted with his demon eye.

Like before, it enlarged the scene.

He sucked in a sharp breath.

Bovyans were boarding six—no, eight—of the fishing boats at the docks. If they'd found someone who could negotiate the Jaws, they were likely headed toward the island.

No doubt they would've expected Sathis and Fethos to report back by now. And of course, they would've been able to see Lydath's Golden Bowl shift from the explosion.

Sofia and Maria were in danger.

He had to get back home, but how?

Even from the gorge, it would take hours to reach the village—and he first had to reach the gorge. Going back up the shaft didn't make sense, not with the Temple of Lydath collapsing on itself.

Climbing down the mountain? He peered over the ledge again. With the way it jutted out, it was impossible from here, even with Sabine's help identifying crevices. Maybe he could tie some vines together...no, that would take too long, and a mistake could send him tumbling to his death.

Hells, he'd taken enough risks, so what was one more? Break the ledge off, and there might be an easier way to climb. He went back into the cave, about thirty *pedes* in. With a deep breath, he tied up the hem of his robe around his waist. Then, he pulled a gemstone from the sleeve. If only the Bovyans hadn't taken his slingshot! He squeezed the crystal until it flattened.

It lit up and whined.

He hurled it out onto the ledge, then turned and bolted back toward the crater.

Sliding face-first down the side, he climbed over a dragon rib and covered himself under the robe.

Light flashed. The explosion roared. The ground shook.

After a few seconds, Tomas sat up and patted himself. Still alive.

Heart racing, he scrabbled up the crater and ran back to the cave opening.

At the mouth, the orc bones had vaporized. Outside...

His gut wrenched.

All the greenery was gone. Some of the ledge had broken off, but not entirely. He advanced toward the new edge, stomping on occasion to make sure it didn't collapse beneath him. Lying on his stomach, he peered over.

Dust stung his real eye. He blinked several times to clear it.

Sabine spoke again, the tone again a question.

Tomas nodded. After all, the last time hadn't gotten him killed.

A translucent red line curved across his vision. He lifted and turned his head to follow it, and found it led back through the cavern toward the shaft.

Trying to guide him someplace unpleasant, perhaps? Tomas laughed bitterly to himself. "No, Sabine." He shook his head, but the line remained. He looked back over the edge.

The remains of the ledge were still about thirty *pedes* thick from where it had broken away. The overhang still jutted out too far from the sheer cliff face for him to reach, unless he trusted his grip enough to attempt an upside down, transverse climb.

He still had four gems, though. Again, ignoring the red line, he returned to the cave and squeezed a gemstone. He hurled it out and sprinted into the crater.

Again, the light flashed, the explosion roared. There wasn't as much of a rumble, however. When he went out to investigate the ledge, not much more had broken away. Maybe if he tried two at a time? That would only leave him three.

He looked over the side again.

His heart soared. Down below, sitting on another ledge close to two thousand *pedes* below, the Egg had shifted, well above the water line. The fallen part of the ledge lay partially submerged, and given its position, it must've knocked the Egg from its spot. Not only that, but the shift had exposed another cave opening. Sabine's red line across his vision emerged from the hole, ending in a blinking red dot.

Did the line lead there? Perhaps she wasn't trying to lead him to doom, but needed him to survive. He turned and tracked it. It still ran back down the corridor to the shaft.

Maybe, just maybe, it led to that cave opening on a lower level. His good sense of direction and distance would help, if Sabine tried to lead him astray.

He had to get back before the Bovyans reached the village. Gritting his teeth, Tomas turned and ran back in, following the red line in his vision around the crater and down the hall. His sight shifted to blues and reds again, this time without Sabine asking him. He squeezed through the double doors, where the demon eye again changed, showing the ladder rungs in a lighter color from the shaft walls. The red line headed down.

It was as if she knew his thoughts. He resumed his descent, keeping track of distance. Each set of double doors had a larger warped opening than the previous one. At not quite three thousand *pedes* beneath the summit, he'd reached the bottom of the shaft.

However, the floor rippled. How strange. He lowered himself and tested it with a toe.

Water.

The red line turned into the space between partially submerged double doors. Though the opening was wide, only about two *pedes* of it was above the water.

He might be a strong swimmer, but based on how far the corridor above had stretched before reaching the outside, he might have to swim several thousand *pedes*. Who knew if it was all above water?

His chest squeezed tight. Of all the ways to die, drowning was very low on his list of preferences. Hypothermia wasn't particularly high, either.

Still, the Bovyans were going to invade his village. He dove through the hole and breast-stroked through the corridor, following Sabine's red line.

The priest's robe proved to be too much of a drag, so he folded it up and stuffed it into his shirt. It might make him look pregnant, but it proved to be buoyant. And, if it looked like he would drown, he could always squeeze a gemstone and blow himself to pieces.

But no, he had to survive. For Sofia.

His heart soared as the passage sloped upwards. Before long, he was wading through, his feet sloshing over the uneven surface.

Uneven surface? His heart plummeted back to his stomach. The corridors he'd explored above had all been smooth. Here, they weren't flat and straight, but rather roughhewn into the rock. Shallow now, the path could very well dip later. Some parts might be completely submerged.

Just as he feared, it twisted and descended. Ignoring several side tunnels, he followed the path Sabine provided. Thank her, but also the gods, for his sense of space, which helped him keep track of directions.

The ubiquitous humming sound in the shaft and the corridor to the dragon's lair had silenced. He continued, and about five hundred *pedes* south and thirty *pedes* east of the central shaft, the tunnel sloped down into the water. Sabine's red line continued right through it.

Did she know humans couldn't breathe water? Or did she just mark a path out, without considering obstacles?

Death by drowning. Death by eventual starvation. Gods above, he really had no choice.

Though it was generally the women who dived for shellfish in the lagoon, the boys often tried to compete. He could hold his breath to a count of about three hundred. He took a deep inhalation and dove in.

The cold water stung his skin. Underwater, he opened the demon eye. It was impossible to distinguish the walls from the water; they must be the same temperature. Still, the red line served as a beacon. He counted as he kicked and swam. At a count of a hundred, his thoughts raced. He could still turn back...but then he'd probably die of hypothermia, unless he could climb back up two thousand *pedes* to the dragon lair. If he could pick it out from all the other doors in the shaft.

No, he'd have to soldier on along Sabine's red line. Thankfully, it started to arc up. At two hundred seconds, his vision flashed red several times. Sabine sounded her warning. His lungs burned, and every nerve screamed for him to breathe. He fought to hold his breath, and kicked. He was already past a count of three hundred.

His head broke the surface, and he gasped for air. The demon eye's vision shifted again, revealing a small cave. Patches of the wall and ceiling glowed blue, the same shade as the Blue Moon. It was about as bright as a night when the Blue Moon was open to full.

Following the red line, he paddled until his body scraped against the floor. He picked himself up. Teeth chattering, he hugged himself.

He pulled the priest's robe out from under his shirt. Holding the sleeves so the gemstones wouldn't slip out and give him way too much heat, he snapped it out. The water rolled off the fabric in beads. He tightened it about his shoulders, and tied the hem around his waist. He jogged along the red line in his vision, his ankles sloshing through water and bare feet scraping over the rough floors.

After several twists and turns, he'd lost track of the distance and direction. His toe bashed into something. Pain flared, and whatever he'd kicked clinked less than a *pede* away. He peered into the water, and the demon eye outlined shapes.

Chisel blades. Hammer heads. A short crowbar. If only he'd had them in the temple on the mountaintop, he could've pried out some of the gems. Then again, maybe they would've exploded, like the gemstones in the robe. He reached down and pulled out what looked to be a trowel head. It didn't look corroded or rusted, even though it must've been down here for a long time.

This had to be part of the old dwarf city. Continuing his walk, he collected several items and stashed them into the robe's magic pouch. Before long, metal cups and urns appeared, though he only took one small cup; the rest were too bulky.

The tunnel opened up into another cavern. Sabine's red line tracked through it and abruptly dove straight down below the water. How deep, it was hard to tell given the dim light and distortion, but it looked to loop up and disappear. He took a hammer head and dropped it, but within seconds it became a dark shape and vanished in the depths.

How could he find out if it was possible to reach the bottom? He untied the robe's hem and, careful not to spill the trinkets he'd found, folded it up and set it atop a cauldron a few *pedes* away.

Taking a deep breath, he dove straight down. He counted, but his descent slowed, and at ten seconds, he was fighting with strokes of his arm to continue. He wasn't even halfway down the length of the red line. He gave up and kicked back to the surface.

The cold air bit into his wet skin, and he was shivering again. Was this it? It just wasn't possible to reach the bottom of the pit, not with his buoyancy. No, he needed something heavy.

The metal tools? He could form a sack with the robe and let their weight drag him down; but it would take at least an hour to find enough of them. And, all the tools he'd stuffed into the strange pocket didn't seem to add weight.

The cauldron! He heaved with both hands, and it rose maybe a quarter *pede* off the ground before its heft pulled it down. It would definitely get him to the bottom of the pit, if he could get it to the edge of in the first place. With the cup he'd saved, he ladled the water out and tried again.

It was easier to move, but not by much. Tugging and jerking, he worked it over to the side of the pit. Then it dawned on him.

He folded the metal tools into the robe, and set it into the cauldron. He then dragged and scooted it so it was about halfway over the edge of the pit. Grabbing the rim with both hands, he bent over and put his head in as well. He waddled around until his feet found the edge. Thank the gods Sofia wasn't around to see him look so ridiculous.

With a deep breath, he threw himself down into the water, feet first. The cauldron tipped over, and though some water rushed in, a pocket of air remained as he descended. It took thirty seconds until his feet touched the pit floor. With the cauldron resting on his shoulders, he followed his limited view of the red line until it turned upwards.

He took a deep breath, came out from under the cauldron, and used one hand to pull out his robe. Bending his knees, he gave the floor a strong kick off and started rising. Up above, a circle of light blue beckoned, growing larger as he kicked himself higher and higher.

With plenty of air in his lungs, his head broke the surface of the water into another flooded cavern lit in luminous blue. Clutching the robe under his arm, he swam in side-stroke along Sabine's red line, until the water was shallow enough for him to wade.

He again donned the robe for warmth.

Despite his excellent sense of space, he had no idea where he was in relation to the central shaft. All he could do was follow Sabine's silent directions. The far end of the cavern rose out of the water, and he was never happier to have feet on dry land. The line continued out through another tunnel, which wound left and right without any side passages until it reached a straightaway.

Up ahead, the cave mouth opened, and Sabine's red line ended in a blinking dot.

Tomas' heart soared. With long steps, he strode as fast as he could, until the low ceiling forced him to crawl. The air smelled fresher here. At long last, he shimmied through the hole.

Out! He was finally out! Sabine spoke, perhaps in congratulations.

He deserved it!

He'd touched the Golden Bowl, entered the Temple of Lydath, travelled through an old dwarf city, and had lived to tell about it. He now stood on a narrow outcrop nearly fifty *pedes* above the lake's waterline. Right beside him was the oval-shaped boulder known as the Egg. He must've rowed past this spot thousands of times in in life, but never noticed the cave.

Of course, the Egg would've blocked his view; and in fact, if he imagined this spot from the water, it looked like the enormous boulder might have shifted. The sharp-angled rock shards scattered nearby suggested a recent impact. At the base of the steep slope, the chunk of the ledge he'd broken off now lay partially submerged.

He looked farther up the cliff face. The remains of the ledge hung high above. His current spot rose above the height of the Tooth, providing a view of Lorium across the straits, well to the right. Had anyone been looking at the mountain from town, they would have seen the explosion. No, two explosions.

He squinted with the demon eye past the Tooth, toward Lorium. The image enlarged, revealing eight fishing boats a quarter of the way across. Each held two to three Bovyans, and they were looking at him.

No, not him. The village.

CHAPTER 31:

Illusion of Strength

From astride his horse, Koryn looked over the ranks of his two hundred foot soldiers, deployed around the Tarkothi royal villa. He'd ordered all bauble lamps shuttered, so the lights from the mansion would betray enemy positions, while his own men remained in the dark. He's spread them thin, kept them moving, and brought extra banners, to create the illusion of greater numbers. Based on scouting reports, his men controlled all of Elbahia Island except the docks, and held all bridges from Tarkoth to prevent reinforcements.

Here, the walls were defended by no more than fifty Tarkothi, and though the villa lacked fortifications, Prince Elrayn had apparently retrieved the Light of Solaris from Elbahia Palace. No doubt he was waiting to show it off now, to boost the morale of the defenders. Any assault would lead to heavy casualties.

Koryn looked up to the Iridescent Moon, now waxing toward half. Nine more phases until dawn. Nine more phases with darkness, to maintain the illusion of strength.

Maybe only a quarter of a phase before his promised meeting with Prince Aryn at Elbahia Palace. That promise he'd made to Jie tugged at him now. All her conjecture about Teleri spies planted in the Tarkothi royalty didn't even seem possible.

"Your Highness." Damaryn pointed at a second-floor window.

Koryn followed his finger.

Prince Elrayn stood there, peering into the darkness.

A sense of satisfaction filled Koryn's chest. He'd been Elrayn's prisoner for six days; for now, the tables were turned. At the very least, they'd retrieve Sunblade, which he'd left at the Tarkothi guest house; at best, he'd capture Elrayn as punishment, and ransom him for concessions.

Though did two wrongs make a right? And maybe Elrayn's ultimate goals were actually noble.

He turned to Damaryn. "Did you send word to our little friend to meet me at the palace?"

"Yes."

"Do you think he'll make it in time?"

"We'd already summoned him after you went missing. He must be in Elbahia by now." Damaryn's lips tightened. "Are you really going through with meeting Prince Aryn?"

Koryn half nodded, half shook his head. "I haven't decided."

"Madness, Your Highness." Damaryn's eyes widened enough to tell, even in the dark. "It could be a trap."

"The Elbahia palace guards won't take sides," Koryn said.

Damaryn's mouth tightened. "Even so, we should capture this villa and take Prince Elrayn prisoner."

That was the logical course of action, especially while they had superior numbers. Still... "I promised Jie."

"Can we trust her?" Damaryn asked.

Could they? She was clearly a spy, perhaps an assassin, but so far, she had only helped them. She might be playing a bigger game. "Probably not. But if anyone can sniff her out, it will be our little friend."

"We don't even know if she was able to convince Prince Aryn, or if he got out before we surrounded the villa."

"All logic tells me her theory is impossible. Then again, she has already accomplished the impossible." He sighed. There really never was any indecision. "I will give them a chance, but we will take twenty cavaliers, just in case it is a trap...or to capture Prince Aryn, if it comes to that. Pick out our best riders and meet me in two minutes over there." He pointed to the head of the avenue.

"As you command." Lips tight, Damaryn crossed his fists, bowed his head, and strode off.

Koryn looked again toward the window where Elrayn had appeared. Nobody was there now. He turned his horse and went to the designated spot. In just two minutes, Damaryn joined him with twenty cavaliers.

"Cavaliers on me," Koryn said. He shifted his weight, and though the horse wasn't his beloved Bronze, she was well-trained enough to follow the command and set off down the broad avenue toward the palace.

The rhythmic cadence of trotting horse hooves settled his mind. To think, a month ago he'd been in Cathay—ostensibly to attend their prince's wedding, but really to negotiate purchase of new cast-iron cannons for their ships. Those advanced weapons would've given them the advantage if war with Tarkoth was inevitable; but he'd left without a deal when Cathayi officials levelled preposterous allegations, and demanded to board the *Intimidator* to search for an assassin.

How proud and brash he'd been. Just like Jie had pointed out when she rescued him. Maybe she could be trusted. Then again, given how she'd mysteriously found him, maybe her being here was more than a coincidence.

"Your Highness," Damaryn yelled.

Koryn looked up. Without even realizing it, he'd arrived at Elbahia Palace. Official seat of the Eldaeri Empire before the civil war, its elliptical form, central dome, and four spires were the model on which the three other Eldaeri nations' palaces were based. No great king or lord ruled from here; it was maintained and guarded by Elbahia Island's city government, and only used as a neutral ground for the rival nations to meet. Unlike the others, this one was surrounded by a moat, which was connected to the city's central canal.

Even though they were on the Tarkothi side of the island, there was no sign of enemy soldiers. Strange that Aryn would come here without any guards. Perhaps he'd never left the villa.

The moment his horse stepped onto the palace grounds, they were in neutral territory. He continued across the span, which was illuminated by several light baubles on the stone floor, every six meters. Horseshoes clinked as they passed small blockwood statues mounted to the balustrade, carved in the likeness of the men and women who'd accompanied the first Eldaeri emperor in his unification of coastal Arkoth.

On the other side, they arrived in a grassy yard encircling the palace, also lit by baubles mounted to posts. A single horse was tied to one.

Koryn turned to the cavaliers. "Captain Damaryn will accompany me. Four of you hold this bridge, while the two groups of eight will circle around both sides of the castle, leaving four men to guard each bridge you pass."

The cavaliers crossed their fists and carried out his orders with expected precision.

Following one of the groups, Koryn guided his horse toward the entrance on the south side of the palace grounds. In the main plaza stood three-meter statues of the first six Eldaeri Emperors. Though most had lived to well over a hundred years of age, by custom they'd all abdicated to their sons after thirty years.

He looked to Damaryn. "Are you ready?"

Golden hair rippled as Damaryn bowed his head.

They dismounted and marched through the double doors. Men dressed in the old white imperial regalia crossed their fists and bowed their heads as they passed. Taken from the best royal guards of the three Eldaeri Kingdoms, they'd all sworn neutrality.

Inside, more palace guards saluted as Koryn walked across the marble floors of the central hall, up the grand staircase, and through the double doors to the audience chamber.

Prince Aryn stood in the center, alone, looking straight up.

Koryn followed his line of sight. The dwarf-made, telescoping sky stair was fully extended from the top mezzanine to the center of the dome. The Tarkothi must've used it earlier to retrieve the Light of the Solaris, but not had time to collapse the stair back. He lowered his gaze.

Now, Aryn was studying him. He bowed his head. "Prince Koryn, thank you for meeting me. Let me first apologize for my brother's actions. I didn't condone them, but I couldn't go against my father, who supported your forced marriage."

Koryn nodded. "I could tell that you objected, which is why I agreed to meet with you now."

"Jie," Aryn said, his voice sounding as if had sucked a lemon, "insists that the Teleri have been training elite spies. She says these spies have infiltrated the highest levels of our military, and include my aide, Peris, and my brother's aide, Tharos. That they helped instigate hostilities between our nations so as to keep us divided and weaker."

"You don't sound convinced." Damaryn snorted.

Aryn lowered his voice. "I'm not sure how much I can trust her anymore, and they are very wild claims."

Koryn wondered as well, but kept his expression impassive. "And yet, you are here, talking to me."

"I can hear you," said a high-pitched voice from the first mezzanine.

Koryn looked up.

Elbows resting on the bannister, the half-elf Jie cupped her face in her hands. She grinned.

Aryn looked up to her, and her smile slipped. His expression soured. Whatever had passed between them, it looked like she was no longer his pet. He turned to face him. "Even still, we can't discount the possibility that we are playing right into the Teleri's hands. I wanted to humbly request an armistice, where we both pull our troops off Elbahia Island, to our respective sides of the Valeri River."

Damaryn jabbed an impertinent finger at the foreign prince. "Your brother started this when he kidnapped our prince. Our troops now have him surrounded and most of the island controlled. Why should we cede our superior position?"

Placing a hand on Damaryn's shoulder, Koryn stepped forward. "What the captain says is true. Surrender, and we will consider generous terms."

Aryn sighed. "How ironic that my brother, who's always harbored grand dreams of reuniting the Eldaeri, might have caused a war that divides us further. But if what Jie says is true, he's been manipulated by the Teleri all this time, through Tharos."

Koryn looked up at the half-elf. "As I said before, I've met both Peris and Tharos. Even though they are large, they aren't as big as a Bovyan."

Jie's snort echoed from above. "As I told you earlier, I've met smaller Bovyans, and in each case, they were trained as spies."

"So you say." Damaryn's harrumph was almost as derisive as hers.

Still facing Jie, Koryn held a quieting hand up to him. "For a moment, let's entertain the thought that you are right. That there are smaller Bovyans trained as spies. That they planted them into Tarkoth as youths, hoping they would be accepted into the military, and one day they would rise as high as aides to the princes themselves. That they would be able to manipulate those princes into war. If you were in my position and heard that, what would you say?"

"You'd say she was insane," Aryn whispered. "That she is so desperate to prove her point, she'd say anything."

Koryn nodded. "There are just too many ways it could fail. There could be other reasonable explanations for Peris and Tharos' behavior."

"True," Aryn said. "My brother and I both think Peris is truly in love with our sister, Karyna, and that Tharos helped them escape."

Koryn exchanged glances with Damaryn. The things people did for love—things that he, as prince, couldn't do. A wave of sadness started to creep over him, but he fought it back. "Would they betray Tarkoth for love? Would Karyna?"

Aryn shook his head. "Peris has been as loyal a soldier and friend as I've ever had. Karyna is demure and obedient. I can't imagine her going against our father's will."

Jie spoke; or at least, it was her lips moving, but the voice sounded like Aryn's. "You yourself said that Tharos imitated Karyna's voice perfectly."

Everyone gawked at her.

When Koryn recovered from his shock, he shook his head. "He was quite good at forging. Maybe he was good at voices, too."

Jie spoke again, this time in Koryn's own voice: "He was able to exactly imitate Karyna's, even enough to fool her own brothers." The voice switched back to hers as she turned to Aryn. "Did he ever use that skill before?"

Aryn's head wobbled in slow shakes. Koryn put a hand over his throat, while Damaryn gawped.

"And, he was able to throw his voice to make it sound like it came from inside a room," Jie's disembodied voice said, seemingly from right beside Koryn. "What's the word? Ventriloquism? My...people...practice it, and we are convinced a traitor taught the Teleri Nightblades."

Damaryn shook his head. "It still doesn't discount him doing it just to help his brother."

"In case you've forgotten," Jie said, "Princess Alaena is also missing."

Koryn's sister, who he hadn't seen in years. He met her gaze. "How does Alaena fit into the picture?"

Aryn shook his head. "All we know is that Peris approached her, and she disappeared."

"Why would Peris want her?"

"If he works for the Teleri," Jie said, "he could end any chance of an Eldaeri alliance by getting rid of the princesses. If he made it look like Alaena killed Karyna, there'd be war."

Koryn chewed the inside of his cheek. It'd been so many years since he'd last seen Alaena, but she'd always been a wild girl. Still, even if she didn't want to marry Aryn, no one would believe she'd go as far as killing Karyna. "What do you suggest?"

Aryn crossed his wrists and bowed his head. "I'm not thoroughly convinced, but again, I am requesting a temporary ceasefire. Let's work together and find Alaena and Karyna."

It sounded good, but it meant sacrificing superior position. "My men will hold their positions, but not attack unless attacked. You have until the waning half."

"You're not going to help?" Jie threw up her arms. "The trail is going cold every second we waste."

Koryn looked to Damaryn. "We will provide our best scout."

Jie snorted. "Riders. We need riders. As for scouts, I don't think you'll find anyone better than me."

"You think wrong," called a shrill voice from the entrance.

Grin coming to his lips unbidden, Koryn turned.

Standing a head shorter than even Jie, was the Madaeri chieftain, Fleet. The halfling wore roughspun brown pants and a shirt. He brushed his curly mop of brown hair out of his dark eyes and grinned.

Jie stared at him, wide-eyed, before finally finding her voice. "His legs are shorter than mine. We still need cavaliers if we ever hope to catch up to Alaena. If she's still alive."

CHAPTER 32:

Clues

With only the moons lighting the side yard, Jie's elf vision had taken over, casting the night in shades of grey and green. Wearing her utility suit for the first time in what seemed like forever, she now clung to Captain Damaryn's back as their horse galloped through the streets of Elbahia toward the last place Alaena had been seen: the Korynthi royal villa.

She hadn't thought today could get worse, after having to break Aryn's heart. To her chagrin, tonight was looking more and more like the night where she'd ridden for several phases on the horse relays from her homeland's main port to its capital. Now, like then, it was to find missing royalty. Perhaps it was her cursed lot in life to clean up the messes left by headstrong princesses.

At least this time, others would share in her misfortune. She looked over to Fleet.

Despite his short legs, the Madaeri rode the enormous destrier by himself, with as much ease as the famous Kanin people who were supposedly born in the saddle. He looked more comfortable than even the two dozen cavaliers behind them.

Jie sucked on her lower lip. She knew a lot about a broad range of subjects, but Madaeri were not one of them. Texts from back home spoke of a small people with extraordinary senses. In ancient times, the orcs had kept them as watchdogs against dragons. They now lived in villages dotting coastal Arkoth, under the protection of the Eldaeri kingdoms.

Even if his skill didn't match hers, perhaps his senses would come in handy.

They stopped outside the Korynthi villa, and Damaryn swung out of the saddle with practiced ease. He spoke with the royal guards, who crossed their fists and opened the gate.

Clinging to the horse's mane for dear life, Jie slid off. She fought the urge to kiss the ground when her feet touched it.

At her side, Fleet dismounted with nonchalant grace. He flashed a devious grin at her.

A pit of jealousy sank in her stomach. By the Heavens, she would practice riding if she ever had the chance in the future.

He gestured to the gates. "Shall we? I smell leftover food."

Jie gave a surreptitious sniff. Nothing aromatic. He must've surmised the fact, and not smelled actual food.

After all, logic dictated the Korynthi would've prepared a feast for Alaena's arrival—and that she wouldn't have eaten any, because well, she'd escaped.

They passed through the gates, and she had to grab his sleeve to divert him to the bathhouse instead of the mansion. With a pout, he followed. She waved Damaryn back, to prevent him from further disturbing the scene, and headed to Alaena's suspected point of egress, on the north side of the west wall.

Fleet held out a staying hand. "Wait here, I don't want you messing with the evidence any more than these lumbering hulks did before."

Watching him stride soundlessly over the gravel, leaving no visible tracks, Jie suppressed a pout. Fine, he could move well, but he wouldn't find anything that she hadn't earlier. Indeed, he was headed in the wrong direction, to a corner of the yard where neither Alaena nor Peris had been.

"Here." He pointed to a spot on the east end of the north wall and beckoned her. "Alaena left from here."

Maybe he wasn't so useful. With a snort, Jie headed over and pointed to the right spot. "No, she left that way."

He shook his shaggy head. "She's a skilled ranger. Like a doe that walks back its tracks to throw off predators, she wanted to make her pursuers think that."

Jie raised an eyebrow. "How can you tell?"

"My nose. Her scent is strongest here."

Sniffing the air again, Jie threw up her hands. "My sense of smell is better than any human, and I don't—"

"You are setting the bar quite low. Human noses are useless, save for holding up spectacles." Fleet pushed up on the bridge of his nose.

"My sense of smell is—"

Fleet held up a hand again. "What do you smell right now?"

The evergreen trees, the rich soil, the rocks…those were all obvious. But behind the bathhouse's closed door… "The rosehips in the bathwater, the odor of the sea, mixed with her sweat, in the clothes she left there."

He nodded. "How about the roast pork, rosemary potatoes, and salted pickles cooling in the kitchens? The squirrel poop there, there, and there?"

Maybe, now that he pointed it out.

"To me, they are glaring lights in the dark. Just like Prince Aryn's scent on your pretty lace underwear."

Heat flared in Jie's ears. Could he really smell that? "How could you possibly know about the lace?"

"Oh, I didn't, until you just confirmed it." He rubbed his hands together. "Of course, I knew about your feelings from the second I saw you, just by the way you looked at him. Really, for what you are, your relationship was doomed from the start."

For what she was. Foreigner? Half-elf? Spy? Her face must be red as Tivar's Star during the Year of the Second Sun.

"Now that we have gotten that out of the way," he said, pointing at the spot. "Not only is Alaena's scent stronger here, there's still the minutest amount of heat left from where her large friend had leaned up against the wall."

Jie gaped. "You can see heat?"

"Just like an orc." Fleet tapped beneath his eye.

No wonder the Altivorcs hadn't had a problem seeing her in the dark the time she'd encountered them back home. She squinted at the spot he indicated, but even her elf vision didn't detect anything special.

"Here's a trick: if you ever fight them underground, in the dark, lean up against a wall for a while and let your heat stick to it. They'll run right to it."

Not like she would ever be underground against Altivorcs.

He looked up at the wall. "It's strange she'd go over here."

"Why?" She looked up the wall, which rose over nine feet...three meters by Eldaeri standard.

"It's right up against the north end of the island." Fleet pantomimed a triangular shape with two hands. "The rocks of the breakwater form a triangle."

Jie took three steps back, then ran and pop-vaulted into the corner of the wall and grabbed its top. She pulled herself up and threw a leg over the edge.

"Impressive," Fleet said.

Ignoring the Madaeri, Jie scanned the area. The villa looked to be at the center of the north end of the island. At the foot of the wall, running the length of the one-*li* bank, was a concrete walkway, about a foot long; beyond that, countless enormous rocks jutted into the wide, lazy river, acting as a breakwater. Beyond the jetty were several small wooded isles. The closest one lay about fifty feet away from the end of the rocks.

She squinted. It looked like there was a boat tied to a wooden dock. She pointed. "What's on that little isle?"

Fleet looked up at her. "Which one?"

"The closest one. A little to the west."

"It's technically part of Elbahia, but there's a footbridge into Serikoth. Do you think…?" His eyes lit with mischief.

"There's a boat at a dock over there." She sucked on her lower lip. It didn't prove anything. "It's also possible that she walked along the wall and stayed in the city."

Fleet reached up. "Help me up."

At least he wasn't perfect at everything. Jie leaned over and offered him a hand.

He took an admirable leap for his small size and caught it. He was surprisingly heavy, but she managed to haul him up.

The top of the wall wasn't much wider than half a foot, but it might've been a platform for all the ease with which Fleet skipped across it. Sniffing the whole time, he went only a few feet to the east before turning around and going the other way. Even on the narrow path, he spun around her and continued nimbly on his way.

He sniffed twice. "No, her smell is strongest here."

"The isle, then."

"I'll swim across, you go get the cavaliers and meet me there." He waved back toward the gates to the villa.

"Why don't we both ride?"

"It will take longer for the cavaliers to ride over from Elbahia into Serikoth, then back across to the isle. Unless you'd rather swim?"

Jie sucked on her lower lip. Given the choice between riding a horse again, and swimming in cold water against the current and possibly getting devoured by a river monster, she'd choose the river monster.

Fleet studied her expression and chuckled. "Enjoy your swim, then."

He jumped down off the wall, landing without a sound or even making an indentation in the gravel, despite the height. Waving, he scampered back around to the front of the mansion.

Jie lowered herself down on the river side and landed on the jetty. Elf vision gave her a good view of the boulders' shapes and contours, and the water sloshing between them, but not whether they were slick. With care, she jumped from rock to rock. On occasion, some critter would splash into the river. At the end of the jetty, the water lapped against the rocks.

It was impossible to tell how deep the channel was between here and the isle. Taking off her shoes and putting them in her mouth, she took a tentative step in. The cold water almost made her wish for a horse. With a deep breath, she sloshed ever forward. When the water reached above her waist, at the halfway mark, she dove forward with a splash.

Though slow, the current made the short swim arduous. About ten feet from the isle, she scraped up against the rocky river floor. She pulled herself up and slogged toward the bank. With her cold, wet utility suit clinging to her body, her teeth chattered.

When she reached dry land, she hurried over to the dock, took off her clothes, and wrung them out. She did her best to dry Tharos' throwing stars and her magic knife. Then she inspected the boat. It was large enough for two people, and a pair of oars had been left inside. On closer inspection, she found a strand of long, frizzy hair lay and some cotton fibers. It was impossible to distinguish the colors with her elf vision in the moonlight, but Alaena had curly hair.

With no other clues, she followed the path from the dock. It wound through the trees, and the dried leaves, evergreen needles, and twigs didn't look to be disturbed...until about thirty feet in, where another trail intersected the one she was on.

Having no tracking skills in the wilderness, she'd leave the new path for Fleet. Instead, she continued along her current route, following the new, obvious tracks, and searching for clues with her eyes and a nose which didn't seem as superior as it had just half an hour before. To the west, the rumble of dozens of horse hooves carried over the rustle of the river. No doubt, the cavaliers would soon come to the footbridge between Serikoth and the isle.

She froze. The distinct, heady fragrance of musk, native to her home and used by the clan, carried on the breeze. Sniffing, she followed the scent off the path. It grew stronger until she came to a large tree. Lying at the base was a mitten made from a translucent material, and a balled-up strip of dark cloth. She knelt down.

"What is it?" Fleet said from over her shoulder.

If she had a soul, it would've just about jumped out of her body. Jie turned around and glared.

Fleet blinked innocently. Nobody in the clan could sneak up on her like that.

"How long have you been here?"

"Just now." He reached for the rag. "So, what is it?"

"This flower essence. It's a contact toxin—"

He jerked his hand back.

It was all she could do not to laugh at his wary look. "Don't worry, it only works on females. In small doses, it can lead to a muddled brain and a reverie akin to drunkenness. The victim will lose inhibitions, and generally tell the truth. In larger doses, it can cause unconsciousness. It confirms my suspicion that someone around here was trained in my people's ways."

"By *your people*, you mean...half-elves? Cathayi?"

Clan secret. Jie just shrugged.

"Riiiiight."

She snorted. "In any case, once exposed to air, it quickly loses its potency. I'd say from the concentration, it wouldn't work now."

Fleet snatched up the cloth and grinned. "You never know."

Harrumphing, she pointed at the glove. "Well?"

"It looks to be made of sheep intestine. Waterproof." Realization bloomed on his expression, at the same time it occurred to her.

"A woman used the toxin on another woman," Jie said.

"Smart. And on the trail from the bridge, there were some tracks I didn't understand until now. In fact, they start here." He pointed at the ground.

Jie didn't see much of anything, and shrugged.

"The scattering of the pine needles," he said. "The spacing suggests a woman, but the weight hints at a fairly large man."

"Or a woman, carrying another woman."

He nodded. "If what you say is true about the toxin, I would guess either a woman trained in *your people's* ways used it on Alaena..."

"Or Alaena got it from Peris," Jie said, "and used it on someone else. Like Karyna. But why leave the evidence here?"

"Maybe she couldn't carry it without getting touched by the toxin."

"And maybe," Jie said, "they are trying to escalate the conflict between Tarkoth and Serikoth, and making it look like Cathay is complicit so as to end trade."

Fleet tapped his temple. "Maybe. But the princes could also be right: Peris, knowing he was followed, used Alaena to bring Karyna to him. Alaena would agree to it in order to get out of marriage to Aryn."

"But why use the toxin?"

Fleet laughed. "I hear Karyna is suspicious. Maybe she wouldn't trust Alaena. In any case, whoever this was left a trail."

CHAPTER 33:

There Really is No Place Like Home

Tomas stood on a short ledge at the mouth of the cave and counted the small armada bearing the Bovyan invaders across the straits. They must've commandeered a quarter of the boats in Lorium. Each of the seven craft carried two or three Bovyans: twenty in all. If they rowed as fast as Sathis and Fethos, they could reach the Jaws in half an hour. They'd have to slow and file one boat at a time through the curving gap in the rocks before reaching the lagoon. The logistics might add another several minutes.

He, on the other hand, wasn't even sure how to get back to the village from here. Swimming was out of the question, and not just because he was so tired. The Jaws, which made the approach by boat so treacherous, made swimming just about impossible. Picking his way around the rocks and boulders along the edge of the island could take an hour, half that if he could find a way to bypass the Tooth instead of having to work his way around it.

With either option, he'd have to scrabble down the steep slope. That might take half an hour, even with Sabine's help identifying winding paths and handholds. If the path were more direct...

He looked to the remains of the ledge he'd dislodged from above. Its irregular shape had flattened the slope in places. The Egg by the cave, however, was rounder; and thanks to being hit by the broken ledge, it had shifted. He gave it a shove.

Did it budge? It felt like it might have rocked. He lacked the strength to move it, at least without a tool. The short crowbar he'd found in the old dwarf city might give him more leverage. He took it from the robe, wedged it into the space where the boulder met the ledge, and then simultaneously pushed the rock and stomped on the crowbar.

The Egg rocked, but didn't give. He stuffed a rock under the crowbar and tried again.

The boulder started to tip over the side. He launched his shoulder into it, and it went over. Tomas had to catch himself before going with it. It crashed and tumbled, crushing a path down the slope before coming to a rest at the water's edge.

Tomas set the priest's robe onto the ground and sat on it. Careful to keep the explosive gemstones in the sleeves cushioned, he launched himself down the slope. It wasn't a comfortable ride by any stretch of the imagination, but the loose debris left in the wake of the boulder created a surface which allowed him to glide down. What would've taken a half hour of climbing and walking a winding path took just a minute. With the mental image of him splattering into the boulder and then exploding from the gemstones in his robe, he repeatedly dug his heels into the ground at the sides to slow his descent.

At the bottom, he stood and surveyed the surroundings. There had to be a way to cut the time off the trek around the shore. Wade past the Jaws and swim? He didn't have the energy, and it would take too long, even if he were fresh.

It was the damn Tooth. Once part of an orc-built bridge which connected the mountainside to the edge of the crater, the remains now jutted two thousand *pedes* into the lake toward the Barrows. The sides were too sheer to climb, and even steel tools couldn't so much as scratch the rock's surface. Only the very best divers could swim under it; they reported it to be forty *pedes* deep and ten *pedes* wide. The way the Jaws intersected it, Tomas theorized it was part of the ancient city's defenses.

He started to work his way along the shore, picking his way among the rocks and boulders. As a child, he'd searched for crabs and oysters this way.

At the halfway mark, he looked out to check on the Bovyan's progress across the straits. From the lower vantage point, the Tooth blocked his line of sight, making it impossible.

Now, though, he squinted with the demon eye to where the Tooth met the water. Whereas his own eyes would've never been able to penetrate the tidal pool between the shore and the Jaws, Sabine made out so much more. The underside of the Tooth didn't touch the tidal pool floor, though the encrusting shells didn't leave enough space for even a child to pass under. As he theorized, the Tooth rested perpendicularly on the Jaws some fifty *pedes* from shore before continuing toward Lorium.

In fifteen minutes, he reached the spot where the Tooth met with the mountain ridge, blocking his path. He pressed his palm to its cool, smooth surface, and looked up. It was much too smooth and high to climb, but the demon eye made out minute cracks spider-webbing the surface. Maybe... He pulled the chisel from the folded robe. Steel might not so much as chip the Tooth, but there were cracks here, and this metal was different. He stabbed at the Tooth.

A chunk of rock dislodged, leaving an indentation large enough for his fist to fit in. It was too easy. Heart racing, Tomas hacked into a spot above it, creating another hand hold. He looked up again, and his stomach twisted. He'd have to climb and hack, climb and hack, and then there was the matter of getting down on the other side. He might as well swim around the Tooth.

Or... With several stabs at a spot level with his chest, he dug out a hole two *pedes* deep. When the chisel could no longer reach, he used the crowbar to clear out a niche at the end of the furrow. He paused and panted for breath. This was either a brilliant idea, or one that would get him killed. He didn't even have a slingshot, though even the best village sharpshooter would have little chance of hitting such a small target from a safe distance.

He withdrew one of the gemstones from the robe's sleeves, leaving him with two. He set the gem into the niche, and then stuffed a large rock into the hole.

The gemstone flattened with a crunch. Its whine vibrated through the rock. Holding the robe behind him as a shield, Tomas turned and ran into the water. It meant possibly stubbing his toe on a submerged stone, or tripping in a crevice, but being directly in front of the hole would almost certainly mean getting clobbered by the rock he'd shoved in the hole or incinerated by the blast, or both.

The whine grew louder as he sloshed through the shallows. His vision flashed red, and Sabine warned him with those two syllables he'd heard so often in the last several hours.

The gemstone exploded. The ground rumbled, and the blast wave sent Tomas flying headfirst into the water. A shower of debris pelted into the robe like a hailstorm on the roof of his hut.

An ear-shattering crack rang out, followed by popping and grinding sounds.

Head spinning, Tomas turned to look at the Tooth.

He'd hoped for a hole large enough for him to squeeze through, but this. This was unbelievable.

The hole didn't go all the way through, but it was close. It had left a crater that reached past the top of the Tooth. A few more hacks with the chisel would get him through in much less time than swimming around it.

Another rattling of loud snaps erupted, followed by fissures radiating from the inside of the crater. With an ear-splitting boom, the Tooth cracked.

Then split.

The broken end groaned up into the air.

Tomas' gaze swept along the length of the Tooth. Like a lever, the far end was sinking into the sea, with the Jaws serving as the fulcrum. The near end rose higher, exposing mounds of oysters and barnacles.

Shaking the awe and cobwebs out of his head, Tomas hurried through the gap he'd created. The crater walls curled into globs. The blast must've been hot enough to melt stone.

It should've come as no surprise, given how it had reduced orc bones to ashes, but Tomas gasped nonetheless. He raced to the other side. His village came into sight.

So did the Bovyan armada.

They were three-quarters of the way to the Jaws. Meanwhile, he'd shaved a half an hour off his trip by destroying the Tooth. Many of the Bovyans, as well as villagers, pointed at the structure, which now rose out of lake like a spear borne by Bovyan cavalryman.

He hurried along the narrow beach, picking his way among the rocks and boulders. As he got closer to the village, he came upon several children ankle-deep in the tidal pool. They'd likely been hunting oysters, but were now gawking at the Tooth. Others had paused from target practice with their slingshots. One stood by drying strands of stretchweed on a wood frame.

Tomas waved toward the flotilla. "Hurry back home. The Bovyans are coming!"

The children looked up and followed his gesture.

"Is that your Diviner's Sight?" one of the Castella twins asked.

"No!" Tomas jabbed his finger out at the boats, now narrowing to single-file as they got closer to the Jaws.

The children looked again, and then back at him.

Both Saducci twins shook their heads. "There's nothing there. And what happened to your hair?"

Of course, he'd look ridiculous with the long orc robe and the top of his head singed. But how could they not see the boats? Thomas closed his demon eye.

And gasped.

The boats were gone, replaced by gentle waves.

He switched eyes.

And gasped again.

The boats were all there. In the lead craft was Joacquin, a man who'd left the village for Lorium years ago, but came back on occasion to visit his parents. Behind him sat a man with dark skin, the likes of which Tomas had never seen before. With his skin tone and tight black hair, he was undoubtedly an Aksumi Mystic, from the far South. When the Arkothi Runemasters had unleashed the Hellstorm on the Ayuri Empire, the Aksumi Mystics retaliated with cataclysmic magic of their own, blotting out the skies and ushering in the Long Winter.

That had to be it. The Mystic was using some fell magic to hide the boats from view, and Sabine was helping him see through it.

Though, what was a Mystic doing with the Bovyans? Didn't they see magic as the work of demons? And why did the Bovyans want to mask their approach?

His gut twisted. Surprise, of course. And as long as they controlled the Jaws, no one could get on or off the island. Maybe demons and sorcery were fine, as long as they were the ones using it.

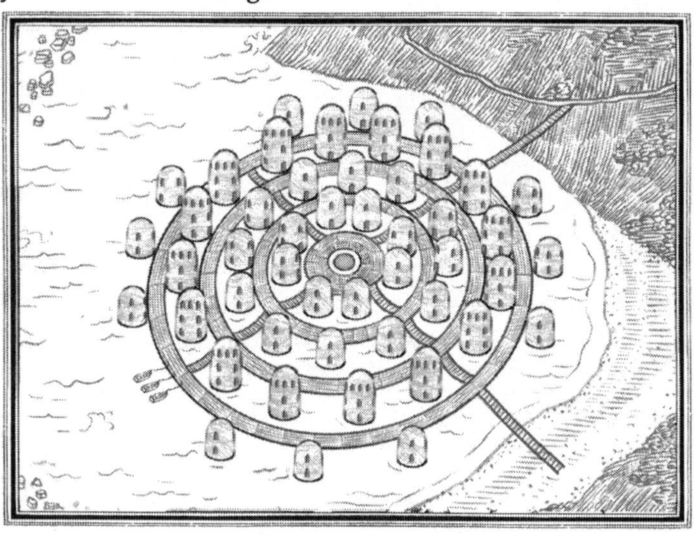

He dashed back to the village as fast as the uneven surface would allow. By the time he made it to the interconnected bridgeways and platforms which wound around the domed metal huts, he collapsed and fought for breath. The weathered planks felt so smooth compared to the gravelly shoreline he'd just negotiated.

Villagers had paused in their daily business, and were now pointing and chattering at where the Tooth was still sinking. Many were bringing their boats in, while others abandoned their work of salting fish or fussing with nets and lines.

"The Teleri are invading!" he yelled. "Gather in the village circle for a council! Bring your slingshots."

The children from before skipped up behind him, slingshots in hand.

Aliya, a middle-aged distant aunt, looked up from where she was repairing a net. Her eyes roved over the priest's robe. "Tomas, you're back! Old Gian said you'd been captured."

"I escaped." Tomas nodded. "Come to the village circle. Get everyone to come. All the elders. Hurry!"

The woman stretched out sun-weathered arms in a yawn. "Why the hurry? Does it have to do with the Tooth?"

"The Teleri are coming!" He pointed to the Jaws.

Aliya cocked her head. "I don't—"

"Diviner's Sight," Tomas said, pointing to his eye. "They caused the explosion."

"Your eye! It changed color! And your head..."

Ignoring the comment, Tomas yelled into the lagoon, where many of the women had been diving for shellfish, or perhaps any of the other ancient trinkets that had ended up there when the Temple of Lydath was sacked. "Get back, get back to shore!"

Heads turned to him, all with looks of confusion.

"The Teleri are coming." He jabbed his finger at the opening in the Jaws. He pitched his voice into a ghostly moan. "I have foreseen it with my Diviner's Sight. Bring slingshots."

Out in the lagoon, the women looked among themselves. Others tugged on diving lines to bring up anyone still underwater.

Lie or not, he was getting the response the village needed. It might not be right, but it had to be done. He turned toward the village center...

...and met Sofia's outstretched arms.

"Oh, Tomas," she said, wide smile showing perfectly straight teeth. "I'm so glad you made it back. I heard they'd captured you."

His heart pattered like a school of minnows zipping through water. He wrapped his arms around hers. Her body was so soft.

She pulled back. "Your eye...what happened to the color?"

He raised a hand to it. He didn't want to lie to Sofia, but the truth would horrify her. "I visited the Temple of Lydath. It happened there."

It wasn't the whole truth. Which was to say, it was a lie. His stomach twisted. Had Sabine twisted his conscience so much that he'd deceive even Sofia?

"That is amazing. And your hair..." Her eyes searched his demon eye. She tugged at the labels of the priest's robe. "This cloth...it's nothing like I've ever seen before."

He nodded. "I got it from the temple."

Her mouth rounded. "How did you even get there?"

"I had the Bovyans bring me to the island, but then tricked them into crashing on the Jaws. They survived, and I tried to lose them in the gorges. In the end, I climbed all the way to the Temple of Lydath."

Around them, people gasped.

"Impossible!"

"How did you do it?"

"Was that the sound?"

"Is that why the Golden Bowl shifted a few hours ago?"

It seemed like a lifetime ago, but he could use the phenomena of the Golden Bowl and Tooth to convince them. Tomas quieted the gathered villagers with a wave of both hands.

He started to speak, but Sofia gazed at him with what looked to be adoring eyes—even though, as a town girl, she didn't know the village lore about all the people who'd tried to climb to the summit. "What was it like?"

Tomas suppressed a shudder. He'd almost been incinerated, crushed, and drowned. And despite the need to warn everyone about the Bovyans, the selfish part of him wanted to impress her. "There were many dead orcs and magic stones."

"What about treasures?" Her eyes glittered. "It's supposedly made of gold."

Tomas nodded. "Yes, but the temple started to collapse while I was in it. I had to escape."

A familiar, dismissive snort silenced the excited chatter. “You? I knew you looked like a monkey, but I didn’t think you could climb like one.”

Tomas turned to the voice.

Antonius stood among a gaggle of the young village women, his arm draped over Tomas’ giggling twin sister, Maria. He was smirking.

“With such long legs,” Tomas said, “you did a great job of running away from the Bovyans.”

Antonius’s expression darkened. “It’s not my fault you couldn’t keep up and got caught. I had to save Sofia. Now, I’m still trying to figure out how a fisherman managed to climb up to the summit.”

Fire rose to Tomas’ face. If not for this bastard abandoning him, he wouldn’t have gotten caught, lost his eye, or had a demon pushed into his head.

Antonius looked from Tomas to Maria. “I still can’t figure out why you are so ugly, and she is so beautiful. Are you really twins?”

“Yes.” Maria tossed her brown hair over her shoulder.

“Well, you must’ve stolen all his good looks in the womb!” Antonius leaned back and cackled.

Maria giggled yet again.

Tomas ignored her, instead turning back to Sofia. “I hope you found the village welcoming?”

If Maria’s fawning on Antonius cast dark clouds over his spirit, Sofia’s smile felt like the sunlight breaking through. “Yes. Your parents have been so kind to me.”

As if on cue, a familiar thud on the wood planks approached from the far end of the village center.

Tomas' shoulders tightened with dread as he turned.

As always, Pa wore the same disappointed expression, punctuated by his grizzly brown beard and mustache. Unkempt hair, streaked with white, bounced with each step. A leg injury from his days as a mercenary, hidden by brown woolen trousers, forced him to limp. He draped a bare arm over Ma, whose urgent, tear-filled eyes locked on Tomas.

"Oh, Tomas!" Ma flung off Father's arm and ran to him. She took his face in her hands and searched his eyes. "Your eye..."

"It happened on the mountain." Tomas' stomach clenched. Now, Sabine was making him telling half-truths to his own mother.

She enveloped him in a warm embrace. "Oh, Tomas. We're just happy you escaped."

"Caught by the Teleri. Hrrrmph. Don't you wish you'd learned to swing a sword now, boy?" Pa pointed the cane in his other hand.

The cane blinked red twice in Tomas' vision, and Sabine muttered something unintelligible in his mind. Tomas pushed himself out of Ma's arms, and pointed back toward the lagoon. "The Teleri. They are coming now."

Everyone turned and squinted out into the waters.

"I don't see anything," Sofia said.

Ma shook her head. "Me either."

"The explosions," Tomas said. "First at the Golden Dish, then just now. It's a sign."

"Did you get hit in the head, boy?" Pa snorted.

Antonius nodded. "He did. That's how they caught him. Knocked him right out."

Ma covered her mouth.

If his own family didn't believe him, there was no way to convince the rest of the village. Tomas took Sofia's hand and tugged. "Come with me."

"Hey! Where are you taking her?" Antonius swiped for Tomas' arm.

Red flashed in his vision, and the path of Antonius' hand lit up in a red arcing line. Releasing Sofia's hand, Tomas stepped just beyond the end point, leaving Antonius grasping at air.

Ma, Pa, Maria, and Sofia all stared, gawking.

Antonius looked from them, back to Tomas. "Why, you little..." He balled up his fists and cocked back his arm.

Sabine muttered a warning. Tomas' vision flashed. Crisscrossing red lines preceded the barrage of four punches, all of which would have pummeled his head, if not for the forewarning. It was almost as if he moved of his own accord, turning this way and that, without getting hit by the best brawler in Lorium.

Red-faced, fists raised, Antonius glared at him. "How did you do that?"

"Diviner's Sight?" Tomas couldn't keep the question out of his tone. After all, maybe Sabine really could see the future, and Diviner's Sight had a much less ominous tone than Demon Eye. He took Sofia's hand and ran. It was time to retreat to the gorge.

Sofia laughed as they picked their way among the huts. "That was amazing! I've seen Antonius beat up so many people."

Maybe that was because Antonius was actually a good fighter, or perhaps the locals knew better than to lay a finger on the mayor's son. Tomas only grinned.

They passed by the village's central platform, surrounded by the elders' single-story homes. Standing around the opening in the middle, men added firewood to the large metal dish rising up from the sea floor.

"Is it true?" Sofia pointed at the plate. "That it came from the Temple of Lydath?"

That was the story the village told, and certainly his own visit to the Temple had shown such a huge piece of metal was possible. Now, though, it was used for cooking and heating stones for warmth in the winter. "It was the centerpiece of the Arkothi emperor's summer villa."

They continued past the two-level buildings on the second ring to the three-story homes on the third, and finally made it to his home on the fourth ring. Motioning for her to wait, he pushed aside the stretchweed-braided cover and climbed through the oval door. Dashing past the rubberwood furnishings, he climbed the steps winding up around the walls, pushed open the hatch, and climbed into the bedchamber.

He retrieved his other slingshot from beneath his bedding, then went over to the north window. Pushing aside the reed curtain, he peeked out to the east. The other homes blocked his view of the village center, but the panicked voices sounded clearer now.

"Look over there!"

"The Bovyans!"

"Tomas was right!"

"His Diviner's Sight is always right."

The buildings blocked the view of the lagoon, but all the chatter left no doubt the Bovyans were landing. Running down the steps and climbing out, he met Sofia's worried expression. With a tilt of his head, they continued past the fifth ring. They reached the end of the village, where the platforms met the mountainside. Behind them, villagers now shouted and screamed.

Tomas ran up the winding mountain path to a vantage point high enough to see above the domed rooftops, through the village circle, to the docks—but not so far that he couldn't hear what was going on. He dropped down below a thick shrub and looked.

The flotilla had cleared the Jaws and now approached the platform. While some elders went out to the docks to greet them, several of the villagers ran into their homes. Tomas craned his neck, looking toward his family home. There was no sign of Sofia, Mother, or Father, but from the cacophony of footsteps, they were likely hiding.

Sofia dropped down beside him, her breath ragged. "What's happening?"

Thomas put a finger to his lips, then lifted his chin to the docks.

The Bovyans tied their boats to the pylons and climbed up. Unlike Sathis and Fethos, these wore hardened leather cuirasses, while the Aksumi Mystic wore a black tunic. Much shorter and slimmer than his compatriots, he had coarse black hair coiled tightly to his head. Joacquin, who'd led them, stayed back in his boat.

One of the elders bowed low. "Welcome to Twins Island. What may we do for you?"

The largest of the Bovyans thumped a fist on his chest. "You are now subjects of the Teleri Empire. Assemble the villagers."

All the elders bowed several times. One gestured the brutes deeper into the village, though the Aksumi hung back, his eyes taking in the surroundings.

"I wonder what the Aksumi is doing," Tomas whispered.

Sofia turned her head. "Aksumi?"

"The small, dark-skinned one in back."

She shook her head. "Are you sure your head is okay?"

Tomas closed the demon eye.

The Aksumi was gone, replaced by a Bovyan.

As soon as Tomas opened the demon eye, the Bovyan form shrunk back to Aksumi. Was Sabine trying to deceive him? Or was she showing him the truth?

With the help of the gutless elders, the Bovyans fanned out and ushered everyone into the village circle. Father, Mother, and Maria huddled among the five dozen murmuring people at the near end of the fire plate. That coward Antonius was nowhere to be seen. While the leader remained near the front, with an aide, the others spread out to cover the bridgeways.

Tomas' heart sunk. This was going to be just like when their cavalry occupied Lorium. Neither Father's sword nor all the village slingshots could stop the invaders. Despite his warning, only a handful of people even carried them now.

The Bovyan leader's eyes raked over the crowds. "Where are the one-eyed boy and our two scouts?"

Cold ran up Tomas' spine. Of course they would be looking for him, and the men he'd tricked, poisoned, and stranded.

The villagers exchanged glances.

"There's no one-eyed boy here, Your Exaltedness," one elder said.

Tomas blew out a breath. Right, nobody on the island knew what happened to him in Lorium, beyond getting captured and his subsequent escape. They'd seen him just now with both eyes.

The Bovyan leader turned and conferred with the man by his side, their voices too low to be heard from this distance. He turned back and spoke louder. "I see the rumors are true, that there are many twins here."

"Yes, Your Exaltedness." The midwife bowed her head. "Autumn children, born here, beneath the Temple of Lydath."

The Aksumi spoke with an accent thick with the South. "The banished orc goddess of fertility."

The midwife nodded.

"So it's true," the Aksumi said, "that the magic potion sold in this region is water running off of Lydath's Bowl?"

The midwife's lip trembled. "Y-Yes."

Tomas gritted his teeth. There was no magic potion, just like he was no true Diviner, but rather, the very shrub above his head, whose seedling Father had brought back from the Kanin Wars three decades before. The village kept its berries secret, selling the juice in Lorium and beyond. Meanwhile, men looking to improve their virility, and women who had trouble getting pregnant, would visit the island and bathe in the pools.

He suppressed a gasp. Everything made sense. Keris' interest in twins on the island. What the healer in Lorium had said about women only being able to carry one Bovyan pregnancy. Twins would increase the soldier population. They'd be twice the threat to the world.

A threat he could stop by burning this bush to the ground. Though that would dry up outside gold coming to the island...

"Good," the leader said. "Soon, we will bring architects and engineers over to expand your village. It will make you all even richer."

The villagers all whispered among themselves, frowning and scowling.

"You will take me to the supply of temple water now." The leader peered at the midwife, then gestured to the Aksumi. "For the rest of you, Melas has another important matter to discuss."

With the midwife guiding, the leader set off with one of his aides down a bridgeway and disappeared between the domes.

They'd pass by Tomas' hiding place soon, and all he had was his slingshot. He tapped Sofia's shoulder, and started to back out from under the shrub.

In the village circle, the Aksumi man cleared his throat, his words lilting with a foreign accent. "Historical records say that the last Runemaster Imperator came to this location to invoke the Hellstorm."

Tomas froze.

The villagers chattered among themselves. It was an old story, perhaps a legend, but one which many believed. Some of them even claimed the Last Imperator as an ancestor.

One of the elders cleared his throat. "Yes, he was trapped here once the waters rose. After a few years, he died."

The coffin! Perhaps the man in there was the Last Imperator, whose cabal was powerful enough to summon the Hellstorm. Maybe Sabine... Tomas raised a hand to the eye.

Down below, the Aksumi withdrew a scroll from his tunic and unfurled it. Tomas squinted with the demon eye, and the image enlarged: it was a crown, with a multifaceted jewel, not unlike the ones from the Temple of Lydath, set in the stud above the brow.

"The Imperial Crown," the Aksumi said. "What happened to it?"

The crowd broke out into murmurs.

An elder bowed his head. "Our legends say it was cursed."

A Bovyan spat. “Undoubtedly, a demon was housed in the gem.”

The Aksumi pursed his lips, but continued. “Does this village have it?”

Looking among each other, the elders passed some silent message between them.

“I grow impatient.” The Aksumi drew a dagger and flipped it through his fingers.

One shook his head. “When the Last Imperator saw his folly, he renounced his magic and cast the crown into the lake.”

“It could be anywhere,” another elder said.

“I can find it,” the Aksumi said. “How fortuitous it is, that this village is famous for divers.”

Tomas’ sister, Maria, was the best.

And now, the midwife and the two Bovyans’ footsteps were about to round the corner of the mountain path.

CHAPTER 34:

Measure of a Woman

With night falling, Alaena huddled at the edge of the clearing where she'd tied Princess Karyna to a sablewood tree. Now, if the pampered brat would hurry up and awaken, they could continue on to meet Peris, and they could all get on with a life of their own choosing.

At least they were in the forest. She took a long sniff. The moist, evergreen smell filled her with a sense of nostalgia. Of a carefree childhood. This was where she belonged. Not trapped in a castle, receiving dignitaries and signing orders.

With a sigh, she listened for sounds of Peris. There was no sign of him, only the murmur of rustling water mixed with the wind in the trees. The moons hung low, their light filtering through the branches and leaves. Darkness had arrived, and with it, hungry forest predators that would probably find at least one of the princess' meat juicy and tender.

Karyna's. Though thin, she was nothing but soft flesh. She probably never had to lift a pinkie to do any work, and instead spent her days looking pretty. With her abnormally pale complexion, she probably never saw the sun.

Anger now thrumming in her ears, Alaena picked up a stone and withdrew her slingshot. Acquired from a market in the distant town of Lorium, its stretchweed band could make even a small pebble deadly, so Alaena took care not to pull the rock too far back. She aimed and released.

It hit Karyna in the gut. The pasty girl let out a small squeal. Her lids fluttered open, revealing particularly light-brown irises. They roved this way and that. Panic bloomed in her expression, and she started tugging at her bindings.

To her credit, she didn't call for help. However, that meant she needed to struggle a little longer for Alaena's plan to work. Not that it wasn't fun to see the spoiled girl squirm a little.

Alaena stepped into the clearing and set her expression into one of surprise. "By Solaris, are you all right?"

Karyna froze. Her eyes locked on Alaena. A hint of caution, but mostly relief, filled her expression. "I...I think so."

The hesitant, high-pitched voice made Alaena cringe. She used a question to deflect suspicion. "Who did this to you?"

"I...I don't know. Where am I?"

Alaena pointed with her chin toward the sound of rustling water. "The woods along the Valeri River."

"The...Valeri River?" Karyna's chest pitched in rapid heaves. She resumed her struggle, only managing to tangle her dress between her legs.

"You're just making it worse," Alaena said with a roll of her eyes. "Take a deep breath and calm down."

"Oh please, don't let it be the Serikothi side." The Tarkothi brat's eyes locked on Alaena as she squirmed in the ropes. "I'm Karyna Corivar, princess of Tarkoth. You have to help me."

Foolish girl, revealing her identity to a stranger. Alaena could have been anyone, and in that, she had the advantage. It was time to weave a story and gain trust. "There's a band of brigands around here that's kidnapping young women."

"So close to Elbahia?"

Maybe she wasn't as clueless as she looked. Alaena nodded. "They're a brazen lot."

Karyna's expression darkened. "The Serikothi are so corrupt, I bet they are colluding with the local authorities."

It was tempting to rebut the insult to the land of her birth, but Alaena held her tongue. If that's what Karyna believed, Alaena would use it to make her story more plausible. She drew her knife. "I'm going to cut your bonds."

Karyna gave a tentative nod, even as she still struggled.

"Keep still."

Karyna shook her head like a dog drying itself. "You don't understand. If the Serikothi catch me, there's no telling what they'll do."

Alaena snorted. The Serikothi should've been the least of the girl's worries. Careful not to damage the tree's bark, Alaena sliced through the rope. "I'm going to take you to safety."

If Karyna nodded any more enthusiastically, she'd make sea lions jealous. Once she slipped free of the bonds, she rubbed her right wrist. Then winced and stared. The rope had abraded her skin, leaving a streak of red. Eyes rounded, she wavered.

"Don't faint on me." A growl caught in Alaena's throat as she strode over and slapped the dainty princess again.

"Oh," Karyna said, panting. "This is horrible. That will leave a scar."

Alaena had several. Rolling her eyes again, she knelt and made a show of examining the crushed leaves and scattered pine needles. It was time to find out how much her counterpart remembered. "How did you get here? What is the last thing you remember?"

"I was walking along a path in a park near Elbahia Island..." Karyna's voice started wistful, then her brows furrowed. "Then there was a musky scent... After that, I don't remember."

"What were you doing all alone?" Even though she knew the answer, Alaena forced incredulousness into her tone.

Karyna's cheeks flushed an interesting shade of crimson. "I...I... Elbahia is safe!"

"Apparently not." Alaena's lips twitched in spite of themselves. There was little danger to one's physical well-being on Elbahia Island; the politicking, on the other hand... Well, this pampered princess didn't know about that yet, but would when she learned her own brother had promised her to the Crown Prince of Serikoth.

Something rustled in the near distance. Every muscle tensed for a second as Alaena evaluated. No metal from armor, not loud enough to be a bear. Relaxing, she pointed east. "Based on the sound of the river and position of the Iridescent Moon, we're in Serikoth. Tracks come from the south, so that is the way you got here."

"Tracks? Are you a woodswoman?"

Alaena shrugged. "I know my way around the forests. I can tell you that at least four men were involved in your kidnapping, and you were carried here."

"Where are they now?" Karyna's eyes narrowed.

Thankfully, Alaena had thought of a good story. "The brigands use secret drop-off points to prevent authorities from tracking them."

Karyna's expression bloomed in understanding. "Thank you for finding me. You will be richly rewarded if you can take me back to Tarkoth's royal villa on Elbahia Island."

Alaena harrumphed. That was the last place she wanted to go. And it wasn't as if there was anything the Tarkothi could offer that she wanted. She set off toward the northeast, heading to the river. "Come on. I know somewhere safe."

Behind her, Karyna hurried to keep up. She stepped on every twig and dry leaf along the way. "Slow down. Ouch!"

Alaena looked back. Karyna sat on the ground pouting, staring at her leg. Thank all the gods in heaven that there really weren't brigands prowling the area, because they would've heard this little princess. Alaena threw up her hands and stomped back. A bruise discolored the delicate flower's shin. "If you want to get home safe, you're going to have to grow up."

Tears welled in Karyna's eyes. "You...you don't understand. I'm a princess."

"So am I." Against her best judgement, she revealed it. Maybe it would get Karyna to stop acting so spoiled. "Alaena Vardamcar."

The Tarkothi princess raised an eyebrow and studied her. "Princess of Serikoth and heir to Korynth?"

"Yes." Alaena nodded. "Your soon-to-be sister-in-law if your brother gets his way."

"What?" Lines creased Karyna's pretty forehead again. Then she pointed. "Your hair. It's so...messy. And red and frizzy."

Alaena ran a hand through her tangles. The color was unheard of for their people, leading to hushed whispers questioning Mother's honor. "On your feet. You are a disgrace to our ancestors. When they came to this continent, they conquered all the land that is now Tarkoth, Serikoth, and Korynth with no more than thirty thousand people. Men and women. We fought alongside our brothers, with sword and crossbow, and on the backs of rocs."

Karyna glared, defiant, as she climbed to her feet. "That was three hundred years ago. I grew up in a palace learning etiquette."

"So did I." Alaena turned around and took a step. Her head jerked back. And she looked.

Clenching a fistful of red hair, Karyna snarled.

"I'm glad you have a little fight in you." Alaena punched Karyna's wrist. When the helpless princess' grasp loosened, Alaena slid a leg behind her and torqued her hip.

Karyna hit the ground with a ladylike squeal. Tears now flowed freely. "How did you get so...so mean?"

Mean? Alaena shook her head. "My father, King of Serikoth, trained me to be a pretty, submissive doll, like you. When I didn't play his games, he gave me up to the Queen of Korynth. I'm sure you remember, since you were presented to her as well. For me, my father had hoped to influence the Korynthi court and gain an ally against your country. I was sent as a political tool."

Frown softening, Karyna cast her gaze into space.

Of course, there was more to the story, maybe a lesson to strengthen this soft girl. Alaena said, "The old queen had raised her late daughter, her only child, to rule. She did the same for me."

Karyna's mouth formed an O. "I understand now. My brother wants Aryn to marry you so that he can claim the Korynthian throne."

Maybe she wasn't as vapid as she looked. Alaena nodded. "And no doubt, he arranged your marriage to Crown Prince Koryn as a way to influence Serikoth."

"What?" She shook her head, sending her brown locks waving. "No, I was supposed to...supposed to..." Karyna's lips trembled, and she fell silent.

Alaena shrugged. "It sounds like he has grand plans, but I don't want to be any part of them."

"If that's what Elrayn wants..." Cheeks flushing, Karyna sighed the wistful sigh of a woman in love. "I have to comply. I have no choice."

Not like Alaena cared about such things. "I've made mine. Don't let others make yours for you."

"I want to be strong. Like you."

"It's not too late." It probably was. Alaena offered the pampered girl a hand.

Karyna puffed out her chest. "I can ride a horse and shoot a bow."

Ignoring her, Alaena held up a hand. Rustling came from the nearby brush. A pair of deer, from the weight.

"Come on. It's already night. You have more to worry about than an arranged marriage."

Before long, they made it to the river. The ground squished beneath their shoes, and Karyna put on a brave face in spite of it all. Alaena almost felt sorry for her. Almost.

"I don't think it was brigands who kidnapped me," Karyna said.

Alaena clenched her jaw. Maybe she shouldn't have mentioned Prince Elrayn's machinations, because it appeared this girl wasn't so dumb. "If not, then it was someone who doesn't want to see our kingdoms reunited through political marriages."

Karyna nodded. "The civil war didn't split the empire asunder for nothing. I guess there are still bitter feelings."

If only she knew the whole story. Alaena pursed her lips and quickened the pace along the banks.

And then stopped. With frantic waves, she motioned for Karyna to hide behind a tree. Not far in the distance, horse hooves clopped and armor jingled. Chest constricting, Alaena studied the bend in the river. She and Karyna now approached the spot where the highway met the river, at the ruins of the old bridge—destroyed over a century ago during the Eldaeri Civil War. They needed to get across the road and beyond the bridge undetected.

"Princess Karyna!" One of the cavalrymen yelled in the distance. "Princess Alaena!"

Peering out, Karyna's eyes brightened.

Alaena scowled and gestured her back. "We need to be certain it's not an enemy trying to draw us out," she whispered.

The voices and sounds faded in the distance, moving away from the bridge.

"That could have been our rescue!" Karyna hissed.

"Do you want to risk it?" Alaena jabbed a finger. "This is my homeland. I know a safe spot. Now come along."

Lips pursed, head hanging, Karyna trudged a few steps behind.

Alaena harrumphed. To think that once upon a time, she'd been a spoiled, sulking brat, too. And just when Karyna was starting to show some spunk.

Where the road cut across the forest, right at the riverbank, charred stone footings marked where the bridge had once been. There were many such remnants of crossings to the north, all silent scars memorializing the folly of ambitious men who tore the Eldaeri Empire apart. Burnt bridges, literally and figuratively.

Peeking out, Alaena listened. No sign of patrols or search parties, save for the sound of more horseshoes well to the south. Beckoning Karyna to follow, she dashed across the road and back into the cover of the woods. She looked back.

The Tarkothi hitched up her skirts and teetered across like a dancer.

Another sigh catching in her throat, Alaena shook her head. "Hurry up. It's not far now." The roll of her eyes would be difficult to see in moons' brittle light, but she didn't keep irritation out of her tone.

They hiked farther through the woods, the darkness making it difficult to negotiate. Their ancestors had intermingled with elves thousands of years before on a distant continent, but those traces of elf blood only made them slim, short, and long-lived compared to other humans, without conferring night vision or magic. Now, only the light blue of Ayara's Eye filtered through the leaves.

Up ahead, a soft white glow illuminated a glade. Alaena placed a hand on Karyna's chest to stop her. "Wait here while I investigate."

Picking her way through the trees, Alaena came to the edge of the clearing. In the middle stood Peris. A robust man, his strong chin and nose were lit by the bauble lamp on the ground. Gone was his green uniform coat from earlier in the afternoon, replaced by brown trousers and a grey tunic. A broadsword hung at his side.

"Peris." Alaena stepped out.

Further back, Karyna drew a sharp breath. "Peris?" She hustled over faster than any time in the last two hours. Pushing past Alaena, she burst through the glade and careened into Peris' embrace. Their lips mashed together in a sloppy kiss that sent Alaena's stomach churning.

When she leaned back to gaze at the officer, her adoring eyes were just as nauseating. Her voice was just too chirpy. "Your note told me to come to that island north of Elbahia!"

Peris grinned. Karyna pouted.

With a snort, Alaena stepped into the clearing. "Your family suspected your affair and kept a close watch on you. Peris asked me to kidnap you, using a contact intoxicant he brought from back from Cathay. That was the musk you smelled."

Karyna glared at her. "Why didn't you just tell me?"

"Because you don't know the first thing about sneaking around."

"Then why the ruse with tying me up at the tree?" Karyna put her hands on her hips.

"The intoxicant was wearing off, and I needed you to trust me when you woke." Though the gullible girl probably would've, without the deception. Still, it wasn't worth leaving to chance.

Karyna searched her eyes. "What do you have to gain from all of this?"

"Would you believe me if I said I was a sucker for true love?"

Karyna shook her head. Maybe she wasn't so gullible after all. Or maybe it was just that obvious.

Alaena laughed. "With you running away with Peris, the deal between our countries to exchange princess brides is null. I get my freedom. Now, I will be on my way. I suggest you shutter your lamp and enjoy each other's warm embrace tonight. While there really aren't any bandits roving this area, I don't recommend travelling the forest in the dark. In the morning, if you head north along the riverbank, you can disappear for good."

"Thank you." With one arm extended, Peris approached with a broad smile.

There was something fake about his expression, and he held his other hand behind his back. A musky smell hung in the air.

The contact toxin she'd used on Karyna. Alaena backed away, reaching for the knife tucked into the back of her breeches.

Peris froze. His lips twisted into a malevolent grin as he drew his own blade.

"What are you doing?" Karyna stumbled over and grasped his arm.

"Our secret dies with her."

Karyna shook her head. "No, no. You can't hurt her. She helped us. She doesn't have a reason to betray us now."

Peris gave the naïve princess a hard shove, sending her to the grass. He locked his gaze on Alaena. "You don't stand a chance. Just surrender, and I'll make it quick."

"You wouldn't ask me to die quietly if you thought you could beat me so easily." Alaena pointed the knife at him, though little good its length would do against his sword. Her only hope would be to escape into the woods. But that also left Karyna. If he treated her so roughly—

A rag came hurtling at her. Alaena weaved out of the way, but a musky drop grazed her cheek. A sword hack followed, and she just managed to sidestep the blow.

"No!" Karyna shrieked. "Stop!"

Alaena's head spun, as if the musk formed a haze over her mind. Peris chopped again, and it was all she could do put her knife in its path. The blow wrung her hand and sent the weapon flying. He rammed his shoulder into her and she slammed into the ground, knocking the air out of her.

His massive weight crushed her chest. He bent over and clawed for his sword, which had somehow slipped from his grasp. "Karyna, bring me the cloth."

No! Alaena's word came out as gasp. If Karyna touched the contact toxin, she'd be knocked out, too. Maybe that was this vile man's goal.

For now, though, Karyna was pulling at Peris. "Please, let her go."

Not even looking, he backhanded her in the face, sending her flying. She landed with a thud somewhere behind him. She let out a dainty whimper.

He'd straightened in order to hit her, which took him further from his sword and gave Alaena at least a slight chance. She squirmed and kicked as she reached for his weapon, but he shifted his weight back. It all but squeezed out her breath. It was impossible to think through the mental haze. There was nothing to stop him from killing her, nothing to—

Peris choked. Blood flecked his lips. He collapsed, burying her under his weight, and after two more rasping breaths, lay still.

Head spinning, Alaena squirmed out. Her knife protruded from his back, a lucky shot which must have punctured his lung. Standing above him, a blanching Karyna offered a blood-slicked, trembling hand.

Then immediately withdrew it. She keeled over and vomited.

She'd stabbed her own lover in the back. That was the only way to explain it. Head still reeling, Alaena worked her way out from under Peris' body. How ironic that she owed a spoiled, pampered princess her life. She staggered to her feet and patted Karyna on the back. "Are you all right?"

Tears pooling in her eyes, Karyna looked up. "I...I loved him."

"He would have killed you, too." Probably. The malevolence in his eyes said as much.

Karyna nodded. "I realized that, as soon as he told me to get the cloth."

Wobbling on her feet, Alaena beckoned Karyna to follow. "Let's get back to the highway."

Karyna shook her head. "We can't just leave him here."

"We have to. Now come on." She took Karyna's wrist and pulled her along.

With Peris' lamp lighting their way, they made it to back to the road quickly. Again, at the bridge ruins, voices and horse hooves sounded in the distance.

Alaena held the lamp up to Karyna. Her gaze looked vacant, her face frozen in shock. Each step plodded. She'd probably never be the same after tonight.

Whether she descended into depression or rose up with gritty determination might rely on the right words.

"It gets easier," Alaena said.

Karyna blinked, breaking the blank stare. "What does?"

"Fighting. Killing." Who knew if those were the right words? Somehow it mattered, even for an enemy.

Karyna's focus shifted from Alaena to the sound of approaching horse hooves and jangling of armor.

Following her gaze, Alaena saw several riders on Serikoth's magnificent chargers. The burnished cuirasses sparkling in the lamps and crimson capes billowing behind them marked them as cavaliers. It'd been years since she'd seen them, and she'd forgotten just how dashing they were. All save for a Madaeri and a girl who clung to him as if her life depended on it. The formation slowed to a stop.

The blond leader, a captain by the insignias on his armor, swung out of his saddle. He crossed his arms over his chest and bowed to Alaena. "Your Highness. Are you unharmed?"

"We are fine." Alaena nodded and pulled Karyna forward.

For all her earlier fear of being caught in Serikoth, Karyna strode forward with her chin held high.

The man crossed his arms again and bowed. "Princess Karyna, your people uncovered a plot to kidnap and murder you and frame it on our Princess Alaena."

Alaena's stomach clenched. Peris had tricked her, just as much as he'd deceived Karyna, possibly for years. She'd been complicit in the kidnapping, though like Karyna, she'd failed to see through Peris' deception until it was almost too late.

Karyna looked back and gave her a slight nod.

"We are here," the captain continued, "to capture the conspirators and escort you back to your people."

Karyna squared her shoulders and held up her bloody hand. "Thank you, Captain. The traitor is dead."

"How?"

Alaena cleared her throat. "By her hand."

The soldier nodded and crossed his arms again. "We would expect nothing less of an Eldaeri princess." He guided his horse forward. "Can you ride?"

Swinging up into the saddle, Karyna looked...regal. Valiant. More like the Eldaeri women of old than the wretched girl from just a couple of hours before.

Alaena was just happy the shadows hid her smile.

CHAPTER 35:

To Know Your Enemy

Koryn waited with Prince Aryn in Elbahia Palace, as messengers came and went with updates. By the time the ceasefire had begun, Serikothi soldiers—all full-blooded Eldaeri, of course—had captured most of Elbahia and the bridges into Tarkoth. Still, they would be stretched thin until reinforcements came from deeper in Serikoth. And there was still no update from the docks, even though the cannon fire had fallen silent a while ago. More concerning was that there was no word about the missing princesses.

He found Aryn in his peripheral vision.

The prince stood still, lips pursed.

Koryn cleared his throat. "Prince Aryn, I plan on telling my father to raise an objection to your marriage to my sister. I believe the Queen of Korynth will respect his wishes in this regard."

Aryn's eyes fluttered before their gazes met. "Let us hope we find her, first, so that you can raise that objection."

"Of course." Koryn nodded. "That said, in light of this incident, I feel that there is a gulf between our countries that will not be narrowed any time soon. I am afraid we must see an alliance between Korynth and Tarkoth as a hostile act." Though one which would give his life meaning.

"Just when I was entertaining the idea." Aryn chuckled.

Koryn studied his expression.

Not truly amused, the forced smile hid a lot of hurt. The half-elf was clearly more than just a plaything to him, and something she had said or done had upset him.

Boots clacked on the marble floors. A Serikothi courier ran in and crossed fists over his chest. "Your Highness, horrible news. Tarkothi troops under an unknown lieutenant have scored a resounding victory at the docks."

Koryn chewed the inside of his cheek. How was it possible that a mish-mash of mongrels could win? It had to be the Light. "Did they hold the Light of Solaris? Did the Tarkothi continue fighting after the announcement of the ceasefire?"

The messenger shook his head. "No, Your Highness. They did not have the Light, and they were overwhelming our position. If not for the ceasefire, they might've captured the *Intimidator* and *Solaris' Spear*."

"What is the current status?" Koryn looked sidelong at Aryn.

"Our marines were forced to abandon the docks. They are holed up on the two ships. None of the Elbahia tug crews are around to pull them out into the harbor, nor does either ship have a large enough crew to sail."

The Serikothi fleet was small compared to the Tarkothi, and the *Intimidator* was its flagship. If it fell into Tarkothi hands... With the bulk of Serikothi forces surrounding the Tarkothi royal villa and the bridges, they'd have to wait for reinforcements before trying to retake the docks. Gritting his teeth, Koryn found Aryn in the corner of his eye.

Only a hint of a smile flicked across his otherwise expressionless face.

He was here, unguarded. If Tarkoth captured the *Intimidator*, maybe they would trade it back for their prince. Then again, to bargain with a hostage was no better than Elrayn trying to arrange marriages at swordpoint.

And of course, there were the missing princesses. If Karyna turned up dead, as Koryn's gut told him would happen, it would mean all-out war. If Alaena were killed as well, not only would he lose a sister he hadn't seen in over a decade, but Korynth would side against whomever they blamed for her death.

"I hope Karyna and Princess Alaena are all right." Aryn tugged at his sleeves. Perhaps he was thinking along the same lines.

Koryn studied him again. "Were you serious about entertaining the idea of marrying Alaena?"

"If anything, this incident has taught me that maybe we do need to come closer together. To prevent brother from killing brother."

It was a novel idea, though it would take more than a few political marriages.

Another Serikothi runner rushed in. "Your Highness, Princesses Alaena and Karyna have been safely recovered."

The tension fled from Koryn's shoulders. He blew out a long breath. "Where are they now?"

"Captain Damaryn is riding back with an escort of cavaliers. They'll cross onto Elbahia Island at the Flaviyan Bridge."

Koryn turned to Aryn. "Will you join me in greeting them?"

"I'd like to get a look at my possible bride." Aryn smirked.

"Me too?" With a chuckle, Koryn strode out of the audience chamber, down the stairs through the grand hall, and out to where a soldier waited with his horse.

Aryn followed, and went to where his horse was hitched. He really had come alone.

Koryn gestured to the four cavaliers holding the south bridge, and mounted up. They fell in behind him and Aryn, and he circled around to the west bridge. With his nod, the four cavaliers guarding it joined in the escort as well. They crossed over in tight formation and turned north.

Smoke and sulfur hung in the air, and though Elbahia was typically quiet at night, it might as well have been an abandoned ruin for all the shuttered and boarded homes. Every so often, they passed groups of Serikothi soldiers, some bearing litters with the wounded.

Koryn's stomach knotted. Even without Teleri machinations dividing the Eldaeri realms, he would have taken the same measures to punish the Tarkothi for kidnapping him. This conflict was Prince Elrayn's fault, and men had died because of it.

On his order, they came to a stop at the Flaviyan Bridge, the span farthest to the north, which crossed into Serikoth. He looked up to the Iridescent Moon, now waxing toward full. Almost midnight; seven phases of darkness left. Seven phases before his men outside the Tarkothi royal villa would lose their advantage, if he decided to pursue punitive action.

No, he wouldn't. Despite the capture. Too many of Solaris' Chosen had died tonight.

Up ahead came the rumble of horse hooves. Bobbing lamps illuminated the crimson capes and feathers of the cavaliers, with Damaryn's golden hair fluttering in the wind. It mingled with frizzy red hair, where Alaena clung to his back.

Koryn's heart skipped a beat.

Behind them, another horse bore two riders, one whose slim build and billowing dress revealed her to be Princess Karyna.

The one Elrayn wanted him to marry. Whose marriage his own father had endorsed. Perhaps both men had hoped to influence the other country. Perhaps it could actually provide cover for Koryn's affair with his lover: as long as he made a baby with Karyna, everyone would be happy.

He shuddered. He'd have nothing to do with that. Shaking the notion out of his head, he locked his gaze on the bridge.

Damaryn was crossing now, and up close, Alaena looked wobbly in the saddle. Behind them, eyes closed, Princess Karyna's head rested on a cavalier's shoulder.

Damaryn pulled up, and swung out of his saddle like a poet would draw a quill across paper. In the same smooth motion, he helped Alaena off his mount.

How strange that free-spirted Alaena would allow the help, even if she needed it. When her feet found the ground, her legs wobbled like a soldier in his first battle. Something was clearly wrong.

Koryn dismounted and strode toward her. "Alaena, are you all right?"

Her head bobbled, reminiscent of the Ayuri merchants in Ayudra, making it unclear if she was shaking her head or nodding. She staggered.

Damaryn's arm swept under her with effortless grace, providing innocuous support. Such was his veneration of the royal family that he wouldn't want her to lose face.

Koryn reached her side and slid an arm under her. "Alaena, it's been so long. I'm glad you're safe. What happened?"

"The Tarkothi, Peris," she rasped. "He used some kind of intoxicant on me."

The bastard! Koryn looked back for Aryn, who wasn't there. He looked left and right, then found the foreign prince helping Princess Karyna off the back of a horse, some five meters away.

Sobbing, she threw her arms around her brother. "Oh, Aryn. I'm so sorry. I'm so sorry. It's all my fault."

"It's our fault," Aryn said. "Peris fooled me all these years. I took him for a friend, and it got you kidnapped."

"And almost killed," the half-elf chirped out of nowhere.

"I thought he loved me. But then...then... He was about to..." Karyna wilted, and then broke into sobs.

Koryn harrumphed in spite of himself. To think Elrayn wanted to control Serikoth by marrying this delicate flower into the royal family. Perhaps wedding her would actually be the solution to all his problems. But no, this weak-willed, lovestruck woman wouldn't last in the Serikothi court. It would be unfair to her. He pulled Alaena back, putting Damaryn's horse between them and the Tarkothi.

At his side, Alaena bobbled her head again. When she spoke, her voice was hoarse. "I also share the blame. I didn't want to marry their prince, and Peris tricked me into thinking I could get out of it by helping Karyna escape with him. He really wanted to kill us."

"That's what I said," Jie muttered under her breath. The half-elf and Fleet had positioned themselves halfway between the respective princes and princesses.

"But now," Alaena said, "Peris is dead. Killed by Karyna."

It didn't seem possible. Koryn looked around the horse at the fragile girl. Perhaps she wasn't so fragile after all.

Who Karyna was or wasn't didn't matter now. For the moment, they'd averted a crisis. Koryn left Alaena in Damaryn's care and walked around the horse. Karyna's back was to him, enfolded as she was in her brother's embrace.

The foreign prince gave him a nod. "I think things are settled now?"

Koryn nodded. "I shall order my men to withdraw across to our side of the river, once I have word from Prince Elrayn that you have done the same."

"I shall return to our villa and implore him to do so."

"Then—"

Two horses galloped toward them, the closer one bearing a Serikothi flag, the other with a Tarkothi flag, just a few lengths behind.

The first leaped off his saddle even before the horse came to a stop. He crossed his fists and bowed. "Your Highness, trouble. A flotilla of river boats bypassed our positions on the bridges and delivered Tarkothi soldiers along the east bank. They have deployed near their villa. Our generals say they can break our siege with ease."

Koryn clenched his fists. It was a blatant breaking of the ceasefire.

"Also, three of their frigates have arrived in the harbor." The courier motioned behind him. "Their messenger wishes to parley with you."

Koryn looked over at the other courier, who'd dismounted near Aryn.

Head shaking, Prince Aryn was scowling. He grabbed the messenger. "No, that is madness. The Serikothi had nothing to do with it."

The man crossed his fists. "I am just the courier. I have orders to deliver the ultimatum to Prince Koryn."

Ultimatum? Ice ran up Koryn's spine. All their positions were threatened, and their ships were in more danger of capture now. Had the ceasefire all been a ploy for the Tarkothi to reinforce their beleaguered troops? And just what would Elrayn be demanding?

Holding the courier back, Aryn hung his head. "I will deliver the message, then."

The rider crossed his fists and bowed his head, but followed a step behind the prince.

Trudging over, Aryn bowed low, like a servant. "Prince Koryn, I have the unenviable responsibility to deliver an ultimatum from my fool of a brother."

Koryn stiffened. After being held prisoner, he had no patience for Elrayn. "Go ahead."

Aryn blew out a long breath. "My brother's words, not mine. He believes that you took the Light of Solaris during the night's confusion. He demands its return in half a phase, or Tarkoth will consider it a breach of the ceasefire."

"What?" Anger flared in Koryn's face. He spoke through gritted teeth. "You moved reinforcements onto the island during our ceasefire. Not only that, the Light has been missing since even before I was able to escape from Tarkoth."

"I'm sorry." Aryn bowed his head. "If you will allow us to leave, I shall return to our villa and implore Prince Elrayn not to continue down this path."

Koryn chewed on the inside of his cheek. Taking Aryn prisoner would be well within Serikoth's rights for Tarkoth's breach of the ceasefire. Still, he'd acted in all sincerity, and Koryn wouldn't take him hostage... It would make him no better than Elrayn. He nodded. "Please. We have shed enough Eldaeri blood tonight."

"Thank you, Prince Koryn." Aryn craned around, looking in the direction of Alaena and Damaryn, but then turned back to him. "If my brother doesn't back down, I will marry into your family and work towards rebuilding bridges between our three nations."

Koryn nodded. Still, no matter what happened, the Light of Solaris—the most important heirloom of the Chosen People—was missing. All this time, he thought the Tarkothi had already retrieved it from Elbahia Palace, to use against his troops.

A pit formed in his stomach. Tharos was still unaccounted for. If he really was a Bovyan, as Jie suggested, the treasured relic of their people had probably already fallen into the hands of a race that wanted nothing less than the extermination of Solaris' Chosen.

CHAPTER 36:

Temptations of a Succubus

Heart pattering, Tomas motioned for Sofia to follow as he scooted back out from under the berry shrub. Any moment, the village midwife would lead the Bovyan leader and his aide around the bend. Indeed, the hurried footsteps and jangling sword grew louder.

"We need to get deeper into the island." He gained his feet and helped Sofia up.

Before they had a chance to run, colors danced at the turn in the path.

Tomas' heart just about stopped.

Antonius stumbled into view. "Wait!"

Him! The constable's sword banging against his thigh would give away their position. If the Bovyans found them, he would no doubt sell Tomas out again.

Sofia's hand tightened around Tomas'.

It was all the sign he needed. He turned and ran with her into the gorge.

"Wait!" Antonius yelled so loud, a deaf person on the other end of the island would be able to hear.

Sofia ground to a halt. "Let him catch up. Otherwise he'll continue squawking."

She was right. Tomas turned and beckoned. "Hurry up! Hold on to your sword!"

Nodding excitedly, Antonius clasped his weapon. He loped over.

Tomas poked him in the chest. "Now listen. Be quiet. Don't speak unless spoken to. Otherwise, I'm going to lose you in the gorge."

"All r—"

Tomas hissed.

Antonius pantomimed sealing his lips.

Satisfied, Tomas continued on the path. Before long, they came to a split, with a treacherous path winding up to a ridge, and an easy trail descending into the ravine. Falling water sounded from within.

Tomas started upward.

"Wait." Antonius pointed down. "This way is easier. Some small shrubs, but no trees, see? They've all been cut down to stumps."

It was also the way to the pools, the Bovyan's destination; and with no trees, there was also no cover. Over the centuries, the villagers had harvested all the lumber for the bridgeways, platforms, and boats. They'd stand out like a solitary cloud in a clear summer sky.

Tomas bit back a sharp retort about the constable's stupidity. Instead, winking at Sofia, he said, "You're right. You lead."

Sofia's expression bloomed in understanding.

Puffing out his chest, Antonius worked his way down.

He'd gone about ten feet when Sofia bent over. "Wait, I twisted my ankle."

"Come back," Tomas said. "We need to help her. The Bovyans are almost here."

Without breaking a stride, Antonius looked over his shoulder. "I'll scout ahead."

Tomas hid his smirk. He'd made good measure of the man. He turned back to Sofia, only to find her testing a shrub trunk as she climbed up to the higher path. She'd hiked her skirts up and tied them between her legs for better mobility. Smart girl.

He followed her up. His vision outlined the shrub she'd grabbed, then another. A rock she was about to step on flashed red. "Stop. Step over it."

Her foot hovered over the rock for a second, then she hopped over. When he reached it himself, he gave it a light kick.

It shifted. Had someone put their full weight on it, they might've tumbled into the gorge.

Once they'd gained a level ledge some thirty *pedes* above the ravine floor, they ducked down beneath some thick shrubbery and looked down.

"It's beautiful." Eyes wide, Sofia covered her gasp.

Tomas had been here thousands of times, but the demon eye made everything stand out in sharp relief.

Every twig and leaf and rock seemed more colorful. A narrow waterfall tumbled over rocks to the ravine floor. The water pooled, the algae within giving it a red tinge. Antonius was hurrying past one now.

"An escapee!" a Bovyan voice bellowed.

Heart leaping into his throat, Tomas tracked the words to the source, at the head of the gorge.

The enemy leader was pointing at...

Tomas tracked his finger downward to Antonius.

He blew out a breath. Of course, he and Sofia were up and well-hidden.

Beside the leader stood the village midwife, hand over her mouth. The aide was striding down the path toward Antonius.

Tomas' gut wrenched. For his own safety, and Sofia's of course, he'd intentionally used Antonius as a diversion. Maybe the selfish, cowardly constable deserved it, but still... It must be Sabine, yet again, bringing out Tomas' most evil thoughts. Even worse, she seemed to be tempting him with yet another possibility: two Bovyans were here, separated from the others and the Aksumi in the village. Kill...er, disable them, and draw the others in one by one, and the entire village would be safe, as long as no one brought more Bovyans back through the Jaws.

He felt for the last two gemstones on his sleeve, but then stayed his hand. The midwife was down there too, and it would be better to save the explosive for a time when more Bovyans were clustered together.

Below, steel rasped from scabbards.

Tomas looked down.

Standing in a threatening stance near one of the pools, the aide brandished his arming sword.

Antonius pointed his rapier back. The thin blade wobbled in his trembling hands. Eyes darting around, he took two steps back. "I...I am the best swordsman in Lorium. Stay back!"

"Drop your weapon," the aide said, "and you will be spared."

Even at this distance, the demon eye picked up the sweat beading on Antonius' brow. He licked his lips. Then he threw down the sword.

"Coward." The aide claimed the distance between them, and kicked the rapier away. He slapped Antonius across the face, knocking him to the ground with a squeal.

Sofia covered her mouth.

The leader strode up and delivered a sharp kick to Antonius' gut. "You're wearing the uniform of the Lorium constables. You must be the deserter who fled the first day. Where's the girl?"

Antonius' eyes shifted back to the head of the gorge. No doubt, the wretch planned to sell Sofia out to save his own miserable hide. For now, he hadn't looked up.

Scanning the path ahead, Tomas locked in on a ledge, which Sabine outlined in red. He squeezed Sofia's hand and whispered, "I have an idea. See that outcrop over there? Walk around to the other side and scream."

She looked at him, expression incredulous for a second. Then she nodded. Shimmying out and picking herself up, she worked her way toward the ledge. She looked back, stopping when he motioned her to do so.

"There she is!" Antonius yelled.

Tomas looked down again.

Antonius was pointing up, while the Bovyans and midwife followed the gesture.

The leader's eyes narrowed. "Go, get her."

Thumping his chest with a fist, the aide hustled up the path, back to the entrance to the ravine. He climbed to the ledge and loped along the trail. His focus remained locked on Sofia the whole time.

It would be easier for Tomas this way. He held his breath as the brute came closer. He glanced back down, to where the leader, Antonius, and midwife followed the soldier's progress. If anyone caught sight of Tomas, hiding beneath the shrub...

The soldier was just five paces away now.

Four paces.

Tomas' palms sweat as he got ready.

Two paces.

One pace.

Tomas shot his arm out, snagging the man's front leg just as the weight was shifting off of it. So firm and heavy, it was like hitting a tree trunk. Tomas' shoulder jarred.

Still, the soldier stumbled and fell. He threw his hands out. One landed on the trail, but the other slipped at the edge of the ledge.

Scrabbling out from his hiding place on all fours, Tomas shoved the man.

He went over the side. His scream was cut short by a crash on the rocks below.

Tomas hazarded a glance down.

His victim was crumpled in an unmoving heap. Not far from them, the midwife held both hands to her mouth. Antonius gawked.

The leader locked his gaze on Tomas. “You!”

“Run!” Tomas waved frantically at the midwife.

Antonius, of course, ran deeper into the gorge. The midwife came out of her shock and followed.

The leader swiped at her with his hand, but missed. He started to run after her.

Tomas snatched up a rock and set it in his slingshot. He pulled back and aimed. Tingles shot through his head. He stifled a gasp at the red rune that appeared in his visual field, encircling the Bovyan’s form. It interfered with his concentration, but he released the stone.

A red line trailed behind the spinning rock. The red rune shrank by the second, until it covered the middle of the leader’s back.

The Bovyan reached again for the midwife. The rock struck his leather armor and bounced off, but it was enough to make the man stumble a step. He spun around.

Tomas picked up another stone and pulled back. The rune appeared again, smaller this time, now on the leader’s head. The rune shrank as he pulled, then started to enlarge again. Sabine must be helping him aim. He released a little bit of the tension, and the rune contracted. He released.

The pebble slammed into the leader's face, inside the red rune. It knocked him to the ground. Holding his nose, his other hand on the ground, he staggered as he tried to stand, and then collapsed onto his butt.

Tomas retrieved another rock, and pulled back. When the red rune appeared, it was now no larger than a dot. He squinted, and the Bovyan grew in size. He adjusted the aim, setting the dot over the man's eye, and released.

The rock zipped through the air and slammed into the leader's eye socket. He toppled over, and lay unmoving.

"Wow." Sofia sidled up to him. "I didn't realize you were so good with the slingshot."

Neither did Tomas. He'd always been among the worst shots in the village. He grinned and beckoned her to follow him to the ravine floor.

Sofia looked at the pools, then tracked the trickle of water from the mountaintop. "Does the water really help girls step into womanhood, and barren women get pregnant?"

"Yes." Until he married her, Sofia would be an outsider, and the berry's secrets needed to be kept. Or was that Sabine, getting him to lie? Would he have answered any differently two days ago? "The water runs off of Lydath's Golden Bowl, picking up its residual magic, before tumbling down to here."

Tomas cringed at the falsehoods spilling out of his mouth. He now knew for certain that the water didn't actually run off Lydath's Golden Bowl. He'd been to the top himself, and seen it. He found Sofia in the corner of his eye.

She stared at the waters, wide-eyed. She'd asked for some of the water, which was what had brought him to Lorium's marketplace the day he lost his eye.

Tomas patted his pocket, where he'd kept the vial of berry juice. The shards now lay crushed on the beaches of Lorium. Had she wanted it for herself? He'd taken the last of the previous year's harvest. Now, it would be autumn before they could gather more.

He busied himself with climbing over the aide he'd pushed over the ledge. The body lay broken backward across a small boulder. Its eyes stared wide and lifeless. Tomas' stomach churned, and a sour taste rose to his mouth. Yet another man he'd killed. Swallowing hard, he retrieved the belt with the dagger and sword. The latter was too heavy, and probably the only villager skilled enough to wield it was Pa.

Climbing down, he slipped past Sofia, who was dangling her hand in the water, and headed over to the leader.

The midwife was returning from the other side. "You must've been practicing with your slingshot since I last saw you use it."

Tomas offered a feeble grin. With his slingshot at the ready, he slinked over. He gave the Bovyan's leg a nudge with his foot and jumped back.

The leg wobbled, but flopped to its original position, unmoving. Unconscious?

Tomas edged around the inert form and leaned over. He gasped.

Blood oozed from where the stone had lodged deep in the man's eye socket. A shot Tomas could've never made before. Maybe even the best village sharpshooters couldn't. Sabine, for all that she was doing to his soul, was making him into more than he could ever have become with his own two eyes.

A rapier drove into the leader's throat. The man's body spasmed, a guttural sound escaping his lips, before falling still again.

Heart jolting, Tomas fell on his butt. The slingshot slipped from his hand. He scuttled back and looked up.

Antonius stood there, weapon in hand, face red with fury. "That will teach that bastard to challenge me!"

Tomas shook his head. "You didn't— "

Red flashed in his vision. Sabine spoke words of warning.

The rapier tip pointed at him. He stared up the weapon's length.

Antonius snarled. "You monkey-faced freak. If you contradict me, ever, I will run you through, just like him."

"Antonius!" Sofia scrambled over. Kneeling by Tomas side, she pushed the blade away. "Please, don't hurt him."

The constable harrumphed. "Monkey Face just got lucky. The Bovyan wasn't even moving." He scooped up the slingshot with his sword and let it slide down the blade. With a yank, he sliced through the stretchweed band.

Hand outstretched, Tomas gasped.

The midwife slapped Antonius. "You fool, Tomas needed that. There are still eighteen more of them in the village."

Well, seventeen, plus the Aksumi. Tomas squeezed his hands tight. He had the other Bovyan's dagger, but that would be useless against a rapier.

Antonius harrumphed. "Monkey Face got a lucky shot. It was useless. He—"

The midwife held up a quieting hand. "Well, until we get rid of them, no one is safe. You two have to get along."

"Don't blame me." Tomas clenched his teeth. He'd tried, and Antonius betrayed him at every turn.

She looked from him to Antonius. "Well, what's done is done. We need to do something about the Bovyans."

"We need to do something about Joacquin, too," Tomas said in a low voice.

Sofia covered her mouth and stared at him.

Tomas swallowed hard. It must be Sabine, whispering evil suggestions into his mind. "He helped the Bovyans get through the Jaws. We need to keep him from bringing over every fishing boat in Lorium, loaded with those monsters."

The midwife nodded in slow bobs, while Antonius puffed out his chest.

Sofia... She was shaking her head. "There has to be another way than hurting poor Joacquin."

Tomas nodded. “I think I have an idea.”

CHAPTER 37:

Lore of the Land

Jie studied the body of the Elbahia palace guard standing on the stairwell landing between the second and third floors. No doubt, Nightblades were involved in the theft of the Light of Solaris, which made this squabble among these Eldaeri princes her business. Track down the thief, and she'd be closer to the clan traitor.

After hearing Prince Elrayn's outrageous ultimatum, Fleet had dragged her onto a horse, yet again, and brought her to the palace to help investigate. Still comforting Princess Karyna, Aryn had watched her go, wordless. If they survived the night, there would be a reckoning with him.

With a sigh, Jie shook his betrayed expression out of her head and looked at this unfortunate guard. Aryn had said the Elbahia palace guards were some of the best swordsmen, chosen from all the Eldaeri Kingdoms. And yet, this one had been slain. There was no blood on his white uniform or steel cuirass. The method for propping him up was similar to that used on the two bodies at the Tarkothi guest house, where Koryn had killed the Bovyan Nightblade—only this time, the assassin had secured the remains to a light bauble sconce with a thin silk thread. The bruise marks under his high collar indicated death by strangulation.

Despite her protests, Fleet had climbed up to her shoulders and was studying the thread. "This is silk. It only comes from your country."

Jie would've nodded if his foot wasn't on her head. "We export a lot of it, but this fine grade..."

"It only comes from a rare species of silkworm living in the mulberry groves of the Black Lotus Temple." He jumped down.

Hand straying to her magic knife, she stared down at him. How could he possibly know about silkworms at all, let alone about the temple? Only a handful of the realm's highest officials knew it existed, and only the Emperor's family knew its name. Could Fleet be involved with the Nightblades? It seemed highly unlikely, but...

He grinned. "I've travelled the length and breadth of Tivaralan, and beyond. You couldn't begin to fathom how far I've been."

That still didn't explain how he would even know how to find the temple. Still, if he worked for the Teleri, he wouldn't have helped her find Alaena and Karyna. Unless that was part of their plan, to have spies gain trust by betraying other spies.

"You are either constipated, or your pretty little brain is trying to figure out how I know the Black Fists, and how I know you are one." Fleet shrugged.

Her hand left her knife, but didn't stray far. "Well?"

His voice changed, sounding a lot like her own. "Surely your clan has oral histories which tell the origins of your skills. Like imitating voices and throwing them, as you did earlier. Those talents go back to before the War of Ancient Gods."

Jie just about had to pick her jaw off the ground. "The Elf Angel Aralas bid the Madaeri, who were also slaves to the Tivari, to teach us."

He nodded.

"That was over a thousand years ago."

"Would you believe my great-great-great-great-great-grandfather..." Fleet counted on his fingers. "No, add two more greats. Or three? Oh, it doesn't matter. My ancestor taught the first Black Fist adepts stealth. After the war, he helped create the Black Lotus sect, and lived in the temple for a few years before moving east."

Such coincidences didn't seem possible. Could it possibly be Fleet, and not some clan traitor, who was the mysterious teacher of the Nightblades? No, there were so many more skills Peris, Tharos, and the others had used, that the Black Lotus had developed themselves. For now, Fleet was a potential resource. "Can I trust you with a secret?"

He rubbed his belly. "My people's promises are usually sealed with food, but I'll collect on that later."

"We suspect a traitor to my clan has taught some Bovyans our art. I was sent to track him down."

"Are you sure it's a him?"

Was she? The clan had confirmed the whereabouts or deaths of all operatives in the last eighty years, though her own experiences had shown deaths could be faked. "No. We don't know much of anything. All adepts and masters are accounted for. Unless..." She studied him. Maybe the Madaeri really had taught the Bovyans.

He blinked innocently.

She continued up the steps, and he followed without a sound.

There were bodies propped up on the next two landings as well. With all the bright light, and the guards' lines of sight, it wouldn't be easy to sneak up and kill them without raising the alarm. How would she have done it? Thrown her voice to get the guard to turn his head? The Nightblade must've visited the palace to know where guards were placed. An important royal aide like Tharos or Peris would certainly not have aroused suspicion on a scouting mission.

Jie froze in place. There was a smudge of blood on the wall behind the last victim, yet none anywhere else that she could see. Tharos, maybe? He'd been bleeding from the broken window. She sniffed up at the garrote which had been used to strangle the unfortunate guard. Mingling in with the man's own scent was another. The musky smell that had clung to Tharos' bedcovers, the same one she'd picked up when she'd met Prince Elrayn and Tharos in the cold warehouse.

If her nose could pick it up... She cupped her hands to form a stirrup and looked to Fleet. "Get a whiff of the musk."

He waved her off. "I can smell it fine down here."

"Tharos, Prince Elrayn's aide. I'm sure he's a Teleri Nightblade."

Fleet sniffed the air. "His scent is diffuse enough that he's long gone. However, the smell grows stronger the higher we go."

Jie nodded, and they continued their climb. They arrived at the top level and went out to the mezzanine. As they rounded the balcony, they came across three more of the palace guards, all lying dead in pools of their own blood, none propped up like the others. Tharos had acted swiftly in these cases, dispatching elite warriors by slashing their throats.

Jie eyed the balcony overlooking the central hall. He must've stayed low along the balustrade, out of their line of sight until he was ready to pounce.

She came to the telescoping sky-stair, which extended up to the cupola in the dome, where the Light of Solaris had been kept, visible throughout the island.

She turned to Fleet. "I noticed the stair before. I imagine it ruins the view from down below."

"It's usually folded in on itself. Dwarven ingenuity. Whoever used it was in a hurry to leave, and didn't return it to its closed position."

"Or, he escaped out through the cupola." Jie pointed to the niche.

"And slid down the outside of dome?" Fleet's head swept in slow shakes. "It would've been easier to leave the way he'd entered."

"You said yourself, his scent was stronger higher up." Jie tested the air with her nose, but didn't detect the musk.

Fleet shrugged and sniffed again. Like a wild boar snuffling for truffles, nose close to the ground, he headed to the sky stair and ascended.

Jie followed, eyes sweeping the area for any evidence, and also looking down at the mezzanine balconies and grand audience chamber below. At least four Elbahia guard positions should've been able to see someone using the stair. "Fleet, does this sky stair make much noise when it's opened?"

The Madaeri shook his head. "Probably not. Well-lubricated gears. Did I mention dwarven ingenuity?"

They made it to the cupola and climbed through the niche, out into the night.

Cool air and distant shouts greeted her. She suppressed a gasp. The view was stunning, even in the muted grey-green of her elf vision. As shown in the maps, the island appeared to be a perfect oval, sitting where the Valeri River widened into a natural harbor, before continuing its path toward the sea. As the Serikothi messenger had said earlier, three small ships floated in the harbor, their prow cannons pointing at the larger *Intimidator*.

Several river barges were docked along the eastern side. The Serikothi surrounded the Tarkothi royal villa on three sides, while they themselves were surrounded by the Tarkothi reinforcements.

The only thing that would prevent bloodshed was the Light of Solaris, which was supposed to be in this very spot. She pointed to the empty pedestal. "What is so special about this Light, that Prince Elrayn would go to war for it?"

"They say it holds a spark of Solaris' divinity." Fleet's voice sounded doubtful.

"You don't believe it?"

"It doesn't matter what *I* believe. Soldiers will fight and die if *they* believe. They see a light that never goes out..."

She patted one of her interior pockets, where two light baubles were stashed. "Nothing special about that. Aksumi Mystics enchant hundreds of light baubles a day, and you can buy them cheaply in any marketplace in the world. Can we make a copy?"

He shook his head. "No, the Light is different. Sorcerers and wizards have tried to extinguish it. It has survived falls and fires, and its light has never even dimmed. Don't underestimate humans' power of belief. The Eldaeri, who claim to be the Sun God's Chosen, see it as symbol of their invincibility. None of their armies have ever been defeated in battle when it has been held aloft."

"And now, the Teleri have it."

He nodded. "And since the Bovyans claim descent from Solaris' mortal son, they will treasure it as much as the Eldaeri."

"Then we'd better find it." Jie ran a finger over one of the cupola's columns, pausing at the blood. "He was here."

Fleet shook his head. "Not anymore, and I don't smell any sign of him."

She swept her gaze over the dome. There, a discolored streak. If it were daylight, she'd wager it was Tharos' blood. And right now, it was their only clue. She pointed. "He slid down here."

"Let's check it out." Fleet started to step out.

Jie grabbed him. "It might be slippery."

"If our Bovyan friend did it, so can I." He laughed.

True enough. She snorted.

He sat down and slid down the dome, running his finger over the blood stains that he passed. His speed increased, and he looked back halfway down, his expression lit up in delight.

He was enjoying himself!

Landing on the outer rim, he balanced himself. He looked up and beckoned to her.

Gritting her teeth, Jie sat down and followed. The dome was cool through her clothes, and she glided down quickly. Too quickly; much faster than the Madaeri. The smooth fabric of her stealth suit didn't create enough friction compared to his roughspun trousers. Her speed built as the curve steepened. She shot out her bare hands onto the smooth surface to try to slow the slide. When that did little to arrest her descent, she flipped over onto her belly and splayed her limbs out, using her bare hands to increase friction. She might've decelerated a little.

Now, though, she didn't have a good view of the end of the dome. She had to be close—close to the precipitous, four-story drop. She hazarded a glance over her shoulder. She was there. Turning back over, she brought her legs together and bent her knees as her feet hit the narrow ledge between the rim of the palace's outer wall and the dome.

The landing happened too fast. Her balance teetered, and her center of gravity shifted over the rim. She waved her hands in wild circles to regain equilibrium before she went over. Down below, the ground gazed back up at her, waiting eagerly to be decorated by half-elf splatter.

A firm grasp wrapped around her wrist and pulled her back.

Her heart raced like the gallop of horse hooves. Letting out a gasp, she turned and looked up at Fleet.

"You're welcome," he said.

She nodded. "Thanks."

"So much for Black Lotus grace." He grinned.

She pursed her lips, but then looked back up the dome. "I can't imagine Tharos being able to slide down without going over the edge."

He took her sleeve between his fingers. "Maybe his clothes weren't as slick as yours."

"When he fled the Tarkothi villa, he might've been naked. The slide probably left a burn on his ass."

Fleet grimaced. "Can't unsee that."

She chuckled. "Now, assuming he was able to survive the slide, how did he get down?"

"You go that way." He gestured counterclockwise. "I'll go the other, and we can see if there are any clues."

It was a sound idea. With a nod, she worked her way around the rim, looking down for any clues. Or, if they were fortunate, Tharos' broken body.

No such luck. Instead, along the northwest end of the palace, a set of spikes descended the wall to the courtyard below.

"Over here," she yelled, then started down.

Like the spikes outside the Tarkothi villa, these were spaced for a tall man. Still, she was able to stretch and use them to reach the bottom with ease.

She looked up to find Fleet nearly upon her. That someone with such short legs was able to move so fast around the rim, and then descend with hand and footholds spaced so far apart, was hard to believe.

When she finished gaping, she finally found the words. "How do you do that?"

"Look so handsome?"

"No, move so quickly and quietly?"

He studied his nails. "We are small people, requiring even better senses and faster reflexes than elves in order to survive. When the Tivari subjugated the world, they used us to keep an eye on their human slaves, and also as watchdogs against dragons. We also don't fear much, so a ride down a dome is kind of fun."

Jie gawked. Shaking the explanation out of her head, she pondered. Why had Tharos chosen the northwest end of the palace to descend? Lines of sight, perhaps. Here, he'd be less visible from the bridges. She scanned the area. Her elf vision detected no sign of the Nightblade, and her nose found no trace of his scent.

She paused. A drop of dried blood. Then another, just six *chi*–two meters by Eldaeri standards—farther, and then another, after seven *chi*. They formed a straight line to the end of the palace yard ten *chi* beyond, where the foundation dropped fifteen *chi* to the moat below.

Walking to the end, she looked over the edge. There were no signs of climbing spikes, and given the lack of seams in the foundation, it didn't seem possible spikes would penetrate the strange rock.

"He must've known the secret passage." Fleet's voice, right beside her, nearly caused her soul to jump out of her body.

"Secret passage?" She looked down at him.

He nodded and pointed back the way they'd come.

She doubled back, and stopped at the last blood splotch. Its outer edge was a smooth, straight line. A hatch of some sort.

"This was an escape route from the time the Eldaeri ruled from Elbahia, though it has probably been around since the elves raised the island out of the water. Only a handful of people know about it."

"Including you." Jie afforded him a suspicious raise of her eyebrow. "How would Tharos know?"

The way Fleet's face scrunched up, it looked like he was constipated. "He's an aide to Tarkothi royalty, after all."

Snorting, she looked for any handholds. "Ok, how do we open it?"

Fleet knelt down and ran his fingers along the unseen seam. His hand froze, and he pressed down. Three crescent-shaped panels of a circular door swished open, from the center out.

She gawked. "I've never seen..."

"Have I mentioned anything about dwarf ingenuity?" With a grin, he disappeared into the hole.

"Many times." Jie looked down. Ladder rungs jutted out from the side of the wall, spaced almost too close for a grown human male. Hand under hand, she descended.

Her feet landed lightly on the ground, right next to large footprints in the thick dust layer. Though there were no signs of light, she could see as if it were dusk. The tunnel looked to be made of braided tree branches. Large gemstones crusted the walls at regular intervals, some sparkling with a light of their own. She ran her hand over one of the bulbous beams, which felt rough and gnarly.

"Don't touch!" Fleet called.

Jie pulled her hand back, just before it reached a gemstone. "We have to be below the waterline. How come these tunnels aren't flooded? Just what is this place?"

"Do you know the old legends of the Twilight of Istriya?" Fleet kept sniffing and walking through the corridors.

Keeping pace, following the obvious tracks and blood drops Tharos left, Jie shook her head.

"Of course not." He sighed. "Humans reckon history from the overthrow of the Tivari, just a thousand years ago. But for thousands of years before that, they were slaves to the orcs. And before that, the world belonged to the elves, and they called it Istriya."

Jie nodded. Black Lotus history dealt mostly with her homeland, and specifically the last hundred years. Still, there were fairy tales from ancient times, before the War of Ancient Gods.

"The struggle between elves and orcs for control of Istriya went back and forth for years. It strained even the elves' capacity for magic."

Jie nodded again. She'd seen how sorcery taxed Aksumi Mystics.

"At one point, when they were close to losing, the elves rediscovered these glittering caves, and in them, starbursts."

"In Tokahia," Jie said, "I saw a statue of the First Diviner, holding a starburst. I thought it was just a divining tool."

"No, starbursts focus energy, so the channeler can recover quickly from using magic. Some believe the starburst set into the Crown of Arkos helped the Runemaster Imperator with his magic. For sure, it helped the elves turn the tide in the war against the orcs, until the Year of the Second Sun."

"I thought that was just a legend." Jie looked around. They'd taken so many turns, she'd lost track of where they were in relation to the buildings above.

"The orc god Tivar appeared in the heavens, shining like a second, red sun, day and night, for a year. Magic failed the elves and the orcs massacred them. The survivors went into hiding."

"How do you know all this?"

"Hang out with elves long enough, and they'll sing you a song or fifty about it."

Jie shuddered. She'd never seen a full-blooded elf before, except maybe as a baby when her good-for-nothing father left her at the gates of the Black Lotus Temple. No, she had no desire to ever meet an elf, let alone hear one sing.

He stopped in place and studied her. "Sore topic, eh?"

Where had her ability to hide emotions fled to? She set her expression into detached indifference.

He chuckled.

"Wait," she said, hurrying to keep up. "You just mentioned the Crown of Arkos. Prince Elrayn was looking for it, and Peris found mention of the last Runemaster Imperator fleeing to Lorium after the Hellstorm. If he knew, then Tharos knows, too. Bovyans have no use for magic. What if..."

"The Teleri want it as a symbol of legitimacy." Nodding, Fleet looked over his shoulder at her. "To cast themselves as the rightful heirs to the Sundered Empire."

"And now," Jie said, "they'll replace the starburst with the Light of Solaris, to symbolize their bloodline to the Sun God himself."

Fleet blew out a breath. "Which means..."

"The conflict tonight, the kidnapping of the princesses, it was all a distraction."

"It's a sound theory." Fleet stopped and pointed. "His scent is strong here."

Jie looked around. More tree branches in the wall formed a ladder heading up. On the floor, several sets of large footprints had come and gone. "Do you know where we are?"

"I'd guess we are beneath the northern part of the island, just outside the Korynthi royal villa."

"So, not far from the bridge where we met back up with Prince Koryn after finding the missing princesses." And by now, Elrayn's ultimatum deadline had long passed. Perhaps the Serikothi and Tarkothi were already killing each other, keeping them divided. Ready for the Teleri to swoop in.

He nodded and started up the ladder. He applied pressure to the ceiling. Like before, the three-paneled door whooshed opened from the center.

Dirt and sod fell in. Far in the distance, cannons roared and men yelled.

Not breaking the surface, Fleet looked out. His ears twitched. Then, he flashed Black Lotus hand signals. *Someone approaching. Get ready.*

Sucking on her lower lip, Jie palmed a throwing star.

CHAPTER 38:

Unwelcome Guests

The sun hung low in the west, sending a ray of orange into the waters of the sea. Though Sofia, Antonius, and the midwife squinted as they huddled on their stomachs under the shrub at Tomas' side, the demon eye let him see the scene below clearly.

A dozen boats bobbed just outside the Jaws. In one, the Aksumi Mystic held up a clear crystal, dangling from its chain. Spread out around him, villagers worked in pairs, with one matted-haired woman holding the rope while another dove. Every couple of minutes, a diver would bob up with some kind of trinket—but no crown, if the frowning Mystic's shaking head were any indication—and switch places with the one in the boat.

Tomas squinted with the demon eye. All kinds of new treasures lay piled in the boats: bracelets, tiaras, head circlets. The divers had brought up more valuables in the last couple of hours than they did in a month.

He shifted his attention back to the village. Three of the Bovyans stood guard at each of the ramps which led to the west and south beaches, and the gorge. Ten circulated through the village. Three more walked with the elders on the west beach, with one pointing and drawing in the air with his fingers. Wearing even more sour expressions than usual, the elders all nodded each time the Bovyan stopped speaking.

"What's your plan?" Sofia asked.

If it were possible to get all the Bovyans together, in the gorge, without any of the villagers nearby, he'd use one of his unholy gems. That didn't seem likely, though. Tomas turned his head to her. "We need to lure them into the gorge, one at a time."

Antonius stopped ogling the divers and scoffed. "How do you plan to do that?"

"Our midwife will go to the sentry nearest to the gorge and tell him their leader needs him. She'll guide him in, and Antonius will kill him."

Antonius blanched. "I... I... It wouldn't be fair. I won't do it."

Sofia looked past Tomas, sidelong. "You didn't seem to care about fighting fair when you stabbed their leader through the throat."

"That...that was different."

Tomas growled. "It's only an hour to sunset. We need to do it soon. Otherwise, they'll go looking for their missing leader. We need to make sure it is one at a time."

Antonius shook his head. "I'm not going to dishonor myself."

"Fine." Tomas looked to the midwife while pointing at the guard on the path to the gorge. "You need to rush down to him, making it seem urgent, so he doesn't have time to get his friends. Take him up to the ridge instead of down to the pools. I'll be hiding and push him over the edge."

The midwife's head nodded in slow bobs. "All right."

"That's a stupid idea." Antonius smirked. "Where can you hide on that ledge?"

Tomas pointed from the sun to the ravine. "There's a niche which will be in the shadows right now. I'll hide there."

"You're so smart." Sofia beamed.

Antonius' lips twisted into a frown. "Just lucky."

Tomas gestured back the way they'd come. "Sofia, you go hide in the ravine."

"I'll protect her," Antonius said.

"From what?" Tomas muttered under his breath, but gestured them on.

They all backed out from beneath the shrub. Tomas, Antonius, and Sofia all scrambled up the trail toward the gorge opening. At the fork, Tomas hustled them toward the path down.

"For luck." Sofia leaned in and kissed him on the cheek before refusing Antonius' hand.

Heat flashed in Tomas' face. To hide it, he looked over his shoulder.

The midwife was talking to the Bovyan, gesticulating wildly, pointing in this direction.

He ducked back in, then climbed up the ledge. The dark afternoon shade would've made such a brisk pace dangerous, if not for the demon eye's clarity. He squeezed past where the ledge narrowed, to the niche. Before squeezing in, he searched the ravine floor for Sofia.

She and Antonius were pulling the leader's body to a crevice. Such good thinking on her part!

Careful not to put pressure on the gemstones on his sleeves, Tomas backed in and took a few deep breaths to settle his heart. If this didn't work, if the Bovyan checked the niche, then Tomas was stuck there, with no way to avoid getting a sword stuck in his gut.

"He's up there! Hurry, before it gets too dark." The midwife's voice echoed from the entrance to the cavern.

Tomas peeked out.

"Wait." The Bovyan reached into his pouch and withdrew a light bauble.

Again careful with the gemstones, Tomas pressed back into the niche. Didn't the Bovyans view magic as the work of demons? He looked straight out, but it was still dark. He craned his head out again.

A sphere of white light spread out around the soldier and midwife, but didn't reach his hiding place or the ravine floor. Sofia would be safe. Tomas ducked back in and held his breath.

The footsteps came closer.

"He's just up ahead," the midwife said.

"Hurry, woman."

They had to be only a few paces away. Sweat gathered on Tomas' brow, and every muscle felt stiff as wood. He could just let the Bovyan pass and not risk it.

No, he had to act. For Sofia. For the village.

The midwife passed, her head turning just a little toward the niche.

Would the Bovyan see it? Would he look, too?

Tomas' heart just about stopped.

The big body lumbered by.

Tomas sprang from the crevice and shoved the man.

It was like hitting a stone wall. The Bovyan stopped in place to regain his balance. He turned his head and his eyes widened.

Red flashed over the man's sword, hanging on his left side. Tomas grabbed the hilt and shoved it so the scabbard slammed behind the Bovyan's knees. In the same motion, he threw his shoulder into the Bovyan's chest.

The Bovyan teetered, hands waving wildly to regain his balance. He swiped at Tomas, the arc of the attack flashing in Tomas' vision.

Tomas caught hold of a rock in the crevice and pulled himself back. The Bovyan's fingers sent a swoosh of air into Tomas' face, and he fell backward over the side. The scream lasted only a second before the man thudded into the rocks below.

Panting, Tomas patted his chest. He'd almost gone over, too. Odds were he wouldn't survive sixteen more encounters; and that was assuming the Bovyans were stupid enough to come one at a time. He craned over the edge.

Though deep in the afternoon shadows, the sprawled, contorted body appeared clear in the demon eye.

Tomas' gut wrenched. He'd sent two men to their deaths today. A third, if Sathis died from the mushrooms. A fourth, including the leader, even if it'd been Antonius who'd delivered the killing blow. Their lives, snuffed out. He wasn't even sure where Bovyans' souls went after they died. "Did you make me do this, Sabine?"

The succubus remained silent.

"Who is Sabine?" the midwife asked.

Swallowing hard, Tomas pulled himself back and met her eyes. "Nobody. I'm just rambling."

"Are you all right?" She studied his head.

"I...I think so."

She patted him on the back. "I can't imagine how you're feeling. But, just think, each of those men has raped and murdered, and would have continued to do so."

It was easy for her to say: she wasn't the one who did the actual killing. With a sigh, he found Sofia huddling in the shadows of the ravine floor. At least she was safe.

Gritting his teeth, Tomas gave a firm nod. "Sixteen more, and the Aksumi."

"Aksumi?" The midwife cocked her head.

"Never mind. Seventeen more. We need to figure out what to do about them before they come looking for their friends." Tomas picked his way along the ledge and climbed back down to the mouth of the gorge.

Sofia threw her hands around him. "Oh, Tomas. Are you all right?"

No matter the guilt that weighed on his shoulders, her soft body felt so comforting against his.

Antonius snorted from behind. "What, did he crack a nail?"

Sofia turned on him. "You coward. You've been useless since this invasion began. No, you've made things worse."

Even in the late afternoon shadows, his face flushed an interesting shade of crimson. He smacked Sofia across the side of the face. "Bitch. I killed their leader. I—"

Fire raged in Tomas' head. He shoved Antonius with both hands, sending him stumbling back.

Snarling, the spoiled constable drew his rapier. "You little shit. I'm going to mark your face with enough scars, you won't look like a monkey anymore."

The tip would've slashed across Tomas' face, but his vision flashed, and Sabine spoke in his mind. His head pulled back, just out of reach, of its own accord. He bobbed and weaved, avoiding the follow-ups as red lines danced in his eyes.

"Stop!" The midwife cuffed Antonius on the back of his head. "We still have more than a dozen Bovyans, and you two are squabbling."

Antonius snapped his sword into its scabbard. "Just keep Monkey Face away from me. Or next time, I'll run him through."

The entitled ass might be an even greater threat than the invaders. Squeezing his fists, Tomas took a deep breath. If not for Sabine's sense of self-preservation backing him out of the way, his face might've been sliced up. He spun on his heel and crept down the path.

Reaching the same shrub as before, he knelt and scanned the area.

Illuminated by rays from the nearly open Blue Moon on the water, the village boats were filing through the Jaws and into the lagoon. The Aksumi had already climbed onto the bridgeways, emptyhanded if his sour expression was any indication.

Two of the Bovyans remained at their previous posts, at the ramps to the beaches. One conversed with elders in the village center, while others ate and a few patrolled. With so few occupiers, it shouldn't be hard to sneak through the village without them knowing. The first order of business would be to get ahold of a slingshot.

He turned back to the others. "I'm going to the village. As far as the Bovyans know, their leader and aide are with you." He nodded at the midwife. "They don't know about Antonius or Sofia, unless the others told them. So stay back. Camp out in the gorge."

Antonius threw his hands up. "What are we supposed to eat?"

"There are plenty of edible plants you can harvest."

Antonius shook his head. "It's dark."

Sofia held up a hand. Light spilled through her fingers. "I got the bauble. Thank Fortuna, it didn't crack."

"I'll bring you back some fish," Tomas said.

The midwife took Sofia's hand. "Come on, let's go. You, too." She glared at Antonius.

Picking his way down the trail, Tomas came to the ramp which led up to the village bridgeways. Night had fallen, though the demon eye made it look like dusk. With a quick scan, he crept up. The scent of roasting fish and vegetables percolated from the communal fire plate in the village center.

Beneath his bare feet, the planks of the bridgeway creaked. There was no way to avoid the sound, but it wasn't out of the ordinary for villagers to walk to and from the fire plate at this hour as they prepared for dinner.

He came to his family hut and peered in. Nobody was home. He slipped in, tiptoed over to Maria's bedding, and retrieved her spare slingshot and some smooth stones from the secret compartment beneath. Testing the stretchweed, he set a stone in the sling and gave it a pull. The red circle appeared in his vision again, large like the first time he'd shot. Sabine must be able to distinguish the difference in the slingshots' tension.

Satisfied, he shrugged out of the priest's robe and added it to a lower layer of his own bedding, but not before pocketing his remaining two gemstones. He tucked the Bovyan's sheathed dagger and slingshot into his belt, behind his back, and let his shirt drape over them.

Above Pa's and Ma's bedding hung Pa's spear and longsword, from his days fighting in the Kanin Wars. Sometimes, it seemed Father was still stuck in an idealized youth, even as his broken body refused to play along.

With a sigh, Tomas snuck back out and worked his way to the village center. Many of the villagers gathered around the thirty-*pede* wide hole, legs dangling over the edge of the platform as they used stakes to roast fish over the fire plate. One Bovyan sat with the elders at the far end, while another eight sat on either side of him, eating. Not far out of their group, the Aksumi lounged between the pretty sixteen-year-old Iacco twins, his arms draped over their shoulders. They both wore desolate expressions, and their parents looked on with frowns.

Tomas clenched his fists. The sooner they got rid of these unwelcome visitors, the better. He came and plopped down next to Ma, who sat nearly opposite the Aksumi. The fire blazing between them provided cover.

She gasped. "Tomas!"

He hushed her. "What's happening?"

"The Bovyan has been talking to the elders about where they will construct more buildings."

Pa growled. "The beaches."

Maria tugged on his sleeve. "What about Antonius?"

Tomas' vision flashed red. He held up a finger. "Shhhhhh."

Three of the Bovyans stood up, their tall heads visible above the fire. Two marched around the circle in their direction.

Chest squeezing, Tomas gritted his teeth. He slouched and hung his head low.

Their heavy footsteps thudded on the wood planks, coming closer.

Just keep low. If they discovered him, they could cover all the exits to the village center and trap him in. He certainly couldn't fight all of them.

One turned to the east, while the other continued around and left down another bridgeway.

Tomas blew out his breath. He looked over his shoulder and followed their progress.

The entrances to the village. They were probably going to change sentries. Which meant they'd find out the one guarding the path to the ravine was missing.

He started to stand, but then looked back. "What about the divers? Did they find the crown?"

"The Bovyan says they are in the right place," Father said. "The women say it's too deep, too dark. They keep finding other things on the slope, but not his precious crown. When they throw light baubles into the water, they flash bright, then blink out."

The soldier who'd just headed toward the gorge came running back. "Lieutenant Teris," he yelled.

The Bovyan among the elders looked up. "What is it?"

"Flovus is missing. There's also no sign of the captain or sergeant."

"Men, to me." Teris climbed to his feet and thumped his chest.

The others around the circle bolted up in unison and thumped their chests.

Teris gestured in the direction of the Aksumi. "Melas, stop your carousing and get over here."

Tomas craned around to get a better view of the Aksumi on the other side of the flames.

Yawning, the man unwrapped himself from the two girls and picked himself up. When he spoke in his thick accent, it sounded thoroughly unenthusiastic. "Yes, sir."

"Block all the bridgeways out of the village center," Teris boomed. "Rufis, Monas, Korus, and Titus, fan out, check all the homes, and bring everyone here. Tokis and Nunes, take a villager into the gorge to look for the captain."

The Bovyans thumped their chests and fanned out, even as the villagers muttered among themselves. Four of the Bovyans hurried down the bridgeways.

Tomas squeezed his fists tight. Sofia was hiding there. He called out, "Lieutenant, it's too dark and dangerous. Can't it wait until morning?"

"Who said that?" Teris tilted around the flames and looked before marching over.

Ma gripped Tomas' arm tight like an eagle's talons.

Keeping his head down, Tomas tried to shake her hands loose.

"Whoever spoke," Teris said, jerking one of the Marcello twins to her feet, "come forward now.

Otherwise, I will whip this girl so hard, she won't be able to lie down for a week."

Tomas fought off Ma's clinging hands and rose. "It's true. The gorge is treacherous at night. Your men are more likely to fall and break their necks than they are to find your captain."

"Not if you are the one leading." Teris gestured him forward.

Tomas squared his shoulders and strode over. He could lead Nunes and Teris up the same narrow path he'd pushed the aide and sentry off of. In the dark, Sabine gave him an advantage.

"I don't recognize you." Teris raised a light bauble, and studied Tomas' face. "Wait…"

Tomas chest squeezed. If they found him out—

"You're the boy we caught in Lorium. Your eye…"

"You must be referring to my twin," Tomas said; never mind all the twins on the island were fraternal. "He's been missing for days."

Teris' head bobbed in slow nods. Tomas held back his sigh of relief.

"No," came a familiar voice from the east bridgeway, where a resolute stride mingled with stuttered footsteps. "That's him."

Heart sinking, Tomas turned.

Fethos, the man who'd shoved the demon eye in his skull, had somehow found a way through the gorge. Filthy and haggard, he was half-dragging Sofia, whose face was streaked by tears.

CHAPTER 39:

Relieved

Pacing the deck of the *Indomitable*, Aelward looked across the quays to where his men had the Serikothi *Intimidator* and *Solaris' Spear* surrounded. With the reprieve the ceasefire had afforded the enemy, they'd holed up on their ships, their repeaters pointing out. Now, after his own forces had lost their momentum, Prince Elrayn had sent specific instructions to capture both if the Light of Solaris wasn't returned by the full Iridescent Moon.

The madness! With his fish-brained scheme to force marriages, it was Elrayn's fault the Light was missing in the first place. Now good marines would die, trying to take a floating fortress. Elrayn had even forbidden the use of cannon, so as not to damage the ship.

Orders were orders. Sailors ran across the deck. Down below, Tarkothi marines were readying their crossbows, preparing to execute his plan. Hopefully, it would minimize casualties. Aelward looked up to the Iridescent Moon. The Serikothi had what, two minutes left?

He turned to Captain Suryn. "Send the signals."

The captain crossed his fists, then waved to the officer in the crow's nest.

The man opened and closed the shutters of his lamp, sending the signal to the three ships in the harbor. All three were within twenty meters of the enemy. Lights flashed back. Oars slid out from their oarlocks.

Aelward gritted his teeth. One minute.

"Crown Prince Elrayn on board!" yelled a marine.

Soldiers snapped to attention.

The Light must've been recovered. Aelward blew out his breath and looked over.

With several royal guards in tow, Prince Elrayn marched toward him. He didn't look to be carrying anything.

Oh, please let it be his bad eyes. Craning his neck, Aelward squinted. No, the prince didn't have the Light. No doubt, they would've returned the Light to its niche. Aelward looked north toward Elbahia Palace.

The palace dome glistened in the moon, but the Light wasn't there.

He snapped to attention as the Crown Prince stopped two meters from him. Aelward crossed his fists and bowed his head. "Your Highness, are you here with good news about the Light?"

"Unfortunately, no, Lieutenant. I'm here to oversee the assault."

A pit formed in Aelward's throat.

Elrayn turned to Captain Suryn. "Is everything prepared?"

The captain bowed his head. "Yes, Your Highness. I believe the lieutenant has come up with a plan that gives us the best chance of success."

Elrayn turned and studied him. "Did he now?"

Crossing his fists, Aelward nodded. "With what little time we had, I conferred with all available officers."

"Well then, the deadline has passed. Begin the attack."

Aelward exchanged looks with Captain Suryn, who then gestured to the crow's nest.

Lights flashed again, answered by the ships at sea.

Yells erupted from the Serikothi ships.

"Shoot!" barked Tarkothi marine commanders on the docks.

Repeaters clicked in a rhythm, and bolts flew into the *Intimidator's* stern and flank. Its marines sent out one volley, but then ducked below the incoming swarm. Its aft cannons roared. In the distance, *Solaris' Spear*'s cannons fired as well. Wood on the approaching ships splintered and cracked. Men screamed.

Elrayn stared at him. "This was your plan? Our ships are taking fire."

"With all due respect," Aelward said, "You forbade us from using our own cannon. There was no way to prevent the first shots, but our volleys will slow their reloading." Hopefully.

Their ships were close now, and the oars reversed as the vessels crowded closer together. Their main decks stood some five meters below the *Intimidator's* sterncastle poop deck. Grappling hooks flew up into the bulwarks and rigging, and the Tarkothi marines started climbing up. Some jumped over to the stern balcony. Serikothi marines bobbed up from behind cover to shoot. Men screamed. Others plunged into the water. Before long, metal clashed on metal as swords flashed in the moonlight.

Elrayn turned to the captain. "Will we be able to capture their ships?"

He nodded. "The lieutenant's plan put us in good position. Now, it is a matter of who wants it more. If you allow us to use our cannon, I can almost guarantee minimal casualties."

The prince shook his head. "I want their ships captured undamaged. Another *Intimidator* class vessel will make a fine addition to our navy."

It would, but it seemed too good to last. Aelward cleared his throat. "If I may, Your Highness, what if the Serikothi demand its return?"

"Then they will have to surrender the Light of Solaris."

Men grunted and yelled. So many were dying over this squabble. More would, if it wasn't resolved soon.

Aelward clenched his jaw. "What if they don't actually have it?"

"Of course they do." Elrayn scoffed. "Their Princess Alaena kidnapped our Princess Karyna to create a distraction, so they could steal it."

Mauls and Maelstroms, what? Aelward cocked his head. That didn't sound like the Alaena he'd come to know. "She's heir to Korynth."

"But she was born to the Serikothi royal family. She is undoubtedly still loyal to them."

Aelward shook his head. From everything she'd said, she didn't seem interested in being royalty at all. "I brought her to Elbahia. I don't know how she could've possibly communicated with the Serikothi."

"Were you watching her at all times?" Elrayn arched an eyebrow.

Almost, because she clung to him, and would've slept in his cabin had he allowed it. He shook his head.

The prince gave a knowing nod. "A woman can beguile a sailor to pass messages. Or maybe it was planned well in advance. In any case, how else can you explain the missing Light?"

"Was it not our own Peris and Tharos who were involved?"

Elrayn frowned. "We will get to the bottom of that soon. Messengers have said Alaena is back with the Korynthi. Tomorrow, when the smoke has cleared, I will go and demand answers."

"I don't think—"

"No, you do not think." Elrayn jabbed a finger at him. "I do not appreciate your questioning. You are relieved as mission commander. Captain Suryn, you are in charge."

Aelward gawked. His plan was working, and now he was to be relieved?

The captain crossed his fists and bowed his head. He turned to Aelward. "I'm sorry, Lieutenant. I do think the battle is well in hand, though, thanks to your sound planning. And the men certainly remember you rallying them before we lost the initiative with the ceasefire."

Jaws clenched, Aelward gave a stiff bow and stomped across the deck to the gangplank. Marines and sailors all saluted him with crossed fists as he passed. He looked back.

Tempests! Elrayn wasn't even paying attention to him, instead chatting with the captain.

With a sigh, he descended to the dock. As always, when he reached solid ground, dizziness made his knees wobble. Where to now? There was a naval officers' villa on the Tarkothi side of the river, but that would be a long walk. Back to his cabin on the *Sea Dragon*? Close, but...

No. He needed answers. If Alaena had gone to the Korynthi villa, that's where he'd go. Even if Elbahia Island was a raging battlefield, he'd find his way over there.

He broke into a run, his dry-land balance returning quickly. Tarkothi marines saluted him as he passed, but he soon left the dock area and ran north up the central boulevard.

In a couple minutes, he'd crossed over the channel demarcating the neutral port area. In the distance there were cries, horses' hooves, and the clash of weapons, but the streets he took were all but deserted. With the south bridge to Elbahia Palace unguarded, he ran over the moat, around the castle yard and to the north bridge. It, too, was curiously unguarded.

Tides and Tempests, had the Elbahia royal guards broken their oaths of neutrality and joined in with their respective nations' forces?

The Korynthi section of the island was eerily quiet, with only the occasional sound of distant battle. The streets were lit only by the Blue Moon. He paused at the southeast corner of the Korynthi villa's walls. Hands on his knees, he panted to catch his breath. Sweat ran down his temples and soaked his uniform. He'd run over a kilometer, which was about a kilometer more than he ever ran. A few minutes' rest would make him more presentable to the guards at the front gate.

Cold steel pressed against his neck. He froze.

A voice hissed in his ear. "Why are you here, Tarkothi?"

A familiar voice, though no longer sultry. Lethal. And maybe a little sleepy.

Aelward's heart lurched. "Lass! I was coming to see ye."

Alaena let out an excited squeal.

Then, she cleared her throat, and her sarcastic tone returned. "Well, I would hear you from the other end of the island, the way your boots echo on the pavestones." The blade retreated. Hands turned him around. Alaena stood there, a lock of frizzy red hair in her face. She looked like a cleaner version of the lass he'd met in the royal palace in Korynth a week before. She wore comfortable breeches and a shirt, their color hard to determine in the moonlight. A bow and quiver were slung over her shoulder, and a shortsword hung at her side. Her half-lidded eyes studied him, somewhat vacantly.

Brushing away the knife, he wrapped her in an embrace. She tensed at first, but then melted into him. Her cheek rested on his shoulder.

"I heard that ye were found. What are ye doing out now?"

She pushed herself out of his hug. "It isn't hard to sneak out and climb over the wall."

"But why? Did you really create a distraction so your brother could steal the Light of Solaris?"

"What?" Her glazed eyes took on a lethal glint. "How could you believe that?"

"I didn't." He shook his head. "That's just what the Crown Prince of Tarkoth is saying."

"Yes, that's the rumor that bastard is spreading."

Aelward grimaced. He was the true bastard, even if Elrayn was acting like one. No matter, it was reassuring for Alaena to confirm she wasn't involved. Still... "They said ye conspired with Peris to kidnap Princess Karyna."

She stared at the ground. "I can't deny it."

"But why?"

"You don't know?"

The lass must've still been in a daze. She was talking in circles. He threw up his hands. "How could I?"

"I told you." She pouted.

Told him? He shook his head. "When?"

"Do you have jellyfish for brains?" She sighed. "I told you many times. I don't want to marry Prince Aryn.

Princess Karyna didn't want to marry Prince Koryn. Peris told me it was a way to get out of it, a way no one would get hurt."

Aelward's head spun, and he shook his head in slow arcs. "I don't understand."

"Me either. It made sense at the time, but now I realize he was just tricking me. He tried to kill me." Her voice cracked, and she fell into his arms again.

Elrayn was clearly wrong about suspecting her. Aelward ran a hand through her hair. "I'm so sorry."

She pulled back. "Anyway, that's why I am out. I want to prove my innocence, by recovering the Light."

"By yourself?"

"No one will help me."

"I will."

She choked down a laugh. "Oh, Aelward, you are so adorable."

Indignation rose. "What is that supposed to mean?"

"If we were on a ship, you'd have my full confidence. But here..."

He harrumphed. "I can still swing a sword."

"I guess so." She shrugged.

"Well, how were you trying to find the Light?"

She took his hand and pulled him along the villa wall. "Peris approached me in the rear yard. He came in over the east walls, right here. There were handprints in the dirt on the top, where he went over."

"So, he came out here. You don't even know which way he came or went, or even if he was involved with the theft." Poor lass was sweeping her hand through the ocean in hopes of catching a fish.

"While you were lumbering over, I was looking for any tracks he might've left."

He stared at the paved road. "On stone?"

"Tracks aren't just impressions in dirt. It could be broken twigs, displaced dust…there." She pointed at the wall. "Here, extra dirt in the crease between the pavestones. It's pointed right at the wall, and is too wide to be an Eldaeri's foot."

It didn't help that the only light was from the Blue Moon. Aelward squinted. "I don't see anything, lass."

She drew her finger in a straight line to a grassy square, notable only for the bench surrounded by shrubs. "If he passed through there, it will give us clues."

And then what? He nodded to provide optimism he didn't feel, then followed as she jogged over.

They'd just about reached the grass when a circular hole behind the bench opened with a hiss. Alaena shot a hand out, holding him back.

From where they stood, five meters away, the space below looked utterly dark.

Alaena pulled her sword from its sheath without a sound, and staying low, circled around the hole.

He couldn't draw his own without eliciting a rasp. Instead, he followed.

She held up a hand, then twirled her finger in a circle, gesturing for him to go around the other way. He watched her as he worked his way around, and froze when she held up a staying hand. She pointed two fingers at her eyes, then one at the opening, now about two meters away.

Dropping into a crouch, she held up five fingers, then started counting down.

Four. Bending low, Aelward could swear there were dark shapes down there.

Three. He gripped his own sword hilt, ready to draw.

Two.

One of the shapes sprang from the hole at him. Another followed, darting at Alaena.

Aelward started to pull his sword, but something hooked behind his ankle. Pain burned in his shin, sending him backward. He hit the ground with an *umph*, and whoever it was rolled on top of him. A calloused hand cupped his mouth, and for the second time in a few minutes, a blade pressed to his throat. He went stiff.

Somewhere to his left, Alaena tumbled to the ground.

"Don't move," an unfamiliar voice hissed in a lilting accent from the other tangle of bodies.

The surprisingly light weight on his chest shifted, and the silhouette of a head leaned over him. A male voice whispered, "Hands away from your weapon. I'm going to uncover your mouth, but if you yell out, I'm going to slash your throat. If you understand me, blink twice."

Aelward stretched his arms out behind his head and blinked twice.

The interloper's hand withdrew. "Now, why were you trying to ambush us?"

"These aren't Nightblades," said a female voice to the left. "At least, yours isn't. He moves like a drunk troll, and that might be an insult to all the drunk trolls in the world. Actually, this one is...Princess Alaena."

"Princess Alaena?" His captor's voice sounded excited. The weight on his chest lifted.

Aelward blinked twice and looked. The silhouette was that of a child... No, with those tapered ears and thick build, a Madaeri. Tides and Tempests, how humiliating. Overwhelmed by a Halfling. Thank Sargasso his shipmates hadn't witnessed it.

The Madaeri skipped over to Alaena, where a lithe figure was helping her to her feet.

Aelward picked himself up and tugged his uniform straight.

"Master Fleet!" Alaena said. "How good to see you!"

Master? Aelward studied the Madaeri, whose features were hard to make out in the moonlight.

"You're just saying that now?" Fleet put his hands on his hips. "I was there when you were rescued."

"She was drugged, remember?" said Fleet's partner. She was thin, no more than a strand of seaweed, and the pointed ears gave away her identity as an elf.

Drugged! Aelward gasped. How come he was the last to find these things out? And an elf? They never left their secluded forest realms.

"So you were there?" Alaena asked.

Fleet nodded. "Yes. What are you doing out? You should be resting."

"The Light was stolen because of me. I am going to find it."

The elf girl burst out laughing. "You are trying to track down Teleri Nightblades. They'll hear this lug coming from a mile away." She jerked a thumb at Aelward.

Aelward scowled. "Look here, lass, I am—"

"—wasting time," Fleet said. "We are tracking Tharos, who we suspect stole the Light."

"He came out through the tunnels." The elf pointed to the hole from which she'd emerged.

Tunnels? In Elbahia? Aelward peered at the hole in grass.

Fleet nodded, and started sniffing. "Fan out, look for clues. He was barefooted. You, navy boy, don't get in the way."

Aelward growled. He might not be able to track sneaks on stone, but at least he could protect Alaena. She...

She was now spreading out with the others, looking at the ground, as systematic and efficient as seasoned cannon crew.

"Here." The elf girl knelt by the edge of the grassy area and set her palm into the turf. "Unless there are many huge, barefoot humans around, I think this must be Tharos."

Alaena sauntered over to the indicated spot and studied it. The way her brow furrowed in concentration made her look so serious. So unlike the sultry siren in Korynth, so different from the defensive little girl just a few minutes before.

And even more beautiful.

If he could capture that image, he'd have it carved into a masthead for his own ship. One day.

"Not bad, Jie. Partial toe print." The Madaeri looked up from the spot to the elf, then pointed east. "He went that way."

Aelward shook the fanciful ideas out of his head. He'd never be in position to commission a ship, but at least he'd hold on to the memory of Alaena's expression. Guard it, like the Pirate Queen guarded her treasure.

Now, she took off after Fleet and this Jyeh. Her hips no longer sashayed like a tacking ship, but stayed straight and true as if blown by a gale.

He hurried to follow. He'd follow her into a maelstrom.

CHAPTER 40:

Unenviable Choices

With the Bovyans closing in around him, Tomas scanned for escape routes. His vision flashed red as several drew their swords with ominous rasps. They blocked every rope bridge, while others moved to cover the openings to the nearby homes.

Tomas took three steps toward the center of the platform, then dropped into a slide. He swept over to the fire plate hole and squeezed into the gap between the wood and the hot metal. Heat off the dish coursed through him in waves. Taking a deep breath, he let go and splashed feet-first into the water.

All sense of heat vanished, and it was all Tomas could do not to scream out his air from the frigid water.

Something—no, two somethings—splashed in after him.

He dove deeper, and reached the sea floor—the now mud-covered roof of the ancient imperial villa, actually—some ten *pedes* down. Swimming beneath the platforms and rope bridges was nothing new: every villager did. Doing it at night, however, was unheard of. The darkness made it impossible to see the submerged parts of the towers.

Impossible for someone without a demon eye. For Tomas, the bases appeared even clearer than during the day. Tiny runes flashed through his visual field, blinking on barnacles and oysters that clung to their sediment-encrusted surfaces. What was Sabine trying to tell him?

The runes flashed over the several oval openings that led into each tower, all windows before the Great Flood. He looked over his shoulder to gauge the pursuit.

One of the Bovyans floated suspended in the water, unmoving; another's legs dangled motionless near the surface, his body lodged in the gap between the platform and fire plate. A third kicked furiously near the surface. He sank, and kicked again.

Two more down, leaving fifteen Bovyans, including Fethos, plus the Aksumi. Swimming eastward until his lungs were close to bursting, he pushed through an opening and into the base of the tower. In the darkness, Sabine spoke, and his vision was again cast in shades of blue. A school of small fish squirmed and flitted around him. He kicked up until his head broke the surface.

Like all of the basements, the flooded chamber was a single room. Steps wound up along the wall to a hatch, which led into the living chambers. It was impossible to tell whose home he'd come up in, but he had to be at least two platform rings away from the village center.

That close, it would be the house of someone important. He doggy paddled to the steps, on the lookout for any human excrement the fish might not yet have devoured.

He climbed up and pushed the hatch up just enough to peek through. No sign of anyone. No doubt everyone was in the village center, under the Bovyans' watchful gaze. He opened it all the way and climbed up. When his vision shifted to normal, he took a quick glance around.

The standard twelve-*pede*s across, with four goatskin-covered oval windows at each of the cardinal directions, the chamber had cushioned rubberwood furniture surrounding a reed-woven carpet. Shell artwork decorated the wall. One of the many multi-level homes, it had another set of steps winding up.

Tomas took the steps up to the bedchambers, again with smaller oval windows in the cardinal directions. The number of bedrolls suggested a family of six. Another set of stairs went to a third level, making this one of the few three-level buildings in the village, all on the third ring from the village center. Based on the direction he'd swam in, and the family size, it belonged to the Iacco family. Meaning two of those beds belonged to Liya and Maya. Their undergarments would be folded underneath.

He shook the dirty thoughts out of his head. No doubt, Sabine trying to seduce him again. Footsteps clopped on the bridgeways, and voices boomed outside, though the goatskin muffled them. Tomas hurried to the west window, moved the curtain aside, and peeked out.

The next two homes over blocked the view of the village center, but with the goatskin out of the way, Lieutenant Torus' words sounded much clearer.

"Hurry, get the body up."

Right below, a Bovyan jogged past along the bridgeway.

Tomas ducked back. Maybe the third floor would give a better view. He climbed up the steps. The next level had eight windows, all open. Like all the other families on the third ring, the Iaccos used the top level as a sun roof. Potted plants lined the walls. Staying low, he crept over to the northeast window, eased up, and looked out. Of course, with the fire so far away, he'd be shrouded in darkness, but it didn't hurt to be careful.

The higher vantage point and better direction provided a partial view of the village center. Bovyans blocked off the bridgeways, while several thudded along the platform rings. Torus stood at the far end, half of his body visible. The central fire sent flickers of shadows across the villagers' worried expressions.

Of the fifteen Bovyans, plus the Aksumi, nine were visible from here. He took out his slingshot and several of the rocks. They stood far beyond the range of the village's best sharpshooters, but none of the villagers had a demon eye to help them. He set one stone in the sling and drew it back to its full length.

A large red rune appeared in his sight, covering half the rooftop of a first-ring hut. He raised the angle for an arcing shot, and the rune grew larger. When he shifted it over, it was twice Torus' size. Careful to make sure no one else was in the target circle, he centered it over the Bovyan lieutenant the best he could, and loosed.

The rune shrank over Torus, and the track of the stone painted an arcing line behind it. It struck the man in the shoulder, sending him staggering back three steps with a grunt.

"What the—?"

Heads snapped in Torus' direction.

Tomas loaded and took aim again. The red rune now appeared the size of a head. Torus' head. He loosed again. The stone left an arching red trail in his vision. It slammed into Torus' cheek, knocking him to the ground, unmoving.

Shouts and screams broke out.

When Tomas aimed at another Bovyan, the rune appeared even smaller, half the size of his face. The shot smashed into the brute's forehead, and he collapsed.

"Get down, get down," Fethos yelled from somewhere out of sight.

Villager and invader alike ducked low, eyes shifting this way and that.

Not even having to focus his gaze on the slingshot itself, Tomas took aim at a third, huddled low with his sword drawn. The rune appeared about the same size as the rock. Tomas shifted the slingshot until the red patch encircled the Bovyan's eye, and loosed. It hit true, knocking him to the platform.

"It came from there." From behind one of the Iocca twins, the Aksumi pointed at the tower to the left.

Heads snapped in that direction. The Aksumi's lips moved, though the surrounding commotion drowned out his voice.

A bright white light flashed on the rooftop.

Bovyan and villager alike gasped.

"The boy really is a sorcerer," said one of the Bovyans.

They must not have seen the Aksumi do it, and thought Tomas had summoned the magic. Not like he'd have a reason to do so. Outside the edge of the light, he aimed at the real sorcerer. The squirming Iacco twin kept getting in the way. He shifted to another Bovyan's eye and released. The stone dropped the man like a heavy rock in water. Four down, eleven and the Aksumi to go.

"Secure that tower," Fethos yelled.

Which tower? Had they seen him?

Five Bovyans approached, sending the bridgeway shaking.

Up to now, all his targets had been stationary, but at least these were coming closer, to a more reasonable range.

Tomas took aim...and Sabine spoke in her strange but soothing language.

Just as she'd shown him the way out of the dwarf city, Sabine drew a rune in front of the running Bovyans.

He stifled a gasp and placed the rune over the first's eye; but then a second rune appeared on the lead soldier's line of approach. Sabine must be telling him where to aim. Though the flashing circle moved, Tomas adjusted the angle of the slingshot to place the solid rune over his target's path. When the blinking rune met the solid one, he loosed.

The Bovyan's head snapped back, and his feet kicked up. The second ran into him, though the next three jumped out of the way and continued their mad dash.

Six stones left. Using Sabine's help to lead the running men, Tomas took two quick shots, felling two more.

Excitement surged through him. Sabine was making him invincible. The remaining two Bovyans went to the tower...next door. One climbed in, while another stood guard outside. Tomas shot him as well, leaving only the one inside, plus the five in the village center, the two guarding the ramps onto the beaches, the Aksumi...and one unaccounted for.

The soldier appeared in the tower's third level, outlined by the sorcerer's light. It was almost too easy. Tomas shot him through the eye, and turned back to the village center.

Fethos, though still hidden, cursed every orc god. Homes blocked the view of the other Bovyans, except...

The Aksumi...

Tomas gritted his teeth.

The sorcerer held a knife to the Iocca girl's throat. "Surrender, or I will kill her."

Would he?

No, the Bovyans needed women. And if he surrendered, there was no hope for the village at all. The Bovyans would drown every diver to get their precious crown, and then turn the village into breeding grounds. Tomas aimed at the Aksumi, waiting for a clear shot.

"Take hostages!" Fethos yelled.

A Bovyan appeared from cover and strode toward an elder. The soldier's skull cracked as Tomas used his second-to-last stone.

A scream started, but then cut short, followed by more screams. And pitiful wails.

Tomas turned back to the Aksumi.

The Iocca girl slumped in his arms, blood gushing from her throat.

Gasping, Tomas covered his mouth. A pit formed in his stomach. He hadn't believed the threat, and that had cost the girl her life. Oh, Sabine. This was all her fault. He raised the slingshot. The Aksumi would pay...

But no, the sorcerer had disappeared behind the cover of a building. No matter, all Tomas needed was some more stones, and he would kill the rest of them, one by one. With just seven remaining, and the Aksumi, he'd rid the village of the invaders, and the traitor, Joacquin. It would cost the village a few people, but they'd be free. They'd forgive Tomas. No, they'd hail him as a hero.

His chest began to swell. That's right, he'd be a hero. First he'd liberate the village, then go back to Lorium. He'd kill every last Bovyan, one by one. The townsfolk would realize what a fraud Antonius was, how it wasn't fair that the mayor was a bumbling fool who only held his position because he married the right woman. They'd respect Tomas, maybe even listen to him above the useless mayor.

No no no. Tomas shook the thoughts out of his head. This was Sabine whispering temptations in his ear, even if she wasn't actually speaking in his head in her strange demon language.

Still, he had to get rid of the Bovyans in the village, even if it cost a few lives. It was the only way to ensure the village's safety.

"Surrender!" Fethos yelled. He came into sight, a blade set to Sofia's neck.

Tomas' chest squeezed as Sofia's scream pierced the night. Her body stiffened. Fethos was pressing the knife point deeper into her neck. The demon eye made out the thin line of blood there.

Of all the people...why couldn't they have grabbed one of the elders, who would die in a few years anyway?

He admonished himself. Sabine was trying to corrupt him again.

"If you don't indicate your surrender in three seconds," Fethos yelled, "the girl you helped escape Lorium is dead. One."

Sweat gathered on his brow. Give up now, and the Bovyans would control the village forever.

"Two."

They'd kill him for sure. "I surrender," he shouted.

Fethos and the Aksumi craned their heads, squinting into the darkness.

"I'm coming down now," Tomas yelled. "I'll be there in a moment."

He went down to the ground floor, but instead of going out the front door, he climbed through the back and ran to his home. He dashed up the steps and stashed the slingshot and the explosive gemstone into that strange pocket of the priest's robe.

With nothing but several slingstones, he jogged to the central platform.

Hundreds of eyes fell on him.

His shoulders slumped as he trudged through the villagers. Still, he took note of the Bovyans' positions. Seven remained, though only three were visible.

"You!" Mama Iocca snarled. "You got my daughter killed."

Papa Iocca pushed past the others, cocked back his fist, and swung.

Tomas' vision flashed red. He stepped back out of the red-lined arc of the punch, and raised his own fists to defend himself.

"Stop!" Fethos bellowed. "Get over here, boy."

Pa gave him a firm nod as he passed, but Ma's eyes welled with tears.

Squaring his shoulders, Tomas walked around the fire plate hole to the head of the central platform. Fethos still held the blade to Sofia's throat, and her eyes were wide with fear.

"You." Fethos studied him, then gestured at the neat line of unmoving Bovyans lying to the side. One's head was charred. All had their arms folded across their chest, weapon in hand. "You've proven resourceful. I assume that was you who killed the captain and the others in the ravine? That makes what, at least ten men, maybe more. And of course, Sathis."

So Sathis had died. He hadn't been as cruel as Fethos.

"Maybe you really are a sorcerer." Fethos had yet to release Sofia. His eyes roved over Tomas, before straying to somewhere behind him.

Tomas looked over his shoulder.

Two Bovyans approached, both with two bodies slung over their shoulders.

Fethos lifted his chin. "All dead?"

"Yes," the two answered in unison.

With a sidelong glare at Tomas, Fethos gestured them to place the bodies among the others. When they'd done so, he jerked a finger at Tomas. "Seize him."

The two Bovyans marched over. Sabine sounded a warning and his vision flared red just before they grabbed both of Tomas' arms. Memories of when they first caught him on the beach flashed in his mind, and his body seized up, unwilling to obey.

"Bring him here." Fethos withdrew the knife from Sofia's throat and gave her a shove. She stumbled toward the villagers, where Pa caught her.

As they dragged him over, Tomas took a few deep breaths to calm his nerves.

Fethos leaned over and held up a light bauble lamp to Tomas' face. "The governor was too lenient on you. Sathis died, because he let you live. I shall not make the same mistake. First, I want to know: how did you get back here? I saw your tracks lead in the opposite direction."

"I climbed to the summit."

The villagers again broke out in chatter.

Fethos silenced them with a hand. "So you are the one responsible for the Golden Bowl's change in angle?"

"Yes." Tomas nodded. "There were hundreds of gemstones and gold in the temple. I can show you the way."

Fethos harrumphed. "I remember the last time I trusted you as a guide. No, we will find our own way up. Now, you die." He grabbed Tomas' shirt and set the dagger at his throat.

Tomas' vision flashed red.

Ma wailed.

"No!" Sofia screamed.

"Wait," Tomas said, heart pounding in his ears. He turned his head toward the Aksumi. "The Crown of Arkos. I know a way to get to it."

More murmuring in the crowd.

The Aksumi pushed his way through the villagers. "Can you, now?"

"He's not a diver," one woman said.

Curse her! Tomas' heart sunk.

Fethos looked up, searching for the speaker, before his gaze settled again on Tomas. "I think you are stalling."

"No." Tomas shook his head. "I made it from the summit of the mountain, through the sunken dwarf city. I can find it."

Snorting, Fethos looked to the Aksumi. "I guess there is no harm in trying. What do you think, Melas?"

The sorcerer grinned. "Yes, you can always kill him afterwards."

"Wait." Tomas held up a hand. "If I do this for you, I want you to swear that you will leave this village, and that you won't harm or kill me or anyone else."

"You ask too much." Fethos shook his head.

"We are in agreement," Melas said.

Fethos locked a glare on the Aksumi.

"You know my orders." Melas tapped his own nose, a strange gesture.

Fethos thumped his chest. "And you know mine."

The two stared at each other, seemingly engaged in a battle of wills with their eyes. Did the Bovyan know Melas was really an Aksumi sorcerer? To reveal him now might help turn the two against each other; but keeping the knowledge secret might be safer.

At last, Fethos thumped his chest. "Very well. A deal is a deal. Bind his hands and put him in that house until morning."

"I will do it now," Tomas said.

The crowd let out a collective gasp.

"It's too dark," one diver said.

"The ghosts," said another.

Tomas turned to the sorcerer. He'd been holding some kind of dangling device in the boat. "I understand you are close, but haven't found the spot."

The sorcerer nodded.

"I've also heard the light baubles all flare for a second, then go out."

"Yes. The crown's power overloads them."

Tomas turned to the villagers. "Bring me a dozen light baubles. Prepare a boat for diving."

The people hurried back to their homes, too many for the Bovyans to control, while others went to the docks.

Tomas pointed at one of the bronze cauldrons near the fire plate. "I will need that."

Fethos' eyes widened. He exchanged glances with the Aksumi, whose expression bloomed in understanding. Another Bovyan lifted the cauldron and followed Tomas to the docks.

The Aksumi trailed just a few footsteps ahead. "Can you really find it in the dark?"

If it was based on diving alone, there were several women who were far more talented; but none had a demon eye. Tomas gave a confident nod. "I will need my diving coat, from back at my house."

The villagers looked among themselves, but neither Fethos nor the sorcerer showed any sign of distrust.

Fethos gestured to one of his men. "Accompany the boy."

The soldier thumped his chest and followed Tomas back home.

All the running back and forth had been tiring. Maybe it would be better to rest before diving, but there was little chance of convincing Fethos of that.

Back in his house, he retrieved the robe. If not for the Bovyan looking over his shoulder, he would've double-checked the orc gems and slingshot in the pocket. With a nod, he headed toward the dock, taking the ring road so as not to surprise the villagers with the priest's robe.

Fethos, Melas, and his family all waited there, and indeed they all stared at his clothes. Another Bovyan was climbing into the boat, carrying the caldron as if it were a bowl. Tomas went next, followed by the Mystic.

Tomas scanned the boat, noting the rope, anchor, rock weights in the pouches of a cloth belt, and dive bags. "I'm going to need a—"

"I'll do it."

Heart sinking, Tomas looked back to the dock.

Ma stood there, silhouetted by the moon. She held a bag, the light spilling from between the seams suggesting light baubles were inside.

No no no. If she were in the boat, a virtual hostage, his plan wouldn't work. "Ma, you shouldn't. I can teach the Bovyans to work the lead rope."

"What good am I, if I can't protect my son?"

Not like she could protect him from these vicious barbarians. Tomas gritted his teeth. Now, his naïve mother, his dear, naïve mother, just let the Bovyans know who she was. "Please, stay back."

"No," the Aksumi said, grinning. "You'll join us. And his girl will stay here, in the village."

Sighing, Tomas extended his hand and helped Mother onto the boat. Following his directions, the Bovyan paddled the boat out toward the Jaws. The moonlight danced in the ripples of the lagoon, and every now and then, the wind echoed in the Golden Dish, moaning like tortured souls. Ma shuddered, but the Bovyan just scoffed.

When they cleared the Jaws, the Aksumi held up the dangling crystal. It listed slightly northward. Ma sucked in a sharp breath, and the Aksumi pointed. Tomas squinted to see what was pulling it.

Reading his mind as always, Sabine spoke in her demon language. Tomas blinked.

Wispy streaks of blue light appeared to be pulling the medallion. Indeed, hundreds of thousands of thin blue veins danced across the sky, crisscrossing each other like a moving spiderweb.

He could only gawk at the beauty. "Those lights are a beautiful color, the same shade as the Blue Moon."

Mother pulled back and looked at him with a scrunched forehead. "Did they hit you in the head?"

Closing the demon eye, Tomas looked. The medallion still listed to the north, but all the lights had disappeared. He opened his eye, and the beautiful display reappeared.

If only Sabine could speak Arkothi, so he could ask what she was showing him. Then again, even if she could, it would look like he was talking to no one at all. Ma really would believe he'd really been hit in the head.

The Bovyan rowed in broad strokes, propelling them through the sea incredibly fast, given the load.

"Out a little," Tomas said, gesturing past the rocks which appeared so clear in his vision. "You'll get too close to the Jaws."

"Slow down. It's near here." The Aksumi's medallion hung at a gentler angle, and the blue lines of light continued to waver off it, until they reached vertical. It remained that way, even as the boat floated another thirty *pedes* to a stop. He turned to Tomas. "Okay, boy, it's somewhere around here. Let's see if your plan works."

Tomas withdrew several of the light baubles and tossed them out in different directions. He counted as their soft white light sank deeper and deeper, refracted by the sea's ripples. To the north, one flashed brighter, then blinked out at twenty seconds.

"That way," Tomas pointed.

With occasional glances at the Aksumi's medallion, he threw more baubles forward as the Bovyan rowed in the indicated direction. When one didn't flash, Tomas tossed another eastward. It did flash, and to the Bovyan's credit, he headed that way. After about half a phase of the Iridescent Moon, he'd triangulated the spot.

Tomas dropped a light bauble straight down and watched over the side. At twenty-three seconds, it flared bright, then went dark.

Mother shook her head. "We're too far out. It's too deep. Not even one of the women could reach the bottom, find the crown in the dark, and then make it back up. Then, there's the ghosts."

"That's a risk I'm willing to take." The Aksumi snickered.

She glared at him.

The Aksumi chuckled. "Just be sure to tie the crown to your lead rope so that we can retrieve it."

"I will find it, and make it back up." First tying the dive belt with its stones, Tomas pointed to the cauldron. "That will get me down faster, and there'll be a pocket of air."

The Bovyan's eyes went wide.

"Smart boy." The Aksumi nodded appreciatively.

All this assumed that the same magic that snuffed out the light baubles didn't destroy Sabine. Tomas tied the rope around his waist. If only Ma weren't here. He'd originally planned to leave the knot loose and untie himself and escape. Now, though, she was a hostage.

He jumped over the side of the boat. The cold bit into his skin, but he treaded water through the weight of the rocks in the dive belt. He held up his hands. "Put the cauldron over my head."

With the least amount of effort, the Bovyan lifted the cauldron, leaned over, and set it over Tomas' head. It was so much easier than flipping over the pot in the ruins of the dwarf kingdom. His vision shifted to the same blue as when he was in the depths of the mountain.

The weight sent him sinking through the frigid water.

Ten seconds.

Would this really work?

Fifteen seconds.

What if the crown did the same thing to Sabine that it did to the light baubles?

Twenty seconds.

What if there were really ghosts?

Twenty-three. Twenty-four.

His cold vision still worked. Tomas blew out a sigh of relief.

At a count of thirty-two, his feet hit the sea bottom. How deep that was, he wasn't sure, but the water squeezed him like a grape in a press. The cauldron sat heavily on his shoulders, but still much lighter than trying to lift his sister on dry land. The air tasted hot and stuffy. Like a coffin, maybe. He took a deep breath, and heaved the pot above his head.

The cold water pressed in on him. He opened his eyes. Rocks lay scattered across the sea floor, mixed in with everything from cutlery to jewelry, all their contours appearing clearly in dark blue. If there were any ghosts, Sabine didn't reveal them.

Tomas scanned the area. There were so many artifacts down here, how could he possibly pick the crown out from all the other debris? No wonder not even the best divers could f—

The wispy blue lines, barely visible with the blue backdrop, danced across his vision and reached back up toward the boat. Squinting, he tracked the lines to their source. Several bulky shapes lay outlined against the sea floor, dozens of *pedes* away—it was impossible to tell exactly how far, underwater.

Arms aching, Tomas lowered the cauldron onto his shoulders again, and breathed in the warm, sticky air inside. He slogged in the direction of the blue lines, occasionally ducking out of the cauldron to make sure he was on the right path.

One last peek; he had to be close. He ducked his head out to find the squiggly blue lines just several *pedes* away. Pulse racing, he pushed through the cold water.

The rope around his waist went taut.

Balancing the cauldron, he reached with his right hand and gave the line two sharp tugs. If she was still the one holding the rope, she'd know the signal to either let out more slack, or row the boat in the right direction. The line pulled back at him in a long, firm tug.

He dug his heels into the muck. He was so close. Why would they be pulling him back…unless…

Ghosts at the surface, protecting an ancient artifact? A chill ran up his spine.

He took a deep breath of muggy, hot air. It couldn't be ghosts threatening the boat. They were only ever seen underwater. If there really were any, they would have claimed him by now.

The rope slackened about his waist. Blowing out a sigh, he trudged the last distance to the source of the blue light and ducked below the cauldron again.

The rays stabbed into a mound of dirt. He tried to scrape away at the mud with his toes, but the cauldron was too unbalancing. He'd have to use his hands. Which meant setting the cauldron down. Without beefy Bovyan arms, there was no guarantee that he'd be able to lift it off the sea floor again. It would be far easier to claim that he'd failed.

No, the Bovyans had made a deal, and no matter how evil they were, they were famous for keeping their word. This was the easiest way to save the village. The air inside the cauldron felt stale, anyway.

He took a deep breath—maybe his last ever—came out from under the cauldron, and shoved it to the side. A large bubble of air drifted out and toward the surface.

Dropping to his knees, he dug through the cold mud. His fingers lodged on what looked to be a bone. Ribs. He moved further up, digging more. His hand caught on a fine chain of some sort, attached to a medallion. He thrust it, and a ring and some bracelets, into the dive bag.

Sand now floated in a cloud, making it hard to see, even with Sabine's help. He continued digging and sifting upward, even as his chest grew heavier and heavier and his hands grew numb.

At last, they closed around something that felt like a crown. Through squinted eyes, he peered. The blue waves of light emanated from it. He ran his arm through the circlet, and emptied the rocks from the belt's pouch. Then he coiled his knees and thrust himself up.

The rope now tugged on him in uneven yanks. His lungs burned. He wasn't rising fast enough. The dive bag, full of trinkets, weighed him down. Priceless treasures, which might cost him his life. Black encroached on the edge of his vision. Every nerve screamed for him to breathe.

All went black.

CHAPTER 41:

Cold Trails

With only the Blue Moon's light illuminating the streets, Alaena studied the way Fleet sniffed and examined the road. Though her nose and ears would never compare to a Madaeri's, she could still learn more about how to find tracks in cities.

It was a skillset she would not have to use in the future, if she had it her way and was able to escape to the forests—but better to know and not use it, than to need it and not know.

Without looking back, she brushed Aelward's hand off her shoulder. "Stop, you're breaking my concentration."

"Why don't ye just follow the little guy? He clearly knows what he's doing."

"You can learn a lot from a Madaeri." She turned to look back at him. "Especially this one."

"Yeah?" Dubiousness hung in his voice.

She nodded. "Fleet has served Serikoth for as long as anyone can remember. He teaches scouts and rangers when he's not off exploring."

"Mmmmm." Aelward didn't sound impressed. Of course he wouldn't, seeing that he was a navy man. He'd never understand the wonders of the tiniest track telling a story.

What did she ever see in him and his ridiculous word choices? She turned back to focus on what was important.

Fleet now knelt by road.

The mysterious half-elf, Jie, crowded over his shoulder. "What is it?"

Alaena craned over his other shoulder to see.

He was running a hand over a pavestone. "Our friend made a mistake. Up to now, he's been stepping in the middle of the pavestones."

"How can you tell?" Alaena asked.

"He's barefoot, and stepping in the cracks would rub off skin."

Jie's lips rounded in a cute way. "I thought you were following his blood."

"He stopped bleeding a while ago."

Alaena cocked her head. "What was the mistake, then?"

"This pavestone is slightly cracked. He scraped his foot on the surface. We are on the right track."

Pressing her cheek to the cool stone, Alaena looked. The crack was almost invisible, and there didn't seem to be any blood or skin. "I don't see anything."

"Of course you can't." Fleet grinned. "The key is, the width of this exfoliation, compared to the width of his foot, suggests he was heading northeast at the time."

Since it was impossible for human eyes to see the flakes of Bovyan skin, Alaena straightened and peered northeast. Her line of sight went straight toward an alley between the backs of rowhouses, a hundred meters away.

Jie came to her side and grumbled. "I don't have good memories of alleys in this city."

"Let's make some new ones." With a grin, Fleet padded off.

Alaena followed with Jie. Aelward trailed several steps behind, though not so far as to keep his thudding boots from giving away his position. How annoying!

Ahead of them, Fleet skidded to a stop and held up a hand.

At her side, Jie's ears twitched. "Cavalry," she whispered, pointing up the street where they were headed.

Peering through the moonlight, Alaena listened, but heard nothing but the sound of cannon and indistinct shouts in the far distance.

Fleet waved frantically and darted toward the closest alley, some twenty meters away.

She hurried after, and even with Jie's shorter legs, the half-elf kept pace. Now, the sound of horse hooves crystalized from faint to clear. They were still ten meters from the alley. The dark shapes of mounted soldiers came into focus up ahead.

They reached the alley and joined Fleet in pressing their backs against the closest house. Alaena blew out a breath and looked back.

Aelward was still a good ten meters away, in the middle of the damn street. Those stupid heavy boots and his sea legs made him so slow!

She peeked around the corner in the opposite direction.

The horses were almost upon them. And now, the steel caps and capes marked them as Serikothi cavaliers. A patrol of two.

And Aelward was in his Tarkothi navy uniform.

Alaena pulled back into the alley and looked to Fleet and Jie. The two were tapping on each other's wrists, scowling and shaking their heads.

The cavaliers rode past, with no sign of seeing them.

But Aelward...

"You!" barked one of the cavaliers. "Stop!"

Alaena grimaced and looked.

Aelward had frozen in place as the cavaliers approached, naked sabers in hand.

He was such a liability, but then again, he'd drawn their attention. And he was cute. She started out.

A hand closed around her wrist.

She looked back.

Jie shook her head.

Alaena tried to break free of Jie's grip, but the half-elf adjusted each time, sticking to her like a wet leaf.

Reins snapped. "He's a Tarkothi. Yah!"

"Wait!" Aelward yelled.

The horses broke into a canter.

"Let go!" Alaena snarled. Aelward was the only person who genuinely cared about her, and the hell if she'd let one of her countrymen trample him. She yanked her arm, dragging the lithe half-elf out with her as she surged into the street.

The cavaliers were bearing down on him from either side. His naval saber was out, but there was no way he could survive the charge.

"No!" Alaena yelled.

Their blades swept in arcs.

Aelward stepped to the inside of the cavalryman to his right and chopped at his arm. The rider screamed. A sword clattered to the ground. Whose?

Bellowing, Aelward got knocked onto his ass. Had he been trampled? Slashed by the other man? It was impossible to tell in the jumble of dark shapes.

Jie had since let go, and Alaena was now running toward her fallen friend, unslinging her bow.

Friend? She shook the notion out of her head. "Stop!"

Now, both cavaliers wheeled with the precision of a crane's mating dance. One was holding his arm. Some fifteen meters in front of them, Aelward climbed to his feet. He held his naval sword and a cavalry saber in either hand.

None of the men heeded her order to stop, and even if they couldn't hear her, why would they?

"Stop, by order of Princess Alaena of Serikoth!" Alaena fit an arrow to the string. She'd have to hurt, or even kill, one of her own countrymen. Or worse, one of the horses. All for a clumsy enemy sailor. Taking aim at the one with the sword, she pulled it back until the fletching tickled her ear. If he charged...

The soldier reined in his horse. "Princess Alaena?"

"Yes," she said. "Stand down. He's my friend."

"A Tarkothi is your friend?" The other clutched at his arm. "We're at war. And the bastard cut me!"

Alaena scoffed. "You attacked him. What did you expect, for him to just stand there and let you run him down?"

"It can't be her," the first said to his companion. "We delivered her to the Korynthi villa just half an hour ago. And why would she aim at us for a Tarkothi?"

Aelward took several stumbling steps back. Jie was hurrying toward him.

The first snapped his reins and the horse started forward.

Alaena loosed the arrow and nocked another.

The first knocked the cavalier back, but plinked off his armor.

She loosed the second.

It zipped through the air and lodged in his sword arm.

He let out a groan and pulled back on his horse. "Bitch! We'll be back with reinforcements."

"Good," Alaena said. "Tell Crown Prince Koryn that we are close to finding the Light of Solaris."

The two turned their horses and galloped away.

She blew out a breath, and hurried over to Aelward. "Are you all right?"

"Just a shallow cut." Jie looked up from where she was examining his back. "Lucky."

"Skilled, lass." Aelward grinned.

Alaena fought off a smile. Jie's assessment seemed more likely.

The half-elf shook her head. "Still, we'll need to clean it and stitch it up."

Alaena looked at the wound. The saber had sliced through his coat, but he must've either partially deflected it, or just been in a fortunate position.

"The trail is growing cold," Fleet said.

"I'm fine, lass." He sheathed his sword and threw the cavalry saber down. "Let's go. Ye be needing me."

"No, we won't." Jie and Fleet said in unison.

"You two go ahead, we'll catch up." Alaena sighed. She was going to miss out on a chance to see how Fleet tracked Tharos, just for an awkward sailor. She hooked Aelward's arm over her shoulder. At least he smelled good, despite his crash to the ground.

"I'm fine, lass. It's just a scratch." He hurried after Fleet and Jie.

They came to the alley, where the Madaeri was studying the wall of a house. "He leaned up against this wall for a while."

"More skin flakes?" Alaena peered at the smooth blockwood.

"No, but I can see the heat he left."

Alaena whistled. No amount of training would let her track like that.

Jie shuddered. "Whistling at night will attract ghosts."

"Only Cathayi ghosts," Aelward said, "and I'd wager there are none in Elbahia."

"So, where did he go from here?" Alaena scanned the area.

Fleet lifted his nose to the air. "His scent lingers here, stronger than in the other places. We are on the right track. He probably waited in this spot, with his back against the wall, while a patrol passed."

Alaena looked back into the street. "Which way did he go, then? Along this road, or down the alley?"

Eyes roving around the area and sniffing, Fleet headed deeper into alley. Unlike the smooth paving on the main roads, the uneven cobblestones left patches of mud. There were no signs of huge, bare feet mixed in with the wide bootprints crisscrossing the area.

Fleet stopped at a door, where many of the muddy prints came and went, and held a finger to his lips. Sniffing, his face contorted.

"What is it?" Alaena whispered.

"Altivorcs."

"Altivorcs?" Incredulity hung in Jie's voice.

Alaena shuddered. Her misadventures had all started when Altivorcs had tried to ambush her, back in Korynth. Now they were in Elbahia.

CHAPTER 42:

Ultimatums

All was lost. Koryn spurred his horse through the streets of Elbahia Island, galloping toward the Tarkothi royal villa to challenge Prince Elrayn to a duel. Tarkoth had landed troops in defiance of the ceasefire, had won every engagement with overwhelming numbers. At the docks, they had captured the *Intimidator* and *Solaris' Spear*. On Koryn's orders, his troops were pulling back over the river into Serikoth, prepared to cede their district on Elbahia.

It didn't seem possible. Tarkoth's mongrels overwhelming the pureblooded Eldaeri of Serikoth. It was all his fault.

His fault for agreeing to the ceasefire when he held a stronger position. His fault for getting captured in the first place. When the history of this misfortune was written, he'd be remembered as the one who failed, while Elrayn would bask in the glory of victory.

That in itself didn't matter, but the future looked bleak. War would likely escalate, and after tonight, Serikoth would be in a poor position to wage it.

More importantly, there was no hope in spending a lifetime with his love. Better to die today, and take treacherous Elrayn with him.

"Koryn!"

Koryn looked over his shoulder, to where Damaryn tried to keep pace, despite explicit orders to stay back and organize the retreat. He'd never catch up; not with the speed of Koryn's destrier.

With a sigh, Koryn pulled up and waited. Now, without horse hooves drowning out other sounds, the noise of muted battle rose.

Coming to a stop next to him, Damaryn crossed his fists and bowed his head.

"I won't tell you again." Koryn jabbed a finger at him. "Escape into Serikoth, and defend the bridges. Tarkoth will use tonight as an excuse to escalate hostilities."

Damaryn shook his head. "My place is with you. Please, tell me what you are planning."

Koryn searched his eyes. "I'm making sure the last of our men gets word of our retreat."

"You're lying. You are going to challenge Elrayn to a duel."

Koryn laughed. "You know me too well."

"Even if he did accept, what would beating him accomplish?"

"If he agrees to single combat, then no one else has to get hurt."

"You know he won't accept. He knows he has the advantage in the field." Damaryn laughed. "So, that leaves your real motive. Revenge for him taking you hostage. Revenge for his treachery contributing to our loss tonight. But you also know, after he refuses the challenge, you'll go charging in as always, and it will probably get you killed."

Koryn chewed on the inside of his cheek. Damaryn knew him too well.

"I have another solution: marry Princess Karyna, and in exchange, demand the return of our ships and land."

A shudder ran down Koryn's spine. That would be as shameful as surrendering. So many men had died already. They would've been better off had he just accepted the marriage from the start. And still... "We will be pawns to Elrayn's machinations."

Damaryn shook his head. "From what I saw when we rescued her, Karyna is quite malleable. She'll make for an obedient bride. Elrayn won't be able to manipulate Serikoth through her."

"But what about—"

"I imagine you'll still be able to continue with your covert rendezvous." Damaryn gave a conspiratorial grin. "None will be the wiser, especially not her."

Koryn chewed the inside of his cheek again. It was an easy solution. Still, it wouldn't be fair to Karyna. Solaris had demanded absolute faithfulness in marriage of his Chosen. All these times Death had never found him on the field, he'd consigned himself to be faithful to his future wife...even if it meant giving up on his true love.

"I'm going to do it my way," he said. "Perhaps Elrayn will accept my challenge, but if not, I expect to die."

Damaryn shook his head. "I can't—"

"You must. Live." Koryn shifted his weight on the horse, and it took off into a gallop. He looked back to see Damaryn spurring his mount on, as well. The stubborn man was too faithful; a paragon of the tenets of Solaris.

Up ahead, the Tarkothi royal villa came into view. Just a few hours ago, his men had it surrounded, ready to assail them and demand Prince Elrayn's surrender. Now his soldiers had pulled back west, most already across the river into Serikoth. If only he'd ordered the assault sooner. Or just let his kidnapping go unavenged. A chasm into Tivar's hells threatened to rip his stomach apart.

A line of Tarkothi crossbowmen guarded the front gates. Though all stared in awe, they leveled their repeaters at him.

A captain stepped forward and thrust out a staying hand. "Halt."

Koryn pulled up. "I, Koryn, Crown Prince of Serikoth, challenge Crown Prince Elrayn to single combat."

The captain crossed his fists and bowed. "Your Highness, I am sure our prince would be happy to oblige, but he went to lead the capture of the docks."

Happy to oblige, indeed. Koryn looked into the villa's main building. The lights were now shuttered. There was no reason for the captain to have lied. Koryn sighed. This mad dash through the night had been for naught. And now, he had no reason to go wading into the Tarkothi to fulfill his death wish.

Damaryn pulled up on the side, his horse's nostrils flaring. "Your Highness—"

Never breaking eye contact with the captain, Koryn held up a hand to Damaryn. "Captain, I would confer with Prince Aryn. Certainly he has returned with Princess Karyna by now."

The captain looked back to the building, then gestured to a messenger. "Tell Prince Aryn that Crown Prince Koryn of Serikoth wishes to speak with him."

"Your Highness," Damaryn said. "You aren't going to challenge Prince Aryn, are you?"

Koryn shook his head. Unlike Elrayn, Aryn was honorable.

"Then what do you hope to accomplish?"

"Prince Aryn has proven quite reasonable. He also wanted to prevent hostilities."

Damaryn shook his head. "Prince Elrayn is still in command, though."

The doors to the villa opened, and Prince Aryn marched out.

Koryn swung out of his saddle. He handed his sword up to Damaryn, sad now that he remembered he'd left his own blade, heirloom of the House of Vardamcar, in the Tarkothi guest house. Yet another loss in this senseless conflict. Tarkothi guards made way as he strode to the gate.

A soldier opened the gate, and Prince Aryn passed through. He greeted him with a bow of his head. "Thank you again for your help in securing the rescue of Princess Karyna."

"Your brother used the distraction to betray our goodwill."

Aryn bowed deeper. "I am very sorry for that. Unfortunately, he is the heir. His commands are considered second only to my father's. By the time we made it back here, he had already left, so I was not able to convince him to stand down."

Koryn chewed on the inside of his cheek. Karyna... Agree to marry her, and it would resolve the conflict. He'd get back the ships, the land, Sunblade. At the same time, he'd throw away his love, condemning himself to a future without happiness. Koryn looked back to Damaryn. "If Elrayn returns, inform him of my formal challenge. I await his answer at the Flaviyan Bridge."

Even in the dark, it looked as if Aryn paled. "He will not accept. He understands he has the advantage in the field."

Koryn looked sidelong at Damaryn.

His aide shifted, lips quirking ever so slightly, body language screaming *I told you so* for anyone who knew how to read it.

Koryn hung his head for a moment before looking up again. "Then tell him, I will agree to marriage with Princess Karyna, on the condition that he returns our ships and my family sword; and also that Elbahia returns to its neutral status for the Three Kingdoms."

Aryn stared at him, wide-eyed. "Are you sure?"

No. Princess Karyna deserved more than to be a pawn, especially after being in love with a spy who died at her own hands. He and his lover would lose their chance to be together. Still, what was the sacrifice of three people compared to the prosperity of Serikoth? Of Solaris' Chosen People? He nodded. "Yes. I will be waiting at the Flaviyan Bridge for the next phase."

"I'm humbled by your decision. It is hard to give up on someone you love." Aryn let out a wistful sigh. Was he thinking about the half-elf? Did he love her?

Koryn turned to Damaryn. "Come, Captain. We will round up any stragglers on our way to the bridge."

"Yes, Your Highness." Damaryn crossed his fists and bowed his head, then offered the sword back.

Koryn received it and swung back into the saddle. He turned his horse and tapped his heels into its flank. As they rode north and east toward the bridge, he couldn't meet Damaryn's eyes.

The sounds of battle had all but died down, and the streets were quiet. Yet up ahead, they came across a pair of riders straggling southward. Though it was dark, the size of their horses and the plumes and caps gave them away as cavaliers. Both appeared to be cradling injured arms, and one was missing his saber.

"Cavaliers," Koryn called.

Their heads turned to him. "Your Highness," they answered in unison, crossing their fists, though one winced as he did so.

"We are retreating into Serikoth for now." Damaryn gestured west.

Koryn studied their wounds. "What happened to you?"

"We attacked a lone Tarkothi naval officer."

It didn't seem possible for cavaliers to be defeated by… "Just one?"

"It was an ambush. He miraculously survived our charge and injured my arm."

The other nodded. "A female archer came out of nowhere and shot me in my shoulder. We couldn't pull our bows."

Koryn frowned. Cavaliers could be foolhardy and arrogant at times, exposing themselves to unnecessary danger. Perhaps they were a reflection of him, their commander. "We are fortunate they didn't press their attack."

The first cavalier let out a nervous chuckle. "Actually, the archer claimed to be Princess Alaena, and she said to tell you she was tracking the Light of Solaris."

The foolish girl! Gawking, Koryn exchanged a shocked look with Damaryn, then back to the cavaliers. "Where did you see her?"

"I'm sure it wasn't really—"

Damaryn clapped once. "His Highness asked you a question."

"They were in the Korynthi district, working west on Flaviyan Road."

Was it even possible for Alaena to track down the Light? If so, he had to help. Koryn gestured west. "Hurry to the Flaviyan Bridge and muster all available cavaliers. Take them to where you saw the princess."

The soldiers crossed their fists and bowed their heads, then spurred their horses into full gallop.

Koryn looked to Damaryn, and yelled over the galloping horses, "If we can recover the Light, then I can use it to negotiate more favorable terms."

CHAPTER 43:

Double-Dealing

Head throbbing, Tomas sat straight up and vomited.

Kneeling by his side, Mother leaned forward to rub his back. He was sitting in the boat, and he had to close the demon eye to see if it really was twilight, or if he'd been unconscious through the night.

Darkness loomed around them, with shouts echoing over the sloshing of waves.

He looked to the source of the shouting.

Melas stood at the stern, desperate eyes shifting from Tomas to the prow.

There, the Bovyan stood with a naked blade in his hand.

With Tomas and Ma caught in between.

"What's happening?" he asked.

"Melas," Ma said. "He's not Bovyan."

Tomas closed the demon eye and looked.

Now chanting in a foul language and waving his hands, Melas had dark skin and tight coiled hair. He pointed his finger at the Bovyan.

Nothing happened.

Except for Melas' shoulders slumping. His chest heaved for air.

Ma searched Tomas' eyes. "Right before we pulled you aboard, he...changed."

Giving a tentative nod, Tomas studied the crown in the crook of his elbow. Moonlight shone on the bluish-grey metal, untarnished despite hiding beneath the waves for three centuries. Mud caked the runes on the inside.

It didn't look exactly like all the paintings, thinner and having a single tine instead of three. The clear, plum-sized gemstone in the tip looked almost the same. Blue wisps radiated out from each of the countless facets, bending toward the Aksumi's medallion. His illusion must've flashed out, just like the light baubles when they came too close to the ancient artifact. Tomas closed the demon eye and looked again. The blue lines around the gemstone and in the sky were gone.

"Out of the way!" Scowling, the Bovyan brandished his sword, rocking the boat.

"Give me the crown." Melas' voice came out weak, urgent.

Tomas looked again at the crown, then back. "I made a deal with the Fethos. This will save my village."

Melas laugh came out a little stronger. The medallion hanging at his neck glowed brighter. "No, you made a deal with me. The Bovyans are true to their word, but Fethos was careful to let *me* do the talking. As you can see, I am not Bovyan."

Tomas met the Bovyan's gaze.

"Give me the crown, or I will kill your mother, then you." The Bovyan raised his sword.

Tomas' vision flashed red. He unhooked the crown from his arm and started to pass it to the soldier.

When he reached for it, Tomas rocked the boat.

The Bovyan's sword went overboard as he fought for balance. On the other side, Melas crouched and clutched the side of the boat, fingers rigid like the dead, wide eyes staring at the water as if it were more dangerous than the soldier.

Despite the rocking, the Bovyan didn't go overboard. He'd found his sea legs and drew a wicked dagger.

Heart racing, Tomas passed the crown to Melas.

The Aksumi stared at it for a second, look of terror transforming into recognition. He reached out, and no sooner did his hands wrap around it than he set it atop his head. He barked out guttural syllables. The gemstone in the crown glowed a pale blue. He pointed.

Spikes of fire formed in midair and darted at the Bovyan. He let out a bellow as they slammed into him, and tumbled overboard with a splash. His head bobbed to the surface, eyes locked on the boat.

"Row, fool!" Melas pointed at the oars.

Tomas grabbed them, set them in the water, and rowed. Still, the Bovyan was close, and reaching out.

Melas grunted more words, like the sound of dogs fighting for scraps. Sparks sizzled from his fingertips and into the Bovyan. He convulsed, went rigid, and sank.

Covering her mouth, Ma could only stare.

With several heaving breathes, Melas looked into the waters as if Sargasso himself would reach out and snatch him. "Now, boy, to Lorium."

"What about my village? There are still five Bovyans there." Unaccustomed to all the weight in the boat, Tomas' arms ached.

Melas shrugged. "It's not my problem. I got what I wanted, and more."

"You just came here for the crown?"

"No, boy. I made a deal with the Teleri First Consul. He gets the crown, I get the starburst. Millennia ago, when the elves were losing their war against the orcs, they found a handful of these in glittering caves. They helped them recover from using magic by funneling the Resonance of the World into whoever holds them." He ran his hand over the glittering gem.

"How did this one become an heirloom of the Arkothi Imperators?"

"The Elf Angel, Aralas, gave it to his lover and the First Diviner, Tatiana, and it was passed on to her descendants in Tokahia. When the Arkothi Empire conquered the Estomar, they took the starburst."

And now, the Bovyans wanted it, because of some prophecy about the Imperator returning with the crown. "Why risk double-crossing the Bovyans?"

"The opportunity arose, and now I have both. In any case, I would've had to wait until the Orc King separated the starburst from the crown."

Such a valuable artifact—one which any magic user would covet, one which the locals believed would return, borne by a new Imperator. Thus, one which the Bovyans coveted, and could be bartered for his village's freedom. "If the Bovyans catch you..."

"Yes. Which is why we must get going. Row." Melas pointed back toward the village.

Tomas followed his finger. Near the docks, Fethos shared a boat with Joacquin, who was rowing. The remaining four Bovyans were split among two other boats. They'd probably seen the fireworks, and recovering the crown apparently took precedence over occupying the village. Then again, the island wasn't going anywhere, and as long as Joacquin was willing to take the Bovyans through the Jaws, they could come back at any time.

No, there was still a way to solve this problem, the evil solution which Sabine constantly whispered in his ear. Tomas resumed rowing, eyes locked on Fethos. Behind him, Melas gulped.

With their beefy arms, the Bovyans covered the lagoon in half the time as the most experienced fishermen. The slowed only as they prepared to pass single file through the Jaws. Once they made it through, they would catch up before Tomas made it a quarter of the way to Lorium.

Tomas looked toward Melas.

The Mystic was chewing his lip.

"You look worried. Can't your magic defeat them?" And maybe kill Joacquin, too...

"It depends on how fast they close, and if they have their crossbows..."

No matter how smart Melas thought he was, he hadn't thought his betrayal through. "Can you make an illusion?"

"I could turn us invisible, but that wouldn't keep them from seeing our boat."

Tomas pulled the oars in.

"What are you doing?" Melas snarled. "They'll catch up sooner."

"I'm going to take care of them." Tomas drew his slingshot and one of the crystals. Infused with orc magic, they were hopefully like Sabine, and immune to the crown stealing their power. If they worked, he'd need to wait until the boats had gotten far enough away from the Jaws that the blast wouldn't damage the natural protection.

Melas' eyes locked on the gemstone. "What is that?"

"Watch." Saying a silent prayer to every god he knew, Tomas took a deep breath and squeezed the crystal. Like before, it compressed. When he released the pressure, it glowed and whined.

It still worked, despite the proximity to the crown. He set the crystal into the sling.

"Fool. You may be a great shot, but that's too far."

Much too far for a straight shot. Aiming at the Jaws, Tomas pulled the sling back. The red rune appeared halfway between them and their pursuers, and then moved toward him as he lifted the slingshot up. The crystal's whine grew louder.

"Are you mad? How can you possibly guess where it will land?"

Tomas couldn't, but Sabine could. When the rune reached the lead boat, now well clear of the Jaws, he released the crystal.

The white light arced through the night sky, the whine's pitch changing with its flight. In his vision, it tracked along a curved red line.

The crystal struck Fethos' boat. It blossomed in reds, oranges, and yellows. A roar rolled over the waters.

Ma covered her eyes, but the demon eye adjusted.

The three boats and their occupants were gone, reduced to ash like the orc bones in the Temple of Lydath. All dead.

By his hand. His gut twisted.

"What have you done?" Ma's voice sounded aghast. "Joacquin was on that boat."

Tomas swallowed hard. He'd murdered a man whose only sin was collaborating with the Bovyans. And really, it had been more like a cold, logical decision than Sabine trying to corrupt his soul. This was him. All him.

Waves from the explosion sloshed against the boat, propelling it forward.

Holding to the side of the boat as if his life depended on it, the Aksumi whistled. "Amazing. That was an impossible shot, with whatever that was. Where did you get the crystal?" He held up the medallion, which still listed toward the crown.

The truth might endanger the village more—Melas clearly lusted for magic artifacts, and if the way he had fondled the girls was any indication, he'd be more of a threat than even the Bovyans. Tomas feigned enthusiasm. "Sometimes we find them in the lagoon. The traders in Mykos say they are old orc weapons, and mining companies will pay top *draka* for them. I just found that one near the crown on the sea floor."

Brow tight, Melas studied him.

Tomas fixed his expression into innocent confusion. If he didn't believe...

Looking first up at the Iridescent Moon, Melas turned next to the island, then toward Lorium. "Back to rowing. Get me to the town as fast as you can."

Crossing her arms, Ma turned her back.

Tomas gritted his teeth. Hopefully she'd forgive him. Eventually. It was for the village, after all, and for now, it was safe. He resumed rowing. The further Melas was from the island the better.

Then again, there was no stopping him from returning in the future. The lure of treasures, magic artifacts, and pretty village girls would bring him back.

"Wait," the Aksumi said. He extended his hand. "Your slingshot."

Without the slingshot, his plan for Melas slipped from his fingers. And, they'd be defenseless. Tomas hesitated.

"Now, or I will do to her what I did to the Bovyan." Melas pointed at Ma.

Heart lurching, Tomas handed it over. At least the Aksumi didn't search for the other orc gem.

Melas stuffed the slingshot into his belt. "Now go."

Tomas resumed rowing. The oars sloshed through the dark waters. With the boat laden by so many people, it was slow going. Tomas turned and looked to Lorium's docks to gauge his progress.

Over a dozen torches flickered there. There'd never been anything like it before—the townsfolk were usually at home at this hour. If they did come out, they would've used a light bauble. In all likelihood, the townsfolk –and Bovyans—had seen the explosion.

He squinted with the demon eye, and the torches enlarged.

Beneath them stood a dozen Bovyans, including Governor Keris, his spyglass aimed at them.

If Tomas continued to the docks, Melas would have to confront the Bovyans; though who knew what magic he would use to get out of the situation, now that he had the crown? And he would no doubt leave Tomas and Ma to fend for themselves.

Tomas pushed back on the oars, slowing them. It would be safer to deal with this on his own terms.

"What are you doing, boy?" Melas glared.

"There's a welcoming party." Tomas pointed back to the docks. Hopefully, this would work. All of Melas' body language up to now suggested it was so.

Melas turned around.

Tomas jumped up and lunged at the Aksumi.

Screaming, the Mystic went overboard with a splash. Tomas threw his hands out to catch the side of the boat and keep from joining him in the water.

The Mystic sank, thrashed back to the surface, and flailed at the water. As Tomas had gambled, Melas was too busy struggling with the water to be able to cast some fell magic.

"What did you do?" Ma hammered on the back of Tomas back with both fists.

Ignoring her protests, Tomas extended his hand over the side of the boat and snatched Melas' wrist.

Melas threw his other hand out and clawed at Tomas' arm. "Help! I can't swim!"

Pulling the Mystic toward the boat, Tomas plucked the crown from his head. He hooked it into his elbow again.

The Aksumi's terrified gaze contorted to anger. One hand released Tomas' arm and thrust into the water.

Tomas' vision flashed red. Sabine issued her two-syllable warning. He shoved Melas away. Both of the Mystic's arms flailed into the air again, this time sending a knife flying through the air. It splashed into the sea, followed by the Aksumi, who sank again.

Maybe it would be better to let him drown. It would mean one less threat to the island. They could row back there now, behind the safety of the Jaws.

Melas bobbed to the surface again and floundered. Dread creased his face. "Help!"

"Help him!" Ma shook him. "I taught you better than that."

Sabine was bringing the worst out of him. Cold logic, devoid of human empathy. With a sigh, Tomas handed her the crown. "Take this. As long as we keep it close to the Aksumi, without him actually wearing it, we can prevent him from using magic."

She searched his eyes, then nodded and took the crown.

He turned back, reached out, and took Melas' hand. "I'm going to help you grab the side of the boat. You're going to work your way to the rear, and stay hanging on while I row to shore."

Hatred burned in Melas' eyes, but he nodded.

Tomas pulled him up, enough that he could grab hold of the bulwark. The man's fingers clenched tight. Oar in hand, ready to smash him if he tried to climb aboard, Tomas watched as he worked his way to the stern.

"Now what?" Melas asked, eyes fixed on the crown in Mother's hands. "Keris wants the crown."

Tomas motioned Ma toward the front of the boat, leaving him between the two. "Why does he want it?"

"Not him, the First Consul. Your peoples' stupid prophecy about the Arkothi Imperator returning with his lost crown."

Tomas gave a slow nod. "Legitimacy, then. What made you think they'd really give you the starburst?"

"The Bovyans are always true to their word, though they are like a snake-tongued barrister. If you make a carefully-worded deal with them, they will honor it."

Tomas shook his head. "Without the starburst, though..."

"They were planning to replace it with the Light of Solaris."

Whatever that was.

Melas could apparently read his expression, and snorted. "They say it has a spark of your Sun God's divinity. Since the Bovyans are descended from him, it will give them more legitimacy than a sorcerer's stone."

"Is it here?"

The Aksumi looked at him as if he were feebleminded. It would be tempting to let him drown. "No, it's the heirloom of Tarkoth. Last I saw, the Bovyans had already stolen it from Elbahia."

Tomas' head spun. Elbahia was days away. The way the Teleri coordinated operations over such a broad area didn't seem possible. How could he keep the crown out of their hands?

He looked to the docks, still far away, where more and more Bovyans gathered. They wanted this crown, and that would be his way to free Lorium, as well. He extended his hand. "Give me back my slingshot."

CHAPTER 44:

Old Friends

Standing outside the locked door to the suspicious rowhouse, Jie studied her lock picks. Now that Fleet had pointed it out, Tharos' musky scent mixed with the unmistakable heady smell of Altivorcs.

She tried not to shudder. Her third of only four previous experiences with the turquoise-skinned bipedals, who'd once enslaved all of humanity, was back home when they'd plotted with a rebel lord to attack an imperial wedding. That plot was likely tied to the assassins she was tracking.

They'd circled the block in opposite directions before returning to the back door. Bird chirps emanated from the building's attic again. They sounded just like the Eldaeri messenger birds aboard the *Indomitable.* Given its small size and unassuming architecture, it was highly unlikely that this was the Tarkothi admiralty headquarters. No, it was the Nightblade safehouse, and they had their own stock of messenger birds.

Her fingers just about tingled with excitement. There was no telling what kind of correspondence they'd find. She selected the appropriate pick, inserted it into the lock. It yielded in seconds.

Fleet nodded appreciatively.

"Can you teach me to do that?" Alaena whispered.

Aelward turned and gawked.

Jie flashed her a grin and shrugged. Maybe not all princesses were bad, after all.

Fleet held up a hand to the two Eldaeri, then pointed to her and himself, two fingers at his eyes, then into the building.

Even a child could understand such simple gestures, but then again, who knew when dealing with royalty and military men? She nodded at Fleet.

She applied pressure on the door and its hinges glided without a sound. Muffled voices percolated out.

On the Madaeri's signal, she slipped in and to the left, and Fleet followed to the right.

Though the light baubles were shuttered, her elf vision picked out the brick oven and chimney, counters, and cooking tools. A set of stairs led up to darkness. Light shined in from under the door to the room beyond, and with it came the voices.

Jie flashed clan signals. She'd go listen, he'd sweep the perimeter, then go upstairs.

He studied her hands, and gave a slow nod. He signed back. *Old.*

Of course, Black Lotus signals changed subtly over time, and dramatically since the discovery of a possible traitor. She switched to the set the clan used previously, from before they learned of the existence of the Nightblades, back when she'd been a courtesan-in-training in her homeland's red-light district.

Fleet shrugged and gave a more definitive nod. He started searching around the kitchen.

Jie crept over to the door and put her ear to the crack below.

"Peris is late," said a guttural voice with a heavy accent. An Altivorc, in all likelihood.

"He'll be here." That voice belonged to Tharos.

Were the two really brothers? They must've been planted in Tarkoth at an age old enough to be trained and indoctrinated, but young enough to pass as orphans. In any case, Tharos would be waiting a long time for Peris.

"It shouldn't have taken him too long to kill two females," said a second Altivorc voice. "If he isn't here..."

"Then he could be dead, like your other friend." The first's tone didn't sound the least bit sympathetic, though perhaps Altivorcs expressed sympathy differently.

The first let out a snuffling laugh. "At least he won't be dead wearing a dress like that one."

So her suspicion was correct. The assassin sent to kill Prince Koryn was also a Bovyan Nightblade.

Tharos growled low, but said nothing. Given the acoustics of the conversation, the adjoining room was likely an interior room with no windows, probably taking up a third of the first floor.

"We can't wait much longer. Our window to leave this island undetected is approaching."

"Peris and I can meet you later. Our identities have been compromised, so our initial plans have changed."

"What were those?" the first Altivorc asked.

"We were ordered to defect to Serikoth, with our knowledge of Tarkothi military operational procedures, to make sure they weakened each other."

"Now what will you do?"

"Await orders here. We can operate out of this safehouse for months by stealing food and water at night. No one will ever see us."

Jie sucked on her lower lip. Part of her wanted to hang out here every night and read his correspondence when he went out to forage. It would bring her closer to the master of the Nightblades. Then again, as long as they had this base of operations, they could undermine the Eldaeri, and possibly put Aryn in harm's way.

"We can't wait any longer," said the Altivorc leader.

Tharos sighed. "You have the Light of Solaris. You're sure your king can modify it to fit in the Crown of the Sundered Empire without extinguishing the Solaris' divine spark?"

"Of course, but he'll only be able to finish after Peris brings us the Sparkling Orb of Cathay. And the crown."

Jie's head spun. The Sparkling Orb of Cathay was an imperial heirloom from back home, belonging to the Founder's Consort. Peris must've stolen it during his visit, along with information on how to find the Crown of Arkos—which the Teleri wanted to find and alter. And then, there was the king, likely the Altivorc King, who'd ruled over the Tivari since even before the War of Ancient Gods. He was said to be beautiful, as beautiful as an angel, so unlike his hideous minions. Why would he care about human struggles for power?

Ten sets of heavy Altivorc boots rumbled closer.

Jie looked from the stairs to the back door. The former would be a perfect hiding place, but Aelward and Alaena were waiting outside, in the path of the Altivorcs. There was no way for her to reach the door without being seen. She darted to the stairs.

The door to the middle room swung open. Altivorcs lumbered out. Though shorter than the average human, they were as stocky as Bovyans. These wore leather armor, and broadswords hung at their sides. While they had blunt, heavy features, their leader might've been as handsome as an elf with his high-bridged nose and high cheekbones. Unarmored, wearing only a leather longcoat, he held a fist-sized object wrapped in cloth. Rays of light peeked out from it.

The Light of Solaris.

Recover it, and perhaps the Eldaeri would end hostilities.

The column marched through the middle of the kitchen, with Tharos behind them. Thankfully, he was now clothed. An arming sword and dagger hung at his side. Eleven enemies in all.

Strategic sense said to stay hidden and track them; but there was still the issue of Alaena and Aelward waiting outside, unaware of the danger.

A tap came at her shoulder.

She nearly jumped out of her skin, but turned back.

Brows bunched up, Fleet jerked a finger at the warriors.

Jie shook her head, holding up ten fingers and one, then followed by four. Eleven to four. Ten of them Altivorcs. One of them a Nightblade, and fighting in his own home. Even though the tight confines would keep them from getting surrounded, the odds were bad.

Fleet slipped past her.

Drawing her magic knife, she hurried to catch up, tapping signals on his back. *Don't kill Big Man.*

Hopefully he would understand the older code. If not, Tharos would take his secrets to the grave.

Though then again, Fleet was awfully small. He probably couldn't hurt—the Madaeri hopped up onto a counter, picked up a cup and hurled it at the back window.

The cup shattered the glass on impact, sending shards everywhere.

The Altivorcs and Tharos turned toward it.

Fleet leaped off the counter, disappearing beneath Altivorc legs.

The back door burst open, revealing Alaena, arrow fitted to her bowstring. Aelward pushed past her, broadsword in hand.

Jie's chest squeezed. In the dark, frail human eyes wouldn't be able to distinguish friend from foe.

Alaena's arrow *thwipp*ed through the air, headed toward Tharos.

He sidestepped and drew his own sword.

Reaching into her sleeves, Jie flung two throwing stars at him.

There was no way he could see them in the dark, but he must've heard the telltale whirling. He dropped to the floor, and the stars thunked into the far wall.

More arrows zipped through the kitchen, lodging into the huddled mass of Altivorcs. It didn't keep them from drawing their swords in a collective rasp and swinging their blades toward the floor.

Fleet hopped and dodged their attacks with blinding speed, as hard to track as the Ayuri Paladins she'd once seen fight. In a deft motion, the little Madaeri pulled the dagger from the leader's hip, adding an element of danger to his deadly dance.

Swords now clashed as Aelward engaged with the closest. His swordsmanship was surprisingly good, despite injury adding to his usual clumsiness. Even though his opponent tried to press him, he didn't give ground.

With only one throwing star left, Jie hefted her knife. Disabling, but not killing Tharos was the first order of business.

An Altivorc sword swept toward her head, forcing her to duck into a roll. No, surviving was the first order of business. She stayed low and slashed at his ankle. The magic knife which she'd acquired in Tokahia sliced through his hard leather boot, flesh, and Achilles tendon.

The brute tumbled to the ground, and she bounced to her feet.

All Altivorc eyes fell on her.

"*Grzk trl mm.*" The leader looked pointedly at her.

She flipped the knife through her fingers. "Speak Arkothi."

The leader barked out more foul syllables and pointed his sword at her.

The Altivorcs turned away from Aelward, Alaena, and Fleet. All seven charged toward her. Behind them, Tharos stared, dumbstruck.

"What just happened?" Aelward said.

It was déjà vu all over again: whenever she'd faced Altivorcs, they'd been busy fighting someone else, but then broke off to attack her. Maybe they hated half-elves.

"Just kill them!" Alaena loosed more arrows into the Altivorcs' backs. At least one more at the rear of their mob collapsed.

"Take Tharos!" Jie backed away, twisting out of the path of stabs and sidestepping hacks. The Altivorcs left openings with their attacks, but their comrades' follow-ups made it impossible to counter. In seconds, she was back in the stairwell. At least it created a bottleneck, and Alaena could pick them off with her archery.

"I'm out!" Alaena yelled.

Of course she was.

Lights flared on, nearly blinding Jie.

The lead Altivorc thrust repeatedly with his sword, forcing her to jump up and back, higher up the stairs. They were all crowded in the stairwell, the heat and stench of orc sweat making her head roil.

She lurched back onto a landing, where the steps curled up to the right...well, left, since she was moving backward. It would be a tactical advantage against right-handed people, but all the orcs held their weapons in their left.

Down below, swords clanged against each other. Just like she used the narrow stair as a bottleneck, so did the rear Altivorc. The leader had been toward the back, though it was hard to tell now over the mass of angry creatures.

The next attack swept at her, the breadth of the landing giving her opponent more room. She ducked below the blade and punched her knife into his armor, through flesh and bone. His eyes widened, and black blood drooled from his lips. Another stab came from the other side of him, and it was all Jie could do to avoid it.

The orc hurdled over his comrade and slipped past her slash to block her ascent. The high ceiling of the second floor allowed for the next one to chop down at her, forcing her to press her back into the far corner.

Trapped like a rat.

Downstairs in the kitchen, the back door opened, letting in the sound of approaching horse hooves, before slamming shut. No more sounds of clashing blades rang out. Tharos must've escaped.

The one blocking the way down reversed his chop with an upswing, while the one obstructing the way thrust up with his stab.

She spun out of the line of both attacks, which left gashes in the blockwood walls. When they went to recover, she took two steps and pop-vaulted in the corners of the stairwell landing, up over the balustrade to the second floor.

The new vantage point provided a better view of the entire stairwell. Behind the one at the head of the landing, three more waited to push past. The leader was at the bottom of the steps, parrying Aelward's skilled attacks. The one who'd blocked the way up was now rushing up the stairs to engage her. The others followed suit, hustling up the steps in a cacophonous rumble.

Jie took a moment to scan the second floor. It was all one large room, running from the front of the rowhouse to the back, with two large windows on both the front and back walls. There were two desks with paper, inkwells, and quills, and a single cot.

She gasped. Notes were pinned to one wall, connected by strings. It was so much like the way a certain clueless spy back home organized his thoughts...a web of interconnections which looked like it had been spun by a spider addicted to Ayuri gooseweed.

The jostling footsteps came closer, and she looked over to see the Altivorcs, save for the leader who covered the rear bottleneck, rounding the landing and clambering up. They came around the balustrade, blocking her from the rest of the second floor, and sank into fighting stances.

Grinning, Jie waved. She leaped back over the bannister and alighted on the landing. Not waiting for them to process what had just happened, she ran down the steps.

The leader was no longer there.

Aelward sat with his back to the wall, panting.

"Are you all right?"

He gave a tentative nod. "Aye, lass. He shouldered past me, and chased after the halfling, Alaena, and Tharos."

Doubtful. More likely he was making off with the Light of Solaris. Jie offered him a hand.

Aelward stared at it for a second before taking it. He pulled himself up, nearly yanking her down with his weight.

"Come on," she said, heading for the door.

She pushed it open and froze.

Outside, the Altivorc leader stood, gripping a magic wand in one hand. In his other, he held the Light of Solaris aloft.

It shed light on a dozen Serikothi cavaliers, Prince Koryn among them, arrows fitted to bowstrings.

Tharos, Fleet, and Alaena were nowhere to be seen.

Twelve cavaliers, their prince, Aelward, and her, against an Altivorc. The odds had shifted, unless the magic wand—

The Altivorc barked out a guttural word. The magic wand flashed. A bolt of blue lightning struck one of the cavaliers, sending him tumbling out of his saddle with a moan.

In quick succession, three flashing bolts slammed into three more.

The Altivorc leveled the wand at Prince Koryn.

CHAPTER 45:

Explosive

Alaena dashed after Tharos, but the traitor's long legs gained distance with his huge lopes. Fleet sped ahead of her, but even his frenetic pace didn't make up for his short limbs. If only she hadn't expended all her arrows, or had retrieved one from a fallen Altivorc.

It had happened all too fast. One moment, she and Aelward had been waiting outside the door; the next, the window shattered. She'd taken that as a sign to enter, and Aelward had pushed past her, trying to defend her yet again. In the chaos of the kitchen, the lights had flared on and Tharos had made his escape. She'd given chase, but now it looked like he was getting away.

Possibly with the Light of Solaris.

And with it, her chance to redeem herself.

Behind her, hooves thudded on the pavement and mail jingled. Cavalry? Or cavaliers? Maybe the ones they'd run into earlier had come back. Or even...Koryn? Maybe she could borrow a horse and run Tharos down.

Light flashed behind her... a light bauble? No, it was much too white.

She turned, just in time to see crackles of blue light strike several cavaliers. They fell from their horses and writhed. She skidded to a halt and gaped. The Altivorc must've had some kind of magic wand. He was now pointing it at Koryn.

Heir to Serikoth.

Her brother.

Pulling a knife from her boot, Alaena raced back. Cavaliers urged their mounts forward. Some fitted arrows. The blue bolt flashed again.

A soldier threw himself into the line of fire, and the magic struck him, sending him tumbling to the ground.

With a guttural snarl, the Altivorc pointed the wand at all the closest cavaliers, unleashing its magic in quick succession. More men fell.

In seconds, only Damaryn was left nearby to sacrifice himself for Koryn. The dashing, handsome young man jostled to interpose himself between the two, but Koryn, in his foolishness, boxed him out with his horse.

Several of the cavalrymen loosed their bowstrings, but their arrows ricocheted off the Altivorc's surcoat as if it were made of metal.

Though nominally close enough, Aelward just stood there gawking; Jie pressed her back up against the door.

The Altivorc pointed the wand.

Now close enough, Alaena hurled the knife.

It hit the Altivorc's arm, just as he grunted the words of magic.

The knife didn't penetrate the coat's sleeve, but the force was enough send the magic astray. It struck the building's wall, splintering the blockwood.

The Altivorc turned and met her gaze, then pointed his wand at her.

And unlike Koryn, she had no one to protect her.

* * *

Aelward had pushed past Jie, who'd skidded to a halt right outside the door. Now, he gawked as the Altivorc leader sent elite cavaliers flopping to the ground with magic worthy of a sea witch. They writhed like fish dumped onto a ship deck.

Then he pointed the wand at Alaena.

Shouting a challenge, Aelward leaped toward the Altivorc and hacked with his broadsword. The blade should've sheared the cloth with ease, and yet it felt like hitting a stone wall. His hands rang from the reverberation.

"Don't shoot," Koryn yelled. "Get out of the way!"

The Altivorc rounded on him, wand leveled.

Aelward chopped again, aiming for the orc's outstretched wrist. The wand flashed, just as the sword bit into the fleshy part of the leader's thumb and cut into his middle and ring finger.

The blue bolt would've hit Aelward square in the chest, but instead struck his right bicep. Pain flared as his entire arm tightened and twitched. His fingers tightened around the sword hilt, then went limp. The weapon slipped from his grip just before it tightened again.

Snarling, the Altivorc shifted the bundle of cloth from his right hand to his left underarm, then transferred the wand to from left to right.

Right arm still numb, Aelward bent over to retrieve the blade with his left. The Altivorc boot slammed into the sword, sending Aelward's knuckles into the pavement. A knee to Aelward's chest knocked the wind out of him.

Staggering back, he gasped for air.

Jie had her back to the door, but a violent thud into it sent her lurching into him, and three Altivorcs pushed out. She steadied him with two hands, then sidled around.

Their leader shifted his aim from Aelward to her, even as Alaena resumed her charge.

Blue light flashed.

Jie dove into a roll, then came up right beside the Altivorc, a black knife in hand.

Not that it would do anything, not if his sword hadn't cut through the magic cloth. "Don't—"

Jie stabbed into his gut. The point punched through the surcoat as if it were made of...cloth. The Altivorc cried out as she yanked the blade through his abdomen. Black blood spurted out.

Despite the pain he must've been in, the orc pointed the wand at her.

Letting go of her knife, Jie caught his wrist and twisted as blue light flashed past her and into the Altivorcs emerging from the house. With the back of her hip to him, his elbow on her shoulder, she jerked down. His joint made a sickening pop, and she swept his legs out from under him. She caught her knife, even before he hit the ground.

Alaena skidded to a halt, gaping. Aelward, too, froze. Who would've thought a little half-elf girl could fight so viciously?

The remaining Altivorcs could've stabbed him in the back, but now pushed past him, swords raised, ready to cut Jie down.

* * *

Koryn had watched in awe as the half-elf not only succeeded in cutting through the Altivorc leader's armor, but also broke his elbow and sent him sprawling. Still, she'd left herself open to the three Altivorcs surging past the useless Tarkothi naval officer.

Tapping his heels into his horse, Koryn charged. A horse-length behind him, Damaryn followed.

The Tarkothi naval officer lunged forward, tackling the rear Altivorc. To the right, Alaena came to her senses. Her sword swept out just in time to block a hack that would've taken the half-elf's head off...had the half-elf been there.

She had spun out of the way and slashed into the left Altivorc's sword arm. With Alaena's backstroke, she cut through the first Altivorc's leather armor and into his flank. The Tarkothi climbed onto his opponent's back, grabbed his hair, and slammed his head repeatedly into the ground.

Koryn galloped by, taking the closest's head off with a sweep of his sword. On the far side, Damaryn cut down the one engaged with Jie. Koryn wheeled around and reassessed the situation.

Though his victim wasn't moving, the Tarkothi continued to ram his head into the pavement. Alaena stared dumbstruck at the Altivorc that Koryn had beheaded, while Jie had already turned from her fallen foe and looked at the leader.

Koryn followed her gaze.

The survivor sat cross-legged, bundle of cloth tucked into his underarm. He fiddled with the wand in his lap.

"Get away!" Fleet's voice yelled from a distance. "Get as far away as you can!"

The Madaeri was the most knowledgeable individual Koryn knew. As if to confirm Fleet's warning, the injured Altivorc cackled, and the wand emitted a low whine. It got louder by the second.

Spurring his horse, Koryn leaned over and caught Alaena up under her arms. Her weight and the horse's momentum nearly yanked him out of the saddle, but he managed to stay on. Damaryn was several horse lengths behind him, but Jie caught his arm and swung up behind him.

"Aelward," Alaena yelled, still dangling in his arms, trying to get a foot over the horse. "You need to get him!"

Koryn looked over his shoulder. "Who?"

"Aelward!" She gestured back the way they'd come.

She must be referring to the Tarkothi. Why did she even care? Still, he was clearly an ally in this fight. In a smooth motion, he wheeled his horse and eased her off. The momentum sent her into a stumble. Not waiting to see if she was all right, he bolted back toward this Aelward.

He was gaining his feet above the sprawled-out Altivorc, and stretched his arm out. The high-pitched whine of the wand grew louder. In the distance, dogs whimpered.

Koryn slowed the horse as they approached and reached out with his own hand. Their arms caught, but Aelward was too heavy. His hand dug into Koryn's wrist, his weight jerking Koryn back, nearly out of the saddle. He was leaning back, barely holding on with one hand on the reins and his feet in the stirrups.

"Jump, dammit!" Koryn tried to bend forward, to re-center his balance, to no avail.

Aelward stumbled along, his feet unable to find purchase on the ground.

It was impossible, and now, the drag pulled Koryn off the horse. He skidded across his butt, while Aelward fell into a head-over-heels roll onto him, knocking his breath away. The horse galloped on without them.

He choked as Aelward pulled him to his feet and tugged him into a lumbering lope. "Come on, Your High—"

Blue light pulsed past them, like a ripple on a pond. It sounded like a giant bell tolling, followed by splintering wood and shattering glass. The hot shockwave crashed into them, slamming them forward through the air.

Koryn had been thrown from a shying horse a few times as a youth, but never had it felt like flying. Never did his clothes singe with searing heat. The air gushed past him and bit into his face. Up ahead, the wall of a house raced to meet his head. He raised his hands just before careening into it. He bounced off the wall and fell back.

He turned over and sat up. His head spun, and his ears were ringing. He blinked several times to clear his vision.

At his side, Aelward lay unmoving. Back where they'd come from, two—no, three houses had lost their rear walls and looked to be on the verge of collapse. Above the building the Altivorc and Alaena had emerged from, birds twittered. The houses on the opposite side of the alley had splintered walls, looking as if a galley had rammed them.

Several of his cavaliers lay as blackened skeletons in steel cuirasses. And Damaryn? Where was he?

Golden hair flashed among the milling soldiers beyond the blast site, and pushed forward. Damaryn!

Their eyes met, and the faithful captain ran over. Alaena followed a few steps behind.

They passed the Altivorc leader…now incinerated to a pile of ash.

Oh no. The Light of Solaris…

A puff of wind gusted through the alley. A ray of white light soared skyward from the ash mound.

Damaryn skidded to a stop, his eyes wide. The murmurs fell into silence.

Surely, this was a sign from Solaris himself. A beacon. Koryn pressed his palms together and bowed his head. The surviving cavaliers did the same.

He lifted his gaze to find Alaena rushing past him, back to where Aelward lay.

On wobbling legs, Koryn stumbled over to the Altivorc remains, dropped to his knees, and sifted through the ashes. The Light of Solaris shined bright beneath.

"Are you all right, Your Highness?" Damaryn skidded to a stop, his eyes wide.

"Yes." Koryn gave a tentative nod before reverently taking the Light in two hands. "You?"

"Yes, Your Highness."

Koryn smiled. "Go to Prince Elrayn. Let him know that we have the Light, and he will have to meet me at the Flaviyan Bridge if he wants it back."

CHAPTER 46:

When Plans Fail

The wider visual field and improved night vision allowed Tomas to keep an eye on the treacherous Aksumi Mystic, while affording a view of the Bovyans as they followed the boat's progress. They probably thought he was looking for a safe place to go ashore.

They'd be wrong. He gauged the distance to the highway bridge to Mykos. Everywhere ached from rowing.

Ma's gaze strayed in the general direction of the island. "Why don't we just go home?"

"I don't want him anywhere near the village." Images of the Aksumi fondling two of the girls mingled with Sofia's face.

She held up the crown. "He won't be able to use his magic with this nearby."

"Maybe. But we'd have to keep it close, and the moment he isn't holding on for dear life, he'll try to take it from us."

"I swear," Melas said. "I won't try to take it. Just let me go."

"Oh, I plan to. But on my terms." If only he could take Ma to safety first. Tomas looked to shore again.

At least a hundred of the Bovyans, including Governor Keris, had mounted up onto their horses, some riding far ahead along the coastal road. Since the crown was their primary mission, they weren't taking chances.

The deep thud of a drum carried across the water.

Tomas' soul just about jumped out of his body. The beat picked up, and he tracked it to the source.

Lorium.

With his vision seeming like twilight even in the dark of night, the shape of a huge Serikothi galley formed against the town's outline far in the distance. He squinted, and as before, the image enlarged.

The Serikothi bireme, now flying the Teleri standard, glided through the water. Its double banks of over a hundred oars churned in rhythmic beats.

Pulse racing even faster than the bireme oars, Tomas shifted his gaze back to the bridge. Still another league, and although the Teleri vessel was four times the distance away, it would only build speed. Sabine spoke, but whatever she said might as well have been gibberish.

"Show me what you mean," Tomas growled.

Ma shot him a concerned look. "What?"

She probably thought him mad. Then again, she couldn't see the red lines in his vision.

One ran from the boat to the bridge. Another, from the bireme to the bridge. What was Sabine trying to say? Tomas snarled.

Sabine spoke in his head, voice calm as ever.

"Calm down, Tomas," Ma said. "Just tell the Teleri the truth. You found the crown, and the Aksumi tried to take it."

Tomas' eyes strayed to Melas, whose lips twitched into a grin. Thinking about some way to twist the story around, no doubt.

How would a Bovyan perceive what they'd seen? The explosion had gotten their attention, and they'd already spotted Ma and him in the boat and maybe Melas clinging on. The Aksumi had used magic fire as a weapon; maybe it would be possible to say he'd killed all the Bovyans. Surely they wouldn't believe a fisherman could do it.

No, this was all a backup plan. He considered the slingshot, hoping the stretchweed wasn't too wet, then locked eyes with Melas. "Kick with your legs, or I'll leave you behind."

Melas scowled, but started kicking. At the very least, it could tire him if they had to deal with him later.

"Just surrender." Ma tugged at Tomas' sleeves.

"Only if I have to."

She gave him a curious look.

His vision flashed red. Sabine spoke again, demon language unintelligible as usual. The line from the bireme shifted slightly. Tomas tracked it back to the bridge.

He gasped. Sabine's line from the bireme now intersected with the line from the boat to the bridge. What did it mean? That the bireme would get there first? Heaving for breath, he rowed faster, while looking to the coastal road. The Bovyan soldiers onshore continued their march, clearly able to see him despite the clouds occasionally obscuring the moon.

Sweat gathered on Tomas' brow. The beat of the bireme drums grew louder, as the red line shifted more. He looked back to find it intersecting his boat's line even sooner, and he had to get to the other side of the bridge. It didn't take Sabine to tell him the bridge lay out of range of even a dry stretchweed slingshot. It also didn't take her to say the bireme was gaining: it loomed larger. The soldiers' outlines formed on the deck, as well as a head and a pair of shoulders rising out of a recessed area in the middle. Arms rose and dropped to the beat of the drum. No, *setting* the beat.

Tomas gulped hard. One orc gem. He could destroy the galley or the bridge, but not both. Or maybe there was still a way. He continued his rowing, even as the ship came closer. His own boat neared the shore. Before long, Melas' feet would be able to reach the sea floor, and he might try to take control. For now, though, he was busy kicking and wouldn't know.

"What are your intentions, boy?" Governor Keris' voice sounded like a disembodied ghost as it carried over the water.

Melas' turned his eyes toward shore, then looked up at Tomas. "Give me the crown, and my magic can solve all your problems."

"How?"

"With enough time, I know how to craft the illusion of a Serikothi warship with a full crew. I've done it before."

Tomas snorted. "Serikoth's warships sail in the oceans, not on the Inland Sea."

Melas looked over his shoulder at the bireme. "I have other magic."

Tempting, but the only thing reliable about the Mystic was that he would turn on them in a moment. Just like he'd betrayed the Bovyans. "All right. I'll tell you when I need your help."

"Hurry, because all this paddling is tiring me out." The Aksumi's panting suggested he was telling the truth, which meant the plan to exhaust him was working. Of course, it could all be an act.

The bireme loomed even closer now. He scooted over and gestured to Mother. "Take the oars."

"What are you going to do?" She stared at him wide-eyed. "I can't row as fast as you."

"I'm going to try and slow the bireme down." He scooped up the slingshot and tested it. The stretchweed was still wet, but had spring to it. Hand reaching into the robe's strange pocket, his fingers wrapped around some metal ring from the dwarf kingdom.

He set it into the sling and aimed at the bireme. According to Sabine's runes, it hadn't come close enough. Moisture must've loosened the stretchweed. He released the tension and waited. The red lines in his vision shifted as the boat slowed and the larger vessel gained. Over his shoulder, the bridge lay out of range, and the advance Bovyan cavalry had already crossed the bridge.

With desperate breaths, he puffed on the stretchweed, willing it to dry out. "A little faster, Ma!"

"These old arms can't row any faster!"

"Let me help," Melas said.

Ignoring him, Tomas took aim again. With a high arc, just like his shot on the three boats earlier, Sabine's rune just about reached the prow. He found his target, took aim, and shot.

Sabine tracked the curve of the trinket's flight. It picked up speed with its downward descent. Tomas held his breath.

The ring struck the drummer in the head. He collapsed, and the beat went silent. The red line shifted.

"How could you possibly...." Melas gasped.

Tomas took over the oars and rowed, all the while squinting at the bireme.

Its oars now hung out of the water, motionless, even as the bireme itself continued its pursuit. Above, a Bovyan held one of the drumsticks while searching the deck around the drum. Another Bovyan was pulling the drummer's body away.

The boat pitched a little as it came even with the river that emptied into the Inland Sea. Tomas scanned the shore. Bovyans now lined the bridge, with several now on the other side. Almost.

The drumming resumed, albeit at a slower, less consistent beat. It was gaining on them, nonetheless. A flurry of activity erupted on deck as Bovyans formed up and loaded crossbows.

Tomas looked back to the highway. Well over half the Bovyans had spilled over the bridge. Under Keris' orders, they were forming up in ranks and loading crossbows. Could the bolts reach the boat? Tomas withdrew another metal trinket, set it in the sling and tested the range. Sabine's red rune didn't reach his target. He'd have to go closer to shore.

"Boy," Keris yelled, much clearer now. "Surrender the crown, and you will be rewarded."

It was tempting, so tempting, but as Melas had said, Bovyans would find a way to twist any deal. Tomas took several deep breaths. The bireme would soon be in range. On shore, the first rank of crossbowmen now pointed their weapons to arc in the boat's direction. A rain of bolts would end them.

Keris raised his hand. "Ready..."

Standing, Tomas waved both his arms back and forth. "Don't shoot! I surrender. We are coming to shore."

"No tricks," Keris said.

Tomas turned to Ma. "Start rowing in."

She beamed. "I'm glad you came to your senses."

"What about me?" Melas said.

"Keep kicking." Tomas reached into his pocket and found the orc gem as they closed in on the shore. One chance, and one chance only. Up above, a patch of clouds floated toward the moons.

He held the slingshot low, to obscure it with the silhouette of his body in the low light, then pulled back on the sling. Not quite yet. To the left, the bireme closed. They'd be in crossbow range soon enough.

"What are you doing?" Melas growled, eyes on the slingshot. With no Bovyan witnesses to his attempt to take the crown, he would just pretend to be victim and still get his starburst.

"Here's your chance to get the crown. Trust me." Tomas afforded him an emphatic stare before testing the range again. Almost there, about a hundred *pedes*.

On the shore, Keris watched with his scope. If he could see the slingshot, he didn't take it to be a threat. And why would he? It wasn't like a regular rock could cause much damage. He'd dismissed it when they first captured him, when Tomas still had his own eye.

Now, it would be their undoing. They reached sixty *pedes* from shore, maybe eighty from the bridge. It was in range. Tomas would be the hero not just of his village, but also of Lorium. He squeezed the gemstone flat. It emitted a low hum and white light. He lifted the slingshot, pulled the sling and watched Sabine's red rune glide across the water toward the bridge.

"What's he doing?" someone yelled from shore.

The red rune was almost to its target.

Voices carried across the water.

"What's in his hand?"

"Slingshot?"

"What's he even aiming at?"

The rune reached the bridge.

The stretchweed snapped. Both ends of the band whipped back and stung his face, luckily missing his eye.

"What is that?" Melas started climbing onto to the boat, causing it to rock. "Another gem?"

The gem now whined louder, the light growing brighter. Any second now, it would reduce them to dust. It was over. Tomas could only stare.

"Tomas!" Ma screamed.

Shaken from the dread fascination, a new plan formed in his mind. The bireme was accelerating again, Sabine's line showing they planned to ram him toward shore. Gauging his position relative to the bridge, he tossed the crystal in the opposite direction. He dropped to the seat, took the oars, and started rowing toward the bridge. Forty *pedes*. Thirty.

Several twangs emanated from the Bovyan ranks on the highway.

Tomas' vision flashed red. Red lines crisscrossed through the air, the only consistency among them being the general direction. Crossbow bolts *thwipp*ed by, most splashing into the water. A few lodged into the wood.

Ma yelped.

Melas ducked low. "Dammit boy, give me the crown! Oh!"

The Aksumi must've realized his feet could touch the sea floor.

Orange and reds bloomed out from where the gem hit the water, followed by a roar. Waves jerked the boat toward the bridge. Twenty *pedes*—it was close!

The churning current from the river mouth caught the boat, lurching it back toward the sea, and right into the path of the bireme. The huge ship now bore down on them, its drums thundering louder now. Its ram was just visible above the water line, ready to gouge the boat's hull. Above, the crossbowmen on deck shielded their eyes from the afterimage of the flare.

At the last second, Tomas rowed hard to starboard, into the line of the oars. Tomas ducked under one, then another, but then their backstroke smashed into the boat's stern. Ma, too, had stayed low—

No. A bolt had lodged in Mother's chest. Her breaths came labored, and her face paled. What had he done? Tears filling his eyes, Tomas crouched down, under the sweep of oars, and held her hand. It was clammy.

"No!" someone shouted from the highway. "Stop! Stop!"

The bireme listed portside, slowing in the river's current.... But not slow enough.

"Oars out," yelled a man on deck. "Oars out!"

The bireme crashed into the bridge. Timbers splintered and cracked. Men screamed. The cacophony of destruction.

EPILOGUE:

Converging Paths

Though every muscle and joint ached, and fatigue weighed down his head and limbs, Koryn sat straight in his saddle as the sun peeked over the horizon. Cavaliers and Serikothi soldiers stood around him at the head of the Flaviyan Bridge, which Prince Aryn and his own honor guard were approaching on horse.

Koryn lifted the Light of Solaris, wondering at its beautiful brightness. Perhaps it would be better to keep it in Serikoth.

But no, by right and treaty, it belonged to Tarkoth. More of Solaris' Chosen would die in the struggle to regain it.

Koryn dismounted and met Aryn in the middle of the bridge. "Good Morning, Your Highness. I expected the Crown Prince to meet with me."

"The king has given me authority to negotiate the return of the Light." Aryn proffered a scroll, sealed with Tarkoth's royal crest.

Koryn received it, broke the seal, and read. Indeed, the King of Tarkoth had invested royal authority in Aryn. "Why not Prince Elrayn?"

"Our father has ordered him confined to the villa until he arrives in person to remonstrate him." Aryn gave a wry smile. "I'm worried I might be the new Crown Prince."

If only he knew the burdens that went along with the title. Still, an earnest man like Aryn would make a better king than the ambitious Elrayn. Koryn smiled back. "It would suit you well."

Aryn shrugged. "I never wanted it."

"Wise man. Now, I am willing to surrender the Light, in return for the two ships you captured, Sunblade, and the return of Elbahia Island back to its original position."

"I agree in principle. Let us draft up a treaty with those as our guidelines."

Koryn nodded. "Now that we know the Teleri are trying to stoke hostilities between us, we must also include language that improves our lines of communication, to avoid a repeat of last night's disaster."

"Yes. Let us meet for tea sometime soon. You can tell me what it means to be Crown Prince."

First and foremost, it meant putting one's own needs aside for that of a nation. Putting duty ahead of love, even if it made life miserable. A frown tugged at Koryn's lips.

* * *

The stairs to the Nightblade safehouse had been destroyed in the blast, and in the early morning sun, the building itself looked ready to collapse. Still, that had not been enough to prevent Jie from climbing the walls to reach the attic.

Roosts lined a surviving wall, and a handful of the messenger birds remained, including one she'd seen on the *Indomitable*. The opposite wall had been claimed by the blast, but what remained looked to be shelves of notes. She'd only recovered a few dozen: some were official correspondence between the admiralties of Serikoth and Tarkoth; others, messages meant for both nations' kings. These she sorted and would give to Aryn and Koryn, in hopes that they would begin to understand the enormity of the security breach, and perhaps capture any other Teleri operatives.

The book Peris had stolen from Cathay had also survived. It turned out to be the record from the previous dynasty's ambassador to the Arkothi Empire. The official had made it home during the Long Winter, bringing with him the story of the Last Imperator's departure for Lydath's Golden Bowl. There was no mention of the crown, but that would be the first place Jie would look. No doubt, Peris had informed Tharos long ago via messenger bird, and their superiors knew as well. Perhaps they'd already secured the crown. These details mattered little to Cathay's security.

More important were the rest of the Nightblade messages, written in a coded language similar to the Black Lotus Clan's. The clan traitor must not have been smart enough to change the codes. If only she could fly like a bird. Then she could find out where the outbound messages were headed, to root out all the operatives who communicated with this nerve center.

But no. Now that Tharos had escaped and their command center had been compromised, they'd likely go to ground.

As she did now. Hand under hand, foot under foot, she made her way back down to the first floor. She picked her way through the rubble and out into the alley.

"I thought I'd find you here." Aryn was leaning against the house across the way.

Jie froze. Her heart fluttered as she dipped into a curtsey, even if her stealth suit had no skirts to clasp. "Your Highness."

His expression darkened. "Who are you, anyway? Not just a Cathayi translator. Don't lie to me. You owe me the truth."

"Your Highness, I have never lied to you." Heavens, her tone was so...pleading. "You asked me to translate for you, but I was never an official translator."

"Half-truths are still lies."

Heat rushed to the tips of her ears, and she stared at the ground.

His expression softened. “Oh, I can’t hate you. You’re just too adorable.”

How much of the truth could she reveal? She reached into a secret pocket of her suit and withdrew the bundle of messages intercepted and copied by the Bovyans from the Tarkothi admiralty. “Tharos and Peris were Teleri Nightblades. Their cell had been intercepting Tarkoth’s official messages for at least three years. Here are the ones I recovered.”

Aryn looked at her outstretched hand, but made no move to take them.

She sucked on her lower lip. “I suspect there are more Nightblades like them. Like those two, they are smaller than the average Bovyan, but larger than anyone else, and were probably planted years ago.”

His expression betrayed no interest. “What was I, to you?”

What was he? A passing fancy? A fun way to wile away a sea voyage? To think so would be lying to herself. And still, there was a clueless spy back home. She searched his eyes. “Your Highness, you are devilishly adorable. I wish I could stay by your side. However, I am tasked with tracking down the Nightblades.”

His lips pressed into a tight line. “Where will you go now?”

“Arkos.” Where an informant had suggested the Nightblades trained.

“Be safe.”

Accompanied by an Ayuri Paladin, an Estomari Diviner, an Aksumi sorceress, and maybe one more… "I'll be fine."

* * *

Aelward groaned as he opened his eyes. The haze of bright light filled his vison, revealing a shock of red hair.

Alaena's face came into focus.

Aelward bolted up in his bed, his body aching from the effort. "Lass, where am I?"

"In the Korynthi villa." She was dressed in a light blue dress, which revealed all the right curves, but didn't mesh with her rugged exterior.

"What am I doing here? I need to report to the *Sea Dragon*."

"I had our villa doctor examine you. It looks like you'll make a full recovery. In the meantime, I sent word to the Tarkothi admiralty that you are convalescing here. They responded, saying you are up for a commendation."

Aelward sighed. All he ever wanted was to advance in his career, maybe one day make captain. But with Alaena here… "What will ye do?"

"The wedding is off. I'm guessing the queen will want me to return to Korynth, but…" A grin tugged at her lips.

"But?"

"I think I'm going to accompany you."

He nearly choked. "Where to?"

She held out a rolled-up scroll with a broken seal. "A message from Prince Elrayn."

Him. Aelward frowned. "Ye read it, didn't ye?"

She nodded. "He's been confined to the Tarkothi villa, but he has an order. No, *request* is a better word. He wants you to go to Lorium and look for some crown."

He snorted. "Elrayn's a royal twat. Why would I help him?"

"He said he will ensure you are promoted to captain if you succeed."

Tempting, but if Aelward were to earn captain, it would be by his own merit.

Her grin widened. "And remember, I promised to take you to a place where the goats are said to be in demand."

Goats? Realization dawned on him. Their conversation in Korynth. "Arkos?"

"Yes. We can hitch a galley ride across the Inland Sea from Lorium. And, Jie and her friends are going there."

* * *

Sitting on the docks of his village, Tomas turned the Crown of the Last Imperator over in his hands. His heart felt like a rock in his chest, grief from Ma's death squeezing out his lungs' attempt to bring in fresh air. A week had passed, and yet, the pain felt fresh as yesterday.

It was also times like this, when he was alone and brooding, that Sabine's whispers fell silent, and she didn't try to communicate with the red flashes in his vision. Maybe she knew he was thinking of ripping her out of his head.

"Tomas!"

He looked up.

Sofia beamed at him from a boat. Old Gian was rowing it through the Jaws.

The girl he'd always wanted. Even her smile couldn't lighten the burden. Not with Pa constantly berating him. Not with the Ioccas blaming him for their daughter's death. All because of a demon eye that the Bovyans had shoved into his skull.

She tossed him a rope as they pulled up, and Tomas tied it down to a post.

"The townsfolk want you to come visit. Well, everyone except Antonius."

He gave a slight nod. With Sabine helping him, he'd led ambushes on the Bovyan garrison that had remained behind when Keris had led his troops across the bridge in pursuit of the boat. Antonius had fallen out of favor, and the townsfolk hailed Tomas as a hero. It'd be nice to bask in their praise instead of drown in the villagers' scorn.

And Lorium still needed him. The Bovyans who'd survived the bireme's crash into the bridge had set up camp on the opposite bank. The Bovyans wanted the crown, and they'd find a way to cross the river.

Evil as Sabine might be, Tomas needed her to fight them.

Join my mailing list at **BookHip.com/KCRNRA** and get a FREE copy of **Prelude to Insurrection**, a story about Jie two years before **Crown of the Sundered Empire**. It leads to **Songs of Insurrection**, Book 1 of the **Dragon Songs Saga,** where you can see how Jie meets Aryn.

We first meet the illusionist, Melas, in **Masters of Deception**. Featuring Jie, it takes place two weeks before Crown of the Sundered Empire.

Pick up **Thorn of the Night Blossoms** to learn more about Jie's life as a courtesan-spy in her homeland. It takes place twenty years before **Crown of the Sundered Empire**.

APPENDICES

Celestial Bodies

White Moon: Known as Renyue in Cathay, and represents the God of the Seas. Its orbital period is thirty days.

Iridescent Moon: Known in Cathay as Caiyue, it is the manifestation of the God of Magic. It appeared at the end of the war between elves and orcs. It never moves from its spot in the sky. Its orbital period is one day, and can be used to keep time.

Blue Moon: Known in Cathay as Guanyin's Eye, it is the manifestation of the Goddess of Fertility. Its phases go from wide open to winking.

Tivar's Star: A red star, a manifestation of the God of Conquest. During the Year of the Second Sun, it approached the world, causing the Blue Moon to go dim.

Hunter Kor: A constellation, always in pursuit of the White Stag

Lycea the Betrayer: A star, avatar of the Goddess of Betrayals

White Stag: A constellation, always hiding from Hunter Kor

Fortuna: A constellation of the Goddess of Luck

Time

As measured by the phases of the Iridescent Moon:
Full = Midnight
1st Waning Gibbons = 1:00 AM
2nd Waning Gibbons =2:00 AM
Mid-Waning Gibbons = 3:00 AM
4th Waning Gibbons = 4:00 AM
5th Waning Gibbons = 5:00 AM
Waning Half = 6:00 AM
1st Waning Crescent = 7:00 AM
2nd Waning Crescent = 8:00 AM
Mid-Waning Crescent = 9:00 AM
4th Waning Crescent = 10:00 AM
5th Waning Crescent = 11: 00 AM
New = Noon
1st Waxing Crescent = 1:00 PM
2nd Waxing Crescent = 2:00 PM
Mid-Waxing Crescent = 3:00 PM
4th Waxing Crescent = 4:00 PM
5th Waxing Crescent = 5:00 PM
Waxing Half = 6:00 PM
1st Waxing Gibbons = 7:00 PM
2nd Waxing Gibbons =8:00 PM
Mid-Waxing Gibbons = 9:00 PM
4th Waxing Gibbons = 10:00 PM
5th Waxing Gibbons = 11:00 PM

Human Ethnicities

Aksumi: Dark-skinned with dark eyes and coarse hair. On Earth, they would be considered North Africans. They can use Sorcery.

Ayuri: Bronze-toned skin with dark hair and eyes. On Earth, they would be considered South Asians. They can use Martial Magic.

Arkothi: Olive-skinned with blond to dark hair and light-colored eyes. On Earth, they would be considered Eastern Mediteraneans. They can use Rune Magic.

Bovyan: The descendants of the Sun God's begotten son, they are cursed to be all male and live only to thirty-three years of age. They are much taller and larger than the average human. Their other physical characteristics are determined by their mother's race. They have no magical ability.

Cathayi (Hua): Honey-toned skin with dark hair and eyes. High-set cheekbones and almond-shaped eyes. On Earth, they would be considered East Asians. They can use Artistic Magic.

Eldaeri: Olive-skinned with brown hair. With features and small frames, they are shorter in stature than the average human. In a previous age, they fled the orc domination of the continent and mingled with elves. They have no magical ability.

Estomari: Olive-skinned with varying eye and hair color. They are famous for their fine arts. On Earth, they would be considered Western Mediterraneans. They can use Divining Magic.

Kanin: Ruddy-skinned with dark hair. On Earth, they would be considered Native Americans. They can use Shamanic Magic.

Levanthi: Dark-bronze skin and dark hair. On Earth, they would be considered Persians. They can use Divine Magic.

Nothori: fair-skinned and fair-haired. On Earth, they would be considered Northern Europeans. They can use Empathic Magic.

Acknowledgements

First, I would like to thank my wife and family for the patience they have afforded me as I pursued my childhood dream of fiction writing.

A shout-out goes to my old Dungeons and Dragons crew: Jon, Chris, Chris, Paul, Conrad, and Julian, for helping to shape the first iteration of Tivara twenty-five years ago. Huge thanks to Brent, who contributed so much backstory to the new literary version.

A huge thanks to my sister Laura for her spectacular job with the maps.

And finally, an even huger thanks to my faithful readers who make it all worth it. Frances Phelps, Samantha Mikals, Brittany Timmins, Lana Turner, Anne Loshuk, Bethany Rheanne Hausen, Katie Tomas, Carole Harris, Pat Wicks, Bettie Womble, and Ticiana Marques deserve special mention.

ABOUT THE AUTHOR

JC Kang's unhealthy obsession with Fantasy and Sci-Fi began at an early age when his brother introduced him to The Chronicles of Narnia, Star Trek, and Star Wars. As an adult, he combines his geek roots with his professional experiences as a Chinese Medicine doctor, martial arts instructor, and technical writer to pen epic fantasy stories.

Made in the USA
Columbia, SC
16 August 2024

40075297R10357